T0143658

THE SWABIAN AFFAIR

Also by Ray Gleason
From Morgan James Fiction
The Gaius Marius Chronicles
De Re Gabiniana: The Gabinian Affair (2015)
De Re Helvetiana: The Helvetian Affair (2016)

Also

A Grunt Speaks: A Devil's Dictionary of Vietnam Infantry Terms (2009)
The Violent Season (2013)

THE GAIUS MARIUS CHRONICLE
BOOK III

THE
SWABIAN
AFFAIR

De Re Suebiana

RAY GLEASON

NEW YORK

NASHVILLE • MELBOURNE • VANCOUVER

THE GAIUS MARIUS CHRONICLE BOOK III
THE SWABIAN AFFAIR
De Re Suebiana

© 2017 RAY GLEASON.

All rights reserved. No portion of this book may be reproduced, stored in a retrieval system, or transmitted in any form or by any means—electronic, mechanical, photocopy, recording, scanning, or other,—except for brief quotations in critical reviews or articles, without the prior written permission of the publisher.

This is a work of fiction. Names, characters, businesses, places, events, and incidents are either the products of the author's imagination or used in a fictitious manner. Any resemblance to actual persons, living or dead, or actual events is purely coincidental.

Published in New York, New York, by Morgan James Publishing. Morgan James and The Entrepreneurial Publisher are trademarks of Morgan James, LLC.
www.MorganJamesPublishing.com

The Morgan James Speakers Group can bring authors to your live event. For more information or to book an event visit The Morgan James Speakers Group at www.TheMorganJamesSpeakersGroup.com.

Shelfie

A **free** eBook edition is available
with the purchase of this print book.

CLEARLY PRINT YOUR NAME ABOVE IN UPPER CASE

Instructions to claim your free eBook edition:
1. Download the Shelfie app for Android or iOS
2. Write your name in **UPPER CASE** above
3. Use the Shelfie app to submit a photo
4. Download your eBook to any device

ISBN 978-1-68350-179-4 paperback
ISBN 978-1-68350-180-0 eBook
Library of Congress Control Number:
2016912730

Cover Design by:
Rachel Lopez
www.r2cdesign.com

Interior Design by:
Bonnie Bushman
The Whole Caboodle Graphic Design

In an effort to support local communities, raise awareness and funds, Morgan James Publishing donates a percentage of all book sales for the life of each book to Habitat for Humanity Peninsula and Greater Williamsburg.

Get involved today! Visit
www.MorganJamesBuilds.com

To "Sock,"
Jacqueline Frances Marmion Nohilly,
30 March 1936 – 3 October 2016
My darlin' "Big Sister" and "Little Mom."

"So long as men can breathe, or eyes can see,
So long lives this, and this gives life to thee."

I miss you evey day, sweetheart!

TABLE OF CONTENTS

DRAMATIS PERSONAE

Gaius Marius Insubrecus Tertius, our hero, known variously as follows:
- *Arth Uthr*, "Fearsome Bear," by his Gallic comrades
- *Pagane*, the "Hick," by his Roman army mates
- Gai, by Caesar, Labienus, his family, close friends, and his few girlfriends
- Insubrecus by his army colleagues and casual associates
- *Prime,* "Top," but that's much later in his military career

Gaius Iulius Caesar, *Imperator* and commander of the Roman legions in Gaul; Proconsul of Cisalpine Gaul, Transalpine Gaul, and Illyricum; ex-Consul of the Roman Repubulic and *Triumvir* with Gnaeus Pompeius and Marcus Licinius Crassus; *Patronus* of our hero, Gaius Marius Insubrecus

Caesar's Legates in Gaul:

Titus Labienus, a professional soldier and Caesar's right-hand man; second in command of the army who saved Caesar's bacon at Bibracte

Publius Licinius Crassus, Iunior, one of the two sons of Caesar's colleague and fellow *triumvir*, Publius Licinius Crassus, Senior; appointed to Caesar's staff as a favor to his father and sent to Gaul by his father to keep an eye on his partner, Caesar

Publius Vatinius, served Caesar in Rome as his pet tribune of the Plebs, a political appointment

Caesar's Military Tribunes:

Tertius Gellius Publicola, a *laticlavus*, the senior tribune of the Ninth Legion; the younger son of an ex-consul, a member of the *Optimates* in the Roman Senate

Lucius Vipsanius Agrippa, an Italian from Asisium; an equestrian, a social and political nobody, but a good officer, serving as Caesar's quartermaster; older brother of Marcus, who eventually makes it big

Tertius Nigidius Caecina, an *angusticlavus*, a junior tribune, serving as Caesar's adjutant; the nephew of the Senator Publius Nigidius Figulus

Quintus Porcius Licinius, the *laticlavus* assigned to the Eleventh Legion; allowed to stay at Bibracte during the Swabian campaign; no relation to Cato the Younger, so considered by Caesar to be politically safe

The Centurions:

Quintus Macro, our hero's mentor, with the rank of *centurio ad manum Caesari*; serving as the commander of the Roman military port in Massalia

Tertius Piscius Malleus, the "Hammer," *Centurio Primus Pilus* of the Tenth Legion

Spurius Hosidius Quiricus, Quercus, the "Oak," *Centurio Primus Pilus* of the Ninth Legion

Volesus Salvius Durianus, known as *Durus*, the "Hard Case"; commander of the Second Century, First Cohort of the Tenth Legion; Malleus' "number one"

Other Roman Officers:

Manius Bruttius de Castris, *Tesserarius* of the Third Century, Second Cohort, Tenth Legion; a *mus castrorum*, army brat; called *Risulus*, "Chuckles," by his mates because of his sunny disposition

Appius Papirius Cerialis, head engineer of the Ninth Legion

Manius Rabirius, aka, Mani *Talus*, Mani "Knuckle Bones," because
of his uncanny luck at dice, especially when using his own; serves
occasionally, when not occupied with his gambling career, as a *decurio*
in the cavalry detachment of the Ninth Legion

Gah'ela, the Gauls

The Aedui, the *Aineduai*, the "Dark Moon" people:
Duuhruhda mab Clethguuhno, *Uucharix*, tribal king of the Aedui, and
Pobl'rix, clan leader of the *Wuhr Blath*, the Wolf clan of the *Aineduai*;
known to the Romans as Diviciacus
Deluuhnu mab Clethguuhno, brother of Duuhruhda; *Dunorix* of the
Aedui, commander of the garrison of Bibracte; known to the Romans
as Dumnorix
Cuhnetha mab Cluhweluhno, *Buch'rix* or "Cattle King" of a small
settlement east of Bibracte; *Pobl'rix*, clan leader of the *Wuhr Tuurch*,
the Boar Clan of the Aedui; a pretender to the throne
Morcant mab Cuhnetha, leader of ten in the Aedui cavalry; a prince of
the Boar Clan; oldest son of Cuhnetha
Tegid mab Davuhd, Morcant's shield bearer and cousin; brother of
Rhonwen
Rhonwen merc Gwen, niece of Cuhnetha; a sassy redhead who caught
Insubrecus' eye in the previous tale and whose memory clearly lingers
on in his mind
Rhuhderc mab Touhim, a veteran warrior in Morcant's troop who chances
only to play a murder victim in this story; hoped to marry Rhonwen,
but never quite managed to, hence the ancient Gallic proverb, "A quick
death is preferable to a long marriage with a redhead."
Teguhd, one of Morcant's warriors and a plot device

The Sequani, the *Soucanai*, the people of the river goddess Soucana:
Athauhnu mab Hergest, *Pencefhul*, leader of a hundred, commander in
the Auxiliary Sequani Cavalry; known as *Adonus Dux* to the Romans

Emlun, Athauhnu's nephew

Guithiru, a troop commander in the Sequani cavalry with the Roman name of Caeso

Rhodri, a Sequani scout

Ci, the "Hound," a troop commander in the Sequani cavalry; known also by the Roman name of Caius

Idwal, a friend of Emlun; a rider in Athauhnu's troop

Aneirin mab Berwuhn, a leader of a hundred serving under the *Cadeuhrn*, the Battle Lord of Vesantio

Dai mab Gluhn, Aneirin's lieutenant, a leader of ten.

Arion mab Cadarn, one of Athauhnu's new recruits who is accused of Rhuhderc's murder

Nuhnian mab Seisuhl, *Buch'rix* or "Cattle King" of a small settlement at the confluence of the Arar and Dubis; self-styled *gouarcheidouad uh cresfannai* or "Keeper of the Crossings"

Bearach mab Nuhnian, eldest son of the senior wife of Nuhnian mab Seisuhl

Drust, a member of Athauhnu's *fintai*; a scout

Bran mab Cahal, the *Cadeuhrn*, or Battle Lord, of Vesantio

Duglos and Ewuhn, scouts in Dai mab Gluhn's troop

Dramatis Personae Aliae, **the Other Players:**

Gaius Valerius Troucillus, Caesar's envoy to Ariovistus; a Roman citizen and member of the order of knights; a prince of the Helvi, a Gallic tribe in the Roman *Provincia*

Marcus Metius, a shifty Roman who claims to be a merchant and who has had dealings, shady and otherwise, with Ariovistus and the *Suebii*

Bulla, a *sicarius*, hitman from Rome, who travels with Metius but whose allegiance lies with someone else altogether

Aderuhn mab Enit, *Barnuchel* of the Helvi, whose Roman name is Gnaeus Curtius Helvius; travels in the *comitatus* of Caesar's emissary to Ariovistus, Gaius Valerius Troucillus

Gabinia Pulchra, "Gabi," the daughter of Aulus Gabinius and our hero's putative "one-and-only"

Rabria Vesantionis, the "Lady of Vesantio"; Roman wife of Bran mab Cahal, the *Cadeuhrn* of Vesantio

Grennadios, the "Trader," a Greek merchant from Massalia, who seems to lead, at least, a double life

Evra, Grennadios's woman, from a mysterious island west of Britannia; not a redhead, but formidable nonetheless

Crocius, the "Croaker," a Roman trooper in Manius's *ala* from the Eighth Legion, with a bit of a soft spot for Dido, the former queen of Carthage

Roscius, another *sicarius* from Rome who works for. . . oh . . that's a surprise for later

Aulus Gabinius, Senior, a senatorial mid-bencher who does well and is elected consul

Aulus Gabinius, Iunior, Gabinius's oldest son and political heir, who backs the wrong *triumvir*

Cleopatra VII Philopator, *The* Cleopatra, whom Gai refers to as the "Macedonian"; appearing in this story only as part of Gai's guilty conscience

Gnaeus Pompeius Magnus, a *triumvir*, a partner of Caesar, and an *eminence grise* in this tale

Marcus Licinius Crassus, a *triumvir*, a political partner of Caesar; too intent on going off to conquer Parthia to pay much attention to what Caesar's doing in Gaul

Ebrius, the "Drunk," Caesar's head military clerk and self-appointed taster of Caesar's wine and *posca* collection

Clamriu, a horse

Beorn, another horse who, as his German name suggests, may be in cahoots with the enemy

PRAEFATIO

My people, the Gah'el, have a saying, *pediooch buth eithigeth choth:* never challenge a gift. Apparently, the ancient ones of my people knew nothing of *Romanitas,* the Roman game."

Romans never seem to grant *gratia,* gifts, without strings attached. Every ostensible act of generosity has some obligation attached to it. And, so it is with *Augustus,* our exalted one down in Rome, granting me the position of *praefectus municipii mediolani,* the prefect of his little experiment in the extension of Roman citizenship to Mediolanum.

The Gah'el also say, *mai chufeloor wasanaitoo canoo dau penai:* no warrior can serve two chiefs, which is exactly where I find myself.

Octavius expects me to keep a lid on things in Mediolanum. He wants a smooth, peaceful transition from Medhlán, the conquered Gallic city, to Mediolanum, his new shining light of *Romanitas* in the midst of savage Gallic Insubria. He also expects me to submit detailed monthly reports on crime, violence, sedition, *and* the gratitude of the "natives" for the generosity of his "gift." I sometimes fear he doesn't even recognize the incongruity of his own expectations.

In theory, however, I am also responsible to the *triumviri* that Octavius appointed to govern his newly minted Roman *municipium.* *They* insist that I go through *them* in all matters, especially when it concerns Rome and *Augustus.*

That, of course, can never happen.

Also, the *triumviri* also insist upon the rule of Roman law in the streets of Mediolanum but are unwilling to part with a single brass *as* to make it happen, which just goes to show that squeezing funds out of rich men is about as easy as squeezing wine out of a raisin.

So, most of my time as prefect is spent discussing irresoluble logistics in budget meetings. Where are we going to get enough public slaves to man the fire brigades? How do we feed said slaves? What equipment is needed, and where will it come from? Where do we establish the stations in the town? Do we use the urban cohort to patrol the streets at night, or do we hire freedmen?

Each meeting seems to be a repeat of the last. Nothing's solved; nothing's decided; no funding is allocated. If the Roman army operated like this, the Romans would still be deliberating what to do about the Sabines.

The only good news for me is that my old comrade, Macro, has agreed to serve as one of my tribunes. He and Rufia, who has retired from active participation in her many "interests" around the town, are now living together in their town house, a whole city block really, in "snob hill," the northwest quarter of the town.

They are raising their adopted teenaged son, whom they named Gaius Macro. When Macro was establishing a military harbor at Salamis on the island of Cyprus to support Octavius's final campaign against Antonius around Alexandria, he found Gaius. The boy was part of a Roman refugee community who had fled Iudea when the Parthians tried to establish a client kingdom in Syria under Antigonus during the chaos of the Roman Civil War. Gaius claimed he was the only survivor a Roman merchant family, a Roman father and a mother of the Iudaioi people, slaughtered during anti-Roman riots in the port city of Iapho.

Macro hired my old tutor, Dion, known as Aulus Gabinius Dionysius since his emancipation, to tutor young Gaius, so he no longer speaks Latin with "that horrible Greek twang," as Macro puts it. I don't think Macro fully undertsands the irony in his hiring Dion to do *that*.

While the various *triumviri*, praetors, quaestors, aediles, priests, sacred virgins, *and* the merchants who pull their strings, are running around in circles, trying to decide how to satisfy Octavius's expectations without spending any of their own money, I am concentrating on my journals of Caesar's compaigns in Gaul.

After Bibracte, we expected that the campaign was over for that year. We had crushed the Helvetii, destroyed the Boii, and put Duuhruhda mab Clethguuhno and his Aedui in their place. More important, we had fought a brutal battle that had killed or wounded almost a quarter of our mates. We were certain Caesar would withdraw the army south of the Rhodanus. There in the *Provincia*, we would spend the rest of the campaign season, collecting rations and preparing for the long Gallic winter.

Caesar had other plans.

De Bello Caesaris contra Ariovistum Charta
Ann Cons L Calpurnii Pisonis Caesonini et A Gabinii
(Map of Caesar's Campaign Against Ariovistus, 58 BCE)

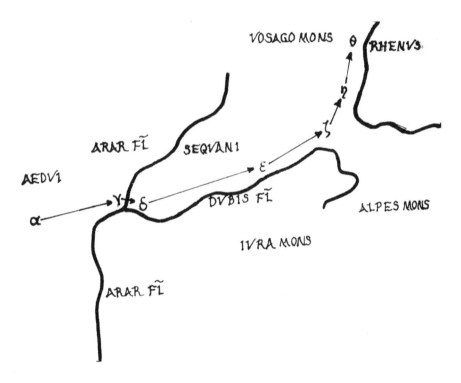

α Bibracte

γ Ventum Cavillonum

ε Vesantio

η Collis pecorum

δ Uh Dun Du

ζ Castrum Bellum

θ The Battle Near the Vosges

I.

Pro Contubernalibus Valete

A FAREWELL TO COMRADES

Ex eo proelio circiter hominum milia CXXX superfuerunt eaque tota nocte continenter ierunt nullam partem noctis itinere intermisso; in fines Lingonum die quarto pervenerunt, cum et propter vulnera militum et propter sepulturam occisorum nostri triduum morati eos sequi non potuissent.

"About a hundred thirty thousand Helvetians survived the battle. In the darkness of the entire night, they fled without stopping. By the fourth day, they had arrived in the territory of the Lingones, but our troops could not pursue them; we were held back for three days by our wounded and the funeral rites for our dead."

(from Gaius Marius Insubrecus' notebook of Caesar's journal)

---

*A*fter the fight with the Boii, Emlun brought me back "to feed the crows."

The nearest aid station was that of the Seventh Legion, where Madog's body still lay, but I didn't want to put myself at the mercy of the crow whose nose I had smashed, so we found the medical station of the Tenth Legion near the Roman right flank.

I didn't think I needed to see the medics, but after taking one look at me, Spina ordered me onto his examining table. While I sat there, he asked me a series of questions in his Aventine *patois*.

Spina asked, "How's yer head?"

"Feels like somebody's beating on it with a hammer," I replied.

"What's yer name?"

"What? You know who I am!"

"But do youse . . . What's yer name?"

"Gaius Marius Insubrecus"

"Did ya lose consciousness?"

"Yes . . . when I was hit."

"Do ya feel dizzy?"

"Only when I stand up."

"Do ya feel nauseous?"

"Yes, I threw up."

"Who's da commander of th'army?"

(Sigh) "Gaius Iulius Caesar, *Imperator*"

"Does da light hoit y'eyes?"

It took me a moment to figure out what he was saying. Finally, I replied, "Yes . . . a little."

"Enough wit' da questions. I got ta'xamine youse."

Spina told me to close my eyes. I did and kept them closed for close to a hundred heartbeats. When he told me to open them, he was nose-to-nose with me and seemed to be looking straight into my eyes for something.

He told me to close my eyes again, and we repeated the drill.

Then, he said he had to examine my head. Before he started, he nodded, and two rather burly attendants, one on each side of me, took hold of my arms and shoulders.

"Dis might sting yas a bit," Spina said.

I would never have thought that an ex-gutter-rat from the Aventine had such a gift for *ironia*.

Spina began to probe my wounded forehead. It felt as if he were cauterizing my skull with white-hot irons. Initially, I squirmed and tried to escape. Spina kept muttering, "Hold still . . . Hold still, almost done . . . Hold still," while his two bully boys did their best to hold me in place.

Finally, he was done. "I got some good news for yas and some utter news . . . Good news foist . . . as far as I can tell wid all dat trauma, yer skull's intact."

I was blinking away the tears after Spina's poking. I asked him, "So, what's the other news?"

"Ya want dee utter news, huh?" he nodded. "Okay . . . ya got what's called *concussus*."

"*Concussus?*" I questioned. "That makes no sense . . . I wasn't shaken . . . I was hit in the head by a horse's hoof! It's not serious, is it?"

Spina shrugged, "Doh know yet. Sometimes it's just a bad headache . . . Sometimes it kills ya."

I stared at him blankly, lost somewhere between "bad headache" and "kills ya."

Spina continued, "We're gonna keep ya heah wheah I can keep an eye on yas for a while. If ya keep vomiting, ya headache gets woise, ya get really sleepy, ya can't talk straight, ya arms go numb, or ya pass out, it means ya got some blood leakin' in ya head. If dat happens, I hafta drill a little hole through yer skull to drain it. If dat don't fix it . . . well . . . donworryboutit. Yule be halfway down to da boatman and won't know a t'ing."

I translated "drill a little hole through yer skull," wondered about "donworryboutit," and nodded dumbly.

Spina continued, "And dis is real important! Don't fall asleep! If ya does, I'll think ya passed out, and when ya wake up, I'll be drillin' on ya head . . . Got it?"

Again, only a nod.

"Hey, look!" Spina finished with his best approximation of a bedside manner, "Yer probably just gonna have a headache for a couple a days. So, forgedaboudit! Okay? Yule be up and around in no time."

Again, a nod, and I wondered about "forgedaboudit."

Spina turned to one of his crows: "Take dis officer to da recovery tent. Tell 'em he's to stay awake. If he goes unconscious, come get me. And, give him plenty a waddah. . . no wine. . . just waddah!"

As the attendant walked me to the recovery tent, Spina said again, "Donworryboutit!"

The crow helped me get settled in the recovery tent. I almost passed out as I tried to take off my belts and *lorica*. There wasn't much of a chance I'd fall asleep; my head hurt too much. At least six times an hour the attendants checked on me—plenty of "waddah," no wine.

Around dusk, Agrippa arrived. He said that he had been searching the army's medical stations for me; the Tenth was his last stop.

Caesar had stood down the Sequani cavalry, telling them they had done enough for one day. The butcher's bill was dear. Besides Madog and Alaw, out of the force of forty-seven riders, there were ten dead, seven wounded, and two missing. Athauhnu was temporarily in command.

But, the battle with the Helvetii wasn't over. The legions had pushed them off the southern ridge, but they had fallen back on their baggage train, which the Helvetii had converted into a stockade. The legions' two assaults had failed to break through. Caesar was considering bringing up his reserves, the Eleventh and Twelfth Legions.

"Why doesn't Caesar just allow them to withdraw?" I asked. "He *has* defeated them."

Agrippa shrugged. "They frightened him. Although he'll never admit it, the Helvetii had set an ambush for Caesar, and he allowed his army to fall right into the trap. Even worse, when the Boii triggered the ambush, Caesar was out of position, unable to control his own forces. They showed him up badly. His ego demands he destroy them completely."

I nodded. Many men would die that night to appease Caesar's wounded pride.

About an hour into the first watch, Spina came into the tent. He was pale, exhausted. His bloodshot eyes had a strange, far-away look in them. A smudge of dried blood dirtied his left cheek.

He gave me a quick physical examination; it didn't hurt as much this time. He did the drill with my eyes again, this time using an oil lamp because of the dim light in the tent. He asked me a few questions: Was I still feeling dizzy? Did my head still hurt? Had I vomited in the last few hours? Did I feel numbness anywhere in my body?

Satisfied with my answers, he pronounced that I wasn't going on any imminent stygian boat rides, and he ordered one of his crows to administer some wine mixed with Morpheus poppy to help me sleep.

And sleep I did.

No sooner had I sampled a bit of Spina's potion than I tumbled into a bottomless, black pit. I did not become aware of my own existence again until I sensed, through the darkness in which I was floating, someone shaking my shoulder. When I climbed out of Morpheus's black realm and my eyes finally cleared, I saw Labienus standing at the foot of my cot. He was dressed only in a military tunic. And, since I was obviously still alive, I assumed that the battle was over and we had won.

"Is it over?" I managed to croak.

Labienus raised his eyebrows and asked the crow, "How long has this officer been unconscious?"

"Since the night before last, Legate," the *capsarius* responded.

"Ah . . . that explains it . . . Please leave us, Soldier," he said.

I watched the man leave. Someone had erected partitions around my cot.

"I'm glad to see that Spina's magic potion worked its wonders," Labienus smiled. "How're you feeling?"

I had to think about that for a few moments. My head still hurt, but the pain seemed to be outside of my skull now, isolated around the spot where the horse struck me.

"Okay," I croaked.

Labienus walked over to a stand next to my cot and poured some water from a pitcher into a ceramic cup. He handed it to me. "Here, drink some of this!" he offered. "Water . . . without drugs . . . that should loosen your tongue a bit."

While I drank, Labienus talked, "Athauhnu credits you with killing the German *thegn*. Technically, his horse killed him . . . rolled over him when he went down . . . saddle horn just about cut him in two . . . but you knocked him off the horse. So the kill is yours."

I put the cup down and nodded. "The battle?" I asked. "The Helvetii?"

"Oh, that," Labienus answered. "We breached their barricade night before last . . . almost into the third watch . . . Had a devil of a time preventing a massacre. The men really had their blood up. Can't blame them really. It was a bloodbath. The survivors, warriors mostly, fled east toward the Rhenus."

"Caesar in pursuit?" I asked.

"Pursuit?" Labienus repeated. "No . . . not yet at least. The army's exhausted. We're bringing supplies down from Bibracte. The Aedui have been pretty forthcoming now that they don't have the Helvetii to hide behind. We're cleaning up the battlefield . . . recovering our dead. The funeral rites will be held tomorrow. Then, we settle with the Helvetii."

"Was it bad?" I continued.

Labienus shook his head. "Worst Rome has seen in a while. Almost four in ten are down in the veteran legions . . . More than half of those dead or soon to be. Spina and his mates have been swimming in a sea of blood."

He began to trail off, then changed the subject. "But, that's not why I came to see you. There's been a development based on the intelligence you brought back from that Greek merchant north of Bibracte. Caesar wanted me to share it with you."

Labienus sat down on the edge of my cot and lowered his voice, "When we breached the Helvetian laager, we captured a Roman . . . almost missed him in the confusion. He tried to blend in with our *muli*, but one of our sharper troopers nailed him from his haircut. Can you imagine that? We brought him back to the *praetorium* for questioning. Arrogant little sod! Let us know straight off that he was a client of Pompeius Magnus, and if we harmed a hair on his head, we'd have to answer to his boss. He confirmed everything we've suspected. Pompeius has been encouraging the tribes to resist Caesar . . . even had his oldest son up here to demonstrate his sincerity to the chiefs and to spread his silver around.

"It seems that Pompeius wanted a military disaster in Gaul to remove Caesar as a political rival and to panic the senate into declaring him dictator and giving him a military command in Gaul. He was willing to sacrifice six Roman legions to make it happen. Had his plan worked, it would have been the massacre of Arauso all over again. His son, Sextus, has been in *Hispania*, putting the legions there in motion to block any potential barbarian incursions south of the Rhonus. Presumably, with Caesar dead or disgraced and Crassus tucked away in Parthia, Pompeius would be the only real power in Rome, and he'd have an army behind him."

"What does Caesar plan to do?" I asked.

"Caesar?" Labienus raised his eyebrows. "At the moment, Caesar plans to do nothing. The military disaster, which was needed to set Pompeius's plan in motion, never came to pass . . . just the opposite, in fact. When word of *this* victory reaches Rome, Caesar's political stock and popularity with the mob will soar. Besides, the word of a traitorous Roman spy is worthless against a man as powerful as Pompeius. Caesar will just watch . . . watch, and wait for his opportunity."

"Did this man have any information about my situation?" I asked.

"No," Labienus shook his head. "We put the question to him. . . but he claimed he'd never heard of you. We're pretty certain that the tribune with the scar was your old friend Aulus Gabinius Iunior. He's supposed to be down in Massalia, supervising the military docks as part of the quaester's staff. He could have taken a road trip up-country with Pompeius *Iunior*. And, *his* father, the consul, has always been in Pompeius' *marsupium*, his purse . . . in more ways than one." Labienus chuckled at his own pun. "So, as the wise men say, 'Where there's smoke, there's probably a fire.' Perhaps there is a connection."

I was not satisfied. "Can I speak to the man?"

Labienus shook his head. "We'll be burning many Romans tomorrow. Caesar thought one more wouldn't be noticed."

I had hit another dead end—in more ways than one.

Labienus stood up. I raised my hand to stop him. "Sir, there's one other thing I don't understand."

"What's that, Insubrecus?" he asked.

"Why did the German attack collapse so quickly?" I asked. "By the time Emlun picked me up off the ground, our *muli* were already mopping them up."

"Oh, that!" Labienus barked a humorous chuckle. "You're new at this. You'll learn that for *pilosi*, the hair-bags, to have any chance of success against us, they need surprise and momentum. The *Grunni*, those Kraut Grunters, almost achieved their surprise when they came up suddenly on our rear, but we were able to stop them. After that, they made no attempt to conceal their movements, which gave us time to counter them. They never had overwhelming strength, and they couldn't gain any momentum against our lines. You saw how the *thegn* couldn't even control his own shock troops . . . couldn't get them moving when we offered the opportunity. Then, he sent his bodyguard cavalry in ahead of the attack to exploit the gaps we had opened in our lines, and they just got tangled up in their own muster-men, who couldn't get out of the way. When the German attack finally got moving, it slammed right into the rear of its own troops and stopped dead. Almost comic when you think about it. Even their favorite god, Woden, couldn't untangle that mess.

"Then, when you got into their rear with the Sequani and put their leader down, the fight just went out of them. That's the way it is with barbarians. I ordered our battle line to advance, but as soon as I did, the muster-men started throwing down their weapons. Then, the rest did the same. The fight left them like wind out of a sail. Amazing, really."

Labienus turned to leave. "Caesar sends his regards and hopes that you will soon be on your feet and back on duty in the *praetorium*. He wants you to review his staff journals concerning the battle before sending them to Rome to announce our victory in the forum. Oh, and I think he's going to offer you command of his praetorian cavalry."

"Command?" I questioned. "What about Valgus?"

Labienus looked away for a heartbeat, "Valgus didn't make it. We'll be honoring him and many other brave Roman soldiers tomorrow at the funeral rites."

The funeral rights for our slain were conducted the next day. On the battlefield, four huge pyres, one for each of the veteran legions engaged in the battle, were built by captured Helvetii and Tulingi. During the fourth watch of the night, the bodies of our dead, after having been washed and wrapped in their military cloaks by their *contubernales*, their tent-mates, were laid by torchlight on top of the pile of well-oiled lumber and brush.

I noticed that the bodies of officers and *muli*, even the tribunes we had lost, were laid together side-by-side on the same pyre. Labienus explained that in

Roman military tradition, there is no rank, no privilege, among the dead. We all cross the river in the same boat.

At dawn, the six legions of the army were assembled on parade around the pyres. Each legionary eagle, carried by its *aquilifer*, his head encased in the jaws of a lion, the paws of whose pelt draped over his shoulders, came center around a platform that had been erected the night before. To the left of each legionary *aquila* stood the *primus pilus*, the top-soldier of the legion. In front of the platform was one of the army's portable altars, and to its right, a stone-lined pit had been dug. In it, a fire burned, constantly fueled from a pile of dried wood and tended by legionary slaves.

As the sun broke above the eastern horizon, the legions remained silent, absolutely still. The only movement in the entire field was the fluttering of legionary crests and unit banners as the breeze accompanying the dawn moved across the ranks of silent men.

To my left, a mournful trumpet call sounded. Then, a procession led by Caesar, in his role as *pontifex* of the Roman state, slowly wound its way toward the altar. With his toga draped over his head, Caesar bowed to the altar and climbed the platform. He stood facing the legions, threw the folds of his toga back off his head, raised his hands in the direction of the pyres, and began the *Laudatio Mortuum*, the Eulogy for the Dead.

"*Infantes!*" Caesar intoned. "Boys! We gather here on this field of honor, consecrated by the sacrificial blood of our comrades, to bid farewell to these brave men, our brothers, who gave their lives so Rome might live."

Caesar spoke for less than a quarter of an hour, but I could see tears forming in the eyes of even the most hardened of our veterans. No one in the army was untouched by what we had endured in order to defeat the Helvetii. Every man on that field knew the name and remembered the face of a comrade now lying on one of the four pyres.

Caesar descended from the platform and took a position behind the altar. He gestured toward a group of *viri togati*, men in togas, their heads covered in the folds of their robes. They herded the sacrificial animals forward, one for each pyre, the *scrofae Cereris*, the sows of the goddess Ceres, mother of Proserpina, queen of the underworld. Caesar again draped the folds of his toga over his head in respect for the gods and the sacred rites he was about to perform.

One by one, the sows were placed on the altar, and with a single stroke of his knife across the throat, Caesar quickly dispatched each of the victims. Even before the sows ceased twitching, the assistants eviscerated them and divided the bodies in two. Half of each sow and its viscera were thrown into the burning pit in sacrifice to Ceres. The other half was carried to one of the four pyres and placed on a spot intentionally left vacant; this was the *viaticum*, the travel rations for the dead for their journey to the underworld.

After the sacrifices had been performed, Caesar washed his hands and arms in a basin of water positioned on the left side of the altar. He then nodded to his assistants. They picked up four torches, which were lying beside the altar, and lit them from Ceres' fire. They carried a burning torch to each of the pyres and waited.

Caesar turned to the altar, raised his hands to the skies, and mouthed a prayer. He paused briefly, then nodded.

He turned toward the assembled army and proclaimed, "*Dea Ceres*, the goddess Ceres, has accepted our sacrifice and is ready to gather our comrades into her arms."

He nodded toward the men holding the torches. They plunged the torches into the pyres. The wood and brush, dried and drenched with oil, immediately ignited. Within a few heartbeats, the pyres were engulfed in orange and red flames that seemed to drive columns of billowing black smoke up into the heavens.

Our entire army erupted in a slow, moaning, ululating chant. Some began to hammer out a slow, pounding, staccato beat on their wooden shields with the side of their fists. Officers in plate *loricae* slapped their palms against their chests to mimic the rhythm. Others stomped their hobnailed *caligae* against the earth, as if to awaken the *dis infernis*, the gods of the underworld.

With the black smoke rising into the heavens, a ghostly Roman legion marched into the realms of the dead.

Later that afternoon, we buried our Sequani comrades.

The smoke was still rising over the glowing embers of the burned down pyres of the Roman dead. When the ashes were cool, our war prisoners would cover the ashes of the fallen, creating a mound of soil.

That was the Roman practice.

The Gah'el practice was to bury their dead in the soil of the battlefield on which they fell.

We picked a spot near our own battlefield, near where we had stood with the Roman line against the Boii and Tulingi. The Sequani themselves dug the graves around the spot where Madog had succumbed to his wounds.

We assumed that our missing men were dead. The bodies of Alaw and those who fell in our first skirmish with the Germans had been hacked to shreds. The Krauts believe if a body is destroyed, the *Wal Ciurige*, the gatherers of the battle dead, will not select that warrior for the *Wal Halle*, the Hall of Warriors.

We Gah'el believe that all brave warriors are welcomed into the Land of Youth. So, we filled Alaw's grave and those of our missing companions with whatever of their belongings we could gather, a jug of mead, some bread for the journey, and the head of a slain enemy who would serve the dead soldier as a slave for eternity.

Madog's grave was in the center of a circle formed by the fifteen graves of our dead and missing comrades. His body had been washed, dressed in his finest clothes, and placed in his armor. Each man placed an offering in the grave: Athauhnu, a ring; the others whatever they had: small coins, metal buckles, even cuttings of their hair. I gave him my dented helmet; Agrippa gave him a *quadrigae*, a silver *denarius* coin bearing Caesar's image as consul. We kept his sword for his son, but we placed the sword of the German *thegn* on Madog's chest and put the Kraut's head between Madog's feet.

After we closed the graves, we drank. We drank mead, beer, and someone even found a jug of *dur*, the Gallic "water of life." As we drank, we told stories and conjured up memories of our fallen comrades.

When we could think of no more stories, we sang. We sang of the heroes of our people; we sang of the gods; we sang of the women of the *lios, merched tuhoouhth teg*, the phantom lovers; we sang of the *gourachod coch*, red-headed sprites who seduce men beside running brooks; we sang of the dark-haired dryads of the forests, *gourachod du*, whose glowing blue eyes can beguile a man with a glance; we sang of the golden-haired fays, *gourachod meluhn*, whose beauty is so terrible that men go mad at the very sight of them.

As we sang, we clapped our hands together and danced. We danced around the freshly turned earth that now embraced our friends. When we could think of no more songs, when we were too exhausted to dance, we drank again.

Sometime during the night, Athauhnu stood me up among the graves, in front of Agrippa and the *Soucanai*, and announced, "This is my friend . . . a strong right arm in battle . . . a steady shield when needed . . . a brother . . . a true warrior of the Gah'el!"

Athauhnu then removed the thick strands of twisted gold he wore around his neck, the five-strand golden *torc* that designated him as *pencefhul* of his people, and he placed it around my neck saying, "He will no longer be known among us as Arth Bek, the 'Little Bear'. . . From this day on, he shall be known among the Soucanai as Arth Uthr, the 'Bear of Terror'!"

II.

De Fine Belli Contra Helvetios

THE END OF THE
HELVETIAN CAMPAIGN

Helvetii omnium rerum inopia adducti legatos de deditione ad
eum miserunt qui cum eum in itinere convenissent seque ad pedes
proiecissent suppliciterque locuti flentes pacem petissent atque eos in eo
loco quo tum essent suum adventum expectare iussisset paruerunt

"Driven by their desperate situation, the Helvetians sent envoys to
Caesar. When the envoys encountered Caesar on the march, they
threw themselves down at his feet. Sniveling, they abased themselves
and begged him for a truce. Caesar ordered the Helvetians to remain
where they were and await his arrival, and the Helvetians submitted."

(from Gaius Marius Insubrecus' notebook of Caesar's journal)

Labienus was certainly wrong about one thing. Caesar had no
intention of putting me in command of his praetorian cavalry.
He told me that I would keep my appointment as *decurio*,
but he would continue to use me as his *ad manum* around the *Praetorium,*

especially for his journals, and he would send me out on freelance missions as the situation dictated.

The day after the funeral rights, Caesar launched the army east in pursuit of the fleeing Helvetii. *Gratias dis*! Thanks be to the gods! The pursuit was short! After my celebrations with the Sequani the previous night, my head hurt worse from the mead and *dur* than from the wound I had suffered in battle. In fact, at first I had no idea why I woke up wearing Athauhnu's *torc*; Agrippa had to explain it to me.

We had marched no more than a few thousand *passus* from the site of the battle when we were met by a delegation from the surviving Helvetii. They abased themselves before Caesar and begged for his clemency. Their surrender was abject and complete.

Caesar then surprised many in the army by refusing to place the Helvetii and their allies *sub corona*, "under the crown," by selling their entire tribe - man, woman and child - into slavery. Not the least shocked were the *muli,* who had been looking forward to a victory *donatum*, a monetary bonus augmented by the sale of tens of thousands of slaves.

Caesar's reasoning was that he needed the Helvetii back in their lands along the west bank of the Rhenus, and he needed them strong enough to act as a buffer against German incursions into *Gallia*. In order to appease the soldiers, Caesar promised to augment their *donatum* out of his own purse. The only ones who would lose out were the slavers, who followed the army, but most soldiers considered them *spuma*, scum, and were not at all sympathetic to their complaints.

Caesar's clemency was tested when a number of his prisoners, a small band of the Helvetii called the *Verbigeni*, staged an escape from the prisoner stockades. They fled east toward the Rhenus with no fixed plan. Caesar sent emissaries chosen from their own people after them, and they soon returned.

Their leaders professed they had been told Caesar planned to sell them all into slavery as soon as they had laid down their arms. The men were to work in the mines, and the women were to be sold into prostitution. When asked who had told them this, they claimed it was a Roman, a noble with a purple stripe who had been accompanied by a prince of the Aedui. Why would they not believe what a Roman told them about the Caesar? And, were not the Aedui now Roman allies?

With that, Caesar knew that Pompeius' agents were still active in *Gallia*. We had little doubt that the "prince of the Aedui" was Deluuhnu mab Clethguuhno, the former *dunorix* of Bibracte, and brother of Duuhruhda, the king of the Aedui. Rumors suggested that he had fled east among the *Belgae* near the *Arduenna Silva*, the great forest which stretches toward the Rhenus.

Caesar established his legionary *castra* in the fields south of Bibracte, a visible and unmistakable warning to Duuhruhda, the king, that he, Caesar, was now the real power in central *Gallia*. The most pressing issue facing the army was replacing the losses suffered by the veteran legions in the battle against the Helvetii.

After a rather stormy officers' council, Caesar decided that he would fill the vacancies in the veteran legions by cross-levelling from the Eleventh and Twelfth Legions, but he would limit the number of replacements from those formations to no more than a thousand *muli* from each. Further, officer vacancies would be filled from within the legion: third-line centurions would be moved up to the second line; second-line to the first; *centuriones posteriores* would become *centuriones priores*; *optiones* would be promoted to the centuriate; *muli* would be promoted to the *tesserarii* and *optiones* vacancies in their own centuries. As quickly as possible, the four veteran legions would be restored to full mission capability.

III.

Massalia Quod Cognovi
WHAT WE LEARNED IN MASSALIA

Caesar left Labienus to supervise the details of the reorganization of the army while he went down to Massalia for a couple of days to take care of the administrivia of governing his provinces. His *quaester provinciarum*, the head of the civilian administration for Caesar's provinces, had established himself there, and a number of issues demanded Caesar's immediate attention.

For their stand against the Boii and Tulingi, Caesar honored Athauhnu and his Sequani by allowing them the privilege of accompanying him to the port. Agrippa was still the titular commander with the title of *praefectus*, but Caesar gave Athauhnu the title of *dux* in place of Madog.

I accompanied the party as Agrippa's *decurio* and Caesar's *ad manum*.

I had never seen the sea. When we rode over the final hills separating the coast from the interior and I saw what the Romans call *Mare Nostrum*, Our Sea, stretching before me right up to the edge of the heavens themselves, I must have acted exactly like a *paganus*, the country hick my mates accused me of being. I wasn't the only one in shock; none of Athauhnu's Sequani had ever seen a sight so spectacular and awesome either.

Agrippa understood. In his elementary Gah'el, he told us it was only water.

In those days, Massalia was still, at least in theory, an independent Greek city over which Caesar had no official authority. Although the military docks and warehouses were located in the harbor area, Caesar established his *principia* outside the city in a villa overlooking the town. Since Caesar had sacked Pulcher, the army lacked a quartermaster with adequate social prestige to interact with the senatorial broad-striper who served as the *quaester* of the Gallic province. Caesar had decided to appoint Agrippa to the army post, *pro tem*, and on this visit, one of his missions was to establish Agrippa's *bona fides* with the official nob from Rome, one Quintus Valerius Flaccus, who counted at least three former consuls in his family line and had every expectation of ascending in time to the curial chair himself.

I was assigned a *cubiculum* all my own in the villa and spent most of my time augmenting and re-writing Caesar's staff journals for publication in Rome. I had been working in the villa for three days when Agrippa and Athauhnu showed up at my door and invited me to accompany them into Massalia to inspect the military stores kept in the harbor. I felt like I needed some air and hadn't really seen the sun for three days, so I gladly agreed.

In truth, my desire to go to the harbor had little to do with sun or air. I had been told the sea was actually filled with salty water. I would never have forgiven myself if I had returned to the army at Bibracte without finding out if it were true. It seemed impossible. Salt was a valuable commodity! How could the sea be full of it?

We rode south from Caesar's villa and picked up the Roman road in less than a thousand *passus*. Then, we followed the Roman road as it approached Massalia from the northeast. Like most Greek cities, Massalia was walled, but as no one had paid much attention to maintaining the walls, they were now crumbling. The gate, on the other hand, was reasonably well maintained because it channeled those entering the town so duties and customs could be collected. As we approached the gate, the city militia could see from our tunics, belts, and weapons that we were Roman officers, so they waved us through.

We found a livery just inside the town gate where we stabled our mounts. After all we had been through, I could almost sense Clamriu's surprise and delight: a short ride of a couple thousand *passus* without armor and a stand down for a grooming and fresh oats!

We walked through the crowded, narrow streets until we came to an *agora*, what the Greeks call a *forum*. Beyond the *agora*, I could see another wall with a wide gate opening up to a sparkling blue expanse I knew to be the harbor. I felt like a child on a holiday outing. It took all of my self-control not to run toward the harbor gate.

With my dignity more or less intact, we eventually entered the harbor area, and when we did, I was immediately overwhelmed by the swirling colors of the crowded quays and the shimmering blue vastness spreading out from the harbor to the horizon. The sea! Equally overwhelming were the aromas. The cool sea breezes smelled of fish and tar, and yes, salt! I must have halted briefly because Agrippa ran up on my heels. But, Athauhnu had simply stopped dead under the arch of the gate and stood gaping at the scene before him.

After stumbling into me, Agrippa recovered his poise and gestured toward the left, saying, "The military docks are this way!"

We walked along the south side of the harbor toward a distant, tall building that seemed to be on fire. Black smoke billowed out of its top.

"That's the *pharos*," Agrippa explained without my having to ask. "The smoke guides ships into the harbor. At night, the harbor's marked by a fire burning on the platform at the top of the tower, although no sailor in his right mind would be caught out at sea at night."

We walked along the bustling commercial quay. Some ships were loading cargoes; others were unloading. Stevedore slaves were hauling bundles and *amphorae* in various directions; overseers were shouting; sailors were cursing; *lupae* were trying to drum up a little business.

I was so distracted that I collided with a group of men, sailors, and to my surprise, one of them had black skin! A black man! In my culture, we only imagined such beings as coming from the other world. My jaw dropped. I gawked at the man.

After a few heartbeats, the black man snarled at me in bad Latin, "What'cha lookin' at, boy?"

I was too stunned to answer.

A couple of his mates intervened. I heard something like, "Roman soldiers . . . don't want to get messed up with the likes of them . . . too much trouble."

The group finally moved on. Agrippa was grinning at me, "Never seen a Numidian before?"

Still in shock, I didn't answer.

"Come on!" Agrippa urged, taking my elbow. "The military compound is just down the way."

Athauhnu hissed into my ear, "Was . . . was that a demon?"

"No," I answered. "He's a—" Then, I realized there was no word in Gah'el for *Numidian.*

"He's a sailor," I explained simply.

Athauhnu just shook his head.

The Roman military harbor was partitioned off from the commercial harbor by a wooden fence. A guard stood at the entryway. He wore Roman legionary equipment, but he looked too well fed and too old to be a *muli,* almost forty I guessed. He was about to stop us, but he spotted Agrippa's narrow purple stripe. He stood back and greeted the officer, "Good afternoon, Tribune!"

"Good afternoon, Soldier!" Agrippa responded. "I am Lucius Vipsanius Agrippa, *quaester* to the army of the proconsul, Gaius Iulius Caesar, *Imperator.* I am here to inspect the military stores."

The guard stiffened a bit at the mention of Caesar's name. He responded, "Very good, Tribune!"

The man then turned toward a small shack on the dock and called, "*Tesserari! Ad portam!* Officer of the Guard! To the gate!"

A soldier emerged wearing the sash of a junior officer. "What is it, Quint? I was right in the middle of my—" Then, he noticed Agrippa. He wiped his mouth off and straightened into something resembling the position of attention.

The first guard explained, "The tribune here is the governor's *quaester.* He's here to take a look at the army stuff!"

The *tesserarius* almost smiled. "We were told to expect you, Tribune! Please, follow me!"

The *tesserarius* led us toward one of the warehouses; it had a large "I" painted on its front in white.

"I will turn you over to the dock supervisor," the soldier explained. "I have to return to my duties at the gate. I'm sure, as a soldier, you understand that."

When we reached the warehouse, the *tesserarius* ordered one of the stevedore slaves lounging in front of a small door, "Go get the dock supervisor, boy!"

The boy, who didn't seem much older than twelve, ran into the warehouse without a word.

While we waited, we all just rocked on our heels. The *tesserarius* gave us an occasional vacant grin.

Finally, Agrippa broke the silence. "Which legion?" he asked the man.

"The Third, Tribune," the man said. "In Syria . . . first under Lucullus . . . then Pompeius. Took my twenty and got out. Pompeius fixed me up with this gig. Easy work. No marching. Climate's not too bad, except when the winds blow out of the South. You wouldn't believe . . . ah . . . here we go."

I saw a man emerging from the darkened warehouse into the sunlight and glare off the water. He was squinting, but I noticed his limp. He looked somehow familiar.

"Macro?!" I heard myself blurt out, even before fully recognizing the man. "Macro! What in the name of Pluto's balls are *you* doing here?"

Macro blinked a few more times, then seemed to recognize me. "Gai! Small bleedin' world, ain'it? Welcome to Massalia!"

"I take it you two know each other," Agrippa announced the obvious.

"Yes! Yes," I rambled. "Oh! Tribune, allow me to present Quintus Macro, former *optio* of Lucullus' Third Syrian Legion. Macro, this is Lucius Vipsanius Agrippa, *Tribunus Angusticlavus* of Caesar's army, my commander, and now the military *quaester*."

"Glad to meet you, Tribune!" Macro nodded to Agrippa. "And, who's the rather large gentleman in the colorful Gallic trousers?"

"This is Athauhnu mab Hergest, *Pencefhul* of the *Soucanai* and *Dux* of Caesar's Sequani cavalry."

"Glad to make your acquaintance, At'a. . . ounou, is it?" Macro butchered Athauhnu's name.

"*Me voces Adonus* . . . You may call me Adonus," Athauhnu smiled. I hadn't noticed how much his Latin had improved since Caesar had promoted him to *dux*.

"I got it from here, *Tesserarius*," Macro dismissed our guard. The man nodded to Agrippa and, ignoring the rest of us, strode back to the gate.

Macro watched the man's back as he walked away. "I knew that *mentul'* in Syria, when he was a *mulus* under Lucullus. Lazy *bustrap*! But, he knew the right arses to kiss. A waste of meat, really. I'd shove a *tessera* up his *tesserarius*-arse for a clipped *denarius*. Now he has his nose up Cicatrix's arse."

A classic Macro performance.

"Cicatrix?" Agrippa asked. "Who's Cicatrix, 'the Scar'?"

"That's what we call Gabinius. Not to his face, of course. That's Gabinius *Iunior*, the consul's son. He's the tribune in charge of these docks . . . my boss," Macro explained. "And, Gai here knows how he got that scar . . . He gave it to him himeself!"

I winced a bit at that. I certainly didn't want to run into Gabinius. Agrippa was giving me a curious look.

"So," Macro concluded, "Cicatrix . . . I mean, the tribune is not about at the moment. Usually doesn't show up until mid-afternoon, if at all. So, let me take you through the warehouses so you can see we're taking good care of Caesar's ash and trash."

Macro led us through warehouses I and II. Everything looked correct, up on pallets, dry, packing undisturbed, amphorae properly in stands—a seemingly well-run operation.

"Warehouse III is being converted for grain storage," Macro explained. "This far north there isn't a decent harvest before September, so the army is bringing in grain from Sicilia, Africa, and even Aegyptus. First grain ships are due next month. We should be ready for them. We're using number IV to store supply wagons . . . The oxen are on a farm outside the city."

Agrippa nodded his head, then asked, "What about number V?"

"Uhhh . . . number V?" Macro hesitated. "Number V's Gabinius' private operation. He has it sealed."

Agrippa stopped walking and faced Macro. "What do you mean *private*? This is a military installation. There's nothing *private* about it!"

Macro shrugged, "Unless you're a consul's son."

"What does that mean?" Agrippa pressed.

Macro decided to give it up. "Okay, Tribune, let me explain how this thing works . . . Cargoes that land on the municipal docks have to pay a fee to dock, a fee to unload, and another fee when the stuff goes out the city gates. Military cargoes are exempt. So, a few *denarii* change hands, and a civilian ship gets shifted over to us at midnight. Our slaves unload the cargo into Warehouse V, and the stuff leaves the city in a military wagon. It's part of . . . uh . . . let's just say it's a *stips*. . . a *donativum* that goes to the tribune in charge of the docks. Plus, he gets to keep part of the cargo . . . a few amphorae of wine . . . a little *garum* . . . some cheese wheels . . . whatever's coming in. And, the boss spreads it around a bit. We all get a small *donatum*, a bonus at the end of the month.

"It's the way things have always worked around here. I make sure it doesn't affect the military operation. The only ones who get hurt are the *Graeculi*, the Greeklings who run the town."

Agrippa thought about that for a while and finally shrugged. "As long as it has nothing to do with the army," he said, then chose to end the discussion.

Agrippa decided to audit the military books, so Macro set him up at a desk in a warehouse office. While Agrippa read, the rest of us walked over to a *caupona*, a wine shop, in the town just behind the military docks.

When we walked in, I saw a couple of our stevedore slaves sitting at a table around a jug of wine. They didn't seem at all alarmed by our catching them there. In fact, Macro greeted them with a wink and offered to go them a round.

"Slow day," he told us as we took a seat. "They have to work like the devil when a ship docks, so why not kick back a bit when it's slow."

We sat down at a table, and the landlord came over to take our order. Since Massalia was a Greek city, I decided to show off a bit.

"*Theloume na exoume mia kanata krasi . . . kokkino, protimo*," I ordered.

The landlord stared at me for a few heartbeats while pulling on the gold earring in his left ear. Then, he said in a semblance of Latin, "You Roman schoolboy, no?"

"No!" I protested. "I'm an officer in the Roman army!"

"Maybe . . . yes," he answered. "But, you talk Greek like Roman school boy. No one talk like that since Achilles in diapers. I bring you some retsina . . . That good, Macro?"

"That works, Linos," Macro agreed. "Thanks!"

After recovering a bit from my embarrassment, I asked Macro, "So, what are you doing up here? What happened to our wine empire?"

Macro's face darkened. "Gabinius screwed me! *Senior*, not *Iunior*. When he realized that my idea might payoff big, he moved in on it himself. He's partnered up with your grandfather, Naso, that bastard . . . No offence to your family, Gai . . . Your mom's a real lady . . . They squeezed me out. Gabinius never forgave me for what you did to *Iunior* . . . Holds me responsible for that . . . Probably holds me responsible for you and his daughter too."

Athauhnu punched me in the arm and gave me an "atta-boy" grin. His listening skills in Latin were improving by leaps and bounds!

"Nothing happened between me and Gabi!" I tried to protest.

Macro was continuing his story. "So, my choice was to hit the road or join up as part of *Iunior's familia* up here in Massalia. I had the experience, and the old man probably understood that if someone wasn't babysitting *Iunior*, he'd totally screw the pooch."

"What is this 'having sex with the dog'?" Athauhnu asked, looking somewhat concerned. But, the landlord arriving with the wine and cups interrupted him.

As Macro poured the wine, I explained to Athauhnu, "It just means making a lot of mistakes . . . fouling things up."

Athauhnu seemed relieved by that.

"Did you know she's here?" Macro asked me.

"She . . . who?" I asked.

"Gabinia, you idiot!" he said. "Who'd you think I meant? She's living up at the villa with her big brother, *Iunior*."

I shrugged, "No . . . didn't have a clue. How would I? Been a bit busy these last few weeks!"

Then, a thought hit me. "You say that *Iunior* doesn't show up at the docks every day, but did he disappear for a few weeks last month?"

Macro thought about it, then said, "Come to think of it, he did. It was when that big shot from Rome showed up . . . Tried to hide his identity . . . Got off a navy dispatch cutter at high noon all wrapped up in a dark cloak. A senatorial. Not only did *Cicatrix* show up to greet him, but he was wearing his parade armor. He even tried to shape those snuffies we pay to guard this place into an honor guard."

"How'd you know it was a senatorial, if he was wrapped in a *sagum*?" I pressed.

"Weren't you listening, Gai?" Macro said. "He was taxying around the *Mare Nostrum* in a commissioned Roman naval vessel. You think the senate loans those things out to just anyone? A rumor went around it was one of the Cicerones or Cato up from Rome to check on Caesar."

"But, that was the time that *Iunior* disappeared, right?" I persisted.

"Yeah . . . exactly!" Macro confirmed. "Like I said, I didn't think much about it at the time . . . Just assumed that *Cicatrix* and the nob were off on a two-week bender."

"Any evidence that *Iunior* had left town . . . went up-country?" I asked.

"*Iunior*? Up-country!" Macro guffawed. "He gets nervous a thousand *passus* outside the city gate, even though there haven't been any wild, long-haired Gauls rampaging through here since Alexander was sucking teat. No offense, Adone!"

"None taken, Macro!" Athauhnu responded, finishing his second cup of unwatered retsina. Along with mastering Latin, he was starting to develop quite a taste for wine.

"Come to think of it," Macro said suddenly. "It was right after our mystery guest arrived that our side racket down on the docks really picked up. Only lasted about a week, but there was a midnight ship docking every night. Ran our slaves ragged getting all that stuff into number V."

"What stuff?" I asked, my interest picking up.

"Don't know," Macro said. "Everything was in crates. I do know the slaves complained about how heavy the stuff was . . . like the crates were filled with iron ingots . . . or farm equipment . . . Damn near broke their backs. The guards were in a hurry to clear it off the docks . . . not that the civilian dock inspectors were any threat to our operation. They get greased, too. Stuff's still in there. Far as I know, it hasn't passed through the city gates yet."

I got a sudden, bad feeling. "Can we get into V to have a look around?"

"No way!" Macro said. "*Cicatrix* has it locked up tighter than a virgin's knees. He keeps guards on the doors night and day."

"We've got to get in there and see what's in those crates," I told Macro. "Let's finish the wine and get Agrippa!"

We left the *caupona* and walked toward the dock gate. A rather sad specimen of a Roman soldier was standing guard. He barely nodded to us as we passed through.

"They all know me," Macro explained. Then, he changed the subject. "You never told me what happened to your head, Gai. Looks like you were in a fight. A jealous Gallic husband catch up with you?"

Athauhnu chuckled. "If a Gaul caught him with his woman, he'd have a second mouth to smile with. A bruise like that, one of our women could give him if he didn't please her!" A sudden amazing grasp of Latin!

"Horse kicked me," I said simply.

"Horses," Macro shook his head. "Never trusted those nasty beasts . . . evil . . . pure evil!"

By then we had reached Warehouse I. We found Agrippa still plowing through the *tabulae*.

"You have a good time at the *caupona*?" he asked without looking up from his work. "You smell like a pine forest. What were you drinking? Some crazy Greek concoction?"

"We have to get into number V and take a look around," I said bluntly.

Agrippa looked up, alarmed. "Why?"

No Roman wants to look too deeply into the private matters of another Roman. *Romanitas*. It just isn't done.

"I hope I'm wrong," I continued. "But, I think Pompeius is stockpiling contraband . . . weapons and equipment for the tribes."

Again, Agrippa resisted. "Why would you think such a thing?"

I told him about the "mystery visitor" and the "midnight ships," how the timing seem to fit with the reports of Romans resembling Pompeius *Iunior* and Gabinius *Iunior* going up-country to visit the Gauls and try to stir things up against Caesar, and how the crates didn't seem to be commercial goods, but something else, something heavy, something made of steel.

Agrippa sighed. "Alright . . . we'll take a look. But, if all we find is cheese and *garum*, we forget about the whole thing . . . *ti' placebit* . . . acceptable?"

"*Mi' placebit,*" I agreed. "Acceptable."

We walked over to Warehouse V. There were two security guards posted at the entry door. They stiffened when they saw us approaching. They noticed Agrippa's purple stripe. They knew Macro.

"Open it, Laeve," Macro ordered.

"You know I can't do that, Macro," the one called "Lefty" responded. "*Cica*—I mean the tribune—would have the flesh off my back if I did."

"I'll have the flesh off your back if you don't!" Agrippa countered.

"You got no jurisdiction over me," Laevus began.

"This is an army installation," Agrippa told him. "And, it's under my jurisdiction. So, open that bleedin' door before I lose what's left of my patience!"

Laevus' barracks-lawyer bravado quickly crumbled. He turned to his mate and said, "Quick, get the *tesserarius.*" Then, to Agrippa, "We don't have the keys, Tribune . . . Only *our* tribune has them!"

"Not an insurmountable problem," Agrippa said. He looked around and spotted what he wanted. "Insubrecus *Decurio,* hand me that crowbar!"

I looked and saw a *vectis* that had been left on top of some discarded packing by a careless slave. I handed it to Agrippa.

"Step aside, Soldier!" Agrippa ordered, now armed with the iron rod.

Laevus hesitated just a heartbeat, then decided on discretion. He stepped away. As he did, I heard him hiss at Macro, "We're all in for it now, you stupid bastard!"

Agrippa had the shackles off the door in no time and kicked the door open. The interior was dim, but there were oil lamps and a flint stored at the entry. We lit the lamps and entered. Laevus stayed outside.

I heard a thud from outside the door, then the sound of something heavy hitting the ground. Macro walked in, rubbing his fist.

He said, "I may not be the brightest lamp in anyone's room, but my papa married my mama . . . and I don't take that kind of shit from no snuffy."

"*Fungulus?*" Athauhnu asked. "*Quid vult dicere 'fungulus?*"

"Incompetent and sloppy soldier," I explained. "*Fungulus* . . . a snuffy."

Athauhnu nodded and chuckled. "Snuffy . . . I like that!"

We looked around the warehouse. It was as Macro had said: wine, some cheeses, bundles of fabric—just evidence of perfectly reasonable and well-organized corruption.

Then, Macro said, "Something's wrong!"

"What is it?" I asked.

"This room's a lot shorter than the building," Macro announced, walking toward the back of the warehouse. Then, after a few heartbeats, he called, "Tribune! Could you bring that crowbar back here?"

We followed the sound of Macro's voice to what we thought was the back of the building. Macro was standing in front of a heavily locked door in what was now obviously a partition across the back of the warehouse.

Agrippa made short work of the locks, and we entered. When our eyes adjusted to the dark, we could see that the room was filled with sealed shipping crates. But, before we could investigate further, the *tesserarius* of the security detail burst in. Laevus was close behind. Even in the dark, the swelling around his right eye was obvious.

"*Fungulus!*" I heard Athauhnu chuckle in the dark.

"What in the name of Hecate's three mutts do you people think you're doing?" the *tesserarius* exclaimed.

"Watch your mouth when addressing senior officers!" Agrippa shot back.

The man stiffened. "Sorry, *sir* . . . Didn't see you . . . This warehouse is off limits."

"Not to Caesar's *quaestor!*" Agrippa corrected him.

The man ignored Agrippa and hissed to Laevus, "Get Gabinius here, *stat*! I don't care if you got to pull him out of a *lupinarium*, just get him here!"

Laevus bounded toward the exit as Agrippa attacked one of the crates. He had the top off in a few heartbeats. I lowered my lamp into the crate. At first it looked like rows of black skulls packed in straw. When my eyes adjusted, I realized I was looking at tarnished *galeae*, military helmets, dozens of them.

Agrippa attacked another crate, javelins. Then another, swords. Then, military tunics. Boots.

"Explain this, Soldier!" Agrippa confronted the guard.

"I've never seen any of this before, Tribune!" the man stammered. "I have no idea."

Just then, Laevus and another man burst into the room. The other wore a white tunic with a broad stripe that appeared black in the darkness. He had a vivid scar across his cheek, a scar I had given him months ago. Aulus Gabinius *Iunior*!

"What is the meaning of this?" he demanded.

"Who are you?" Agrippa shot back.

"I am the commander of this installation!" Gabinius declared. "Aulus Gabinius *Iunior*, son of the consul."

Before he could get too deep into his pedigree, Agrippa demanded, "Can you explain the contraband in this warehouse?"

Gabinius dismissed the question, "I don't have to explain anything to you, a mere *angusticlavus*, from some dirt-farm in the Italian hills by your abominable accent."

Agrippa lowered his voice. "You are addressing the *quaestor exercitus*, the quartermaster of the army of Gaius Iulius Caesar, *Imperator*, proconsul of this province. Again, I demand you explain this contraband in an army warehouse. And, you will address me as 'Sir'!"

"*I* . . . address *you* as 'Sir'?"

Agrippa's patience was at an end. "*Adone, Dux!*" he commanded.

"*Ti'adsum, Tribune!*" Athauhnu responded. "Yes, Sir!"

"Place this officer under arrest!"

"You wouldn't dare!" Gabinius started. When Athauhnu tried to take his arm, Gabinius shook him off and snarled, "Take your hands off me, you long-haired bastard . . . *Tesserarius!*"

Gabinius' guard made a move toward the hilt of his sword. Agrippa saw the movement.

"Freeze, Soldier!" he ordered. "Think about it! The worst that could happen to your boss here is he might spend the rest of his life kicking his heels up around some island in the Bay of Neapolis. You, on the other hand . . . you draw that sword, and I'll see to it you're beaten to death by ten of Caesar's *muli*. I'm sure they'll make a nice, slow job of it when they find out what the weapons in these crates were intended for."

Athauhnu had Gabinius' arms behind his back. I handed him a length of cord to bind his hands. That was the first time Gabinius noticed me.

"You!" he hissed. "Macro's Gallic fancy boy! I should have guessed. Macro, you're a dead man! You're all dead men! You have no idea what you're up against."

"*Adone Dux!*" Agrippa ordered. "Gag the prisoner!"

Before Athauhnu could act, Gabinius raged, "You fools! You stupid fools! You'll never make anything stick! Even Caesar doesn't dare hold me! I'll be back in Rome screwing your mothers before—"

Agrippa hit him. He moved so fast, all I saw was Gabinius down on the ground, the scar on his cheek split wide open.

"Gag the bastard and get him out of my sight!" Agrippa ordered.

"*Fungulus!*" I heard Athauhnu chuckle as he applied the gag.

IV.

De Reconciliatione Gabinia

MY REUNION WITH GABINIA

*G*abinius was right about one thing. Caesar released him from arrest almost as soon as he was notified. However, he did confine him to his villa until he could arrange for his passage back to Rome.

Caesar also asked Spina *Medicus* to see what he could do about *Iunior's* face. Spina did what he could, but confided in me later that *Iunior* would never be called *pulcher*, "pretty boy." I just wish I could have been a fly on the wall when *Iunior* had to listen to Spina's Aventine argot as he stitched up the hole across his face. Caesar decided there would be no official charges—*Romanitas*, of course.

Caesar quickly dispatched a detail from his praetorian escort under Agrippa to secure the military harbor. Agrippa reported that there was nothing out of balance with the military accounts and stores. So, at Agrippa's recommendation, Caesar appointed Macro harbormaster with the rank, pay, and privileges of *centurio ad manum*, answerable to Caesar alone, through Agrippa, of course.

Caesar decided to do nothing about the contraband. He explained that he could use the equipment for his own Gallic allies. As far as the other crates that were in warehouse V, Caesar took no *official* notice, as long as Gabinius' share reached Caesar's purse, through Macro and Agrippa—*Romanitas*, of course.

I received a summons three days later, the day before we were to return north with Caesar to the army encamped around Bibracte. The message was delivered to my *cubiculum* by one of the *famuli*, the household slaves of our host, whom I had never met. It came in the form of an expensive piece of parchment, folded and sealed, smelling strongly of lilacs. It read, "The Lady Gabinia Calpurnia would welcome the pleasure of a visit by Gaius Marius Insubrecus, *Decurio Praetorianus Caesaris*, this afternoon at the seventh hour."

There was no need for a response. The Lady Gabinia Calpurnia could not imagine such an invitation being turned down.

Athauhnu, who didn't have much to occupy himself with—except sampling our invisible host's fine Roman wines and his continuing education in Latin slang—decided to accompany me. We rode over to the villa where Gabinia and her now well-confined brother were staying. The villa was a couple thousand *passus* to the east, situated on a gentle hill with a view of the city and the sea and surrounded by vineyards. We arrived punctually at the seventh hour.

I was excited at the prospect of seeing Gabi again. In my mind, she was still the young goddess, *Dea Diana*, with whom I had taken wild rides up into the green hills of *Gallia Cisalpina* and with whom I had shared kisses in a magical, Arcadian grove.

When we arrived, Athauhnu and I were received by the household staff. Although slaves, they were attired in the finest livery. In fact, the *maior domus*, the supervisor of the household, was well-coiffed and manicured, dressed in a fine linen tunic, and smelled, well, as good as a girl.

Athauhnu was quite impressed. But, since, at that time, Athauhnu still sported brightly colored Gallic *bracae* and kept his hair long and his mustachios bushy and down past his chin, the *maior domus* was significantly less impressed with him.

As every well-trained domestic knows, it is never good policy to insult a *Gallus comatus*, a long-haired Gaul, who shows up on your doorstep with a *spatha* almost three *pedes* in length and a *palmus* in width strapped to his waist, especially when that long-haired Gaul is accompanied by a Roman ruffian sporting an apple-sized, reddish-purple bruise on his forehead and wearing a wide military belt, from which hung a razor-sharp *pugio*.

So, we were immediately led through the *vestibulum*, across the *atrium*, past an *impluvium*, in which shimmering, crystal-clear water gave life to a gold, blue, and green mosaic of frolicking shepherds, satyrs, and fauns, and finally to the *peristylium*. The *pescina* there, which was fed by a bubbling fountain flowing through a satyr's marble lips, was filled with multi-colored carp gliding silently and gracefully under deep-green lily pads.

We were seated behind the pillars, out of the sun, and served a light, slightly chilled white wine, a bowl of black and green olives, and cheeses cut into bite-sized pieces. The *maior domus* announced that he would inform her ladyship that we had arrived. Meanwhile, should we desire anything, the servants would be happy to take care of our every need.

I noticed the long, somewhat worried look he gave Athauhnu as he left the room. I could have sworn Athauhnu gave him a big wink in return.

Athauhnu unbuckled his belt, hanging it on the back of a chair, and also removed his baldric, standing his sword in a corner within arm's reach of his chair. Then, he sat down to enjoy his wine. I removed my soldier's belt and *pugio* and hung them on the back of my chair. I was carrying no *gladius* that day since I assumed that this was a social visit.

Speaking through a mouthful of olives, Athauhnu said, "*Il' puella tu'*, your former girlfriend lives well, eh? Maybe you should give up soldiering and move in here with her."

I looked about and said, "Somehow I think the price would be too high." Athauhnu just shrugged and began sampling the cheeses.

The Lady Gabinia Calpurnia kept us cooling our heels for a good half hour until finally a young *famila*, one of her *ancillae*, her personal maids, came to collect me. We left Athauhnu in the *peristylium*, quite happy among the wine cups, olives, and cheeses. My belt and *pugio* remained on the back of my chair. The *famila* led me back into the house, and we finally arrived at a closed door just across from the *impluvium* we had passed earlier.

When the *famila* knocked on the door, another door to the right opened slightly and a face appeared, the face of a particularly ugly man with a shaved head. The second door quickly closed, and I heard a pattern of knocks, which seemed to be coming from an internal common wall between the two rooms.

Before I had a chance to puzzle it out, I heard a voice, a familiar voice, calling from behind the door before which I was standing. "Are you going to stand out there all day to tease me, you naughty boy? *Intres, carissime*! Darling, please come in!"

It was Gabi!

I entered the room. The *famila* remained outside and closed the door behind me. The room was dimly lit; its one window was covered with a white, translucent curtain, which moved slightly in the afternoon breeze. The atmosphere was somewhat cloying, thick with the scent of lilac and roses and with another darker scent, somewhat familiar, but I could not immediately put my finger on it.

Again, I heard Gabi's voice, "Are you just going to stand there, Gai? Come here to me! I've waited so long for this moment."

I looked deeper into the chamber and saw her. She was reclining on a couch. She was draped in a robe of some shimmering white material, which seemed to cling to her body as if the fabric were moist. She held her right arm up to invite me to join her.

I took a seat in a chair next to her couch.

"Not there, silly!" she playfully scolded, patting a spot on her couch, "Here . . . next to me."

I sat beside her. The fragrance was stronger here, an earthy aroma, moist earth, familiar, but distant, allusive.

She reached across me to a table that stood next to her couch. She handed me a blue-green glass goblet holding a liquid with a slight yellow tint.

"Wine?" she invited. "It's a local Greek vintage, but lovely chilled on a warm day."

She picked up her own glass, clinked it lightly on mine and sipped. I drank. The taste was so light it seemed to evaporate on my tongue. Delicious. I tasted sweetness, a fruity sweetness, peaches, apples, an aftertaste of orange.

"It's horribly expensive, *carissime*," Gabi confided. "But, my man is able to find it for me in Massalia . . . a special place he knows just off the *agora*."

I finally looked at the woman who was describing the wine. I could tell it was Gabi, but she had changed. Into what, I wasn't sure: A woman? A woman of Rome?

The girlish ponytail of my riding companion had been replaced by a careful coiffure, curled and stylishly piled on her head. There were hints of gold in the chestnut hair I remembered from last summer. Her eyebrows were shaped, shaved, and stained black. Her eyelashes were thicker than I remembered, longer. There were hints of light blue above her eyes and a thin line of black kohl below. Her lips glistened, deep red, even in the dim light of the room. There was a slight pink blush high on her cheeks.

I heard Gabi's voice saying, "Are you just going to stare at me like some *rusticus*, Gai? Has the cat got your tongue? Aren't you glad to see me?"

"Glad—" I stammered. "Yes . . . yes, I am . . . I missed you."

MISSED YOU? my mind screamed at me. *Now you really sound like a bumpkin!*

But, Gabi smiled at me. She didn't seem to notice or to mind my infantile response. She placed her hand on my thigh. Her fingernails, long and red as blood, scored my flesh, just slightly. The hint of earthy moisture grew stronger, like a fleeting *foetor*, a faint *putor* lurking just beneath the light fragrances of lilac and roses.

"You're such a sweet boy," she cooed. "And, I missed you too . . . our long rides into the hills . . . our enchanted little grotto . . . reading poetry. And, what we did. Do you remember? Our last ride before Daddy made me return to Rome." Her finger nails slightly increased their pressure.

A wave of heat coursed through my body. I felt as if my face were glowing. The earthy moisture was overwhelming now. It was coming from her, coming from Gabi, so familiar.

"Where are you, *carissime*?" I heard Gabi's voice ask.

"Huh? Oh . . . sorry, Gabi," I stammered.

"I love it when you call me that," she cooed. "Gabi! No one calls me Gabi anymore. Now I'm Gabinia Calpurnia *Matrona. Patronus* to poor Piso's former clients. My friends call me *Pulchra*. Remember when we talked about that in our enchanted grove? *Pulchra poetarum* . . . 'Beauty of the Poets'! What a child I was. You know, I finally met Catullus. Very disappointing. A complete bore."

"Poor Piso?" I asked. "Is your husband—"

"Is he dead?" I swear I heard her chuckle. "Months ago. Ate a plate of his favorite mushrooms and," she snapped her fingers, "right into Charon's boat.

No heirs. At least none that couldn't be handled. So, I have his house on the Palatine . . . the villas . . . his clients . . . the slaves . . . and all the rest. But, why would you care, *carissime?* Piso tried to have you killed. He was a jealous old sod." She giggled again.

"Yes, I knew that. But didn't you—"

"Now that that weasel's out of the bag," she interrupted, "I must apologize for what my silly brother tried to do to you. The boy can't ever do anything right. But, that's no excuse. You *do* forgive me . . . don't you, *carissime?*" She seemed to pout a bit. She was stroking my thigh.

I shrugged, "I paid him back . . . I could never understand why he kept trying—"

"Trying what?" she interrupted again. Then, she realized what I was referring to. "Oh! That wasn't Aulus. He gave up after the first attempt . . . never could see anything through, my brother. That was Milo who came after you in Mediolanum. Not Aulus. You surprised Milo, I think. But, that *scorta* . . . that whore helped you. What was her name?"

"Milo?" I exclaimed. "Why would one of the chief gangsters in Rome want *me* dead?"

Gabi looked away in a pout; she placed both hands lightly over her mouth. Then, she began, "Well, Gai . . . he was doing it for me."

Her right hand shot out and rested lightly on my chest. "He . . . he was jealous . . . and . . . I was angry at you. I said . . . I said something. I don't remember what. But, poor Milo got it into his head that he should kill you . . . to make me happy, I imagine."

"Angry at me?" I began.

"You told that awful man . . . Macro . . . the one who worked for Daddy . . . you told him—"

I swear she blushed.

"You told him we weren't lovers . . . and he told Daddy. You can't imagine how embarrassing that was for me. Clodia and Atia . . . that's Caesar's niece . . . they just told everybody. I couldn't go out of the house for almost a week."

"Because we didn't—" I had to stop. I couldn't think of a word to finish *that* thought.

"I *told* people, Gai! I told them that you were my lover . . . my wild, Gallic brigand!"

Gabi was becoming angry. "All my girlfriends were jealous . . . wild . . . They only had those pasty-faced, inbred patrician boys sniffing around their *stolae*. But, I had you! A wild Gallic rogue . . . carrying me off into the hills. And, you said it didn't happen!"

Gabi had worked her way up into quite a pique. "You said *nothing* happened. And Daddy *believed* you! *Everybody believed you!* I was a laughing stock. I couldn't show my face. That's why I sent that *sicarius* . . . one of Milo's top hitters . . . up to Aquileia."

"You?" I stammered. "The fake slave?" I rubbed the scar on my arm. "You sent him?"

"Of course I sent him!" Gabi hissed.

Then, she seemed to catch herself. She looked away, caught her breath. Then, her shoulders seemed to shake. When she looked up, she had tears in her eyes. She reached out to me, placed her hand over mine.

"I'm so sorry, Gai," she sobbed. "That's why I invited you here. One of the reasons . . . mostly . . . I . . . I just wanted to see you again . . . I had to see you again. But, I wanted to tell you . . . It bothered me so . . . I'm so glad they . . . they . . . didn't hurt you. I know now, I could never have lived with that. . . I . . . I—"

I didn't hear what she was saying. My mind was in an uproar. *Gabi tried to have me killed? No! Not my Gabi! It was* this *woman. This grotesque parody of my Gabi.*

She was talking, calmly now. "But, that's all behind us now, isn't it, *carissime*? We're over that. I'm a free woman. My husband's dead. I have plenty of money. Even Milo's out of my life. I'm sure Pompeius will buy you out of the army. He owes me so many favors."

The hand was back on my leg, the blood-red fingernails, stroking.

"So what are you saying, Gabinia?" I interrupted. "That I should leave the army? Go to Rome with you?"

"Well . . . not right away," she answered. "I need you to do something first . . . not for me . . . for Pompeius. He will be *so* grateful. He's a generous man, Gai.

He has always taken good care of me. Especially when Milo . . . well . . . never mind that. You are Caesar's *ad manum*. Caesar trusts you. You sit in on his war councils. You hear his plans. You even edit his journals."

It began to dawn on me where she might be going with this. She wanted me to spy on Caesar for Pompeius! And, in return, she was offering herself!

"It's not for Pompeius," she was saying. "It's for the good of the *res publica*. Even Cicero and Daddy agree that Caesar—"

"No!" I said flatly.

"What?" she said abruptly as if I were a minor actor, who had stepped on her lines.

"No," I repeated. "I won't betray my commander, my *patronus*."

"Oh Gai," she cooed. "Stop being such a . . . a . . . a child about this. This isn't some boys' adventure . . . some Greek romance novel. You don't have to play the *miles fidelis* . . . the faithful soldier. This isn't some bad drama. This is real. This is me asking. Your Gabi—"

"I won't do it!" I insisted. "Pompeius is a self-serving, treacherous bastard, just like that worthless brother of yours . . . just like—"

"Just like who, Gai?" The actor's mask had fallen away. She was cold. Her eyes were dead. "Like *me*? A ruthless, little *cunna* like me, Gai? Is that what you were about to say? You're a fool! *Stulte!* Idiot! I offer you everything . . . luxury . . . riches . . . Pompeius' favor . . . *me*! And you say no? No one says no to me! Not Piso! Not Milo! And certainly not some smelly, little *paganus comatus*, shaggy bumpkin from Gaul!"

As Gabinia raged, the damp, earthy aroma I had sensed earlier built. It overcame the lilac and roses; it was becoming overwhelming. A *putor*. A stink! Then, I remembered where I had encountered it before. In Mediolanum. The house of the blue door. Rufia's place. It was the smell of sex, *lupinarium* sex, sex traded for money.

Gabinia was not finished with me. "Did you see that man in the doorway before you came in here? The one in the next *cella*? . . . Do you have any idea who he is? Of course not. He's the brother of the man you had strung up in Aquileia. His *brother*, Gai! He'd like nothing more than to stick his *sica* in your gut and watch you for hours, slowly dying. He's quite good at it, Gai. He's had a lot of practice up on the Aventine working for Milo. He works for me now, Gai. I told him he couldn't kill you. Not yet. I still had some use for you. But now, I don't. You're useless to me, Gai. A dead man."

Suddenly, she called out, "*Rosci! Veni! Ad me . . . stat*! Get in here now!"

In less than a heartbeat, the door to her chamber burst open. Roscius must have been waiting outside for her summons. Another thug stood behind him.

I stood to face them.

"Roscius, he's yours," she said flatly from behind my back.

"Here, *Matrona?*" the *sicarius* asked.

"Yes," Gabinia answered. "I want to see it done right this time."

Roscius shrugged and removed a nasty looking crescent-bladed dagger from beneath his tunic sleeve.

I felt for my *pugio*. It was still hanging on my chair back in the *peristylium*!

There was a sudden flurry of movement in the doorway. I heard a sound like two melons being smashed together. Roscius' eyes went strangely blank. The *sica* dropped from his fingers. Both he and his henchman crumbled to the ground.

Athauhnu stepped across the threshold. He had an empty wine cup in his right hand.

"Sorry to burst in on you, *m'amice*," he said blandly. "Ah . . . this must be the lovely Lady Gabinia I've heard so much about."

He made a mock bow in Gabinia's direction.

"I was looking for one of the servants . . . Ran out of wine, you see!" He held up his empty wine cup. "I saw the commotion through the doorway. Then, I saw that nasty little Roman dinner knife."

He bent over, picked up the *sica*, briefly examined it, then shrugged. "I trust you weren't harmed, *me' domina*," he finished, tossing the dagger back on the floor.

I heard an unworldly shriek.

Gabinia was off her couch, coming at me, blood-red claws out! I caught her wrists and quickly pivoted my hips, catching the knee that was meant for my testicles on my upper thigh. I knew *that* would leave a bruise!

She spat in my face, shrieking, "You *mentul*! You *verpa*! No snot-nosed, Gallic, *cunnus* says *no* to Gabinia *Pulchra*."

"Is this how Romans perform foreplay?" Athauhnu asked dryly.

I fleetingly wondered where Athauhnu had picked up the Latin word for "foreplay," but another knee drove into my leg, and I remembered that I had my hands full with a raging Fury who wanted to kill me.

I released Gabinia's hands, but before she could do any damage to my face with her nails, I pushed her shoulders hard. She fell backward onto the couch.

"I think we have overstayed our welcome here!" I said to Athauhnu.

Gabinia continued to scream at me, saying I was a dead man, that she wouldn't rest until she had me killed and fed my body to pigs. Athauhnu and I beat a hasty retreat. We collected our gear from the *peristylium* and left quickly through the kitchens. Athauhnu grabbed a handful of olives on the way out.

As we hurried toward the stables, where we expected to find our horses, Athauhnu chuckled, "Now I know why all you Romans are up here in Gaul!"

"*Pro qua?*" I responded. "Why?"

"With women like that, you need to get as far away from Rome as you can!"

V.

De Proposito Novo Caesaris
CAESAR'S NEW AMBITIONS

---

*Bello Helvetiorum confecto totius fere Galliae legati
principes civitatum ad Caesarem gratulatum convenerunt*

"When the war with the Helvetians was concluded,
envoys from almost every nation of Gaul, the leading men
of their tribes, assembled to give thanks to Caesar."
(from Gaius Marius Insubrecus' notebook of Caesar's journal)

Throughout my military career, the speed at which rumor and gossip spread among the *muli* always amazed me. I don't think we were back in the legionary camps around Bibracte more than an hour before the boys were giving me the big grin, clapping me on the shoulder, and asking questions like, "Hey, *Pagane*! You set the date yet?" Or, "What you give your new bride as a wedding present? Your balls?" Even Emlun, Athauhnu's nephew, walked up to me, shook my hand solemnly and said, "Arth Uthr, if you haven't anyone to stand as a witness for you at the wedding, I would be honored."

I felt nothing as my mates ribbed me, at least not about what had happened with Gabi. At the time, I wondered at my lack of grief over her.

I have discovered in my career that, when a man receives a physical wound, a thrust from a sword or a slashing blow with a dagger, often he feels nothing at first. A deep thrust from a spear can feel no more serious than a punch in the stomach.

During the battle against the *Liberatores* at Phillipi, some *podex* got in around my open side and slashed my forearm with a *gladius* or a *pugio*. He opened my arm down to the bone. I felt the blow, but not the pain. I wrapped the wound in my *sudarium*, my neck scarf, and continued the fight. When the battle was done and my arm began to ache, I was almost surprised when I uncovered my wound. The worst pain I felt was when Spina poured that rot-gut wine of his over my arm and started stitching me up.

The *medici* cannot explain the numbness that comes with a sudden deep wound, other than to shrug and declare that the temporary suspension of pain is a gift of the gods. Spina theorizes that the wound itself does not generate pain; some other part of our bodies registers it. What part of the body and how it might be connected to other parts, Spina has no idea.

I've found that the *motus animi*, the gyrations of the mind that we sense as distress and anguish, act in a similar manner. We receive a blow—the death of a close comrade, the loss of a child—and when the blow lands, we feel nothing. And, in that brief interim between injury and pain, we have a chance to bury the shock of the wound deeply in the dark recesses of the *anima*, where *ratio*, human reason, never goes.

I think I had convinced myself that somehow I had not really lost *my* Gabi. That murderous harpy, Gabinia Calpurnia *Pulchra*, was an imposter, some grotesque parody of my beloved, a changling foisted upon me by the Danu, the dark god. Somewhere *my* Gabi, the girl with whom I took wild rides up into the Gallic hills, the girl whose hand I held in a shady, enchanted mountain glen while she read poetry to me, still existed and still awaited my return.

Perhaps the *medici* are right and this period of numbness is, indeed, a gift of the gods, meant to protect the *animus,* our consciousness, from the crippling awareness of loss and heartache. By the time I realized that my sentiments were wrong, that my Gabi had indeed morphed into a self-serving, homicidal virago named Gabinia Calpurnia Pulchra, I no longer cared. I had other worries.

The mockery and jokes didn't bother me either. When the *veterani* treat a first-campaigner like this, it's actually a sign of acceptance, an acknowledgement that the *tiro*, the rookie, is now one of them.

Besides, we were all in a good mood. With the defeat of the Helvetii, we assumed this year's campaigning season was over and soon we would be moving south into the warmer climes of the *Provincia* for the winter.

Caesar soon demonstrated to us the danger of making assumptions, regardless of how sensible they might seem, especially when they concerned *his* decisions.

During the third hour of our second day back, Caesar asked Labienus to give him a briefing on the state of the army. It was not a *consilium*, a war council. None of the senior officers were present. The only reason I was at headquarters was to try and make sense out of Caesar's journals for inclusion in his dispatches to Rome.

I was sitting at a field desk in the rear of Caesar's *cubiculum*, barely able to see over a virtual wall of *tabulae*, wax tablets, that had been accumulating in my absence. Caesar was seated by the campaign maps hung along the tent walls, while Labienus was standing and reading from the latest adminsitrative and logistics reports.

"So, after cross-leveling, we can field six operational legions, each of which is between 60-63 percent full strength, giving us a battleline strength of 18,787 *muli* and legionary-grade officers. We still have 682 men under medical care. The *medici* estimate that less than half of these will be back to full-duty status in the next sixty days. The rest may need to be mustered out."

"I understand the strength issues, Labienus," Caesar interrupted. "Tell me again about our rations status."

"Certainly, Caesar," Labienus responded. He closed the *tabula* from which he was reading and bent over to find another, which was mixed in a stack of reports on a chair next to Caesar.

Finally finding the logistics summary, Labienus opened it and reviewed it for a few heartbeats before speaking. "Drinking water's no problem . . . plenty of wells and springs in the area . . . We have enough livestock, grain, and sundries on hand to maintain the army at full rations for seven days . . . nine at the most . . . Most rations are being drawn from the Aedui . . . more than enough to sustain us until we move south."

"What makes you think we're moving south, Labienus?" Caesar interrupted again.

At that, I stopped fussing with the *tabulae* on my desk and gave Caesar my full attention.

Caesar's statement almost knocked Labienus off his cart. "Uh. . . with the Helvetii defeated and returned to the Rhenus, I assumed—"

Caesar changed the subject. "On my way back to our camps, I noticed teams of Roman *finitores*, surveyors, at work between here and the Rhonus. *I assume* you ordered this. For what purpose?"

Labienus was totally off script now. The logistics report, from which he had been reading, hung in his left hand at his side. "They are surveying the army's route back to the *Provincia*, Caesar. They are also to locate bridging points on the Rhonus for our crossing and sites on the south bank for camps—"

"*Us'erit*," Caesar interrupted him. "That will be useful, but I want you to change their mission."

While Labienus scrambled to find the *tabula* he used to take notes, Caesar continued, "Instruct the surveyors that I want them to plot the route of a logistics road between here and the river . . . a road capable of supporting heavy wagons . . . bridges over the Rhonus. . . heavy duty and semi-permanent . . . Also, plot the site of a logistics depot on our side of the river, capable of supplying this army . . . Tell them to keep in mind that they have to integrate the depot with the existing road network in the *Provincia*. My eventual goal is to have a *via munita*, a continuous ribbon of Roman paving stone from the docks at Massilia to my supply depot on the banks of the Rhonus . . . and at least a *via glareata* . . . gravel, not packed earth . . . from the Rhonus to our camps here."

Labienus was scribbling feverishly into his wax *tabula*. I had totally abandoned my work, wondering where Caesar was going with this. A dark thought was forming itself in my mind. Our expectations to be in winter quarters south of the Rhonus before the harvest began were evaporating in the heat of Caesar's new enthusiasms.

"Are we abandoning the depot at Lugdunum of the Sequani?" Labienus suddenly asked.

The question stopped Caesar dead in his tracks. I could feel his mind processing the question. "No! No, I don't think so," he answered. "That position could prove quite useful to us in the future."

Future! I thought. *What plans does the imperator have for this army? What would a supply depot that far east be useful for?*

"That's an execellent observation, Labienus!" Caesar continued. "That *oppidum* sits at the confluence of the Rhonus and the Arar. The high ground and bluffs are easily defensible . . . and it borders our *Provincia* . . . No . . . we will not abandon that position. . . It's strategically critical to us . . . Have our surveyors determine whether the Rhonus is navigable by barge to Lugdunum . . . I imagine the natives can tell us . . . If it isn't, can we make it so? . . . Then we will survey the Arar to the north . . . Again, the Aedui and Sequani who inhabit the area have the answers we need . . . I'm especially interested in a river, a tributary of the Arar known as *Flumen Nig'rum* . . . the Black River . . . The Greek geographies call it the *Dubis*. Gai! Since you've been easedropping on this conversation, tell me . . . what is the Gallic name for the Black River?"

I should have known by that time that Caesar had eyes in the back of his head and had seen me sitting there at my desk with my mouth hanging open. "The Black River, *Patrone?* That would be *Uhr Afon Du*," I translated.

"That's it!" Caesar said snapping his fingers. "The natives call it the *Arabondou* . . . That's where the Greeks got their name for it, Dubis . . . I want to know if supply barges can reach the confluence of the Dubis and the Arar from Lugdunum . . . I believe there's a settlement of the Sequani there . . . a small *oppidum* of some sort . . . Yes . . . this could be a prority."

Caesar walked over to his maps. "Here is Cavillonum of the Aedui on the Arar!" he stated pointing at a spot along a squiggly blue line representing the river. He then traced the river to where it intersected with another blue line. "The Dubis and a possible Sequani position," he said, to no one in particular, as his finger traced the second river. The Dubis looked like a blue horseshoe on the map, reaching up into the northeast, then doubling back on itself to the south.

"And, here!" Caesar announced, pointing to a spot near the top of the horseshoe. "Vesantio of the Sequani . . . whoever holds this position controls the valley of the Rhenus and access to central Gaul . . . This is strategically important . . . I must know who controls Vesantio."

Labienus broke Caesar out of his revery. "Caesar, perhaps if you'd share with me what your goals are in the East, I would understand why these places . . . Cavillonum . . . Vesantio . . . are so important to Rome . . . I don't understand."

Caesar seemed to come back into room with us. "My goals . . . ah . . . yes . . . I'm getting ahead of myself, Labienus. My apologies . . . The day after tomorrow, a deputation of Gallic kings, led by our current 'host,' Diviciacus of the Aedui, will arrive here . . . If that works out the way I expect it, all your questions will be answered. Meanwhile, issue the necessary orders to the surveyers in the South. I will send *exploratores* to the Arar. That may be a good mission for Adonus *Dux* and his Sequani. Do you agree, Gai?"

"*Ti' a'sentior, Patrone*," I snapped, "I agree, Patrone!" What else could I say?

"*Bene! Bene!*" Caesar said, bringing that discussion to an end. Then, suddenly, he said, "Gai, *quot'orarum?*"

Since we were under leather in Caesar's praetorium tent, I had to reference a burning candle next to my desk marked with twelve notches, one for each summer hour.

"Half the fourth hour, by the candle, *Patrone!*" I responded.

"Please, remain for this, Labienus," Caesar said. Then, he called out, "*Scriba!* Is the tribune, Agrippa, waiting?"

"*Te manet, Imperator,*" I heard Ebrius's voice call out from the other side of the tent flap.

"Then, send him in!" Caesar directed.

Agrippa, in full armor, his helmet clasped tightly under his left arm, burst smartly into the room: "*Imperator! Lucius Vipsanius Agrippa, Tribunus, dicto paret—*"

"*Laxa . . . laxa,*" Caesar stood Agrippa down. "At ease, Agrippa. Let's keep this thing informal. You're a member of my personal staff. You don't have to be on parade when you brief me."

Agrippa relaxed, just slightly.

"First, some administrative minutiae," Caesar announced. "Agrippa, you are relieved from your assignment with the Sequani cavalry and reassigned to my personal staff as my *quaestor exercitus*, quartermaster of the army. You may have to play hardball with my provincial quaestor and my legates, but I think you have the sand for it after the way you dealt with that broad-striped *mentul'* Gabinius, down in Massalia. I can't put a broad purple stripe on your tunic, at least not until you're appointed to the senate, but the purple sash of my *praetorium* should more than make up for that."

Agrippa's posture stiffened again, "*Imperator, paratus sum* . . . Sir, I am ready."

Caesar held up his hand and continued. "Labienus will brief you on the guidance I just gave him on our logistics goals. We have to remain somewhat flexible until the concept of our next mission develops. Which reminds me . . . Labienus!"

"Yes, *Imperator*," he snapped. I noticed "*Imperator*" had replaced "Caesar" in Labienus' response now that Agrippa had joined us.

"I want you to select a reliable *angusticlavus*, a junior tribune, to serve on my personal staff as an adjutant. His primary job will be maintaining the strength reports of the army and writing my orders. I want to free you from having to count every head and every sack of grain in the army so that you can spend more time in operations planning with me . . . The battle with the Helvetii demonstrated to me I need an officer who is prepared to take immediate command if, for some reason, I am . . . *uh* . . . shall we say, *non ad manum*, unavailable. The chap who commanded the *vexillatio* to the Rhenus, Caecina, may be a good choice for that job."

"*Compre'endo, Imperator*," Labienus muttered while scratching some notes into his tabula.

"Now, Agrippa," Caesar continued, "you said that you had a recommendation for me?"

"'*Abeo, Imperator*," Agrippa snapped. "I do, sir! It has to do with the way the army is conducting its foraging operations. We are being too passive. We rely on our allies to supply us at their convenience. This issue affected our operations during the pursuit of the Helvetii. We were forced to make choices based not on the tactical situation but on our logistical needs."

"I don't disagree with that observation, Agrippa," Caesar said. "Please continue."

Caesar's half-hearted agreement with Agrippa's assessment was enough for him to continue. "I recommend that we form an army-level unit of foragers whose mission is to fan out aggressively around the army's route of advance and acquire the needed rations. If the indigenous peoples agree to donate them, our troops would merely collect, pack, and transport. If the *pilosi*, the hair-bags, are less than cooperative, our men would convince them to part with the goods."

"Where would you get the men for this detail, Tribune?" Labienus asked.

"Legate," Aggrippa responded, "from our last battle, we have a number of wounded whom the *medici* believe will recover but will not be mission capable as infantry. They will not be able to endure the strain of a daily twenty thousand *passus* march *impeditus*, under full pack. I can offer them the choice of joining my unit and staying with the army. They are physically capable of riding supply wagons and providing security for the foraging details. It would be a better option for them than being mustered out with a few *quadriga* in their purses."

"Hmmm," Caesar muttered. "I am intrigued. If we march east, I don't want to find myself in the same postion I did when we stalled south of Bibracte and the Aedui had stripped their settlements of food and livestock."

There is that "march east" suggestion again. I was now sure that Caesar had already made up his mind about it. The deputation from the Gauls was just another one of his show pieces.

"There is another potential benefit to my plan, *Imperator*," Agrippa suggested.

"*Di' mi', Tribune*," Caesar nodded. "Tell me!"

"Our foragers can act as *exploratores, Imperator*," Agrippa continued. "They can collect intelligence about the attitudes of the natives, enemy movements on our flanks and in our rear, things like that."

Caesar was nodding now. "I am intrigued. What do you think, Labienus?"

"We have little to lose and much to gain," Labienus shrugged.

"*Constamus*," Caesar concluded. "We're agreed, then. Agrippa, we'll try this plan of yours, at least to test it. If it works like you think, it will become a permanent detail. If not, we've lost little. Do you have a name for this unit?"

"'*Abeo, Imperator*," Agrippa nodded. "I plan to call my men the *frumentarii*."

"The grain snatchers," Caesar translated. "*Bene*, Agrippa, make it happen."

Frumentarii. That was the first time I ever heard the word. At the time, I had no way of knowing the kind of a monster Agrippa's idea would morph into.

VI.

De Bello Novo Caesaris contra Ariovistum

CAESAR'S NEW CAMPAIGN
AGAINST ARIOVISTUS

Propterea quod Ariovistus rex Germanorum in eorum finibus consedisset
tertiamque partem agri Sequani qui esset optimus totius Galliae occupavisset
et nunc de altera parte tertia Sequanos decedere iuberet propterea quod
paucis mensibus ante Harudum milia hominum XXIIII ad eum venissent
quibus locus ac sedes pararentur futurum esse paucis annis uti omnes ex
Galliae finibus pellerentur atque omnes Germani Rhenum transirent.

"Ariovistus, a German king, settled in the territory of the Sequani and siezed
a third of their lands, the richest in all Gaul. Now, Ariovistus has ordered
the Sequani to hand over another third of their lands because, a few months
ago, the peoples of the Harudes, twenty-four thousand in all, had joined
him, and Ariovistus needs to provide them with living space and homes.
In a few years, the day will come when every Gaul will be driven out of the
land, and there won't be a single German left on the far side of the Rhenus!"

(from Gaius Marius Insubrecus' notebook of Caesar's journal)

Caesar's propensity for theater certainly did not disappoint.

On the tenth day before the calends of *September*, the expected Gallic deputation arrived at the camps of Caesar's army. The long line of Gallic chiefs in their best armor were mounted on prancing stallions and wrapped in the colorful tartans of their tribes. With bodyguards, druids, brehons, poets, musicians, and standards and banners snapping in the morning breeze, the parade seemed more like the arrival of a country fair than it did a serious political mission.

Caesar, his thinning hair topped with the golden leaves of his Civic Crown and his lean frame draped in a pure white magisterial toga with a broad purple stripe, sat waiting in his curial chair of state, elevated on a wooded platform and shaded by a canvas pavilion dyed the blood red of the legions. Behind him stood his legates in full battle armor, their plumed helmets locked in their left arms. Behind them stood the *laticlavi*, the senior tribunes of the army.

On each side of Caesar's platform stood a *centuria* of *muli*, an honor guard drawn from the First Cohort of the Tenth Legion, the biggest men in the legion. Commanding the detail, Tertius Piscius Malleus, the "Hammer," *Centurio Primus Pilus* of the Tenth, had polished and scrubbed these, his best troops, so they sparkled like the god of war himself in the late morning sun. The *muli* of Caesar's honor guard stood *laxantes*, at ease, the points of their *pila* pushed forward, their *scuta* grounded, and their feet apart.

Caesar had established his chair in a field surrounded by the *castra* of his six legions. On the parapet of each camp, the *muli* were assembled under arms; the *vexillia* of the legions snapped in the lively breezes blowing over the *portae principales*, the main gate of each camp, Roman red against the Gallic blue sky.

Caesar sat in the center of Roman power that had established itself before the walls of Gallic Bibracte.

The Gallic deputation, led by Diviciacus, King of the Aedui to the Romans, rode slowly into this stage of Roman steel and pomp. When they reached a point about fifty *passus* from Caesar, they halted. Diviciacus then rode forward alone, holding up his white wand of negotiation, so all could see that he had come to talk, not to fight.

As Diviciacus came forward, Malleus' voice rang out, "*Cohors Prima Legionis Decem!*"

The two centurions of the honor detail echoed, "*Centuria!*"

"*State!*" boomed Malleus.

As one, the entire honor detail pulled back *pila* and *scuta*. Their heels crashed together in a single clap of thunder.

Duuhruhda halted about five *passus* before Caesar's platform, holding his wand of negotiation forward for Caesar to see. The *imperator* acknowledged the gesture with a slight nod.

It was then that I noticed a wooden peg, a *sudis* stake, pounded into the ground exactly where Duuhruhda had pulled up his mount. I looked back to where the Gallic chiefs had halted, and there was a line of pegs marking the farthest point of their advance. There were even stakes marking the positions of Malleus' centuries. Not only had Caesar written the script for this scene, he had blocked it, and had somehow managed to rehearse it!

Duuhruhda began to recite his lines in Latin: "*Imperator! Caesar! Amicus sociusque gentibus libris Galliarum!* Victorious General! Caesar! Friend and ally of the free Gallic peoples! We understand that this war has avenged an ancient wrong perpetrated by the Helvetians on the Roman nation. Now the restless *lemures* of the brave Romans slain through the betrayal and deceit of the Helvetians can rest. We know too that this betrayal touched the very family of Caesar himself. What man could claim that Caesar had no right to vengeance? Who could say that Rome herself had no cause to avenge this ancient crime? Despite all this, Caesar's great victory had no less benefit to the free peoples of Gaul than it did to the Roman nation. The Helvetians, while they were most prosperous and powerful, left their homeland to wage war against all Gaul and to conquer it. In their great arrogance, the Helvetians desired a new homeland in the richest lands of Gaul. The free peoples of Gaul the Helvetians would have held in servitude. We, the leaders of the Gallic nations, freely assembled here before Caesar and the Roman nation, proclaim our thanks and gratitude for Caesar's victory over the Helvetians."

I immediately noticed how much Duuhruhda's Latin had improved. His speech was well coached. When he concluded, he turned his horse and held his wand of negotion up in his right hand toward the assembled host of Gallic chiefs. Despite the fact that most of them had no idea what Duuhruhda had just said, they gave Caesar a thunderous ovation.

Caesar allowed the cheering to continue for a while before standing and holding up his arms for silence. Then, he began, "*Ego, Gaius Iulius Caesar, Imperator, Proconsul gentis Romanae,* I, Gaius Iulius Caesar, Victorious General, Proconsul of the Roman nation, welcome you as friends and allies of Rome. I accept your thanks and gratitude, and I invite you to a great victory feast to celebrate the defeat of the Helvetians and the liberation of the Gallic nations!"

Caesar's generosity with the Aeduan food stocks knew no bounds! The Gallic assembly, despite the fact that most of them had no idea what Caesar had just said, again gave him an ovation.

When the clamor finally began to subside, I heard Duuhruhda say, "Caesar! I beg a favor of you!"

"Speak, King of the Aedui and friend of Rome," Caesar responded.

"Caesar," Duuhruhda continued, "I request that you grant a private audience to me and the leaders of the Sequani. We have information that is critical to all our peoples."

Ah, the plot of this little drama thickens, I thought.

Caesar announced loud enough that everyone assembled on his dais could hear, "I grant you this, Diviciacus. You and the Sequani may join me in my *principia* in one hour. Meanwhile, enjoy the moment of our victory with your people!"

As Caesar turned away to descend the platform, he spotted me standing to the side of one of Malleus' centuries. He gestured to me to follow him. I circled around to the back of the platform and met Caesar as he was shrugging off his toga into the arms of one of his personal slaves. A member of the praetorian detail was bringing Caesar's white stallion forward. Caesar's red general's cloak was drapped across the saddle.

"Enjoy the show?" he asked me with a wink.

"I had a good seat, *Imperator,*" I answered.

"I don't want you to miss the second act," he continued. "Report to my *principia* in half an hour. And, find your friend, Adonus *Dux*. A Sequani chief will be interested in what Diviciacus has to say."

With that, Caesar took the red cloak offered by his praetorian, mounted his horse, and rode away toward the *castrum* of the Tenth Legion.

By this point, I wouldn't have been a bit surprised to discover that Caesar already knew what Duuhruhda was about to say to him. Why shouldn't he? He wrote the lines.

I found Athauhnu with Guithiru and Ci at the Sequani horse lines at the rear of the camp of the Tenth Legion. Guithiru had been promoted to command one of the *alae*, a wing of Athauhnu's *turma*, his cavalry troop. Since the Sequani were equipped with Roman armor, drew Roman rations, were supplied with Roman horses, and were now paid in Roman silver–and the threat of the Helvetii seemed to have passed–their ranks were swelling with young Sequani riders from the East.

Athauhnu was inspecting one of the hooves of a new mount, a gray mare. "See, here. As I suspected, this hoof is bruised . . . It may have been caused by a stone, but I want this horse re-shod. Ah, Insubrecus *Decurio*," he said, switching to Latin, "to what do we owe the honor of your visit?"

I answered him in Ga'hel: "If I can tear you away from your girlfriend here, the Caisar requests your presence at his headquarters. He is meeting with Duuhruhda and some chiefs of the *Soucanai* from east of the Arar."

At the mention of Duuhruhda's name, both Ci and Guithiru spit on the ground. It would take more than a single campaign against a common enemy to overcome decades of enmity between the *Soucanai* and the *Aineduai*.

"Has that *moch*, that pig, surrendered his treacherous, shit-eating litter-mate, Deluuhnu, to the Caisar yet?" Athauhnu asked. Delhuuhnu's betrayal of Caesar's cavalry to the Helvetians was not forgotten by the *Soucanai*, who lost comrades and family members in the ambush.

"I haven't heard of it, my friend," I answered. "The Caisar believes that Deluuhnu has fled to Belgica in the East."

"Pah!" Ci spat. "It's more likely that he's with *Uh Gweleduth* among *uhr Almaenwuhr*, the Germans who stole our lands in the East."

Ci used an expression that surprised me, *uh Gweleduth*, the "Seer." "Who is this 'seer'?" I asked him.

"A *diafol*," Ci answered, "a demon, the bedmate of Hell, the goddess who rules the underworld of the *Almaenwuhr*." Ci further explained, "Some say he's a Belgian from *Arducoil*, the great forest that you Romans call *Arduenna Silva*. Some say he's one of the people of the goddess Ritona, who live on this side of the Rhenus. Others say he came out of the black forests across the Rhenus. He claims that he is the son of Tiw, the war god of both the *Belgai* and the *Almaenwuhr* . . . He seduced the chiefs of the Eastern *Soucanai* . . . For years they were paying tribute to the *Aineduai* for trade along the Arar. *Uh Gweleduth* said he could lead them to victory over their enemies and the *Aineduai* would then be paying tribute to them . . . All he asked in return was some land on this side of the Rhenus for his followers . . . Then he seduced the black forest people you Romans call the *Suebii* with Roman silver and promises of land . . . He and the *Soucanai* crushed the *Aineduai* in a great battle near the *Soucanai* fortress at Amagtobria . . . Instead of freeing our people from one master, he made them the thrall of another . . . Now the *Soucanai* pay tribute to *Uh Gweleduth* with silver and land. Meanwhile, his power along the Rhenus grows as the dregs of the *Belgai* and the *Almaenwuhr* swell the ranks of his followers . . . He tells them that his father, the god Tiw, has promised him all of Gaul as his empire . . . He tells them that even Rome fears him and will not intervene against him."

"I've never heard of this," I stammered.

"Why should you?" Ci shrugged. "*Uh Gweleduth* is far from the Roman lands south of the Rhodanus. The *Almaenwuhr* call him *Alleseher*, the 'All-Seer,' and to the Romans he's known as *Arisvisus*, the 'Vision of Mars.'"

Initially, I didn't give much weight to Ci's legend of a crazed mystic posing a threat on the Rhenus. But, the idea of a threat to the Sequani in the East, coupled with Caesar's interest in logistic routes to Vesantio on the Dubis and his private audience with representatives of the Sequani, could not be a coincidence.

As I was rapidly learning, with Caesar, there were no coincidences.

The next act of Caesar's drama began promptly at the fifth hour of the day. Caesar stood in front of his campaign maps, now in the full armor of a Roman commander. His highly polished plate *lorica* seemed to take on a bottomless, dark shine in the dim light of the tent, and his general's cloak seemed to glow ominously blood red.

For an audience, Caesar had assembled Labienus, all his legates, and the broad-stripe military tribunes; they gathered behind him, all in full armor. Off to the side stood Decius Minatius Gemellus, Caesar's *praefectus castrorum*, with the commanding centurions of all six legions. I stood to the other side with Agrippa, Caecina—Caesar's newly minted adjutant–Athauhnu, and Ebrius, who was keeping the minutes of the meeting in a wax *tabula*.

Athauhnu had managed to wash most of the horse-stink off himself. He had armed himself as a Roman cavalry officer in a red tunic and chainmail *lorica*, wrapped with the sash of a cavalry officer. His long, Gallic *spatha*, his cavalry sabre, hung at his left side from a polished leather baldric; a Roman infantry *pugio* hung from his belt on his right side. Out of recognition for his now elevated status in the Roman world, he had retired his colorful Sequani breaches and replaced them with a pair in plain brown leather, stuffed into a pair of Roman boots. His long hair was braided and tied back behind his head; his mustachios hung down past his chin. He looked every inch a man whose legs were rooted in two different worlds.

Caesar had given his officers no warning of what Duuhruhda's request of him would be. Drama, whether it be comedy or tragedy, thrives on the delight of surprise.

There was a commotion at the entry of Caesar's *cubiculum* as an optio of the praetorian detail entered. "*Imperator!*" the man entoned, "Diviciacus, King of the Aedui, and two chiefs of the Sequani beg an audience."

"*Ingrediantur!*" Caesar delivered his lines.

Duuhruhda entered, still in his ceremonial finery from his last scene. Behind him entered two warriors, Sequani by their blue and green tartans. They did not seem at all comfortable in their parts, looking about Caesar's headquarters as if they expected an ambush to be lurking in every shadow.

Diviciacus assumed an orator's pose before Caesar and began, "Great Caesar, *Imperator* of the Romans, friend of the free peoples of Gaul, I, Diviciacus, King of the Aedui, come before you with a petition from the Sequani."

Caesar nodded and said, "Speak, Diviciacus, King of the Aedui, friend and ally of the Roman People."

Diviciacus launched into his address: "Great Caesar! Despite the great danger that hangs over us like Damocles sword—"

Damocles sword! I thought. *Either Duuhruhda has brushed up on the histories of Diodorus before this meeting, or Caesar's script is painting the flowers!*

I looked around. The centurions were all stony faced, as centurions normally are. A few of the legates and tribunes were nodding encouragement in Duuhruhda's direction. I wondered briefly how many of them were already in on the fix.

"The people of Gaul are divided into two factions, one led by the Aedui in the West, the other led by the Sequani in the East. These factions have struggled for years to gain dominance for trade along the Rhonus. Then, the Sequani invited Germans to join them."

The Sequani in Duuhruhda's entourage stared fixedly at the ground, refusing eye contact with anyone in the room.

"At first, some fifteen thousand Germans crossed the Rhenus. Soon after, because these brutal and savage people lust after the fertile lands and the great wealth of Gaul, hordes of Germans came over. Now there are tens of thousands of Germans in Gaul. The Aedui and their allies fought against them, but we suffered a terrible defeat. All our best warriors and chiefs were slaughtered; our confederation was devastated in this catastrophe. The Aedui were forced to surrender hostages and were bound by a sworn oath never to demand the return of these captives, never to seek aid from the Roman people, never to renounce the domination of the Sequani."

Duuhruhda has obviously brushed up on his rhetoric in preparing his oration, I noted. *His rhetorical conduplicatio and alliteration on numquam. . . numquam . . . numquam . . . never . . . never . . . never . . . is worthy of a speech before the senate itself. Such a rhetorical performance might even be worthy of the magister's notice.*

"I, Diviciacus, am the only chief of all the Aedui who could not be forced into swearing this odious oath or surrendering his cherished children as hostages. So, I alone, bound neither by oath nor obligation, come before Great Caesar and the Roman people to seek help. However, worse has happened to the victorious Sequani than happened to the conquered Aedui."

Duuhruhda gestured grandly toward his two companions in Sequani livery. Both looked away from him, seemingly embarrassed by the gesture.

Duuhruhda continued, "Ariovistus, a German king, has settled in the lands of the Sequani along the Rhenus, the richest lands in all Gaul. Now, Ariovistus demands the Sequani surrender their lands along the river Dubis and their great fortress at Vesantio. He claims that the Harudes, the Marcomanni, the Triboci, the Vangiones, the Nemetes, the Sedusii–the most savage of that savage race, who inhabit the black forests across the Rhenus—have joined him and his *Suebii*. Ariovistus claims he needs to provide them with living space and homes. In a few years, a day will come when every Gaul will be driven out of the land, and there won't be a German left on the other side of the Rhenus! However, not only does this savage threat hang over the Gauls, but also over the Romans."

Ah, I thought, here it comes: Caesar's baited hook!

Duuhruhda raised his right arm and pointed directly at Caesar and his assembled senior officers. "If Ariovistus is allowed to dominate the river Dubis, how long will it be before he dominates the river Arar? If Ariovistus conquers the lands along the river Arar, how long will it be before his savage hordes are camped on the banks of the Rhonus? And, once Ariovistus reaches the Rhonus, do you believe that his greed and ambition will be sated as he stares across at the lush valleys of the Roman *Provincia*? I say no! He and his barbaric horde will pour over the Rhonus as the Cimbri, the Teutones, the Ambrones and the Tigurini did in the days of our grandfathers."

Interesing use of the word "our," I noted. *I don't remember the Aedui siding with the Romans in that war.*

Duuhruhda went for the close. "So my question, oh, Great Caesar, is this: Does the Roman nation want to face this German threat while it is in its infancy or wait until it grows into a hideous beast? Do you wish to destroy Ariovistus on the banks of the Rhenus, or do you want to take your chances on the banks of the Rhonus? This is what I ask, oh, Caesar! This is the favor for which I beg. Smother this threat to Gaul and to Rome in its cradle. March against Ariovistus now!"

Caesar, of course, did not immediately respond. He was waiting for Duuhruhda's heroic monologue to sink in with the Romans he had gathered as an audience. For a few heartbeats, he stared at the ground before him, seemingly pensive. Finally, he lifted his head and responded.

"I hear your words, Diviciacus, *amicus sociusque*, friend and ally. Rome is not in the habit of abandoning her friends. Rome hears the cries of her allies. But, this army is exhausted. We have just completed a monumental struggle against a powerful foe, the Helvetii. The smoke of our funeral pyres still darkens the battlefield where many brave Romans fell defending the land of the Aedui. I must discuss this matter with my officers. I will give you my answer before the sun sets."

Duuhruhda bowed and said, "I can ask no more of the Great Caesar and the Roman nation." His final lines delivered, he turned and exited the stage, herding the two reluctant Sequani bit players off with him.

As they left, Caesar caught my eye and nodded toward the exit through which the Gauls had just passed. I whispered to Athauhnu, "*Dilunooch fi!* Come with me!"

The Sequani had wasted no time separating themselves from Duuhruhda as soon as they left Caesar's presence. As we approached, they looked at us defensively. To them, we were two Romans.

Athauhnu broke the ice. "*A uhw'n wir uhr hun a thuhwedoth uh mochyn o Aineduai?* Is what that Aeduan pig says true?"

Recognizing the accents of the *Soucanai*, the men relaxed a bit. "I see a Roman, but I hear a Soucana," the one on the right challenged.

"I am Athauhnu mab Hergest, a leader of a hundred in the Caisar's cavalry. This is Arth mab Secundus of the Insubres beyond the great mountains."

"Arth mab Secundus?" the Sequani challenged. "Are you a Ga'hel or a Roman?"

"I am a man and a warrior," I told him.

He smiled, "A good answer! I am being rude. I am Aneirin mab Berwuhn, a leader of a hundred for the *Cadeuhrn* of Vesantio. My companion is Dai mab Gluhn, a leader of ten in my troop."

"The Battle Lord of Vesantio," Athauhnu translated. "How do things stand with our people along the black river? Is what that *Aineduai* pig says true?"

"We hold Vesantio," Aneirin shrugged. "The *Almaenwuhr* and *Belgai* in the valley of the Rhine grow stronger, but we still hold *uh porth*, 'the Gate' between the mountains."

"There are *Belgai* with the *Almaenwuhr*?" I asked.

"*Shuh*," Aneirin affirmed. "Yes! And *Aineduai* horsemen . . . and Rhufeiniaid."

"Rhufeiniaid!" I said. "Romans!"

"*Shuh*," Aneirin nodded. "They claim they are merchants. They must pass through the valley of the black river to reach the Rhine. But, for merchants, they travel light. They carry nothing to trade . . . just silver for the *Almaenwuhr*."

"And you said *Aineduai*, too?" Athauhnu pressed.

"*Shuh*," Aneirin nodded again. "A troop of heavily armed *Aineduai* cavalry forced a passage through the Gate a couple of weeks ago. They were led by a prince of the *Aineduai*, called the Deluuhnu."

Deluuhnu, brother of Duuhruhda, I thought.

"How do you know this?" Athauhnu pressed.

Aneirin smiled coldly. "I said the *Aineduai* forced the Gate; I didn't say they all made it through. Some of them fell into our hands and were . . . convinced, let's say . . . to talk to us."

"The leader of the people along the Rhine," I pressed. "Is it the Ariovistus as the *Ainedua* chief claims?"

Aneirin nodded. "Ariovistus is what the *Rhufeiniaid* call him. To the *Soucanai*, he is *uh Gweleduth*, the 'Seer.' He now calls himself *uhn fab i Rudianos*, the Son of Rudianos, the god whom the *Rhufeiniaid* call Mars. He claims that the god, his father, has promised him rule of all the middle lands."

Aris Vistus, I thought, *the Seer of Mars . . . Ariovistus.*

When Athauhnu and I returned to Caesar's headquarters, we discovered that the little drama had not been received as well as the playwright had hoped.

The room was divided with the legates and senior tribunes to one side and the senior centurions to the other.

Gemellus, the camp praefect, was looking on, expressionless, while Malleus, *Centurio Primus Pilus* of the Tenth Legion, spoke, "The Tenth will do its duty, *Imperator*, as I'm sure all your legions will . . . but the battle with the Helvetii took its toll on the men . . . Strength is down; the men are exhausted . . . To march to the Rhenus, where no Roman army has ever gone, may be . . . may be . . . too optimistic a goal for now . . . We can winter on the Rhonus . . . refill our ranks . . . refit and let the men get their legs back . . . Then we can go after these German *verpae* in the spring."

The other centurions were nodding in agreement with the Hammer. The legates and the tribunes remained silent. I noticed the faces of some of Caesar's legates were as white as a *lupa's* face on a forum holiday.

Finally, Crassus spoke up. "Delay is our enemy, Malleus. If those *Grunni*, those grunting barbarians, penetrate the valley of the Dubis and take Vesantio, we'll have all Hades to pay to dislodge them. I say march now! Hit them hard before they're ready for us. Every day we delay, a few hundred more of those hairbags cross the Rhenus!"

I could see Malleus was about to respond when Caesar spoke up. "Gemellus! What's the bottom line on this? Is the army ready to march against Ariovistus?"

The centurions stared at the ground. Gemellus delayed for a few heartbeats. For a Roman officer, there was only one acceptable answer to this question.

"*Parati, Imperator!*" Gemellus stated simply, "We are ready, sir!"

The other centurions slowly assumed the position of attention in front of their general. But, their eyes remained masked.

Caesar nodded in their direction with a grunt. "Very well! Thank you for your advice . . . all of you . . . You will have my decision before the tenth hour . . . Labienus and my personal staff, remain . . . The rest of you . . . *miss'est* . . . you are dismissed!"

As the senior centurions filed out of Caesar's headquarters, none of them spoke. I heard none of the normal bantering back and forth between them about whose boys were choking the dog in training exercises, or whose camp looked more like a Greek resort town than a Roman military installation. Even the

'Hammer,' who never missed an opportunity to give me some shit about being tied to Caesar's cloak, walked past me as if I wasn't even there.

Caesar noticed me in the back of the tent. "*Decurio*! Did you learn anything from the Sequani?"

I went over to where Caesar and Labienus were standing. "*Imperator*, the Sequani report that they still hold Vesantio and a place they call *uh Porth*, 'the Gate.' Ariovistus' forces are still to east and north along the Rhenus but are pressing the Sequani."

Labienus interrupted, "What is this position called 'the Gate'?"

I shrugged and started, "I'm not sure, Legate, but it seems to be between Vesantio and the Rhenus."

Athauhnu, who was standing behind me, spoke up, "The Gate is a passage between the valleys of the Dubis and the Rhenus, where the Dubis turns south for its run to the Arar . . . It's an opening north of the mountains of the forest that you Romans call *Iuria* and south of *Vosego Mons* . . . In the middle of the pass is a small *oppidum* of the Sequani called *Caer Harth* . . . It's called 'the Gate' because it is the portal to the valley of the Rhonus."

Athauhnu now had Caesar's interest. "Adonus *Dux*, can you show me on my map where this . . . this 'ah port' is?"

I saw a momentary look of panic in Athauhnu's eyes. I was sure that he understood the Latin word, *tabula*, but I was quite sure he had never seen an actual map.

"Permit me, *Imperator*," I said, coming to Athauhnu's rescue. I walked over to Caesar's campaign map and found the blue, asymmetric horseshoe representing the river Dubis. I picked up the wooden *sudis* stake used for map briefings.

"This is where the Dubis flows south toward the Arar," I said, pointing to the top of the horseshoe. "To the south, the Jura Mountains; to the north, the Vosges; between them, the Gate, with *Caer Harth* . . . *Castrum Bellum* . . . in the center."

"*Castrum Bellum*," Caesar repeated, "Belfort . . . that's the key, Labienus . . . if I can get my legions in front of Belfort, Ariovistus will have to come to me!"

"There are other matters, *Imperator*," I offered.

"Other matters?" Caesar repeated, turning back to me from Labienus.

"Yes, *Imperator*," I said. "The Sequani report that Dumnorix is with Ariovistus."

"Dumnorix, you say?" Caesar followed quickly. "So much the better. I have some unfinished business with that *verpa*."

"Yes, *Imperator*," I agreed. "But, you should know that the Sequani also report there are Romans with Ariovistus in the valley of the Rhenus."

VII.

Comites Caesari

CAESAR'S COMPANIONS

Paulatim autem Germanos consuescere Rhenum transire et in Galliam
magnam eorum multitudinem venire populo Romano periculosum
videbat neque sibi homines feros ac barbaros temperaturos existimabat
quin cum omnem Galliam occupavissent ut ante Cimbri Teutonique
fecissent in provinciam exirent atque inde in Italiam contenderent

"Moreover, Caesar believed that the Germans would gradually think nothing
of crossing the Rhenus and their great numbers in Gaul would be a menace
to the Roman nation. Caesar concluded that, when the Germans had seized
all Gaul, as the Cimbri and the Teutones had done before, a people so violent
and barbaric would pour into the Province and then invade Italy."

(from Gaius Marius Insubrecus' notebook of Caesar's journal)

---

*W*hen I told Caesar about the Romans, he just stared at me
blankly for a few heartbeats. Then Agrippa broke in, "I'm
sure there are Roman merchants who operate along the Arar
and the Dubis."

"That may be true, Tribune," I responded, "but the Sequani report that *these* merchants travel without trading goods. They also cannot be *Roman* spies, because they travel openly as Romans."

"Will those *mentul'* never cease their plots against me?" I heard Caesar ask no one in particular.

He then seemed to come back to himself and rejoin the discussion. "Neither the Roman presence nor that of Dumnorix is material to our purpose," he stated. "We'll deal with them in due course . . . Labienus . . . I've never seen Malleus so hesitant about advancing when there's an enemy before him . . . Do you have a feel for the temper of the troops? Is the army in as bad a shape as the centurions imply?"

Labienus thought for a few heartbeats before replying. "There is the issue of attrition after the battle with the Helvetii, but all of our legions are mission capable as far as equipment and manpower. The men are rested . . . We are well stocked with rations . . . The equipment is combat ready."

Caesar interrupted, "Then what is it, Labienus? What is compelling my senior centurions to advise delay?"

"From what I hear, a couple of matters are affecting the men's morale," Labinus offered. "First, the men are angry that you released the Helvetians and did not place them *sub corona* . . . After such a desperate battle, the men felt entitled to the silver from the slave traders."

"I need a strong buffer on the Rhenus, Labiene," Caesar started.

This time Labienus interrupted, "*I* understand the strategic issue, *Imperator*, but from the point of view of the troops, they would rather have silver in their purses today and worry about a new battle tomorrow. Also, the *castrones* are stirring up trouble over the cross-leveling."

"The *castrones*!" Caesar barked. "The *mus castrorum*! The camp rats! Army brats! What possible problem could they have? Weren't there plenty of early promotions to fill key leadership positions in the cohorts?"

"That's true, *Imperator*," Labienus continued, "but the new legions . . . the Eleventh and Twelfth . . . were recruited in *Gallia Cisalpina* from the locals . . . The citizenship of many of these recruits is . . . well . . . doubtful . . . and many of the new troops can hardly speak more Latin than they had to learn in basic training . . . The *castrones* resent the new legions in general, but now that we have cross-leveled some of these recruits into the veteran legions, the *castrones* are stirring up the waters against them . . . Already there have been some issues . . . fights breaking out in the camps and the taverns in the *vicus*."

Agrippa must have seen the look of confusion in my eyes. He inclined in my direction and whispered, "The *castrones* are the sons of former legionaries and their camp women . . . They were born into the army . . . Some of them are third generation legionaries . . . They believe that they themselves should judge who is worthy to serve under the eagles . . . soldier or officer."

Caesar was speaking, "This is nothing a centurion's cudgel can't fix, Labienus. Have the legionary officers knock some sense into them!"

"I don't recommend that, *Imperator*," Labienus countered. "That would not put the fire out. The embers would still glow hot under the ashes. The only fix for this is time . . . Once the *castrones* accept the Gaulic legionaries as *dignos* . . . worthy . . . this thing will blow over."

"So you think a winter in camp south of the Rhonus will fix the problem?" Caesar asked.

"It would help sort things out," Labienus agreed, "but there are other issues."

"Continue," Caesar granted.

"The enemy are Germans, Caesar," Labienus said. "Most of these men were brought up on their mothers' tales of those wild, hairy demons from beyond the Rhenus who would put them on spits and roast them over their camp fires."

"Pah!" Caesar dismissed Labienus' concern. "We massacred the Cimbri the last time they dared show their hairy faces in the civilized world."

"That was on the Rhonus with a Marius," Labienus countered. "You propose to march to the Rhenus without—" Labienus then realized his blunder.

"Without a Marius," Caesar completed his thought.

Labienus' face turned as red as that of a victorious general's during his triumph.

"Don't worry, Labienus," Caesar consoled. "I've said it many times . . . *libertas* . . . candor is a Roman virtue . . . I value your frank and candid opinions. Remember that, all of you! Don't tell me what you think *I want* to hear; tell me what I *need* to hear. If this army is to win, I need your honest counsel. You'll have plenty of chances to kiss some senator's *culus* when you're running for office back in Rome."

Caesar's banter seemed to lighten the mood a bit. Then, he said to Labienus, "Let me see if I got it all . . . The men are pissed off because I let their slaves go . . . The *castrones* don't like to share their tents with hicks from Gaul . . . The men are crapping their loincloths over marching to the Rhenus to fight a few shaggy Krauts . . . Is that it?"

"There is one other matter," Labienus vacillated.

"Out with it, Labienus," Caesar urged. "You haven't seemed concerned about protecting my feelings to this point . . . Why start now?"

"It's . . . uh . . . it's a political issue," Labienus hesitated.

"Shall we retire?" Agrippa offered.

"No!" Caesar stated. "None of you can advise me unless you understand *all* the issues! Out with it, Labienus . . . I think I know what you're going to say, but tell me anyway."

Labienus shrugged. "Ariovistus is on this side of the Rhenus because Rome invited him. The senate itself declared him a king, a friend, and an ally of Rome. How can we just ignore that declaration and attack him?"

Caesar nodded. "Good . . . the weasel's out of the bag . . . Everything you say is true, Labienus . . . I myself was seated in the senate when that declaration was made . . . It made sense *then* . . . It does not make sense *now* . . . Ariovistus and the *Suebii* were encouraged to cross the Rhenus because, at that time, the biggest threat to Roman peace in Gaul was the Aedui, not a ragtag bunch of *Grunni* still dripping wet from swimming across the Rhenus . . . During the consulship of Murena and Silanus, my predecessor, as proconsul of Cisalpine Gaul, Quintus Caecilius Metellus Celer, met with Ariovistus personally . . . And Ariovistus served Rome well when he allied with the Sequani and destroyed the power of the Aeduan confederation at Magetobriga . . . That was then . . . Now, the Aedui are our allies . . . There are hundreds of *pilosi* crossing the Rhenus every day, and Ariovistus is pressuring the Sequani to give him lands in the valley of the Dubis. *Ariovistus* is now the greatest threat to the peace and well-being of the *imperium* . . . As far as what the senate may think, I don't give a brass *as* . . . By the time those dithering old fools find out, I'll have Ariovistus and his Krauts under the yoke . . .

And if you're worried about legalities, Labienus, just remember . . . the senate also passed a resolution that the proconsul of Gaul can take *any* measures he sees fit to protect the welfare of the *imperium* . . . I sat in the senate for that one, too . . . A permanent German presence along the Dubis or the Arar is not acceptable to Rome, and that's exactly what we'll be facing unless we act now."

Caesar let his speech sink in.

I heard later that Caesar could out-Cicero Cicero himself in a debate. This was the first evidence I had seen of it. Labienus was left speechless, as were we all. Caesar had already made up his mind on the issue.

Caesar then continued, "Let me propose *this* to you, gentlemen. I will send a message to Ariovistus. I will advise him that I am willing to confirm his status as king and ally of Rome on *this* side of the Rhenus under the following conditions . . . First, all German migration into Gaul *must* cease immediately . . . Second, he *must* send back all tribes that have joined him since he defeated the Aedui . . . Third, he *must* cease harassing the Sequani and the Aedui, who are now allied to Rome . . . Fourth, he *must* return all the hostages he has taken from the Aedui . . . If he refuses, I will enforce the will of Rome with my army . . . I think this will maintain the honor of Rome by reestablishing the conditions of our original agreement with him . . . Will that suffice?"

There was no response as we tried to digest all that Caesar had just offered.

So, Caesar continued, "There are two additional matters that I want you to consider. First, it is my policy to allow no German settlements west of the Rhenus. Allowing Ariovistus and the *Suebii* to remain would be an exception . . . One I am not totally comfortable with, but one I could live with . . . *for now*. Second, I do not expect Ariovistus to accept my terms. His German allies would tear him to shreds if he tried to send them back across the Rhenus. So, we are not waiting for his response. We will march east toward the Rhenus in the wake of my messengers. I want my army established in the Gate at Belfort when I receive Ariovistus' refusal. Then, he will have to come to me, and I will be ready for him."

This, I learned, was Caesar's way of conducting a campaign: strategically aggressive, tactically defensive. Force the enemy to react, then engage them from a position of strength. Make them come to him in a position of his own choosing.

It seemed obvious to all in that room that the decision to advance on Ariovistus had been made. If, on my way out of the tent, I were to ask Ebrius to see a copy of Caesar's message to Ariovistus, I was sure he could have produced it in triplicate: one copy for Ariovistus, one for the army file, and one for the state archives. Our job now was to make the plan work.

Caesar continued, "Caecina, prepare the orders for the legions to march in three days . . . That would be—"

"The sixth before the Kalends of September," Caecina suggested.

"Yes," Caesar agreed. "The day is *fastus*, propitious, is it not?"

Caecina nodded.

"*Bene!*" Caesar continued. "Assign the legates to the legions, same as they were against the Helvetii . . . Young Crassus will stay with the cavalry . . . Tell the *haruspex* of the Tenth Legion to perform the auguries tomorrow at dawn . . . Be sure he understands: I don't care what he pulls out of the guts of his chickens . . . Unless Mars himself appears to me and orders me not to march, this army moves out in three days."

Caecina was nodding as he took notes in a wax *tabula*.

Caesar continued, "We are not abandoning this position . . . Instruct the Eleventh and Twelfth Legions each to detail their Tenth Cohort to man this position . . . Place the broad striper from the Eleventh in command . . . What's his name—"

"Licinius," Labienus suggested, "Quintus Porcius Licinius."

"No connection to Cato?" Caesar quizzed.

"No, *Imperator* . . . different branch of the *gens Porcia* altogether," Labienus stated.

"*Bene!*" Caesar agreed, "Quintus Porcius Licinius it is then . . . Any questions, Caecina?"

"*N'abeo, Imperator*," Caecina answered. "No, sir!"

"*Bene!*" Caesar nodded. "Put the warning order out to the senior centurions of each legion immediately . . . officers' call here, tomorrow morning, third hour . . . We'll give them the written order then . . . I imagine I'll get an earful from the legionary officers then . . . eh, Labienus?"

Labienus shrugged, "They're Romans. Once the decision is made, they'll soldier up to it."

"*Bene*," Caesar agreed. "That brings us to you, Agrippa. What are the surveyors reporting about my supply lines from Massalia?"

Agrippa had to think on his feet. This was the first any of us had heard about Caesar's ambitions on the Rhenus. Agrippa walked over to Caesar's campaign map and began, "The surveyors are still working along the Rhonus, but they believe that it's reasonably navigable from Massalia to Lugdunum of the Sequani."

"Reasonably?" Caesar challenged.

Agrippa answered, "The natives tell us that the current in the river is so strong in the spring months that moving supply barges north may not be possible."

"A road then?" Caesar prompted.

"A road then," Agrippa repeated. "There is a well-traveled native road that runs along the south bank of the river to Lugdunum. This time of year it will support supply wagons moving north from the port at Massalia. For this campaign, we can move supply along the road to Lugdunum. There is no need to build another supply depot south of that location; Lugdunum is capable of supplying our current position here at Bibracte over land and our putative postion at Belfort through the valley of the Arar and the Dubis."

Caesar was nodding. "What if Rome needs to make a long-term military commitment to eastern Gaul? Can I maintain troops north of the Rhonus throughout the winter?"

Caesar now had our complete attention. *Wintering in Gaul!*

Tracing with his finger over the map, Agrippa started, "We already have a *via munita*, a paved road, north from Massalia eighteen thousand *passus* to Aquis Sextus. There it connects to an east-west paved Roman road, which leads to the Rhonus at Arelato, another fifty-five thousand *passus*. From there we pick up the native road going north up the valley of the Rhonus. We believe it's a *via glareata*, a gravel road, as far north as Avennione, say another eighteen thousand *passus*. From there, it's a *via terrena*, a dirt road, all the way up to Lugdunum, about a hundred thirty thousand *passus*."

"A hundred thirty thousand *passus* of dirt road," Caesar repeated, staring at the blue line that represented the Rhonus on his map. "That's six days for a legion. How long to get wagons up it?"

Agrippa did some quick math in his head: "In dry weather . . . thirteen . . . fourteen days from Avennione to Lugdunum . . . two days from Arelato to Avennione . . . *Aquis Sextus* to Arelato on the Roman road . . . two, maybe three days . . . Massalia to Aquis Sextus, a day. So, best case scaenario, about twenty days . . . We get some rain and the dirt road goes to mud . . . thirty days . . . Snow . . . I couldn't guess."

Caesar processed what Agrippa had told him, then asked, "How long by river?"

Agrippa replied, "Right now we have no way of trans-shipping from the docks at Massalia to river barges . . . In fact, we don't have the river barges either . . . So, at least in the short term, river transport is not a viable alternative for us—"

Caesar interrupted, "The delta of the Rhonus is right across the bay from Massalia . . . Could we not send ships or barges directly across?"

"We could investigate that option," Agrippa agreed. "But, I don't know how far up the delta we could get our supply ships, if at all . . . We would still have to trans-ship at some point to river barges, and we simply do not have them."

"So, for this campaign, we are dependent on the wagons and whatever your *frumentarii*, your grain-snatchers, can supply us with."

That wasn't a question, so Agrippa did not respond.

After a few heartbeats, Caesar said, "So, let's finish our business on the Rhenus quickly, gentlemen, so we don't outrun our supplies again. Good work, Agrippa! We shall have all winter to build a viable supply line from Massalia. It's always good to keep soldiers busy . . . even in winter camp."

A viable supply line to Lugdunum of the Sequani, I thought. *Caesar plans to winter his army north of the Rhodonus in Gallia Comata,* "Gaul of the Long-Hairs."

"Again," Caesar was saying, "you are my personal staff . . . *mi comites,* my companions, so to speak . . . When we meet as a group, I want your honest and frank opinions, even if they don't agree with mine . . . Also, we can do away with the military courtesies during our private discussions . . . You may address my as Caesar . . . We can argue all we like when we're discussing matters . . . but once I have made a decision, discussion ends . . . As far as the army is concerned, it is *our* decision . . . Is that clear?"

"*Liquet, Caesar!*" we responded.

"*Bene!*" Caesar said. "You all have work to do, so this meet's over . . . Gai, please remain . . . I have something to discuss with you . . . The rest of you . . . *miss'est* . . . you're dismissed."

When the rest of Caesar's newly minted *comites* had filed out of the tent, Caesar walked over to his field desk. "Please, join me, Gai," he invited.

"*Adsum ti', Patrone,*" I responded rather stiffly.

"Relax," Caesar said as he rummaged for something beside his desk. "I understand you had a birthday. . . The Ides of Quintilis, was it not . . . Your seventeenth?"

I was again amazed at Caesar's attention to details, especially when it came to his soldiers.

"Yes, *Patrone*," I agreed.

"Ah . . . here it is," he said and hauled a clumsy bundle up onto his desk. "It's a birthday gift from your mother."

"*Me' mama!*" I said, so surprised that I almost failed to catch the stack of *tabulae* Caesar upset when he plunked the bundle down.

"Yes . . . *tu' mama,*" Caesar laughed.

"But, how?" I stammered.

Caesar shrugged, "When my couriers pass through Mediolanum, on their way back from Aquileia, I have them look in on your family. My man had a hell of a time balancing this piece of baggage on his horse . . . Well . . . are you going to open it or just stand there staring at it with your mouth hanging open?"

I untied the bundle to reveal a wheel of cheese—from our goats by the smell of it—a pair of new woolen socks, a sturdy-looking blue neck scarf, and a comb.

Caesar picked up the scarf. "Hardly regulation . . . but blue *is* the color of the patroness of my *gens*, Venus. And, please share that cheese with your mates . . . I can smell it from here."

As if on cue, Ebrius, Caesar's clerk, entered the cubiculum with a pitcher and two cups.

"Is that wine up to standard?" Caesar quipped.

"Right fitting for a birthday," Ebrius winked and belched modestly.

"*Bene*," Caesar responded, "put it down . . . uh." Caesar realized that my birthday bundle just about covered his desk. He brushed a few more *tabulae* onto the floor, clearing a space. "Right there!"

Ebrius set the cups and pitcher down. From the way he swayed out of the tent, he had done more than just sample my birthday wine.

Caesar laughed, "I imagine I don't have to worry about anyone poisoning my wine!" He handed me a brimming cup, lifted his cup, and said, "Happy Birthday, Gai!"

As I saluted him and drank, he said, "Ah . . . before I forget," Caesar put down his cup and was again rummaging around behind his desk. He finally came up with a scroll and handed it to me, saying, "Happy Birthday . . . from me this time!"

For a second, I didn't realize that I'd have to put down my cup to open the scroll. When my mind cleared enough to execute that little maneuver, I unrolled the scroll and read the first line of the first folio, "μῆνιν ἄειδε θεὰ Πηληϊάδεω Ἀχιλῆος . . . Sing, goddess, the anger of Peleus' son Achilleus." It was a copy of the *Iliad*!

"*Mille gratias, Patrone*," I stammered.

Caesar just held his hand up, "There's also a copy of Homer's other poem, *Odyssey*, on that scroll. You'll have some time on your hands this winter, and it's about time you found out how this thing ends. Besides, you have to learn how to speak proper Greek, the *Koine*. You never know . . . We may have to pay a visit to Alexandria one of these days."

Finally, Caesar handed me a rolled piece of papyrus tied with a red ribbon.

"More?" I sputtered.

"A letter from *tu' mama*," Caesar mocked me gently. "The red ribbon is for your birthday. Now, I'm sure you want to read what *tu' mama* has to say, so get yourself and this bloody cheese out of my tent before a rumor starts that I'm sharing my cot with a goat!"

Valeria Helvetia Minor, Matrona, to her son, Gaius Marius Insubrecus, Decurio, on his seventeenth birthday, salutem plurimam dicit!

I hope this letter finds you in good health and in the good graces of Bona Fortuna Dea. May the good goddess hold you close to her bosom, as I cannot.

I can hardly believe that it has only been a year since we celebrated your last birthday here at home. Your father and I prosper, as does your brother, Lucius.

Your father was afflicted with the coughing sickness this winter, but I sacrificed a hen to Apollo and offered a pitcher of wine to Vediovis for his recovery. Now, he thrives, dis multissimas gratias! Your brother, Lucius, has become infatuated with my maid Amanda. I am not encouraging this pairing. I'm sure I could find a better match for your brother among the Roman community in Mediolanum, but as I'm sure you understand, who can reason with a young man who thinks he's in love?

Our farm continues to sustain us. Mother Ceres, lauda nomen suum, has been kind to us. The weather since the feast of Cerealia has been warm, with a perfect mix of rain and sunshine. So, this year's crop promises to be bountiful. We also have great hopes for the vines, which we planted last year with the help of your friend Macro.

I may have some bad news about Macro. He seems to have disappeared from the estate of the consul, Aulus Gabinius. We have heard rumors. One puts him with Gabinius's familia in Rome, but another reports that he has been put out on the road for his role in shielding you from the consul's retribution.

We received a strange message from him in early spring through a woman named Rufia, who lives in Mediolanum. It was delivered by her slave, a giant of a man, a German, I think, who did not seem at all pleased to be acting as a courier. The message said that Macro was safe, but it gave no specifics about where he had gone. Also, this Rufia claims that she also knows you! She sends you her best wishes! I cannot imagine what she means or how she knows you. I asked your father about this, but he seemed most reluctant to discuss it. Since he was still recovering from his winter illness, I did not press him. But, I am determined to get to the bottom of this mystery! Rufia, indeed!

Caesar Patronus has been most kind to us. He wrote saying that you are now a member of his staff, his ad manum, as a matter of fact. He has kindly invited me to use his military couriers to carry my correspondence to you, and I took advantage of his kindness to send a small parcel of gifts for your birthday. Caesar also sent us a diploma declaring our family and farm "Caesari in fidem," under the protection of gens Iulia. He assured us that he expects no repercussions from that horrible misunderstanding with the consul, which sent you away from us.

Your Avus Lucius continues to prosper. He has stepped in and organized a syndicate for the wine enterprise since Macro has departed. He is in fidem with the consul himself, so we are confident that there will be no further interference. He believes that we will have a vintage within three years, and after I told him of your relationship with Caesar, he assures me that there will be a place for you in the organization when you leave the army.

We have heard reports that there has been a terrible battle with the barbarians in Gaul, but Roman arms have prevailed. Although we are thankful for the protection of Caesar and our armies, we think of you always.

To Deva Cornisca, Diana Fida, and with both hands on your bulla praetexta, which hangs always at my bosom, I offer daily prayers for the protection of my child.

Di te incolumem semper custodiant! May the gods safeguard you always!

VIII.

De Legatione Caesaris Ad Ariovistum

CAESAR'S EMBASSY TO ARIOVISTUS

Quam ob rem placuit ei ut ad Ariovistum legatos mitteret qui ab eo
postularent uti aliquem locum medium utrisque conloquio deligeret velle
sese de re publica et summis utriusque rebus cum eo agere ei legationi
Ariovistus respondit si quid ipsi a Caesare opus esset sese ad eum
venturum fuisse si quid ille se velit illum ad se venire oportere.

"Because of this situation, Caesar thought it appropriate to send envoys
to Ariovistus. The envoys requested that Ariovistus meet with Caesar at
some neutral location of Ariovistus' choosing for a consultation between
the two of them. They said that Caesar desired to talk to him concerning
the interests of the state and of matters of the greatest importance
to them both. Ariovistus answered the envoys that if he had wanted
anything from Caesar, he would have come to Caesar. If Caesar wants
anything from Ariovistus, Caesar must come to Ariovistus."

(from Gaius Marius Insubrecus' notebook of Caesar's journal)

---

*W*hen I read mama's letter, I was glad not to be in my father's boots when she pressed him about Rufia. In fact, I was a bit intrigued at my father knowing anything about Rufia. Some things are best left undiscovered.

I carried mama's goat cheese over to the mess tent, better to bring it there than to stash it in my tent. I'm sure after one whiff, my tentmates would have tossed it, and perhaps me, out onto the camp street. The cooks were not too sure what to do with the cheese, but neither were they inclined to refuse an odiferous gift offered by a *decurio* wearing a praetorian sash.

I was walking back to my quarters, up the *via principalis*, when I almost literally ran into my former *contubernalis*, a mate from my basic training squad, Felix. I didn't recognize him at first because of the raw, red scar that ran from just below his jaw up past his right eye. He didn't recognize me because, like most *muli*, he only saw my sash of office.

"Good afternoon, *Decurio*," he started. Then, "*Pagane*! Is that you?"

"Felix!" I responded, almost equally surprised. "What happened—" But, I stopped myself. I knew damned well what had happened.

Felix's hand went up to the scar on his face. "You mean this? Some hairbag *mentul'* stuck me with a stabbing spear when we were going over the Helvetian wagons . . . Your face is still pretty . . . You're with headquarters now, right? One of Caesar's boys."

"Pretty much," I answered. "During the fight I was on the left, under Labienus with the third battle line and the Sequani cavalry, holding off the *Grunni* . . . Never got up over the ridge where you guys were."

"You didn't miss much," Felix started. "Damned bastards wouldn't give up . . . Just stood behind their wagons and made us go in after them . . . Lot of good guys wound up on the pyre because of that fight . . . Then Caesar just let them go."

At that moment, Felix seemed to remember who he was talking to and fell silent. Then, he said, "Hey! You got some time? I'm meeting some of our mates at the enlisted-men's *caupona* just outside the *porta sinistra*."

I thought for a second. Since I had discharged my cheese, I didn't have anything until horse stables at the tenth hour. "Yeah . . . that would be great to see the guys . . . Let me run by my tent and get some silver."

Felix went on his way, while I went back to my tent and dropped my kit. The area around Bibracte was considered "secure," so we were allowed out of camp, in the *vicus* at least, without arms. Like most *muli*, I still carried my *pugio* on my soldier's belt.

As I went through the left gate, I gave the daily password to the sentry. The *tesserarius* of the guard demanded my name, rank, and organization. He seemed to lose some of his self-importance when I announced I was a *decurio* in the praetorian cavalry. I imagined he was one of our newly minted junior officers, still getting used to his newly found grandeur. He advised me to reenter camp at this gate so he could cross my name off his list.

Decurio is an odd rank in the Roman army. Granted, it does designate an officer, but a junior officer of the cavalry, in an army whose strength lies in its infantry. A *decurio* certainly is not equal in authority and prestige to a centurion. It hovers somewhere slightly below an *optio* and somewhere above a *decanus* or even a *tesserarius*. But, as far as the *muli* were concerned, it was a cavalry rank; so, it smelled of horse shit. Being a praetorian, though, was a knucklebone throw that always showed Venus, a winner. No junior officer was going to harass a member of the chief's inner circle.

The *caupona* was easy to find. The first thing that gave it away was the noise. For reasons I have never understood, when men get drunk, they get loud. They shout instead of talk, laugh as if they were watching *Pseudolus* in a wind storm, pound tables to get a server's attention, and get into strident, and sometimes violent, arguments over the wind direction.

The *caupona* itself was in a large leather tent, which in its former life was probably a legionary supply room or a hospital bay. How the tent got "discharged" from the army and into the hands of a *caupo* is anyone's guess. Since the afternoon was warm, the sides were rolled up, and the joint was overflowing with *muli* in red tunics. At twenty paces, the aromas of rancid lamp oil, frying sausage, and cheap wine assailed me. It was like every other soldiers' *caupona* in the *imperium*.

No sooner had I spotted the joint when I heard Felix's voice yelling, "*Pagane*! *Pagane*! Over here!" I looked over and saw him waving from a table with about ten other *muli*. The table was well positioned—close enough to the bar to get decent service and right on the edge of the tent to escape the worst of the reek of the place. They must have gotten there early, before the place filled up and all the choice tables were taken.

I skipped around the tent ropes and squeezed onto the bench opposite Felix. The soldier to my left put his giant arm around me and said, "Hey, lil' buddy, stayin' out of trouble?" and I realized it was Minutus, "Tiny."

Felix filled a cup and shoved it across to me. I took an experimental sip. It was not sweet enough to be wine and not sour enough to be *posca*. In other words, fit for consumption by the enlisted grunts.

Minutus yelled in my ear, "You remember Rufus over there. . . Lentulus said he'd be here, but he hasn't shown up yet."

A couple of the guys laughed at that crack. During our basic training, Lentulus seemed to show up late for everything, hence the name, "Slowpoke."

"There's Loquax down the end there, talking the ear off our *signifer* . . . And where the hell did Tulli go?"

"He's out in the back, takin' a leak," a voice answered.

"In the latrine . . . a fitting fate for a newly minted *optio*! And, do you recognize that ugly kisser across from you?" Minutus asked.

I looked and saw the only guy at our table in the dirty-white tunic of a civilian. His face looked familiar, but for a few heartbeats, I couldn't place it. Then, I said, "Mollis! So, your flat feet didn't keep you out of the army after all!"

Mollis raised his cup in my direction. "I'm now the journeyman smith for the Eighth. . . You got anything needs repair, bring it over. . . *nul' donatum*, no "gift" required for a former *contubernalis*, *Pagane*!" Mollis drained half his cup to seal the deal.

I turned to Minutus. "We're missing a few?"

Minutus took a long drink from his cup. "Pustula didn't make it. He and his *geminus* bought it when those hairbag *cunni* charged down the ridge at us . . . Some of them cut all the way through to the second battle line . . . Bantus took an arrow in the shoulder . . . The wound festered . . . Those Kraut *podices* shit on their arrowheads before they send 'em our way . . . He almost lost the arm . . . He's still touch and go . . . To tell the truth about Lentulus, he took a spear in the thigh at the wagons . . . Now he's got an excuse for being slow . . . Leg'll never be the same . . . They'd have mustered him out, but he took up with a new detail they're calling the 'grain snatchers' . . . something to do with foraging . . . He gets to ride a wagon now and steal chickens from the hairbags . . . Strabo got kicked up to the first line . . . Third Cohort, I think . . . Now that he's got that extra silver burning a hole in his purse, he drinks at the officers' *caupona* outside the main gate."

"How you doin'?" I asked Minutus.

"Me?" he answered. "*Decanus*! Third *contubernus*, Third Century, Second Cohort."

"Congratulations," I started.

Minutus continued, "That lowlife sitting next to you is my *tesserarius*, Manius Bruttius . . . His lordship's a *castro* . . . second generation grunt . . . A real celebrity . . . ain't ya, Mani?"

The hulk sitting to my right just grunted and gestured toward me with his cup.

"Hey! That's a proper oration from our Mani Castro," Minutus laughed. "*Pagane*, your cup's dry. Hey! Pass that pitcher down this way! Don't be shy! Help yourself to some food . . . The sausage's first rate . . . The *caupo*, the landlord, must have got to the Helvetian horses before the maggots got all the prime cuts."

While Minutus filled my cup, I examined the "first-rate" sausage, which looked like lumps of gray, gristly meat with a slightly greenish tint, swimming in a lake of congealing fat. Since I didn't want to spend the next few hours of my life bent over the latrine pit, I passed on these delicacies. I did grab a few wrinkled olives; you can't go wrong with olives, I assumed.

Minutus grabbed one of the lumps of meat and popped it into his mouth and asked, "So, *Pagane*, what do you hear in the cave of winds?"

"The 'cave of winds'?" I questioned.

"Yeah, the cave of winds . . . the headshed . . . the mound of muddle, the land where bosses plan and gods piss themselves laughing . . . Whatta you hearing? . . .

We're all ready to head south for the winter, and now we're hearin' about pullin' up stakes and marching east. What in the name of Mar's *coleones* is going on?"

I was on dangerous ground here. Back then, I wasn't sure whether my loyalty to my mates outweighed my responsibility to Caesar. I figured they'd find out soon enough; the warning order had already been issued. But, even back then, I understood army rule number one: protect your own ass. "Hey . . . my job's grooming my horse and keeping my metal bits shiney so the old man feels important . . . I'm hearing much of the same crap . . . It'll be a cold day in Hades when those lisping broadstripers can make up their minds."

"And a blizzard in Tararus when it works out for us *muli*," Manius Castro grunted on my right. "It's half-rations and the Rhenus for sure! And, after we beat some sense into those *pelosi*, Caesar'll have us build bridges over the Rhenus so's they don't get their feet wet skulking back into their forests."

Minutus laughed again. "And, that's why we call Manius here *Risulus* . . . 'Chuckles' . . . If he found a wagon full of silver, he'd complain about the tarnish. He's still pissed off about Caesar releasing the Helvetii."

"Damned right I am!" Manius spat. "We chased those hair-faced *mentul'* halfway across Gaul on half rations! I didn't see any of those purple-striped *verpae* lose any weight while we were chewing leather for lunch . . . Then, it takes us all day and night to finish those hairbags off, round 'em up, and put 'em in a slave-pen where they belong, just to have old *Calvus*, 'Baldy,' kiss 'em on both cheeks of their arses and send them back home. I'm surprised he didn't make us apologize to those dog-eating bastards before they left!"

"*Cac't!*" Minutus countered. "We all got a nice bonus out of it! Right out of old *Calvus'* purse."

Mani was about to answer when a commotion on the other side of the table interrupted us. Tulli, back from the jakes, was trying to squeeze on to the bench between Felix and Mollis. He was about to grab the pitcher when he noticed me. "*Verpa Iovis*! Do my tired old eyes deceive me? Is that *Paganus* I see?"

"Guilty, *Optio*!" I said. "Everything shake out alright?"

Tulli laughed. "When the gods have favored you as they have me, lad, you got to give it a few extra shakes to get it drained! Which reminds me . . . I got some news!"

Tulli let us hang a few heartbeats while he filled his cup and gulped half of it down. He wiped his mouth with the back of his hand and began. "I ran into one of the *corvi* in the latrine . . . one of the field medics from the Tenth . . . The docs think Bantus is goin' to make it . . . He may not recover the full use of his arm, so it looks like the *frumentarii* for him . . . the 'grain snatchers' with Lentulus . . . But it looks like he won't be takin' any one-way boat trips any time soon."

The guys around our table raised a toast or beat the tabletop with their fists at that one. Tulli continued, "I saw how you, Minutus, and Manius were goin' at it. You guys may want to take a whiff of the *herba*, the weed. The *serva* just dropped a fresh pile on the coals. It's in your best interest, *Pagane*, sittin' there right between old Scylla and Charybdis."

"The weed?" I asked.

Tulli gave me a strange look for half a heartbeat, then laughed. "I keep forgetting what a rube you still are, *Pagane*. Weed . . . *herba Bacchi* . . . Bacchus Weed . . . Those crazy Greek priestesses . . . the Sybils down in Italy . . . they use the stuff to talk to Apollo or whichever one of the gods is talkative when tourists show up with silver . . . It grows wild up here . . . If you know what you're lookin' for, all you gotta do is go out and pick it . . . The *caupones* burn it in their places . . . It keeps things mellow . . . fewer fights, less damage . . . They think it makes customers eat more . . . good for business!" Tulli laughed, raised his cup in my direction, and drained it.

I looked back down at the greenish sausage. It would take a lot more than a few whiffs of Bacchus Weed to get me to eat that *merda*!

Suddenly, our attention was drawn to a commotion, shouting and laughing from a bunch of *muli* across the room. They seemed to be trying to lift one of their drunken mates up onto a table.

"The guys from the Seventh never could hold their wine," Felix commented.

"Most of them are *Spani* from the north," our *castro*, Mani Chuckles, dismissed them. "They're barbarians . . . *peregrini* . . . shouldn't even be under the eagles."

I remembered my grandpa talking about "*Spani*," men from *Hispania* in the east, from where Caesar had drawn his four veteran legions.

"*Peregrini?*" I asked Mani. "Foreigners? Then, why are they in the army?"

"Pah!" Manius spat, then took a long drink from his cup. "They're all *in fidem* with Pompeius. He raised the Seventh out of his own pocket . . . stocked it with a horde of long-haired barbarians who lived along the river Durus, near *Oceanus*. If Pompeius farted, they'd line up to wipe his arse. They'd never get away with shit like that in my old man's day . . . had to be a real Roman to raise your hand to the *sacramentum* . . . Now any hair-faced *mentula* can get into the army. Hey! Send that bloody pitcher down this way! I'm dry!"

By the end of Mani's second oration of the afternoon, the boys from the Seventh had one of their mates standing on a table. Then, they started a rhythmic clapping. The others in the *caupona* went silent.

The soldier on the table began to sing:

Vae, vae, vae, filo me

Vae silente, vae rapide

D'ar' e foco, vae

Shi t'exir, m'amate

Fado, fado, troce fado

The words sounded like Latin to me, but I could hardly make them out. Then, one of the guys at our table, one I didn't recognize, said, "Ah! I know this one."

"What's going on?" I asked him.

The soldier looked over towards me, "He's singing a '*fado.*' It's the way those people say *fatus* . . . fate. They believe that fate is inescapable . . . You can only accept it and endure it."

"Pah," Manius spat. "Shaggin' barbarians!"

My new acquaintance ignored the interruption, "This one's about a mother sending her son off to war . . . He's a young man and wants to join the warbands . . . She knows she can't stop him . . . It's her fate."

"What language is that?" I asked.

My new friend laughed, "It's Latin . . . at least it's the Latin those *pagani* from the north of Spain speak . . . The chorus is 'Go! Go! Go, my son! Go quietly; go quickly. From my hearth and home, go! I know you're leaving, my darling. It's fate, fate, horrible fate.'"

By now, the whole room was clapping along with the singer. As he ended each chorus, dozens of drunken voices accompanied him, "*Fado, fado, troce fado* . . . It's fate, fate, horrible fate." I even heard Manius join in.

The singer continued:

Mi fil' ab'ir par montes

Para quer' ei fortuna

Para quer' ei fama

Proqua debe t'ir, m'amate

Fado, fado, troce fado

I was beginning to follow his Latin, "My child has gone to the mountains, to find his fortune, to find his name. Why must you go, my love?"

Then, the entire room joined in, "*Fado, fado, troce fado!*"

When the singer was done, the place went wild. Guys were standing on the benches, cheering; others were pounding the tables with fists, cups, and pitchers. Silver was flung at the *servae* to buy rounds for the boys from the Seventh.

"*Fado, fado, troce fado*" was ringing in my head, a mother's lament. Then, I remembered the letter I had left lying on my cot. I heard my mother's voice, "Just come home to me, my son."

Fado, fado, troce fado.

I filled my cup from our pitcher and drank.

I can't say I remember the walk back to my quarters that evening. Like a dream, I remember the assembly horns bellowing and a detail of *muli* going through the *vicus* policing up their mates and herding them back to camp. In my dream, I couldn't remember the password, but the *tesserarius* at the gate said something like, "He's alright. I remember him from before. Get him out of here before he pukes all over our post and we have to clean it up!" I remember him saying with a wink.

I woke up the next morning at the horn signaling the end of the fourth watch of the night. My mouth felt like an entire legion had force-marched across my tongue. When I sat up, my head seemed to explode. The entire room went black, except for curious yellow spots dancing in the darkness. I barely got out of the tent before I lost whatever dregs of wine and pieces of wrinkled olive were still in my stomach.

I arrived at the *praetorium* during the first hour. Ebrius took one look at me and fumbled for something behind his desk. He offered me a hunk of bread and a wine cup. "The bread's for your stomach . . . Eat it first . . . The wine'll take the edge off your head . . . Try not to breathe on the boss . . . or get too close to an open flame." Then, he just shook his head and laughed.

"*Mille gratias,*" I croaked as I ate the bread.

I entered Caesar's *cubiculum* and sat down behind my field desk. I was hoping no one would notice me in the dark corner, hunkered down behind piles of *tabulae*. No such luck.

No sooner were my eyes closed than Caesar blew into the tent with a senior tribune, a *laticlavus*, in his wake. "Insubrece! *Bene*! You're here. Come with me!"

I rose as quickly as my muddled head would allow. Even at that, I almost lost whatever bile and debris was still sloshing around in my guts. As I rounded my desk, I almost collided with Labienus, who was also following Caesar.

Labienus caught me by my shoulders and steadied me. After one look into my eyes, he chuckled, "So, it's true! You and your mates did try to drain old Corvinus' *amphorae* yesterday. Steady, boy. If a *mulus* can't hold his wine, he's got no future in the Roman army."

I followed Labienus slowly over to Caesar's desk. Caesar was pointing something out to the broad striper on his campaign maps.

"Ah, *bene!*" Caesar said as we approached. "This is Tertius Gellius Publicola. His father was consul a few years back with old Cnaeus Cornelius Lentulus Clodianus . . . Made his name in the senate by killing slaves and pirates—and by kissing Cicero's arse. As a favor to my collegue Pompeius, we're lucky enough to have him serving as the senior tribune of the Ninth Legion while his older brother, Lucius, sits in the senate and votes for anything Cato and the *Optimates* tell him to. Do I have your pedigrees right, Publicola?"

Publicola grunted his seeming assent to Caesar's introductory barbs. I was beginning to wonder why this man was in a position of trust when Caesar continued, "Publicola will be in command of my embassy to Ariovistus. I believe even a hair-faced Kraut who's still wringing water from the Rhenus out of his skivvies will be suitably impressed with the width of Publicola's purple stripe and his consular pedigree."

Caesar saw my look of confusion. "Tertius here is not cut from the same political cloth as his father and older brother. . . He's making a go of it in the army . . . What is it now, Tertius . . . three. . . four years under the eagles?"

Publicola nodded toward Caesar and grunted.

I took a good look at Publicola. He was tall—a good six *pedes* and a *palmus*—and athletically thin, giving the impression of a tightly wound ballista, ready and able to lash out suddenly at anything it was aimed at. His hair color hung between light brown and dark blond, betraying some Sabine or perhaps even Gallic ancestry. And, of course, it was stylishly cut in the Roman fashion, as if he had just come from a posh hair stylist on the Palatine and had not been chasing long-haired barbarians through the hills of Gaul like the rest of us. His eyes were a deep blue that seemed to mimic the depths of a cloudless summer sky, and like those of a god in the firmament, they seemed to miss nothing that happened below. While his nose was aristocratically long, sharp, and thin; his mouth, a bloodless slash across his face, hovered over a well-shaved, sharply cleft chin.

In short, I saw and took an immediate dislike to the consular nob, Tertius Gellius Publicola; I determined to stay clear and never turn my back on the pompous gobshite.

Back then, my judgment of men was quick, shallow, and uninformed. The Macedonian - Caesar's little "Egyptian Kitten," as he called her - had an expression for it. She described her youth as her "salad days," when she was green in experience and cold in judgment. When she said that, she was barely twenty-one, pharaoh of both Egypts, lover of the most powerful man in the Roman world, and carrying his child. I find myself thinking of her often these days. Perhaps her restless *lemur* is reaching out to me from the land of the dead. She has as good a reason to do so as I have to resist her enticements, even from beyond the tomb.

Then, I heard Caesar's voice cutting through my fog of nostalgia and the fumes of cheap wine clouding my brain: "I'm sending an *ala* of legionary cavalry from Publicola's Ninth as an honor guard . . . I want to put on a bit of a show for these hairy *mentulae* . . . I will also need the Sequani cavalry to ensure safe passage east of the Arar to the Rhenus. But, between here and the Arar is Aedui territory, so I've requested a cavalry escort from Diviciacus. Insubrecus

Decurio! Do you believe that mixing the Aedui and Sequani in a single detail will cause problems?"

It took me a few heartbeats to disengage myself from my dislike of Publicola, but I responded, "Combining the Aedui and Sequani might be difficult, even if it might serve a common cause. The warriors are young . . . They seek glory and reputation . . . They listen to their anger and desires, not their heads."

"I will tolerate no petty-minded, trivial disruptions of our mission, *Decurio*," Publicola interrupted. "I will hold *you* responsible for the behavior of your barbarians."

"Tribune, a century of animosity and warfare between peoples can hardly be dismissed as trivial—" I began.

"Please! Gentlemen!" Caesar intervened. "Stay focused! We need both the Aedui and the Sequani on this mission. I'm sure Diviciacus recognizes the critical nature of our embassy and will choose his men carefully. As far as the Sequani go, the *turma* of Adonus *Dux* has served us faithfully throughout the Helvetian campaign. They understand Roman discipline well enough not to be distracted from their mission . . . or at least to be controllable in these circumstances. Do you not agree, Insubrecus?"

I was not at all sure I agreed with Caesar's assessment, but there was no way I was going to do anything to support Publicola's position on this. "*Tecum consto, Imperator*," I nodded.

"*Bene*," Caesar stated. "Enough talk about tribal jealousies. Let's get back to our mission to Ariovistus. Publicola is in nominal command of the embassy . . . He and his men will provide the color and glitz that impresses those barbarians . . . Insubrecus, you will be under Publicola's *mandatum* for this mission and will exercise overall command of the Gallic cavalry . . . You will also act as liason between them and the tribune here . . . You can release the Aedui as soon as you cross the Arar into Sequani territory . . . I have delegated Gaius Valerius Troucillus to deliver my message to Ariovistus . . . Like you, Insubrecus, he's both a citizen and a Gaul . . . a member of the *civitas Helviorum* just south of the Rhonus . . . He speaks Gallic and Latin like a native, so you two have something else in common, and he's an *eques*, a "knight," so there's another purple stripe to wave in front of Ariovistus . . . He'll be accompanied by Marcus Metius . . . He's a merchant who has had dealings with Ariovistus and his people . . . Metius is there to gather whatever intelligence he can from his contacts about enemy strength and intention . . . Any questions so far, gentlemen?"

"*N'abeo*," I mumbled over my dried out tongue. Publicola grunted something that sounded about the same.

I had no specific questions, but something about Caesar describing Metius as a merchant who had had dealings with Ariovistus' band troubled me. I remembered the Gallic contingent from Vesantio suspected that Roman merchants were somehow in league with the *Suebii*.

Caesar continued, "Troucillus and Metius will join you here tomorrow at the first hour, when you will depart for the Rhenus."

Dios gratias, I thought, *a whole day to recover from the wine fumes that are aiming to shatter my skull.*

"I do not think for a second that Ariovistus will react well to my message . . . I don't believe that he'll openly attack an official embassy, but there's no predicting how bararians will behave . . . So, get Troucillus there to deliver the bad news and then get out . . . *Compe'enditis vos?*"

I responded, "*Compre'endo, Imperator!*" Publicola grunted.

"I'm also sending a detail of *fabricatores* from the Ninth Legion under their *praefectus*, Appius Papirius Cerialis . . . I believe you know the man, Publicola?"

Grunt.

"His primary mission is assessing the defenses of Vesantio and the defensibility of the terrain approaching the gate . . . He will also be conducting a general route reconnaissance and identifying sites for our legionary *castra* . . . Optimally, he will identify a battle ground for our confrontation with the *Grunni* in front of Belfort . . . One of your missions, Insubrecus *Decurio*, is to provide security for Cerialis and his men . . . *Nonne liquet?*"

"*Liquet, Imperator!*"

"*Bene*! Publicola! Once you have disengaged with the Krauts, you will fall back to Vesantio with Troucillus, Metius, and the *fabricatores* . . . Send a messenger back to me with Ariovistus's reply to my ultimatum . . . Insubrecus *Decurio*! You and the Sequani will screen the approaches to the Gate from the east until the army arrives or the *Grunni* push you back . . . Try to stay between the enemy and whatever key terrain Cerialis indicates, but don't get decisively engaged . . . If you are attacked, fall back to Vesantio . . . Vesantio must be held until I can get the legions up the valley of the Dubis . . . Publicola! If the Krauts attack the town, you will defend it with whatever forces you can scrape up . . . They will be mostly Sequani, so you'll need to depend on Adonus *Dux* and Insubrecus *Decurio* to assist you . . . But under no circumstances are you to let Ariovistus take Vesantio . . . Vesantio must be held! *Nonne liquet?*"

"*Clarissime, Imperator!*" I actually thought I saw Publicola's lips move that time!

"*Bene!*" Caesar concluded. You are dismissed. I have an officer's call to conduct, and you have much to do to get ready . . . and, Insubrecus!"

"*Ti' adsum, Imperator,*" I croaked.

"Get some sleep! I've seen crucified criminals who look better than you!"

"*A'mperi'tu', Imperator!*" I managed to spit out over Labienus' chuckling.

XI.

De Itinere Ad Ararem

THE JOURNEY TO THE ARAR

We assembled outside the *porta dextra* of the Ninth Legion's *castrum* just as the trumpets marked the end of the fourth watch.

It was quite a circus: Roman cavalry all shined and glittering; two contingents of Gallic cavalry; the Aedui and the Sequani, trying to avoid each other; Roman engineers looking nervously at the horses they would have to ride through the hills; Caesar's emissaries, Troucillus and Metius, each with his own *comitatus* of assistants and slaves; and Publicola and his "command group," whom I dismissed as a gaggle of cooks, bottle washers, boot lickers, and cot fluffers of the Roman senatorial aristocracy.

Off to the side of this gaggle, some of Athauhnu's boys were trying to organize the remount herd for the Sequani. I was riding Clamriu, but I was taking my German horse with me also. It was time to teach that Kraut nag how to be a proper Roman cavalry mount. What the Romans and the Aedui were doing about remounts, I had no idea. If they lost a horse, they could walk back to the army, as far as I was concerned.

I suspected somewhere among the ash and trash we were dragging behind us, the Roman emissaries and our consular nob had packed the pheasant tongues, quail eggs, and fine wines of the Latin hills, items that no purple-striper would go to war without. That was fine with me. My Sequani would be protecting the baggage and would certainly levy a generous tariff from their charges.

I found Athauhnu briefing his *ala* commanders, Guithiru and Ci, the "Hound."

"*A Pen*," I addressed him in Gah'el. "Is your troop ready to move out?"

Athauhnu responded in Latin, "We wear Caesar's steel, receive Caesar's silver, obey Caesar's orders, *Decurio*, so we speak Caesar's language. *Ben' dictu, m'infantes?*"

"*Bene, Dux*," Guithiru and Ci agreed.

"And a proper pair of Romans we have here," I laughed. "Have you taken Roman *praenomina* for yourselves? Ci, you're alright, but no Roman could hope to pronounce 'Guithiru.'"

"Meet Caeso and Caius," Athauhnu introduced, "the two *decuriones* of the First Sequani Cavalry *Turma*."

I nodded toward the newly minted Caeso and Caius, "*Salvete, decuriones!* Adonus Dux, what is the strength of the First Sequani Cavalry *Turma* for this mission?"

"*Decurio*," he reported, "Caeso's *ala* mounts twenty-three riders and Caius' twenty. My command section mounts seven. We are taking sixty-five mounts, all fit and proper."

"*Bene*," I continued my role as the Roman commander. "Supply?"

"The men are carrying five days' rations on their saddles . . . That should be more than enough to get us to the Arar and out of the lands of the Aedui. Once we have returned to our homeland, we will be supplied by our people," Athauhnu reported.

"And the horses?" I continued.

"The horses are fat on Roman grain and will be content once they are again feeding in Sequani grasslands," he reported.

"*Bene, Dux!*" I agreed. "I haven't been given the order of march, but it's a safe bet that you will be marching within the column until we cross the Arar. I know that you have no reason to love the Aedui, but Caesar asks you to bury your animosities and tolerate their presence among us. Until we reach the Arar, they are our allies on this mission."

"*Invidias?*" Caius Ci asked.

"*Casineba*," Athauhnu translated. "Hostility." Then to me, "*A'mperi'tu, Decurio!*"

"*Bene, m'amice!*" I nodded. "Let me go introduce myself to our *socii* from the Aedui."

"Do you want me to hold your purse while you're among those *abactores*?" Athauhnu asked.

"No, my friend, I should be fine," I replied, wondering briefly how Athauhnu had learned the Latin word for 'cattle rustlers.'"

I rode over to where I had seen the Aedui gathering. Compared to my Roman-equipped Sequani, they were a motley looking bunch. Some wore armor of boiled leather and some had only padded jackets; some had various helmets of steel or bronze, while others were bare-headed; some wore long Gallic *spatha*, others short Roman *gladii*, and some carried nothing but *gaea*, the Gallic throwing spears. Few had shields.

I spotted a rider who I assumed was their chief. He wore a chainmail *lorica* and a conical steel helmet with long cheek guards. A *spatha* in a polished leather sheath decorated with a diamond pattern of silver wires hung on his left side suspended by a leather baldric. He wore a thick, four-strand torc of twisted silver wire; a silver armband nestled on his right arm.

When he saw me approaching, he grunted, "*Romana non dico.*"

"I speak Gah'el," I answered him in his own language. "I'm Gaius Marius Insubrecus, *Decurio*. I'm called Arth mab Secundus among my people, the Insubres. The *Soucanai* call me Arth Uthr."

The man looked me up and down. I'm sure he took in my Roman armor and sashes of rank. His eyes hesitated for a brief heartbeat on the five-strand golden torc, the symbol of a warrior and chief, that hung about my neck. Then, he inclined his head toward me.

"*A Pen*," he answered, repecting my golden torc. "I am Morcant mab Cuhnetha, leader of ten. I command these riders of the *Aineduai* under the authority of Duuhruhda mab Clethguuhno, *Uucharix* of the *Aineduai*. My orders are to escort you Romans and those *Soucanai* mutts to the river of Souconna."

The name Cuhnetha was somehow familiar to me, but I couldn't quite place it. So, I answered Morcant, "I thank you, Chief. Those riders of the *Soucanai* are the friends of the Caisar and of the Roman people, who request that they be treated with respect."

Then, I remembered. "Perhaps you would tell me why the *penaf* of the *Wuhr Tuurch* does the bidding of the *Wuhr Blath* as a mere leader of ten."

Morcant's eyes widened for a brief heartbeat, but he immediately recovered his composure. "What do you know of my people?" he challenged.

"What your father, Cuhnetha, shared with me when he offered me and my men his hospitality and a jug of his red mead," I answered him.

Morcant's face reddened, "A fine lot of good that did him! Are yours the band of *Soucanai* pigs who burned his hall?"

"Burned his hall?" Now it was my turn to be surprised. "I rode with the *Soucanai*. His hall had already been burned when we arrived at his *dun*. He blamed the *fianna* of Deluuhnu mab Clethguuhno, your king's brother. Who told you that *Soucanai* attacked your father?"

"Duuhruhda . . . the king himself . . . he came to me as soon as he heard—" Morcant stuttered. "Why would the king lie about such a thing?"

"Who knows why anyone lies?" I countered. "Think about it yourself, Morcant. Does not your father believe that Clethguuhno, the king's father, murdered your grandfather to steal your birthright? Is not Deluuhnu, the king's brother, now a *heroor*, an outlaw, who under our laws is deprived of his head-price and is to be denied shelter and bread by all *Aineduai*?"

"That is the doing of the Romans," Morcant stammered. "The Caisar condemned Deluuhnu—"

"I fought in the battle in which Deluuhnu betrayed his own people and mine to the River People and the *Almaenwuhr*," I persisted. "I watched as his *fianna* abandoned *Aineduai*, *Soucanai*, and *Rhufeiniaid* to their deaths. And, you ask me why his brother would lie to you? You know the answer, Morcant! When is the last time you saw your father? Did *you* ask *him* who attacked his *dun*? Or, do you accept the word of that *sarf*, that snake who calls himself the Uucharix of the *Aineduai*?"

Morcant had no answer. "I was supposed to return home after the River People fled from our lands . . . but Duuhruhda . . . the king himself . . . he came to me and asked me to undertake this task . . . Once I get you to the River of Soucanna, I will lead my men back to my father's *dun*, and he will tell me the truth of this."

"I have told you the truth of it, Morcant, as your father told it to me. There is no *other* truth to be learned." I placed my hand on my golden torc. "Until we reach the river of Soucanna, I am your *penadur*. The *Soucanai* are our companions on this journey. I ask you and your men to treat them as brothers." Before Morcant could protest, I pulled Clamriu's head about and trotted off toward our forming column.

I hoped that I could keep the Aedui and the Sequani apart until we crossed the Arar. I estimated we would arrive on the banks of the river in four or five days, and during that time, the Aedui would be out screening our column and the Sequani riding within it. The tricky part would be keeping an eye on things when we halted for the night.

We almost made it.

Our Roman circus didn't get moving until well into the second hour. Most of the delay was in trying to collect the ash and trash that Publicola and our Roman envoys were dragging along. Publicola, of course, blamed the Gallic contingent, who had been waiting patiently with their horses since the first hour. Which meant, of course, he blamed me.

I was well aware that I was being tested. Caesar had given me my first independent responsibility as the officer in charge of the Gallic cavalry. Essentially, I was now riding in Agrippa's saddle. I wasn't quite sure whether Caesar was testing my ability to lead the Gauls or my ability to get along with such a pompous twit as Publicola. Probably both. I have long since learned that the Roman army has no shortage of such broad-striped, pompous idiots in positions of authority. In order to get things done, it's often necessary for competent Roman officers to be able, seemingly, to acquiesce to the most ridiculous attitudes and pronouncements of a senior officer whose broad purple stripe is blinding his judgment, then conveniently ignore it all in order to get a critical job done, even if it meant abjectly apologizing for having *misunderstood* the intention of an order. It was another aspect of *Romanitas*, the "Roman game," that I was just then learning.

Some might wonder why Caesar entrusted me with such reponsibility when I was so young and inexperienced. I had only turned seventeen a few weeks prior and had been in the army only a few months.

Romans do not believe that leadership ability is gained by experience; it is given by the gods themselves. The gods show their favor to a nation by gifting it with heroes. So, to the Romans, the age and experience of a man is, to a certain degree, irrelevant. If the gods gift him with the ability to lead armies to victory, that leadership manifests itself whenever the opportunity presents itself.

And, the Romans truly believe that their nation is loved by the gods above all others. I have seen no nation so sure of its divine favor, with the possible exception of a people whom the Greeks call *hoi Ioudaioi*. They inhabit a fly-bitten strip of sand north of Aegyptus, where they recognize only one, nameless god, who shows his favor by making their lives miserable. At least, when a Roman is convinced that one of the gods hates him, he can change allegiance to another.

My own experience in the legions over these many years has not fully resolved this issue of leading men. I don't believe for a heartbeat that experience is not necessary in developing a leader. To this day, I'm amazed that I didn't completely bollix the job. I had no experience to rely on; I was making shit up as I went along. *Lauda Fortunam Deam*! Praise the goddess Fortuna for smiling on me in those days. They say she favors youth and fools. Back then, I had both covered.

On the other hand, I have seen men on whom a life's experience is wasted. They couldn't lead a drunk to a *caupona* in the desert. The gods have somehow intervened in their making to deprive them of that flair necessary for men to be willing to follow them.

But, I still had to ask myself, if the gods were so much in love with the Roman nation, why did they place a broad purple stripe and a military tribune's sash on a pompous twit like Publicola?

During the day, I rode forward with the Aedui, screening our march. It gave me control of my most active maneuver element, let me see the terrain that we were entering, and kept me away from Publicola, who rode at the head of the column.

It was our nightly encampments that made me a bit anxious.

The cavalry, unlike the infantry, does not build a fortified *castra* every night. Cavalry has no intention of defending a fixed position and relies on its mobility to escape an attack. Essentially, when going into a night laager, the cavalry chooses ground that is difficult for an enemy to approach stealthily—usually a hilltop—throws out pickets, then circles its horse lines.

Our little traveling circus had four quasi-independent circles: one for the Aedui; another for the Sequani; a third for the baggage; and the last for the Roman contingent. Publicola usually placed his encampment near the center for security, but upwind of everything else so his patrician nostrils weren't offended by the smell of barbarians and mule shit. The Aedui and the Sequani positioned themselves as far away from each other as they could, which suited my purposes just fine. We tried to keep the baggage somewhere between us so no one could sneak in at night and steal any of the Romans' goodies—at least, no one other than us.

Each night, Publicola entertained Caesar's emissaries and the commander of the Roman engineers. They built their fires high—so much for operational security—and swarms of attendants served their every need, lest a grass stain blemish their pristine, lilly-white arses. Needless to say, I was never invited to Publicola's soirées, which, again, suited me just fine.

On our fourth night out from Caesar's *castra*, we were camped on a small hillock about half a day's ride from the Arar. We were going to arrive at the river near the site of our earlier battle with the Tigurini. Since the river could not be forded at that point and we had pulled down the bridges over which Caesar's army had crossed, Morcant planned to lead us north along the west bank of the river to an Aeduan *oppidum*, opposite where the Dubis enters the Arar. The Aedui called the place Caer Carwuhr, the "fortress of the heroes," a place Roman merchants called *Ventum Cavillonum*, the market town of the Cavillones. Morcant said that at this time of year the Arar was fordable just north of the town. We could cross over into Sequani territory; he and his Aedui would then leave us.

I came that close to keeping the peace between the Aedui and Sequani.

In the morning, at the start of the first hour, one of Morcant's Aedui sought me out in the encampment of the Sequani. I knew whatever the issue was, it had to be critical for an Aedui to enter alone into the circle of a people he considered his mortal enemies—and possibly even the very band that had attacked his own *dun*. I was with Athauhnu and Ci inspecting the horses before we pulled out. The young Aedui actually pulled on the sleeve of my tunic to get my attention.

"*A Pen*," he panted out, "Morcant asks . . . he asks that you attend him . . . right away . . . It's important!"

I turned to find myself next to a red-haired boy who looked no more than fifteen. "What is your name?" I asked him.

The boy looked confused for a heartbeat, then realized that, in his urgency, he had violated an important social protocol of our people. "I am Tegid mab Davuhd, *macouid* to the *pendevig*, Morcant . . . Will you come? . . . It is important!"

Macouid, I thought, *a squire . . . a shield bearer. So this boy is to Morcant what Emlun is to Athauhnu. Another father's sister's son,* I wondered. *The red hair . . .* I had a thought.

"Are you Rhonwen's brother?" I asked him.

The boy looked shocked. "Yes . . . I am . . . How did you—" Then he recovered himself. "You must come, sir. The *Pendevig* said it is urgent that you come right away."

"Athauhnu, please come with me," I said. "Ci, you and Guithiru complete the inspection of the horse lines . . . I'm concerned about the right front hoof of the sorrel mare in Guithri's ala."

Ci nodded as Athauhnu and I turned in the direction of the Aedui encampment.

"The summons is for you alone, *a Pen*," Tegid protested. "Not for this Soucanai—"

Before he could finish his insult, I stopped him, saying, "Who accompanies me is not your choice, Tegid, nor that of your *pendevig*, Morcant."

Tegid wisely shut his mouth and began leading us, not to the Aedui encampment, but to a patch of woods about fifty *passus* north of it.

When we entered the woods, we encountered most of Morcant's riders standing about. I could swear I heard them growl when they saw Athauhnu. I was immediately aware that I was not wearing my armor or carrying a sword. All I had was my authority and a *pugio* in case they decided to attack my friend.

Morcant stepped out from the semi-gloom of the woods. "Why did you bring that Soucanai *mochuhn* with you? Does he wish to admire the handiwork of his murdering bandits?"

I ignored Morcant's insult. "You summoned me here, *a Pen* . . . What is so important that I must visit this wood where your riders piss in the dark?"

"Come look," was Morcant's only response, and he led me further into the gloom.

We had walked less than three *passus* when I saw the body of a man sprawled on the ground. "That is Rhuhderc mab Touhim, a warrior of five years, a member of my band . . . He was murdered by a coward . . . from behind . . . His throat was cut . . . He had no chance to defend himself. Teguhd! Show the Roman the knife!"

An Aedui came forward and offered a knife, handle first. I took it. It was similar in design to a Roman *pugio*, a weapon the Gah'el call a *glev*. They were common among both the Aedui and Sequani.

"What does this prove, Morcant?" I asked. I had almost addressed him as "*Ainedua*" in response to his "Roman," but I remembered something my grandpa used to tell me, "When you're surrounded by your enemies, there's nothing to be gained by pointing the fact out to them."

"Look at the marking on the handle," Morcant insisted.

I flipped the *glev* over and saw what appeared to be a series of lines carved into the wooden handle. I heard Athauhnu suck in his breath.

"I know that knife," he admitted. "It belongs to a rider in Ci's band. A new man . . . a warrior named Airon."

"The murderer confesses to his crime," Morcant hissed. His riders seemed to crowd closer to us . . . hands dropped down to knife and sword handles. I was immediately aware that we were in a wood. No one in the camps could see what happened to us here.

"Stop . . . Back away from us!" I commanded.

Fortunately, Morcant seemed to have no stomach for another murder. He held up his hand, and his men backed away.

My mind was racing. "Where is Airon now, Athauhnu?" I demanded.

Athauhnu said, "He was on the picket to the east last night. His detail returned to camp at the end of the fourth watch."

"What time did the picket ride out last night?" I pressed.

Athauhnu shrugged. "At the end of the eleventh hour of the day, so they had enough daylight to get into position."

Athauhnu's answer was consistent with our standard operating practices. "Are you sure that Airon departed?" I pressed him.

"Yes," he insisted. "I dispatch the pickets myself . . . I saw him ride east with his detail."

"Where is this going?" Morcant challenged.

"What time was your man, Rhuhderc, killed?" I asked him.

Morcant looked down at the body as if it might tell him, then looked up at me, "Who could know such a thing, except the Soucana who murdered him?"

The Aedui hummed their assent to that challenge.

"When's the last time anyone saw Rhuhderc alive?" I asked loudly so all the Aedui could hear.

Almost immediately a voice from behind answered me, "Last night . . . he left the *pabel* we share to take a piss . . . He waited until the moon was up so he could see his way."

"There you have it, Morcant," I stated. "Rhuhderc was still alive when the man you accuse of killing him was in the east."

"This proves nothing!" Morcant almost shouted. "The Soucana could have ridden back in the night and waited in ambush for whomever of my people came here . . . Everyone knew we used this spot as a *eudi*."

"I will question Airon and his mates," I countered. "If he abandoned his post, they will know . . . I will also question him about this *glev*."

"Lies and more lies!" Morcant shouted. His men growled their assent. "We know who killed Rhuhderc, and we know what to do when a Soucana dog kills one of ours."

"No!" I shouted back. I was desperate. I was sure that the Aidenuai were about to seize us and take their revenge on Athauhnu. The *Soucanai* would then feel obligated to revenge their chief. It would be a blood bath.

"This is not the way of our people! *Ein cuhfrei*, our laws demand that—" I began.

I was interrupted by a new voice from behind the mob of Aidenuai closing in on me. "Perhaps I could be of some assistance in this."

Everyone in the grove froze. A figure entered our group. The first thing I noticed was the narrow purple stripe bordering his white tunic. *A Roman*, I thought. *An eques . . . but he speaks Gah'el.*

Then, I noticed the five-strand golden torc around his throat. It was Gaius Valerius Troucillus, Caesar's emissary to Ariovistus. He placed his right hand on his torc and said, "The *decurio* is correct. The Gah'el do not take blood vengeance on each other, even for murder. To do so would be *anouar*, uncivilized. You would be acting like the *Rhufeiniaid* and *Almaenwuhr*, not like people of the nations. This issue must be placed before a *barnu*, a judge who can investigate and apply the law justly."

"A *barnu*," Morcant challenged. "The closest *barnu* would be in Caer Carwuhr. But, I doubt he has the status to judge a case of murder."

"The *Soucanai* will not submit to a *barnu* of the Aidenai!" Athauhnu shouted. I was just about to kick him in the ankle when Troucillus continued.

"*A pen*! You, more than most men, should know that our traditional laws go before tribal loyalties . . . They were given us by Chleu Chlaw Guhves before the nations descended from the high places . . . The *barnu* is accountable to the god, Chleu, himself, not to any tribe or to any chief."

I heard mutterings of assent to this statement from the Aidenuai. Even Morcant was nodding in agreement.

"I may be of further assistance to you," Troucillus continued. "I am the youngest son of the *Uucharix* of the Elvai, the hunters of the Rhonus. As such, a *barnuchel*, a high judge, accompanies me on my journeys to advise me on the laws of our people. He is also a *coulour*, a searcher of the truth. If you will present your accusations and evidence to him, he will apply the laws of Chleu to them. And, since the Elvai hate the Aidenuai and *Soucanai* equally, he will favor neither tribe."

The Aidenuai muttered their approval.

"We will hear the accusations of the Aidenuai against the *Soucanai* in the camp of the *Rhufeiniaid* chief at the sixth hour, when the chariot of Chleu Chlaw Guhves is at its highest point," Troucillus pronounced. "Athauhnu, the *glev*, please."

As Athauhnu handed him the knife, Troucillus whispered, "Wait until the Aidenuai return to their encampment. We don't need one of them taking matters into his own hands on you." Athauhnu nodded.

Then, Troucillus said, "Morcant, do you have a *met'uhg* with your troop?" Despite Troucillus' south-of-the-Rhonus accent, I recognized the word for doctor.

So did Morcant. He nodded.

"Good," Troucillus answered. "Please send him here to me."

As the Aidenai left, Troucillus said to me quietly in Latin, "Publicola will not be pleased with the delay, but as the head of Caesar's embassy, I outrank him. He's sure to see this as a Gallic problem and, therefore, your fault. So, I would avoid him as best you can until he calms down a bit. Did you understand that, *Dux*?"

I heard Athauhnu mutter, "*Compre'endo.*"

Troucillus rubbed his hands together and looked around the grove. "So many of the Aidenuai have tromped through this place that I doubt we'll find any useful footprints. Let's take a closer look at the body."

Rhuhderc was lying face down on the ground near a large oak tree. I helped Troucillus turn him, and we noticed that his penis was still outside his *bracae*.

"Whoever did this, caught him in mid-stream," Troucillus quipped. "By the looks of it, the murderer came up from behind to do the deed. Who would be stealthy enough to walk up on an experienced warrior?"

I shrugged, "A hunter?"

"Someone he knew?" Athauhnu suggested. "One of the Aedui?"

Troucillus grunted. "Adonus *Dux*, the Aedui have departed, so it's best that you leave us now. Any participation that you have in the investigation may contaminate the evidence in their eyes."

Athauhnu was about to protest, when I said, "*Dux*, please return to your encampment and stand the *turma* down. Also, take charge of Airon and his companions from last night's picket. We will need to question them about this *pugio* and Airon's whereabouts last night."

Athuahnu muttered, "*A'mperi'tu*," and left the woods.

As Athuahnu was departing, Troucillus was examining where the victim was standing when he was attacked.

Troucillus pointed to the ground, then to the dead man's boots. "Those marks are where he was standing . . . I don't understand why men insist on pissing on the side of trees . . . Here, look at this . . . These marks . . . they were made by his killer . . . It looks like he had to come up on his toes . . . He would have grabbed his victim by his chin from behind . . . lifted and pulled back . . . then drew the knife across his throat. Then, he would have jumped back to avoid the spurting blood . . . very neatly done . . . The killer knew what he was doing . . . but look at these marks . . . You can see the imprints of hobnails . . . The killer wore *caligae*, Roman boots."

"Many of the Sequani wear Roman boots," I said.

Troucillus nodded. "We also have an entire *ala* of Roman cavalry, a detail of Roman engineers, and many in mine and Publicola's entourage who wear such boots . . . No shortage of suspects who fit *that* bill . . . but our man was shorter than his victim . . . How tall would you estimate the late Rhuhderc mab Touhim was?"

I examined the body for a few heartbeats, then said, "He looks to be about my height . . . five *pedes* and about seven or eight *unciae*."

"*Tecum consto*," Troucillus agreed. "Stand up straight for me, *Decurio*."

I did what Troucillus asked. He walked behind me and placed his left hand under my chin. As he lifted my chin, I wondered for a brief, terrifying moment if he were the killer. But, Troucillus adjusted his height until I could feel the pressure of his reach under my chin.

"How high am I standing?" he asked me.

I turned to see Troucillus adjusting his height on slightly bent knees. I examined him for a few heartbeats, then offered, "A good five *pedes* and three . . . maybe four *unciae*."

"*Bene*," Troucillus agreed. "Our killer wore Roman *caligae* and stood about five-four."

It was then that the Aeduan horse doctor joined us.

"Ah, doctor," Troucillus said in Gah'el. "Please, examine the wound of this unfortunate man and tell me all you can about it."

The *medduhg* looked at Troucillus as if he had lost his mind. Then, he shrugged and bent down over the dead man.

When he finally stood up again, he wiped his hands on the tail of his blouse and started, "It's a shallow wound . . . The windpipe is not cut . . . In fact, only the blood tube on the right side of his throat is cut—"

"The right side?" Troucillus interrupted.

The medduhg nodded, "Yes . . . only the right . . . The left is still intact."

"Anything else?" Troucillus asked.

"Yes . . . the wound was made by a curved blade," the doctor asserted, "A *dagr*, I would say . . . The entry wound on the right of the neck is deeper than the exit wound on the left, but a curved blade, I'd say."

Troucillus removed Arion's *glev* from his belt. "Could this blade have made the wound?"

The *medduhg* examined the *glev* for a few moments, then shook his head. "I don't think so . . . This was done by a curved blade . . . a *dagr*."

Dagr, I thought. *The Latin word for that is sica, the type of knife used by a percussor, an assassin.*

The memory of a slave who wasn't a slave back in Aquileia flashed across my mind. Absently, I began to rub the knife scar on my right forearm. Then, I saw the face of Gabinia snarling at her *sicarius* to kill me in front of her so that she knew "the job was done right."

Seemingly from a distance, I heard Troucillus call my name.

"Uhhh . . . yes, uhhh," I responded lamely.

"Just call me 'Troucillus,'" he smiled. "'*A Pen*' if it makes you more comfortable, but among Romans it's just 'Troucillus.' I was asking whether you are a hunter."

I noticed that the Aeduan *medduhg* had left. "A *venator*?" I answered. "No, not really."

"Really?" he answered. "You're a Gaul . . . What is your father?"

"*Me' pater*? He's a farmer," I answered, wondering where this was going.

"An *agricola*!" he repeated. "Your family must be well Romanized down there over the Alps," he laughed. "The Romans are convinced that the noble, peasant farmer is the backbone of their civilization . . . the one true noble calling . . . Then their nobles do everything they can to avoid getting their hands soiled with good, honest dirt . . . We Gauls believe that being a warrior is the noblest calling, the natural leader of the clan . . . The farmer serves to feed the warrior, and the warrior serves to protect the farmer."

I still had no idea where this was going, but Troucillus continued. "When warriors are not on campaign, they hunt to maintain their fighting skills. My people are the Helvi, the hunters of the war god, Rudianos, whose river the Romans call the Rhodanus. I have been hunting since I could ride. A hunter understands that no animal, or man for that matter, can pass across the land without leaving traces . . . tracks . . . broken branches . . . stool . . . even traces of fur in the brambles."

Troucillus' little speech reminded me of my Sequani scouts, who could tell from a horse's tracks whether it was carrying a load or not, whether it was running or walking, or how long since it passed. They could even tell from its *merda* what it had had for breakfast.

While he spoke, Troucillus was bent over examining the brush and brambles around the body. Suddenly he said, "*Euge*!" and stood up holding something between his fingers.

He offered his find to me. "*Ecce*! Look! Our prey has left its trace!"

I looked at what he was holding. It seemed to be some strands of thread.

"This is wool, the material that Roman tunics are made from," he explained. "From what I can see, these strands are undyed. What is our victim wearing?"

I looked down at his body. He had a leather coat and a worn pair of the blue, red, and green woolen *bracae* of the Aedui. "He's not wearing undyed wool," I told Troucillus.

"I didn't think so," he agreed. "We Gauls love our colors . . . wouldn't be caught dead in an undyed tunic . . . I guess that's a bad pun condsidering the circumstances . . . I don't remember any of our Aedui friends, who managed to churn up this area, wearing undyed cloth . . . so our killer could have left this behind . . . Think, Insubrecus . . . who among the Romans is wearing an undyed tunic?"

I thought for a few heartbeats. "The soldiers are wearing red . . . so are the engineers . . . Publicola, of course, wears white and purple, as do you . . . Metius has worn various colors . . . The teamsters? The slaves in Publicola's and Metius's *comitatus*?"

Troucillus nodded. "I think we're done here . . . Let's sum up what we know . . . The victim, Rhuhderc, was last seen heading towards these woods to relieve himself after the moon was up . . . The moon rose late during the first watch . . . There was still considerable activity in Publicola's and Metius's encampment at that time . . . The accused, Arion, left the Sequani encampment around the eleventh hour and allegedly rode east on picket duty with a couple of his companions . . . The body was discovered around the first hour . . . The killer attacked Rhuhderc from behind with a curved-bladed *sica*. The killer was left handed and about five-four. He was wearing an undyed woolen garment and Roman *caligae*. How'm I doing, so far?"

I shrugged, "Sounds right, but Roman soldiers are trained to use both right and left hand in combat. Are Gauls also?"

Troucillus thought for a few seconds, then said, "What you say about the Romans is correct, but as I understand it, Romans use their right hands unless it's incapacitated. I don't imagine our killer would use his non-dominant hand to attack an unwary victim if he didn't have to. So, unless he were trying to throw us off . . . but that would mean he was expecting a competent examination . . . no . . . I believe our killer's left handed . . . And your question about the Gauls . . . they are not trained to the battle line like Romans . . . They use whatever hand is dominant . . . I don't remember noticing any left-handed Sequani . . . or Aedui for that matter. We should be on the lookout for that."

What Troucillus said seemed to make sense.

He continued, "The next step is to ask ourselves *cui bono*, as the Roman Cicero asks: 'Who gains?' The apparent goal, I would say, is to set the Aedui and the Sequani against each other. But, I don't think that's the killer's endgame. What would a falling out between the tribes cause in this situation?"

"The embassy would not reach Ariovistus?" I suggested.

Troucillus thought about that for a few heartbeats. "*Fortasse* . . . possibly . . . then *cui bono*? Ariovistus? Does Publicola have anything to gain in frustrating Caesar? But, this embassy is for show . . . Caesar expects Ariovistus to reject his demands, and Caesar will attack regardless . . . So what would be frustrated by destroying this delegation . . . certainly Publicola understands the situation . . . Caesar was perfectly frank with me what his expectations were."

"Perhaps, someone who doesn't know Caesar's intent," I suggested. "Someone who thinks Caesar's overtures are sincere?"

"Who could that be?" Troucillus mused. "Disloyal elements within the army? My understanding is that the soldiers are not eager for this campaign, so they would want us to succeed with Ariovistus."

Again, Gabi's words came to me, "Someone in Rome," I suggested. "Pompeius is jealous of Caesar's military successes."

Troucillus became thoughtful again, "*Fortasse*," he agreed. "Perhaps. But, that would only work if Pompeius was confident of Caesar's defeat . . . or some adverse political repercussion of Caesar attacking Ariovistus."

Troucillus shrugged his shoulders and sighed, "All this is possible . . . but we have a judgment to prepare for . . . Let's keep our eyes and ears open . . . a five-four, left-handed man in an undyed tunic and *caligae,* carrying a curve-bladed *sica* . . . When we find him, we may get our answers . . . Let's get out or these woods before the *lemur* of this unfortunate man decides that we are the source of his misfortune . . . Please inform Morcant that he is free to do the honors of the dead for his comrade. There is nothing more that he can tell us."

This was my first experience in being a *venator homocidarum*, an investigator of murders. The skill Troucillus taught me in reading the signs left by criminals, and understanding the motivation of these acts, would prove for me both a blessing and a curse: a blessing, in that at times I was able to find justice for a victim; a curse, in that at times I discovered things I did not want to know.

X.

De Jure Galliorum
GALLIC JUSTICE

he hearing, *cuhmooliat*, as the Gah'ela call it, to decide who was guilty of the murder of Rhuhderc mab Touhim began at the sixth hour. As tradition demands, the *cuhmooliat* was held out of doors, so the god himself, Chleu Chlaw Guhves, whose laws were to be remembered, interpreted, and applied, would witness the event.

A chair for the *barnuchel*, liberated from somewhere among the baggage, was set up on a small, grassy knoll. Both the Aedui and the Sequanni were assembled before the chair–the Aedui to the *barnuchel's* left, as the *cuhuthai,* the "accusers," and the Sequani to his right, as the *cuhuthedai,* the "accused." The assembled Gah'ela were dressed only in their tunic-shirts and *bracae*, their armor left behind in their encampment and their swords placed between themselves and the chair of judgment, the pommels toward the *barunchal* as a sign of peaceful purpose and submission to lawful judgment.

I was seated between the two groups, dressed only in my red military tunic; my *gladius* was also placed before the chair. From where I sat, I could see that Publicola had established himself a dozen or so *passus* to my left front. He was dressed in his broad-striped white tunic, and although he was comfortably seated and one of his *famuli* was busy keeping his wine cup filled, he did not look pleased. But, I could not remember Publicola *ever* looking pleased. Troucillus was seated on his right and the prefect of the engineers,

Appius Papirius Cerialis, on Publicola's left. There was no sign of Caesar's other emissary, the merchant Metius.

At Troucillus's suggestion, Publicola had deployed the legionary cavalry to screen the assembly. I can imagine what the Roman boys thought when they learned that they had to spend the day in full armor under the summer sun to protect an assembly of unarmed Gauls involved in what they considered some barbaric ritual. A few of the Cerialis' *fabricatores* were hanging about, waiting for the show to begin.

And, it soon did.

I noticed a flurry of movement from behind. I turned to see a tall, gaunt man in a long, flowing, red robe approaching the assembly. In his right hand, he held a staff at least five *pedes* in length. The staff was of oak, a tree sacred to the gods. On the bottom was the black steel blade of a thrusting spear, while on the top, a silver hand, fingers extended, palm open, similar to the *signum* of a Roman cohort. Since this was a peaceful assembly, the silver hand was held upright in honor of the god of peace and law.

The man was Aderuhn mab Enit, *barnuchel* of the Evai. I learned later that the red robe represented the blood of a homicide, which this *cuhmooliat* was assembled to decide. Behind Aderuhn followed another man dressed in a brown robe and holding only an oaken wand capped on both ends in silver.

As the *barnuchel* approached the chair, the assembled Gah'ela rose, as did I. I noticed that Troucillus and even Cerialis, albeit unsteadily, also stood up. If anything, Publicola seemed to snuggle further down in his chair.

As Aderuhn stood before the chair, facing the assembled tribes, his assistant held up the oaken wand and announced, "*Mai cuhmooliat uh popl bellac uhn decrau . . .* The assembly of the peoples now begins!" I stole a glance over toward Publicola and saw that Troucillus was translating.

Aderuhn, holding the silver hand of his staff up toward the sun and the assembly, intoned his qualifications as *barnuchel*, "*Uhr wuhf uhn Aderuhn, mab Enit, mab Teb.*" Aderuhn listed all his mentors, teachers, schools; at one point, he claimed to have traveled across *Oceanus* to an island called Pridain, the land of the "blue people," and beyond that, to a place called Irioudain, the island of thr goddess, Iriou.

Finally, when Aderuhn's chant ended, his assistant entoned, "*A oes unrhuhw un uhmginnull uhn i che hoon uhn herio awdurdod i barnuchel i benderfuhnu materion hin?* . . . Does anyone assembled here challenge the authority of the *barnuchel* to decide these matters?" When no one in the assembly answered, Aderuhn sat, and the assembly took their seats before him.

Aderuhn spoke, "Who brings a charge before the *cuhmooliat*?"

Morcant rose, but did not speak. Aderuhn's assistant approached Morcant and handed him the oaken wand.

"I am Morcant, son of Cuhnetha, *Pobl'rix* of the *Wuhr Tuurch*, the Boar Clan of the *Aineduai*," he began. "I am *uhr pendevig* of these assembled warriors. I accuse the warrior Arion of the *Soucanai* with the murder of Rhuhderc mab Touhim, who was of my band."

Aderuhn nodded and asked, "Morcant mab Cuhnetha, why do you call Rhuhderc mab Touhim's death a murder?"

Morcant, still holding the wand, described the circumstances of Rhuderc's death until finally the *barnuchel* held up his hand to silence him. Then, Aderuhn asked, "Do any of the *Soucanai* contest the testimony of Morcant mab Cuhnetha?"

No one from Athauhnu's group rose.

Aderuhn announced, "Since none of the *Soucanai* contest the testimony of Morcant mab Cuhnetha concerning the circumstances of Rhuhderc mab Touhim's death, the *cuhmooliat* declares this death a murder and fixes a *cosbcorv* of ten *dai* for the murderer."

The *coscorv* was the "body fine," the penalty for the crime itself. A *da* was a unit of goods offered in reparation for the offense; it could also mean a punitive punishment, a beating with clubs and staves. In the case of murder, the *da* was paid to the victim's wife; or if the victim was unmarried, the father; or if the parents were dead, the victim's chief. The next step was for the *barnuchel* to fix the *cosvanrhuhda*, the honor penalty, assessed based on the victim's status within the tribe.

Again, Aderuhn spoke, "Morcant mab Cuhnetha, what was Rhuhderc mab Touhim's rank among your people?"

Morcant replied, "A warrior of five years."

Aderuhn countered, "Does he have *gleietai*, vassals, in his own right?"

"No!"

"Does his father have *gleietai*?" Aderuhn further questioned.

"No!" Morcant repeated.

"What is his father's status among your people?"

"*Uh duhntir*, a free farmer."

Aderuhn then questioned, "Was Rhuhderc mab Touhim a married man?"

Morcant answered again, "No!"

"Was he betrothed?"

Morcant hesitated for a few heartbeats, then said, "He was supposed to marry my cousin, Rhonwen merc Gwen."

At the mention of the name, Rhonwen, my ears picked up. For a reason my seventeen-year-old mind could not quite grasp, I had become rather preoccupied with that lass, whom I had only met briefly.

Aderuhn asked, "Has Rhonwen merc Gwen agreed to the marriage?"

No? I hoped.

Morcant replied, "Not yet. We had hoped to hold the *siarad oh atewidio*, the betrothal ceremony, in the fall."

The betrothal has not taken place, I silently celebrated.

Aderuhn followed up: "Are there any acknowledged offspring between them?"

"No! Rhonwen merc Gwen is a *feinir*, a maiden," Morcant asserted.

I celebrated that answer too, still not understanding why Rhonwen's maidenhood should mean anything to me.

Aderuhn continued, "Did he acknowledge any offspring?"

"He did not."

"Does Rhuhderc mab Touhim have any brothers?"

Morcant clarified, "He has two: one older and another younger."

"Are his brothers of sound body, able to support their father?"

Morcant replied, "They are!"

Aderuhn was silent for a few heartbeats, then spoke, "Based on your responses, Morcant mab Cunetha, I determine Rhuhderc mab Touhim's status, being a warrior of five years and the unmarried son of a living father who farms his own land and is supported by other healthy sons, to be *benedivig glas*, a "green lord." Do you object to this judgment?"

Morcant shook his head, "I do not."

"I, therefore, set the *cosvanrhuhda*, the honor price of Rhuhderc mab Touhim, at five *dai*," the *barnuchel* declared.

Morcant bowed his head in agreement.

The *barnuchel* then asked, "Morcant mab Cunetha, you have convinced the *cuhmooliat* that the death of Rhuhderc mab Touhim was murder, and you have accused a warrior of the *Soucanai* called Arion of this murder. Is this correct?"

"It is," Morcant agreed.

"Is Arion of the *Soucanai* present in the *cuhmooliat*?" Aderuhn asked.

Athauhnu rose and stated, "He is, Lord!"

"Arion of the *Soucanai* will stand before the *cuhmooliat*!" Aderuhn demanded.

I looked back over my left shoulder and saw a man rise in the midst of my assembled *turma*. He appeared to be no more than twenty. His build was slight, and his reddish-brown hair fell unbound to his shoulders. He was yet to display the dramatic, chin-length mustachios of a veteran warrior of the Gah'ela.

"I am Arion," he announced to the *cuhmooliat*.

Aderuhn nodded to his assistant, who took the oaken wand from Morcant and carried it to Arion.

"State your full name and title," Aderuhn instructed.

Arion answered, "I am Arion, mab Cadarn, mab Brac, a warrior in the band of Athauhnu mab Hergest. 'Tis me first campaign as a warrior in me own right."

"Have you heard the charges made against you by Morcant mab Cunetha of the *Aineduai*?" the *barnuchel* asked.

"I 'ave, Lord!" Arion asnswered.

"How do you respond to these charges?" Aderuhn asked.

Arion held the oaken wand up toward the sun. "I deny 'em," he stated.

There was a low rumbling among the *Aineduai*, which was almost immediately silenced by a stern look from Aderuhn. The *barnuchel* then asked Arion a series of questions similar to those asked about the victim, Rhuhderc. Finally, Aderuhn announced, "I determine Arion mab Cadarn's status to be *benedivig glas* and set his *cosvanrhuhda* at two *dai*. As his *pencefhul*, do you agree with this judgment, Athauhnu mab Hergest?"

Athauhnu stood. "I do, Lord," he concurred.

"Morcant mab Cunetha!" Aderuhn called. "Stand again before the *cuhmooliat*!"

Aderuhn's assistant transferred the oaken wand back to Morcant.

"Morcant mab Cunetha," Aderuhn asked, "Have you heard Arion mab Cadarn's denial of your accusation concerning the murder of Rhuhderc mab Touhim?"

"I have, Lord," Morcant answered.

"Have you also heard my judgment that Arion mab Cadarn's status to be *benedivig glas* and his *cosvanrhuhda* is two *dai*?" the *barnuchel* asked.

"I have, Lord," Morcant again answered.

Aderuhn continued, "Do you understand, although you have established before this *cuhmooliat* that Rhuhderc mab Touhim was indeed murdered, if I determine your accusation against Arion mab Cadarn to be without merit, I will assess his *cosvanrhuhda* against you? And, further, if I consider your accusation against Arion mab Cadarn to be malicious, I will assess his *cosvanrhuhda* three times against you?"

"I do, Lord," Morcant affirmed.

"Do you wish to persist in your charges against Arion mab Cadarn?" Aderuhn asked.

I sensed a slight delay in Morcant's response, but then he said, "I do, Lord!"

"Very well," Aderuhn nodded. "Proceed with your evidence against Arion mab Cadarn in the murder of Rhuhderc mab Touhim."

Holding the oaken wand, Morcant recounted the discovery of Rhuhderc's body in the woods beyond the encampment of his band. He readily admitted that Rhuhderc had been seen alive after the moon rose the night before, but was discovered murdered at dawn. He then stated that near Rhuherc's body was found a *glev* that was later identified as belonging to the accused, Arion mab Cadarn of the *Soucanai*.

When Morcant's testimony was complete, Aderuhn asked, "Is the *glev* allegedly belonging to Arion mab Cadarn here in the *cuhmooliat*?"

That was my cue. "It is, Lord," I stated, rising to my feet. "I have it here." I raised the knife so everyone in the assembly could see it.

Aderuhn nodded to his assistant, who approached me and took the *glev*. He then presented it to the *barnuchel*, who examined it for a few heartbeats.

Aderuhn then demanded, "Identify yourself for the *cuhmooliat*, warrior!"

After being handed the wand, I responded, "I am Arth mab Secundus, mab Cunorud, mab Cunomaro, known by the *Rhufeiniaid* as Gaius Marius Insubrecus. I serve in the *fintai* of the Caisar and am *penevig* of the Gah'ela bands."

The *barnuchel* nodded. "Did you witness Morcant or any of his band discover this knife near the body of Rhuhderc mab Touhim?"

"No, Lord," I answered. "It was handed to me by a member of Morcant's band, at his instruction."

Aderuhn nodded again. "Do you have any knowledge of how this *glev* was identified as belonging to the accused, Arion mab Cadarn?"

"Yes, Lord," I stated. "On its handle are marks, which Athauhnu mab Hergest recognized as the marks of Arion mab Cadarn."

Aderuhn examined the knife in his hand, then gestured to his assistant, to whom he handed the *glev*.

"Athauhnu mab Hergest! Rise before the *cuhmooliat!*" the *barnuchel* demanded.

Athauhnu rose. The assistant handed him both the knife and the wand.

"You have heard the testimony of Arth mab Secundus concerning the ownership of this weapon and how he came into possession of it," Aderuhn stated. "Do you affirm this testimony before the *cuhmooliat?*"

"I do, Lord," Athauhnu stated.

"Arion mab Cadarn! Rise before the *cuhmooliat!*" the *barnuchel* then demanded.

Arion rose. The assistant handed him both knife and wand.

"Arion mab Cadarn! Do you affirm before the *cuhmooliat* that this is your *glev?*" Aderuhn asked.

Arion examined the knife, then stated, "'Tis me knife, lor', but I a lost—"

"Silence!" the *barnuchel* demanded. "You will be given an opportunity to defend yourself after your accuser has fully stated his case."

Aderuhn then waved his assistant back toward Morcant, who was still standing. He was handed the knife and the wand.

"Morcant mab Cuhnetha!" Aderuhn continued. "Do you affirm before this *cuhmooliat* that this is the *glev* that was found near the body of Rhuhderc mab Touhim?"

Morcant examined the knife for a few heartbeats, then stated, "I do, Lord."

At a gesture from Aderuhn, the assistant took the *glev* from Morcant and placed it before Aderuhn's chair. The *barnuchel* then asked, "Morcant mab Cuhnetha! Do you have any more evidence to place before this *cuhmooliat* concerning the guilt of Arion mab Cadarn for the murder of Rhuhderc mab Touhim?"

"I do not, Lord," Morcant bowed.

The assistant collected the oaken wand from Morcant and took a position to Aderuhn's left. At a gesture from the *barnuchel*, we all sat. The *barnuchel* then raised his face up toward the sun, asking the guidance of Chleu Chlaw Guhves in his first decision.

Finally, Aderuhn rose, lifting his staff with the outstretched palm of its silver hand facing the assembly. "I declare that the evidence presented by Morcant mab Cuhnetha before this *cuhmooliat* accusing Arion mab Cadarn of the murder of Rhuhderc mab Touhim is adequate to proceed. I invite Arion mab Cadarn either to present his defense against these charges or to accept his guilt and satisfy both the body price and honor price of his victim."

As Aderuhn retook his seat, a slight moan was heard from the assembled *Soucanai*, which the *barnuchel* chose to ignore.

I stole a glance over toward Publicola. I realized that he had been following the proceedings; Troucillus was translating for him. Publicola actually seemed interested, nodding his head at times and asking questions, which Troucillus seemed to answer.

Cerialis, the engineer, on the other hand, had remained on seemingly to take advantage of Publicola's supply of wine and tidbits. With a somewhat drunken, bemused smirk on his face, he was slouched in his seat, his winecup hanging to the side of his chair in his right hand. Upon noting the wine cup in his *right hand*, I crossed him off my suspect list.

Aderuhn, the *barnuchel*, then stated, "Arion mab Cadarn! You may now present your defense against these charges."

Arion rose from among the *Soucanai* and walked forward to where Athauhnu was seated. The *barnuchel's* assistant approached and handed him the oaken wand. Arion spoke, "I canna ha' killed the *Ainedua*. I was na near the camp when it 'appened. How me knife got there, I got no idea. It was stolen from me before the killin'."

Aderuhn digested the statement, then said, "Is this the total of your defense against these accusations?"

"'Tis, lor'!" Arion nodded.

"Do you have witnesses to support these claims?" Aderuhn asked.

"I do, lor'!" Arion affirmed.

"Then proceed," Aderuhn directed.

Athauhnu rose, took the wand, and testified that, on the night of the murder, Arion was part of a three-man screening mission to the east of the encampment. The riders left the camp before sundown—and before the victim was last seen alive–and did not return until after the victim's body had been discovered. Athauhnu had watched Arion depart on the mission.

Arion's two mates on that mission then confirmed that Arion had remained with them the entire night. Since at no time were fewer than two of them awake, Arion could not have left and returned to the encampment undetected by at least one of them.

Although I felt that this evidence was adequate to acquit Arion of the accusation, testimony continued concerning the missing knife. Rhodri, the Soucani scout who had served with me in the campaign against the Helvetii and had fought in the battle against the Boii, stated that Arion had reported the missing *glev* to him an entire day before Rhuhderc's murder. He and Guithiru had conducted a search and an inquiry, both of which failed to discover the lost knife among the *Soucanai*.

After Guithiru rose and confirmed the testimony of both Arion and Rhodri concerning the *glev*, Aderuhn held the knife up toward them and asked a question.

"This is an ordinary knife. There must be dozens of them within our camps. Why, then, were you all so conscientious about the recovery of this particular knife, which is now connected to the murder of a warrior of the *Aineduai*?"

Arion spoke up, "It were me da's *glev*! And, his da's before 'im! Look on th'andle, lor'! That's the old writin'! 'Tis the sign for *deroo*, the oak. It gives its owner the strength and blessin's of the gods, it does! It gives me the luck!"

Aderuhn looked down at the handle of the knife and saw the characters of the old writing, = which the nations used before the coming of the Greeks and Romans. He understood the power possessed by these signs, if carved, according to the rituals, by a *derouhd*, one of the black-clad priests schooled in the ancient lore.

He nodded and said, "I accept your explanation."

He then held the knife handle up toward the assembled *Aineduai*. I actually saw some of them nod in agreement.

The *barnuchel* then asked Arion, "Does this conclude the presentation of your defense regarding the accusation against you in the murder of Rhuhderc mab Touhim?"

"'Tis, lor'!" Arion answered.

Before Aderuhn could respond, I heard Troucillus' voice speak in Gah'el, "May I have permission to enter the *cuhmooliat*, Lord?"

"The *pendefig* of the Elvai is welcome to speak before the *cuhmooliat*," Aderuhn agreed.

As Troucillus approached the *barnuchel*'s chair, he gestured for me to accompany him. He bent forward to speak to Aderuhn. "Lord, the information I have is relevant to the matter at hand, but it is sensitive because it indicates the murderer of the unfortunate Rhuhderc mab Touhim, and the murderer may be present in the *cuhmooliat*. If you believe that this information is critical to determining the guilt or innocence of the accused, then I will proclaim it before the assembly. Otherwise, it should be heard by you alone in your role as a *coulour*, a searcher of the truth in this matter."

Aderuhn considered what Troucillus was asking, then said, "You must include the chiefs of the Aidenuai and the Soucanai in this. Otherwise, it could undermine the credibility of my judgment in this matter."

Troucillus immediately agreed to this condition and Aderuhn summoned Morcant and Athauhnu to his chair.

When all were assembled, Troucillus explained what he had found at the crime scene . . . the footprints . . . the fibers . . . the position of the body. When Troucillus began to explain the nature of Rhuhderc's wound—that it had been caused by a *dagr*, not a *glev*—Aderuhn asked him who had substantiated the information. When Troucillus identified Morcant's *medduhg*, Aderuhn summoned the man forward to confirm Troucillus' testimony.

Finally, after the medic returned to his seated companions, Aderuhn summed up what Troucillus had offered. "So, based on what you saw, you believe that the murderer is a left-handed man, about five-four in the Roman measurement, who was wearing Roman boots and an undyed, woolen garment, and who had used a *sica* with a curved blade?"

"I do, Lord," Troucillus confirmed.

"And you, *decurio*," the *barnuchel* asked me, "you confirm that you were present when this evidence was identified?"

"I do, Lord," I stated.

Aderuhn then asked Morcant and Athauhnu, "Do you have any questions for the *pendefig* of the Elvai?"

Athauhnu just shrugged, but Morcant asked a series of questions to confirm Troucillus' qualifications as a tracker and hunter. Finally, Morcant stated, "I am satisfied, Lord."

The *barnuchel* then asked them, "Do you have any in your *fintai* who would fit this description?"

Morcant stated that none of his men were left-handed.

Athauhnu admitted that many of his band wore Roman boots and at least four of his men were left-handed. "But none of them are that short," he stated. "That's a stature more common among the *Rhufeinig* . . . and I've seen none of my men wear undyed, woolen *bracae* . . . Our clan colors are blue and green."

Aderuhn thought about what he had just heard, then spoke, "I understand your concern about keeping this information secret, Troucillus . . . and it has no bearing on how I must decide this case . . . So, you will not be obliged to share this with the *cuhmooliat* . . . I ask the chiefs of the Aidenuai and the Soucanai to explain my decision to their men."

Both Morcant and Athauhnu nodded in agreement.

Aderuhn continued, "Now, you all must step away from the chair of judgment, so I may deliver my decision alone in sight of the god."

When we retreated back to our places, Aderuhn again rose from his seat. The assembled Aidenuai and *Soucanai* rose with him. Aderuhn again lifted his staff, the outstretched palm of its silver hand facing the assembly. "I repeat that the claim of Morcant mab Cuhnetha that Rhuhderc mab Touhim was murdered, is valid."

There was a stirring among the Soucanai; Ci placed his hand on Arion's shoulder to steady him.

Aderuhn continued, "The accusation that Arion mab Cadarn killed Rhuhderc mab Touhim is not proven." A grumbling moan was heard among the Aidenuai. This time it was Morcant who silenced them. Aderuhn went on, "So, I cannot impose the *coscorv* and the *cosvanrhuhda* for this crime on Arion mab Cadarn."

There was a stirring among the *Soucanai*. Ci actually slapped Arion on the shoulder. Athauhnu ordered his men to be still.

The *barnuchel* concluded, "Since this was the purpose of this *cuhmooliat*, I will call it to an end, with the assembly's concurrence."

Morcant spoke up, "Lord! May I speak?"

"Proceed, Morcant mab Cuhnetha," Aderuhn allowed.

"Lord!" Morcant protested, "I and my men will return to our homeland tomorrow, after we have guided the Caisar's embassy to the ford across the river of Soucanna. Although we do not protest the decision of the *barnuchel* in this matter, how are we to bring justice to the father and brothers of Rhuhderc mab Touhim for their loss?"

Aderuhn briefly considered Morcant's words, then spoke, "In our laws, when the actual murderer cannot be identified, there is the allowance for a chief to pay the *coscorv* and the *cosvanrhuhda* to the family of a murder victim who was pledged to the chief at the time of the crime."

The Aidenuai nodded in agreement as Aderuhn continued, "Arth mab Secundus! Please stand before the *cuhmooliat*!"

It took me a few heartbeats to realize that Aderuhn had called for me. I stepped forward, not liking at all where this seemed to be going.

"Arth mab Secundus," Aderuhn announced, "the Caisar has appointed you chief over the *fintai* of both the *Soucanai* and the Aidenuai. Is this not true?"

"*Mai'n wir, fuh arglwyd*," I heard myself say. "'Tis, my Lord!"

"Then, Arth mab Secundus, as chief of the sworn bands, are you prepared to settle the *coscorv* and the *cosvanrhuhda* of Rhuhderc mab Touhim with his chief, Morcant mab Cuhnetha, until the true killer is identified?"

My head was spinning: fifteen *dai*! How many Roman *denarii* to satisfy a *da*—ten, fifteen? Then I heard Troucillus speak, "My Lord! May I speak?"

"Your counsel is always welcome, Gaius Valerius Troucillus," the *barnuchel* acceded.

"Lord," Troucillus began. "I speak for Tertius Gellius Publicola, who is a tribune of the *Rhufeiniaid* and the Caisar's *brenin a froouhdrau* for this expedition. Publicola asks that as the *brenin* of both *Gah'ela* and *Rhufeiniaid*, he be allowed to settle the *coscorv* and the *cosvanrhuhda* of Rhuhderc mab Touhim. He offers one hundred fifteen silver *denarii* in compensation to the family of the *milour*, the soldier, who was murdered while serving under his command."

I was in shock. Initially, from being asked to pay the compensation for Rhuhderc's murder, and then, from the unexpected offer of Publicola, whom I would never have suspected of having a bit of concern for anyone other than himself.

When I finally came to my senses, Morcant was speaking: "I accept the offer of compensation from the *brenin a froouhdrau*, and on behalf of my tribe and the family of Rhuhderc mab Touhim, surrender all claim to his *coscorv* and the *cosvanrhuhda* once his murderer is identified."

The *barnuchel* nodded toward Morcant, then toward Publicola. "Now that the issue of *coscorv* and the *cosvanrhuhda* has been settled to the satisfaction of all parties, I declare this *cuhmooliat* ended."

We reached the ford across the Arar by the seventh hour of the next day.

We had bypassed *Ventum Cavillonum*. Cerialis announced and Publicola concurred that it was a sad place—a collection of roundhuts, cattle pens, and a chief's hall, hardly fortified, and on low ground—of no military value at all.

Metius did enter the *oppidum*. He said he had some contacts there from whom he could collect intelligence.

We halted on the west bank of the river. I sent Ci's *ala* across, with orders to procede as far as a Soucanai settlement on a bluff at the mouth of the Dubis. I made sure that Arion was with Ci's troop. I didn't think any of the Aidenuai would try to take revenge on him, but why take an unnecessary risk? Guithiru's *ala* crossed after Ci and deployed itself along the bluffs on the east bank of the Arar to screen our crossing.

The *decurio* in command of the Roman cavalry had just informed me that Publicola was ready to cross the river when Morcant approached where Athauhnu and I were positioned on the river bank.

"*A Pen!*" I called to him. "I thought by now you would be on your journey home."

He smiled. "We are anxious to go, *a Pen*. But, it would be discourteous of me to depart without taking leave of you . . . and of you, Athauhnu mab Hergest."

An Ainedua avoiding rudeness to a Rhufeiniaid and a Soucana! This is new ground, I thought.

"*Bued i'r duwiau uhn eich amdivuhn huhd nes uh buhtoon uhn cifarfod eto,*" I pronounced the ritual of departure, which was echoed by Athauhnu.

"*Huhd nes uh buhtoon uhn coort eto,*" Morcant responded, raising the palm of his empty right hand toward us in a sign of his peaceful intent.

Instead of leaving, Morcant then asked, "Arth mab Secundus, do you have any message for my cousin, Rhonwen merc Gwen?" By addressing me by name, we were now having a personal conversation—a personal conversation about Rhonwen!

"Uhh . . . please tell her . . . uh . . . tell her I grieve with her for her loss," I stammered, trying to sound proper, military, and "Roman."

Morcant looked blankly at me for a few heartbeats, then chuckled. I even heard Athauhnu snicker.

An Aidenua and a Soucana joining together in a prank against a Rhufeiniaid. Will wonders never cease this day?

"Rhonwen and Rhuhderc grew up together," Morcant explained. "They were friends throughout their childhood, but they never had the kind of love for each other that must exist between husband and wife. She will mourn the death of a friend, and the manner of it, but she will not mourn the loss of one she desired as a husband."

I was not wondering why Morcant was explaining this to me—somehow he had discovered my secret—but I was struggling to maintain some vestige of seventeen-year-old, Roman-officer *gravitas* in this matter.

"Why are you telling me this, Morcant?" I asked, trying to keep my face blank.

Morcant laughed and shook his head. "Because of what is written on your face every time Rhonwen's name is mentioned . . . Plain to see by all but you. Am I not right, Athauhnu?"

"As plain as the nose on a Roman's face," Athauhnu agreed, laughing.

By this point, my face was burning. I'm sure it glowed as red as the setting sun.

"I will tell my cousin that you remember her," Morcant said. "Perhaps I will add 'fondly.'" Morcant laughed, turned his horse, and rode off to join his *fintai*.

I tried to channel my embarrassment into my now-well-bruised authority. "If you're done laughing, *a Pen*," I said to Athauhnu, turning my horse toward the river, "it's time we rejoined our men."

"Give me some time, Arth Uthr," Athauhnu said, still laughing. "It would not be good for my men to see me fall off my horse in the middle of a river."

XII.

De Itinere ad Vesantionem

OUR MARCH TO VESANTIO

If *Ventum Cavillonum* of the *Aineduai* was a "sad" place, the *Soucanai* settlement at the confluence of the Arar and the Dubis was downright miserable—essentially a pig pen, a cattle pen, some storage bins, and a large roundhouse with the pretentious name, *Uh Dun Du*, "The Black Fortress." There was no fortress, and I guessed it was called "black" after one of the rivers that flowed by it, the Dubis.

Cerialis, however, was delighted with the place: it was on the highest ground in the immediate area; it had access to an endless supply of potable water; it had flowing water on two sides of a triangular ridge for defense; it offered locations for baths and latrines; it controlled movement along two rivers; it controlled access to the valley of the Dubis from the west and access to the valley of the Arar from the east; it could easily control the fords across the Arar; and, if the top of the ridge were leveled, it could accommodate at least a full legion.

We reached the place during the eleventh hour, and before the sun was down, Cerialis had his boys staking out a legionary *castrum* around the *Soucanai* settlement, which, in Cerialis' mind, had already ceased to exist. Cerialis himself dragged a crate of his engineering instruments down the bluff to search for a place to bridge the Arar.

121

We established our camp further up the ridge from the settlement, blissfully upwind from the pigs. The hour candle had not burned down an *uncia* into the first watch when Athauhnu came to fetch me.

"Arth Uthr," he gestured to me. "The *Buch'rix* of *Uh Dun Du* offers us the hospitality of his hearth for the evening."

For a heartbeat, I thought I caught a whiff of pigsty in my nostrils, but to refuse such an offer of hospitality would be a great insult. "Let me check on the guard mount first, then we can be on our way," I said, trying to put this thing off as long as I could.

"Ci has already attended to that," Athauhnu stated with a slight grin.

I sighed and threw the baldric of my *gladius* over my left shoulder; I still wore my sword like a *mulus*, on my right hip. Then, I strapped on my *cingulum* and *pugio*.

"*Gadeouch i ni fuhnd*," I said finally. "Let's go."

"*Eamus*," Athauhnu echoed me in Latin, "are you sure you want to take that great Roman sword with you?" Athauhnu chuckled, patting the long *spatha* hanging from his left hip. "You might scare those poor, back-country farmers to death."

"*Cac't!*" I dismissed Athauhnu's dig.

"*Cachou!*" he echoed me in Gah'el, then corrected me. "*Cachou moch* . . . pig shit!" he laughed.

We walked a few dozen paces down the ridge toward the farm. I was so focused on the pigs that I almost didn't notice a figure waiting for us in the darkness. My right hand was on the hilt of my *gladius* when I heard a familiar voice.

"Took you long enough! A man could starve to death waiting for you ladies to get ready for dinner!" It was Troucillus.

"I just hope we're not served pork," I quipped. "That would finish it for me."

Troucillus laughed and slapped me on the shoulder. "You've been away from the farm too long, Gai Mari. Here, fresh pig shit is the smell of prosperity!" he laughed.

We were indeed served pork—a thick stew with carrots, turnips, and some other greens I couldn't readily identify. We sat around a fire pit in a round room of wooden posts joined by wattle-and-daub panels. It reminded me of my original home before mama "Romanified" the house with stone and right angles. Our host was burning herbs, which helped to disguise the barnyard smells that surrounded us. The fire vented up through a hole in the conical thatched roof, where I could hear the sound of nesting birds in the eves. I could almost see the shape of gran'pa in the smoky shadows, his feet extended toward the fire and a cup of *couru* in his fist.

Our host was Nuhnian mab Seisuhl, who styled himself the *Buch'rix* of *Dun Du* and the *Gouarcheidouad Uh Cresfannai*, the "Keeper of the Crossings," which gave him the privilege of extorting fees for hospitality and protection from travelers crossing the Arar into the lands of the *Soucanai*. Since we were traveling with Athauhnu's *fintai* and were *Rhufeiniaid*, friends and allies of the *Soucanai* in their wars against the *Pobluhrafon*, the "River People" as the *Soucanai* call the Helvetii, and against the hated *Almaenwuhr*, he declared us exempt from the toll.

The fact that we had almost a hundred heavily armed troops camped around his *dun* had nothing at all to do with Nuhnian's sense of generosity. I wondered briefly if Cerialis had shared with Nuhnian his imminent and compulsory change of locale.

"I hope whatever is affecting the health of your chief, the Roman prince, it departs quickly," Nuhnian was saying to Troucillus.

Troucillus was tearing a piece of bread from a steaming, freshly baked loaf. "I will pass your concern to our 'prince,' chief. He is sorry that he could not accept your generous invitation."

Nuhnian grunted, accepting Troucillus' explanation, publicly at least. Nuhnian's senior wife sat next to him, directing the movement of food among her guests and directing the delivery of food and drink from the kitchen and larders behind her. One of Nuhnian's other wives was busy keeping our cups full, while a younger woman, perhaps a daughter of the house, was busy ferrying loaves of bread and bowls of radishes and sliced apples in from the kitchens, which seemed to be located to the rear of the roundhouse.

The traditional laws of the Gah'ela permit multiple marriages, both for men and for women, although the practice is reputedly more common among men. Most "civilized" Gah'ela, those who have been influenced by Greek and

Roman culture, are monogamous. Certainly, among my people, the Insubres, who have lived under Roman domination for over a century, monogamy is the practice.

I remember my gran'pa snorting in derision at the possibility of having multiple wives. "A man would have to be mad," he dismissed the idea. "All those clackin' tongues surroundin' him day and night! It would drive a *derwuhd glan*, a holy druid, mad!"

Then, he caught a look from Nana and modified his position, "Unless there were more of you walkin' the earth, me darlin'! Then, I'd be a fool not to marry all of you."

That earned him a derisive snort from Nana, who was buying none of what he had to sell, especially after a few cups of potent, brown, winter *couru* that had been perfecting itself in the bottom of an oak barrel since *Tachwed*, the month Romans call *Novembris*.

"Been peaceful in these lands since we smashed the *Aineduai* years back," Nuhnian was saying. "Them *Almaenwuhr* bastards keep 'emselves east of Vesantio fer the most part . . . Me oldest son, Bearach, took five of me best men and an 'orse to serve the *cadeuhrn* . . . Worth it, if it keeps them German pigs away . . . Just needs 'em back by the harvest . . . especially th'orse."

"Has anyone besides merchants been crossing the Arar going east?" Troucillus interrupted.

"Merchants?" Nuhnian belched out after a long swig of beer. He held his cup out for one of the daughters to refill. "Damn few o' those this year . . . what with them River-People pillocks rampagin' through 'ere and the Krauts stirrin' things up in the east . . . Damn few . . . Bad fer business."

He took a beer break from talking, then continued, "The favor of the gods . . . with our warriors comin' back from the Roman war." He gestured with his cup toward me. "And bringin' you Roman boys along with 'im, them sheep-shaggin' Germans'll crawl back into their shit-ridden swamps . . . Wait . . . We did 'ave a *fintai* of them *Aineduai* knob-yankers pass through a few weeks back . . . Fancy bunch, they was . . . Somebody important."

This caught Troucillus' attention. "A *fintai* of *Aineduai*, you say? Going east up the Dubis? When? How many? Who led them? How were they equipped?"

"Like I said," Nuhnian said through another belch, "a few weeks ago . . . Right around the time the last of the cows calfed . . . When was that, Ceana?" He asked one of his "daughters."

"*Choue wuht'nos*," she shot back. "Six weeks."

"That sounds about right," Nuhnian continued, "six weeks . . . There was about thirty of 'em . . . good 'orses . . . about ten remounts . . . Led by a real nob . . . a nasty piece of work . . . a prince he called hisself . . . up from Bibracte . . . Had good armor and weapons, they did . . . Said they was fer the *cadeuhrn* in Vesantio . . . Passed right through, they did . . . Fine with me . . . I didn't want to 'ave to feed that lot."

"Does the name Deluuhnu mab Clethguuhno sound familiar?" I asked.

Nuhnian shrugged. "Could be . . . The pikey bastard didn't introduce hisself . . . not to the likes o' me, anyway . . . In an 'ell of a big hurry 'e was . . . I was glad to see the backs of 'em with me 'ide still in one piece." The thought made Nuhnian thirsty; he drained his cup and yelled for more.

We stayed long enough to be polite. When Nuhnian started hinting that one of his "daughters" might be willing to take any one of us for her "husband for the night," we begged off, saying we had duties in the camp and would be moving out at sunrise. Nuhnian leered and drunkenly fondled the ass of one of the serving women—either wife or daughter—and said it would be our loss. His senior wife, still seated immediately to his left, seemed not to notice. I imagine, as long as he left her alone, she was fine with whatever he did.

As we were leaving Nuhnian's compound, a woman's voice hissed to us from the shadows behind a cowshed. We stopped, then carefully approached a shadowy figure who kept the shed between herself and the roundhouse. When we got closer, I recognized her as one of the women who had served us; it was the one who kept pouring Nuhnian's beer.

"That dodgy git's lyin' to yas," she said with no preamble. "That *Aineduan* nob who come through 'ere a few weeks back give 'im silver to watch who crossed the river, then send 'im word."

"Why'd he do that?" Troucillus asked her.

"Dunno," she said. "The only thing his lordship shares with me is . . . well . . . never mind that . . . Ain't important . . . What's important is that the *Aineduan* nob seemed nervous . . . Why's a rich man with a *fintai* 'round 'isself nervous, I asks meself . . . Could someone be after 'im . . . someone with more men 'an he's got . . . That's what I thinks . . . That pikey bastard in there'll be sendin' a rider out to warn his new friends as soon as 'e's sober enough to remember, 'e will."

We were silent for a few heartbeats, then Troucillus asked, "Why are you telling us this?"

"Why?" she snorted. "Why? I 'ates the poxy bastard, I do . . . Me parents sold me to 'im, and now I have to wait on 'im 'and and foot when 'e's not gruntin' on top o' me . . . I 'ates 'im!"

Troucillus nodded. He reached into his *marsupium* and handed the girl a few coins.

When we had walked a few paces into the night, Troucillus asked me, "Do you think it's this Deluuhnu mab Clethguuhno you asked Nuhnian about?"

"Must be," I answered. "Who else could it be? Now he and his men are somewhere between us and Vesantio."

Troucillus was silent for a while, then said, "No . . . if he's not with the *cadeuhrn* in Vesantio, he's through the Gate and with Ariovistus . . . He couldn't sustain himself in Soucana territory . . . not with thirty men and forty horses . . . Ariovistus would welcome him . . . A prince of the *Aineduai* would be useful to him when he moves west . . . and as far as Deluuhnu is concerned, Ariovistus is Caesar's enemy."

"*Hostis hostis mei socius meus,*" I said. "An enemy of my enemy is my friend."

"*Certe!*" Troucillus nodded. "Indeed!"

The next day by the first hour, we were on the move east toward Vesantio. As soon as there was enough light to see, we had assembled near where Publicola and the Romans had camped for the night. Publicola seemed to have recovered from whatever "ailment" had prevented him from accepting Nuhnian's hospitality the night before. I assumed that Troucillus had briefed him fully on what we had learned.

Publicola, of course, said nothing to me. I coordinated our order of march with Manius Rabirius, or Manius *Talus* as he's known around the camps— Manius "Knuckle Bones"—because of his "luck" with the dice. Manius was the *decurio* in command of Publicola's cavalry escort. We decided that the Roman *ala* would march with the main body. I would split the Sequani *turma* front and back; Guithiru's *ala* would take the point, while Ci's *ala* would provide rear security. Manius himself would ride in the main body; Athauhnu and I would be in the front with Guithiru's boys.

While we were talking, I noticed that Metius had rejoined us from his errand in *Ventum Cavillonum*. Whatever intelligence he had gathered there from his contacts was not shared with me, so I assumed that he had found out nothing of importance to our mission.

It's dangerous to assume.

Then, for the first time, I noticed a member of Metius' *comitatus*, a stocky, somewhat short, swarthy man holding Metius' horse. The man was dressed in a plain, undyed tunic like a slave, but unlike a slave, he didn't avert his eyes away from the glances of the soldiers and freemen around him. In fact, he met their glances with a challenging glare, which would have earned a slave a beating. He held Metius' horse with his right hand, keeping his left hand free. I glanced down and saw he was wearing Roman *caligae*.

"Hey, Mani! You know that guy over there?" I asked.

"Which one?" he responded.

"The guy holding Metius' horse," I indicated.

Mani looked over. "Oh. . . that one. . . I'd steer clear a that *mentul'* if I was you. . . My boys call him *Umbra*, the 'Shadow,' because if you see Metius, you see that little *verpa*."

"He's Metius' slave?" I asked.

Mani shrugged. "Don't think so. . . Doesn't call anyone '*domine*' as far as I can tell. . . Calls Metius '*Capu,'* Boss, and Metius calls him '*Bulla*'. . . sounds like a gutter-Roman to me. I'd stay clear a the little *podex* if I was you."

"Something happen?" I pressed.

"Yeah," Manius admitted. "A couple a nights ago, a couple a my boys went over to the mess tent for their chow . . . That little *verpa* walks by 'em stinkin' a wine an' says, 'What's to eat?' . . . Then, he sticks his fingers in my guy's mess bowl and licks 'em . . . Then, he spits right in my guy's chow and says it tastes like shit . . . My guys jump the *mentul'*, and he kicks the shit outta both of 'em . . . just like that . . . It's like he did it just to start somethin' . . . for no reason . . .

None a my guys had anythin' to do with him before that . . . Next thing I know, I get called in on the carpet by that broad-striped nob we're nurse-maidin' and told to get control a *my* men or I'd find myself scrubbin' latrines for the rest a my hitch. *Quam merdam!* Just stay clear a that *podex* . . . Somethin' ain't right with that one."

"He always carry a weapon?" I asked. "A knife or a sword?"

Mani shrugged, "Never seen one . . . The way he handled my guys, he don't need one."

We were on the road by the time the sun was on the horizon. The terrain was suprisingly rough. We were following a narrow road, which followed the Dubris as it wound through a narrow, wooded valley. It was just wide enough to accommodate the wagons of the merchants traveling east to Vesantio.

In places, the forests and hills pressed in on the road, preventing us from maintaining good flank security. Athauhnu had sent Rhodri ahead, as our scout. He was riding with one of our new men, Drust, who had been a hunter among his people. The Sequani didn't seem at all concerned; after all, they were back in their own lands and the enemy was being held east of the Gate.

That's what they assumed.

It's dangerous to assume.

When the valley opened up, we could see small farms, but no people and no livestock. I asked Athauhnu about it.

"I don't know," he shrugged. "The people could hide quickly if they thought we were a threat. But, the animals are gone too. Farmers will hide their animals when there are raiders in the area, but that has to be planned ahead of time. I don't understand why they're avoiding *us*. We are *Soucanai*, like them."

We got our answer around the fifth hour. We caught the smell first, an odor of wet charcoal, evidence of an old burning, a large one. Drust came pounding down the trail toward us.

"*A Pen!*" he reported. "Rhodri needs you up ahead!"

I wasn't sure which "chief" he was talking to, me or Athauhnu. I spoke first, "Guithiru! Dismount the troop and hold here!"

Then, to Drust, "Lead us to Rhodri!"

Athauhnu and I followed Drust forward. We met Rhodri about a hundred *passus* up the trail. The charcoal smell was much stronger. "Raiders," was all Rhodri said.

That was all that was necessary. In a narrow, clear valley north of the trail were the burned out ruins of what was once a roundhouse, a cattle pen, and a storage shed. Nothing seemed to be moving among the ashes.

"Are we secure?" I asked Rhodri.

"Even the crows have eaten their fill and departed, *a Pen*," Rhodri answered.

"Any survivors?"

"I've found none," Rhodri replied.

We turned north, spreading out in a line, and walked our horses through the stinking ruins. I was keeping my eyes on the ruins and on the woodline behind them, trying to detect any movement that might indicate an ambush. Clamriu rearing backward was all that prevented me from riding over the first body. From the clothing, it had once been a woman. Her skirts were pulled up over her waist, her tunic ripped apart down the middle. White teeth were bared in a silent scream.

"Dead woman here!" I called over to Athauhnu.

I looked over and saw Athauhnu staring down at something on the ground. "She's not alone, Arth," he said flatly.

There were four that we could positively identify as individuals: my woman, two men, and what appeared to be a boy. The boy still had an arrow in his throat. Drust pulled it out and handed it the Athauhnu. After examining it for a few minutes, he said, "*Almaenwuhr!*"

"Germans this far west?" I challenged.

"A thin, metal head," Athauhnu said. "Only those *moch* from across the Rhenus would use a shoddy arrowhead like this. The joints in the shaft are hardly trimmed . . . The nock doesn't end at a joint. The fletching . . . goose feathers glued with bark pitch . . . This is the work of *anouariad*, 'savages.'"

Rhodri rejoined us from scouting along the woodline. "I found tracks . . . They followed a stream in from the north, went out the same way . . . A dozen of them, I guess . . . They were avoiding the road . . . The trail was rained on, so more than a week old . . . Maybe as many as two."

"That all?" Athauhnu questioned his scout.

Rhodri shrugged, "They weren't carrying any loads on the way out. They got nothing from this. It was as if all they wanted was to kill these people."

"A dozen, you say? Over a week ago?" I echoed Rhodri. "They're no threat to us."

"Rhodri!" Athauhnu snapped. "Ride back to Guithiru. Tell him to bring the men forward. Drust, find the root cellar . . . It may be under the burned timbers. . . It should be near one of the entrances of the house."

"Survivors?" I asked him.

"No," Athauhnu said. "We'll drag what's left of these people into the cellar. It's the only burial we can offer them."

By the time we went into camp that evening, we had found three more burned farms. There seemed to be neither rhyme nor reason to the destruction; a devastated farm would be found in the midst of several untouched ones. There was nothing of value to steal from these people. The harvest wasn't in; the livestock were hidden. It seemed as if the Germans killed just for the sake of killing.

There was no evidence of people at the farms that the raiders had spared. The valley of the Dubis seemed as if it were under a curse that had made all the people and animals disappear. The Sequani, who, when we crossed the Arar, had been heartened at being back in their own lands, were now silent and sullen.

We pulled into our night laager around the eleventh hour. We posted security, set up, and pulled horse stables. Athauhnu and I had just posted the night sentries when there was a Roman cavalryman waiting for us, one of Mani's boys. He was still in full rig, so the visit was "official." When he approached us, he seemed confused for a heartbeat, seemingly seeing *two* officers in Roman gear. Being a veteran and wanting to avoid a *castigatio* for offending the *dignitas* of some Roman fuzz-face who thought he was so important that everyone in the army should recognize him, even in the dark, he addressed the larger of the two apparent officers.

"*Decurio!* The legate, Tertius Gellius Publicola, requests that you report to him at his *principia, stat!*"

Athauhnu chuckled, "You obviously want my little Roman friend here. I don't jump for purple stripers."

The man hestitated. In his mind, he had just mistaken a "wog" for a Roman officer, an offense for which he feared he could be beaten into unconsciousness. The irony was that, in reality, he had mistaken one "wog" for another.

Finally, he addressed me, "*Decurio*! The legate—"

I held my hand up to stop him, "I heard the message. Do you have any idea what this is about?"

"*Nescio, Decurio*!" he snapped. "Sir! I do not know!"

I sighed. Missing my dinner for a meeting with a pompous gobshite like Publicola was not my idea of how to end a stressful day. "*Bene*! Take me to him."

The man did an about face and marched off into the darkness toward the Roman camp fires. I followed in his wake, realizing how heavy my *lorica* weighed down on me after a day in the saddle cataloging German atrocities. Even my boots were dragging. I hoped, whatever bug had crawled up Publicola's butt, this wouldn't take too long, even if it were an ass-chewing for some imagined deficiency.

The cavalryman led me to a tent erected in the middle of the camp and stood back as he parted the leather covering the entrance. As I walked by him, I winked and said, "Don't worry about the mixup . . . Everybody mistakes Adonus *Dux* for me . . . Even our mothers have trouble telling us apart."

I couldn't tell if the man appreciated my humor.

When I entered the tent, I met with a bit of a surprise. I had expected Publicola to be dressed in his full senatorial rig, sitting ramrod straight behind his field desk. Instead, there was no desk. Publicola, Troucillus, Metius, and Manius Talus were sitting in a circle, slouched down in their chairs, each with a wine cup in his hand. The look in Publicola's eyes indicated they had been at it since sundown.

The sound of his voice clinched it. "Ah . . . Insubrecus . . . 'bout time you got here! Take off that helmet and *lorica*! This party's strickerly informal . . . My man will help you . . . Take a seat . . . *Famile*! Slave! Pour the *decurio* some wine!"

It took a bit of maneuvering to get me out of my armor without injuring any of the other guests. Despite Publicola's protestation of informality, I rebuckled my *pugio* to my waist and hung the baldric of my *gladius* over the back of my chair . . . I would never again make the mistake I made in Gabi's villa. A dark blue ceramic cup was thrust into my hand, and Publicola's slave filled it with wine. I took a taste. It was a first-rate Italian vintage, not the vinegar that soldiers usually drink. Publicola wasn't traveling light.

Finally, Publicola spoke. "This is an informal meeting of comrades . . . a symposium of sorts . . . So, just address me as Publicola . . . You think you can . . . can 'andle that . . . Insubrece?" he said with a slight hiccup.

"Yes, Trib . . . yes . . . Publicola," I said. I wasn't quite *that* drunk yet.

"*Be . . . Bene*!" Publicola hiccupped again as he held up his wine cup to be refilled. "Just a bunch of *contubernales* . . . army mates, talkin' 'bout the day."

Publicola continued, "I don't know if Gaius Valerius mentioned it—" He gestured toward Troucillus with his wine cup, sloshing the contents over his hand. "But, I was quite impressed with the way you handled the wogs . . . Oh! . . . My apologies, Insubrece . . . the *Gauls* . . . over that nastiness with the killing . . . Killed while taking a leak . . . not a noble way to fall." Publicola laughed at his own pun.

"The entertainment was well worth the silver I paid," he continued. "Imagine . . . being able to pay a fine for murdering someone! If we Romans did that, it would be a new growth industry in the city . . . an instant success . . . The gods know, murder's already a thriving trade . . . Millions would be changing hands! Maybe we could improve on it! Say . . . I'd like to murder your brother next week . . . How much is he worth to you?'" Again, Publicola enjoyed his own joke.

I stole a glance at Troucillus. His face was frozen in a "slightly amused" look. Metius, I couldn't read at all; his face was completely blank. Manius Talus was just enjoying the moment; he seemed as far into Bacchus' kingdom as was our host.

Publicola suddenly changed direction, "So . . . tell me, Insubrece . . . What do you make of these raids? . . . What do your Gauls think is going on here?"

"It's difficult to decipher . . . uh . . . Publicola," I began. Addressing Publicola by his *cognomen* like some Patrician at a cocktail party on the Palatine was still sticking in my throat. "There's nothing to be gained by it. These people aren't rich . . . There's nothing to steal that's worth the effort . . . All the *Grunni* are accomplishing is scaring the piss out of some farmers."

"Perhaps that's the point," Troucillus interrupted.

"Interesting thought, Troucille," Publicola said. "Say more!"

Troucillus began, "The Germans are terrorizing the Gallic population in preparation for Ariovistus' invasion. If they can succeed, they will have defeated the Sequani in this valley before the first sword is drawn. That, and if the harvest is disrupted, the garrison at Vesantio will not be able to supply itself against a siege."

"Interesting . . . interesting" Publicola blurted. "What do your sources tell you, Meti?"

Metius shrugged, "Germans are bad for business."

"'Germans are bad for business,'" Publicola chuckled. "That's rich . . . rich, indeed."

Publicola thought it a joke. I suspected Metius was holding something back.

"What *did* your contacts in Ventum *Cavillonum* have to say about the situation . . . *Meti*?" I pressed him.

Troucillus gave me a slight shake of the head, but it was too late. The question was out there.

"Yes . . . yes," Publicola encouraged. "What did you learn, Meti?"

Metius turned and looked directly at me. His eyes were dark . . . void, but vaguely threatening. I thought for a heartbeat I was staring into Hecate's black pit.

Finally, he spoke in a monotone, "The Aedui do not admit to knowing anything about the problems of the Sequani living in this valley . . . As far as they're concerned, anything bad that happens to the Sequani is well-deserved . . . as long as it doesn't affect their profits."

Publicola shook his head, "*Gratias dis,* the Gauls hate each other more than they hate us! So . . . Troucille . . . you believe it's terror for the sake of terror . . . To me, that sounds a bit too sophisti—" (hiccup) "sophisticated for barbarians . . . Next you're going to tell me Ariovistus has studied the campaigns of Hannibal!"

Troucillis smiled, "I don't know what Ariovistus has read, but I will not permit myself to assume he has not read military histories or that he is not a capable strategist in his own right. Terror for the sake of terror was not the invention of any historian. But, it has been a device of capable and ruthless military leaders. Hannibal used it against you Romans, as did Mithradates when he massacred every Roman citizen he could get his hands on in *Asia*. Crassus used it against the slaves when he crucified thousands of them along the *Via Appia*. One doesn't need to be a philosopher to understand it."

"*Bene dictum*!" Publicola hicupped. "Well said!"

Troucillus' lecture on terrorism seemed to end the conversation about our current situation. Publicola went off on some discourse about rhetoric, which led him to criticize Cicero for publishing speeches he never gave. Troucillus talked about the best way of hunting boar and five methods of testing animal stool for freshness. Metius said nothing; he just stared down at his winecup and sloshed around the contents. Occasionally, I caught him staring at me with his black, soulless eyes. I talked a bit about growing grapes in the Padus valley, to which Publicola was incredulous and Troucillus was unimpressed, since his people had been cultivating grapes along the Rhodanus for at least a generation.

Finally, Mani *Talus* tried to make a contribution to the conversation by saying, "You guys ever hear the one about the rube who was visitin' Rome and walkin' through the forum? He drew everyone's attention 'cause he was the spittin' image of the *dictator*, Sulla, . . . So, Sulla has his lictors drag the poor sod into the *Curia* and stand 'im up right in front of the entire senate. Sulla says to the guy, 'Your mother has ever visited Rome?' The guy says back, 'No, she never has, but my father came here all the time.'"

Manius was in hysterics at his own joke. Troucillis, Publicola, and I were still trying to unravel the father-mother thing through the fumes of a couple of cups of wine. Metius was impassive. I doubted the man capable of laughing at a joke. I was unwilling to imagine what might have made him smile.

Then, from outside the tent, we heard a voice yell, "You! By the tent there! Halt!" There were the sounds of a struggle. The side of the tent immediately behind Troucillus bulged inward then recovered. There was the sound of a blow and a man grunting in pain. Then, silence.

I was the first one out, my *gladius* in hand. Manius Talus tried to follow but was a little worse for the wine he had drunk. When I got around the tent to where the struggle had occurred, I could see the shapes of two men outlined by the dim glow of lamp light through the translucent leather of the tent. One was down on the ground, the other standing over him.

I called for them to halt and moved in closer. The man on the ground was in the armor of a Roman cavalryman, one of Mani's, obviously a roaming sentry. The other turned to me with a snarl. It was Metius' man, Bulla. He was in a knife-fighter's crouch. There was something in his left hand, which he kept low, down by his hip. It was a curved *sica*.

"You think you can take me, boy? Even with that pig-sticker of yours?" he challenged.

Macro always told me that, when skills are equal, the fighter with the greater reach usually wins. A sword beats a knife. Facing Bulla, though, suddenly I was no longer confident with that principle.

Then, I heard Metius' voice behind me: "Stand down, Bulla!"

Bulla hesitated for a couple of heartbeats. Then, he relaxed and straightened up. He slipped the *sica* up under his right sleeve.

Then, I heard Mani's voice slur, "Soldier . . . *Sta tu*! Get on your feet . . . Report!"

The man on the ground lifted himself up and assumed the position of attention. "*Decurio*! I saw this man skulking outside the Tribune's tent . . . I challenged him."

"That doesn't explain why a civilian with only a knife knocked a fully equipped Roman soldier on his arse," Manius shot back at him. "Explain that to me and maybe I won't have you beaten for dereliction of duty!"

The man stammered a bit, but Metius interrupted him. "*Decurio*, Bulla here is not merely a 'civilian.' He's a trained fighter with many years' experience. He serves as my *custos*, my bodyguard. I'm sure he was here only to ensure my safety."

"Your safety?" Manius shot back. "Your safety? In the Tribune's tent? In the middle of a Roman encampment?"

Before Manius could finish, Publicola spoke up. "Gentlemen! I'm sure this is just a . . . a slight misunderstanding . . . Soldier! *Abi*! *Miss'est*! You're dimissed!"

I could sense that Manius didn't consider the issue either a "misunderstanding" or finished. But, before he could protest, Publicola continued, "It's late gentlemen . . . well into the second watch . . . We have an early start in the morning and need to be on our game with these *Grunni* lurking about . . . Go back to your quarters and get some sleep . . . Insubrece! Please come back inside with me . . . I have some unfinished business with you . . . Troucille, you may remain with us if you wish . . . To the rest of you I bid *valete!*"

Bulla glared at me for a few more heartbeats. Then he made a derisive sound through his nose, turned, and walked off into the darkness. I had the distinct feeling that I now had an enemy in him, and he was not finished with me. As I turned and followed Publicola and Troucillus back around the tent, I bid Manius Talus *vale* over my shoulder. Metius seemed to have vanished into the darkness.

I entered the tent, picked my scabbard up off the ground where it had fallen, sheathed my sword, and hung it back over my chair. As soon as my right hand was free, Publicola handed me another cup of wine. I didn't really want it, but I noticed Publicola pouring Troucillus and himself another cup. Macro always told me some drinkers get insulted when you don't drink with them. So, I took a slight sip of the wine as I took my seat.

"Insubrece," Publicola started, "I'm going to let you in on a confidence that the *Imperator* shared with me . . . He told me to be watchful for possible *Roman* interference with our mission . . . Caesar believes that certain elements in Rome do not want him to succeed in restoring peace to our *provincia* . . . He told me that *you* are aware of these attempts to undermine his ambitions for Gaul . . . He mentioned some . . . uh . . . shall we say, unpleasantness in Massalia, which involved the Consul's son."

Publicola stopped to wet his whistle then started again, "That having been said, what is your opinion on the killing of that *Aeduus*? Was it just tribal rivalries? Or, is someone trying to subvert our mission by stirring up the Gauls?"

I thought about my response for a few heartbeats, then began, "It's difficult to attribute the killing to the Sequani . . . When Gauls go after each other, it's face to face . . . The whole thing was too . . . too *Roman* . . . at night, from behind, leaving misleading evidence—"

Troucillus suddenly chimed in, "I think the Aedui understood that. That's one of the reasons they accepted the judgment of the honor and transgression price so easily, and if you don't mind my saying it, it's why they maneuvered the payment of the fine over to you Romans. They knew somehow one of you was to blame."

Publicola seemed to mull over what I had said, then asked me, "Did Caesar share with you his expectations for our mission?"

I was on dangerous ground. I had no idea what Caesar had told Troucillus or how far he had taken Troucillus into his confidence. But, Troucillus was about to put himself in harm's way by carrying Caesar's message, so he had every right to know how Caesar expected Ariovistus to react.

"Caesar has no expectation that Ariovistus will submit to his demands," I stated flatly. "Caesar wants a battle to force the Germans back over the Rhenus."

Publicola nodded his agreement. "That is what I believe, also. Our mission is to delay Ariovistus long enough for Caesar to get the army into the Gate. Failing that, we are to defend Vesantio until Caesar can relieve it. My job is to convince the *Grunni* of Caesar's sincerity by waving my purple stripe in front of them. Ariovistus is supposed to believe that Caesar wouldn't risk a Roman noble on a deception."

We were silent for a few heartbeats after Publicola's admission. It was only when I heard him say it that I realized what a huge risk *he* was taking. If Ariovistus saw through Caesar's deception–and how could he not—Publicola would be the first target of his rage; then, the rest of us who were gathered in that tent.

Troucillus broke the silence. "This is the first I've heard of this, though I suspected Caesar saw no benefit in Ariovistus accepting his terms. It would be impossible for Ariovistus, of course. How could he force the thousands of Germans, to whom he had promised living space, plunder, and riches, back across the Rhenus? I hope these reports of Ariovistus being a 'seer,' the 'all-seeing one of Mars,' are not true. But, he needn't be clairvoyant to see through Caesar's ploy."

Publicola nodded, then asked, "What would you do if you were in Ariovistus' boots, knowing that Caesar's peace overtures were false?"

I spoke, "I'd be moving on Vesantio as quickly as possible."

Publicola agreed, "Yes . . . move through the Gate and take Vesantio before Caesar can arrive . . . Our mission is to get there before Ariovistus can . . . a bit like rushing to our deaths . . . But *pietas*, devotion to duty, is the primary virtue of a Roman soldier . . . So, I offer a toast to you, *m'amici!*"

Publicola rose somewhat unsteadily to his feet and raised his cup to us. "Roman soldiers . . . *Ad mortem fideles* . . . We are faithful until death!"

Publicola drained his cup. We stood and did the same, drinking to "*Ad mortem fideles!*"

Publicola announced, "Early start in the morning, gentlemen . . . Mustn't keep the boatman waiting, eh? I bid you *valete!*"

Publicola's slave helped me back into my rig while Troucillus waited. When we got outside Publicola's tent, Troucillus laid a hand on my shoulder and began speaking to me in Gah'el, so we were unlikely to be overheard. "It's as bad as I feared. Caesar's political enemies are using Ariovistus to destroy Caesar."

"It seems likely," I admitted.

"Don't those fools in Rome understand what they're doing?" Troucillus asked. "If the *Almaenwuhr* get into the valley of the Black River, thousands will die, Romans and Gauls alike . . . Then, they'll pour down the valley of Rotonos into the Roman *provincia* . . . They'll be banging on the gates of Massalia of the Greeks before the snows fall . . . Do those fools in Rome actually believe that they can control Ariovistus once he knows he can destroy Roman armies? . . . Do they really believe that once Ariovistus controls Gaul that hordes of *Almaenwuhr* will not come pouring across the Rhenus to join him? . . . It will be Arausio all over again, except this time there will be no Marius to pull the Roman chestnuts out of the fire—just a fat, old, pompous has-been who still thinks he can live up to his *cognomen e virtute*, '*Magnus*,' the Great One."

I was a bit surprised at witnessing Troucillus so worked up. I shrugged my shoulders and halfheartedly answered, "Do you think Caesar would withdraw the legions from the nations? There are those who believe Caesar would do the same thing to the tribes that Ariovistus plans."

"Sometimes, the only choice available is between two evils," Troucillus said. "And, if forced to make such a choice, it would be madness not to choose the lesser of the two. The nations have lived beneath the shadow of the *Rhufeiniaid* to the south and the *Almaenwuhr* to the east for too long not to expect that this would one day happen. If Caesar intends to conquer the nations, the tribes cannot stop him; some will even embrace him! The *Aineduai* encourage Caesar to attack their enemies, the *Soucanai*, and the *Soucanai* are just as bad. The Gah'ela are too divided and weak to resist a determined effort by either the *Rhufeiniaid* or the *Almaenwuhr*. The difference between the two is that the *Rhufeiniaid* will eventually assimilate the tribes into their culture, as they did with your people and mine. The *Almaenwuhr* will slaughter everyone they don't need and make slaves out of the rest. I'd rather be Caesar's client than Ariovistus' slave!"

Troucillus was silent for a few heartbeats, then said, "If this goes as badly as we fear, Arth, you and your *Soucanai* have the best chance of escape. Ariovistus will slaughter Publicola and his *Rhufeiniaid*, and he'll send their heads back to Caesar in burlap sacks to terrify his army. He may spare me for a time. Having a *pendefig* of the Elvai tied to his saddle may be of some use to him when he invades the valley of the Rotonos. He may not notice, or even care, about a mere *fintai* of thirty-some-odd *Soucanai*. So, put aside your sense of *fhuhtlondebos*, that *pietas* that Publicola treasures so much . . . If things go badly, escape if you get a chance . . . Get back to Caesar and warn him before Ariovistus and his horde catch his army on the march in some narrow valley."

I was wondering how I could run away when my *contubernales* were being slaughtered. How could I explain myself to Caesar? For an insane moment, I imagined how I would shame mama and her sense of *Romanitas* by running away. Then, I remembered Athauhnu gave me much the same advice when we thought the Boii were going to overrun us at Bibracte. When the battle is lost, your ultimate duty is to save yourself and as many of your mates as you can. Besides, if Ariovistus were advancing down the valley of the Dubis, someone would need to warn Caesar and the army.

Then, I remembered holding mama in my arms on the morning I left home to enlist in the legions, and her saying, "Come home to me, my child. Come home safe."

Troucillus was still talking: "He's not really a bad sort, you know."

"What?" I said, snapping back to our conversation. "Who?"

"Publicola. He's not really a bad sort," Troucillus continued.

"What do you mean?" I asked.

"He doesn't really know how to deal with all the broken fragments of his life," Troucillus explained. "Both his father and brother in the senate support the *Optimates* against Caesar. He owes his appointment as tribune to the patronage of Pompeius. Yet, he favors Caesar and his progressive agenda. He was born into a patrician family and is expected to run the political 'course of honors' down in Rome, yet he feels that he has found a home here in the army, or at least the best home available to him. If he had his way, he'd travel to Athens and study philosophy. He says he's only truly happy when he's buried in a room full of scrolls. He even enjoys the smell of decaying papyrus! But, his father let him know in no uncertain terms that he found that kind of life unacceptable—even played the *pater familias* card on him. Threatened to disown him! Like a true Roman, he's to honor the gods, serve the state, and produce a brood of little Roman patricians, preferably males."

"How is it that you know so much about Publicola?" I questioned Troucillus.

"You get to know a man when you drink with him late into the night," Troucillus answered. "He has some difficulty dealing with people like you and me."

"What do you mean 'people like you and me'?" I asked.

Troucillus shrugged, "As far as Romans of his class are concerned, we're just conquered barbarians who traded their trousers for togas to kiss up to our betters. We're tolerated as long as we keep our mouths shut, stay out of Roman politics, and make our patrons rich. But, 'people like you and me'—Romanized *Gah'ela, Eidalwuhr, Spaenwuhr,* and even a few *Almaenwuhr*—are the backbone of the army that Publicola has embraced. He's afraid of being too familiar with us, or we won't respect him as a Roman noble, but he hates the feeling of being too remote, like some useless Roman nob who spends a year pretending to be a soldier so he can get elected to some lucrative office down in Rome. He just doesn't know how to deal with us, but the wine helps!"

"Thanks for the information," I answered. "By the way, did you notice Bulla?"

"You mean Metius' thug?" Troucillus asked.

"The same," I confirmed. "He's left handed! And, he carries a curved *sica*."

"Oh, you noticed that, did you?" Troucillus acknowledged. "The problem we have with that is Bulla's a citizen, and he's under Metius' protection. So, we're going to need more evidence than we now have to drag him before a magistrate for murder. Besides, the man he killed has no standing in a Roman court. The magistrate may accept our evidence and dismiss it with 'So what? One less barbarian in the world!' But, I'd keep an eye out for Bulla, if I were you. He seems to have acquired an intense dislike for you. If he thinks you are in any way a threat to him, he'll come after you."

"What is Metius' story anyway?" I asked. "Why did Caesar send him on this mission?"

"Other than he's had some contact with Ariovistus?" Troucillus asked. "I hope he's a spy because if he's a merchant as he claims, he's the worst merchant in the *imperium*. He doesn't even bother to carry merchandise."

"A spy?" I asked. "A spy for whom?"

"Now *that* asks for an answer worth a thousand *denarii*!" Troucillus laughed. "If he's a spy for Caesar, he's a worse spy than he is a merchant. He's traveling openly with Caesar's embassy! So, if he is not a spy for Caesar, then that leaves Ariovistus or Caesar's enemies in Rome. And, from what I can see, the two interests are not mutually exclusive."

The next morning, we were off at first light. In order to relieve the strain of witnessing the slaughter inflicted by the German raiders on their people, Athauhnu placed Guithiru's *ala* in the rear and Ci in the lead. We kept Rhodri and Drust as our scouts.

Through the first four hours of the march, we saw nothing. The farms we passed were abandoned, but intact. There was no sign of the Germans. I was beginning to breathe a bit easier, trying to convince myself that we would not have to deal with any more atrocities before we reached Vesantio the next day.

Quam erratum me! How wrong I was!

We were moving through a dangerous area. The trail curved around a bluff that thrust itself out almost to the river's edge; the trail had narrowed to the extent that we were forced to ride in single file. There was heavily forested high ground on our left and an almost sheer drop-off down to the river on our right. The trail curved around the bluff so that we could see no more than a few *passus* to our front. Foliage reached across the trail, making it even more difficult to see further on.

I remember thinking that, depite the fact that our scouts had cleared the trail before us, it was a perfect spot for an ambush. Block the narrow trail, front and back; rain spears and rocks down on us from the high ground. We'd have the choice of dying on the trail or letting our armor drown us in the river.

Even that early in my career, I had lost the gift of seeing the forests and hills as places of magic and romance, as I did when Gabi and I rode off into the hills surrounding her villa. Already, I saw terrain as a soldier: set the ambush there; this hill would serve as a good defensive position; we can turn the enemy's flank by advancing up this valley.

I was in the midst of pushing a thickly leaved maple branch out of my face when suddenly I realized there was a dismounted man standing in the trail about three *passus* ahead. I immediately pulled Clamriu up and reached for my *spatha*; my shield was strapped to my back, out of reach. Athauhnu literally crashed into my rear. Before I could unsheathe my sword, I realized that the man in front of me was Drust.

Before I could speak, Drust held his hand up to his mouth to indicate silence. He walked his horse up to me, and so that only Athauhnu and I could hear, he whispered, "*A Pen! Almaenwuhr!*"

I bent down from my saddle and demanded, "Complete report!"

Drust went on, "A German raiding party. . . We saw about twenty. . . They're attacking a farm about five hundred *passus* down this trail. . . The Germans are on foot and not well armed. . . Less than half have swords. . . Few have armor."

"Are they aware of us?" Athanuhnu asked.

"No, *a Pen*," Drust assured him. "Rhodri and I have been most careful." Then, he added, "You must come quickly! They are killing our people!"

Athauhnu turned his head and whistled softly. Ci was up with us in a heartbeat.

"German raiders ahead," Athauhnu briefed. "Keep the men here until I call for you, but be ready to move immediately into the attack."

"*Buhdhoon uhn barod, a Pen!*" Ci responded. "We will be ready, Chief!"

Athauhnu hissed down the column, "Emlun! To me!"

I gave him a questioning look. "We'll need a runner," he explained. I nodded in agreement.

"Signifer, remain here," Athauhnu continued. "Trumpeter, with me."

When Emlun reached us, Athauhnu whispered to him, "Stay close to me."

Then, he told Drust, "Take us to the Germans!"

Drust remounted and led us down the trail at a fast walk. When we got around the bend, the trail turned away from the river and began to descend into a valley carved by a tributary stream. We had gone no more than four hundred *passus* when I could see light through the trees ahead, indicating an open valley.

Then, I smelled the smoke.

Rhoderi suddenly broke out of some brush ahead of us. Clamriu reared back in surprise. Rhodri raised two empty hands in our direction so that we knew he was unarmed and this is where he wanted us to halt.

We dismounted. Rhodri hissed, "Come! See!"

He led us back into the brush. We followed him only a few *passus* into the wood to where it opened into a small valley. There was a small complex of buildings, or at least what was left of them. We could see men running about. Some were thrusting flaming brands into buildings and storage sheds, which were beginning to burn. Others were rounding up young women and older children, corralling them in a *lawnt*, an open, grassy area in front of a large roundhouse. Other raiders were scrambling about, trying to collect anything they thought had value and piling it next to the captives.

There was no military disciplne. No security was established around the raid. In fact, to my disgust, some of the raiders stopped what they were doing in order to attack the women captives. Others were enjoying whatever mead and beer they found. One man seemed to be pissing on a flaming hut and laughing at the irony.

Athauhnu was speaking, "We'll deploy Ci's *fintai* straight down the road, halt, turn the entire column to the left, and sweep across them before they can organize any defense . . . I want these *counai* dead . . . every last one of them, dead!"

I put my hand on Athauhnu's forearm. "One prisoner!" I said, "Save one for interrogation! He may know where the main body of the Germans is."

Athauhnu spit, then said, "One, just one! The rest we give to the *Morgana,* the Queen of Crows!"

I nodded.

Athauhnu called Emlun over. "Go back to Ci. Tell him to bring the troop forward as fast as he can. I will meet him on the trail. Tell him we will go immediately into the attack!"

Emlun nodded and made a move to go, but Athauhnu held on to his wrist. "You will then go back and communicate with the *Rhufeiniaid.* You will tell them that we are in contact with a German raiding party. Tell them that we will destroy the Germans ourselves."

"But, *a Pen,*" Emlun began to protest.

Athauhnu did not allow him to finish. "A warrior of the *Soucanai* does as he's commanded; only a child argues. Which are you, today?"

Emlun seemed to be about to say something, then nodded to Athauhnu and moved back toward the horses.

I was about to say something to Athauhnu, but he was fixated on the slaughter in the valley. His jaw muscles were bulging; the knuckles of his sword hand were white around the hilt of his *spatha.*

Suddenly he said, "We must move back to the trail and meet Ci's *ruhfelwuhr* when they arrive!" He got up and strode back to our horses.

When we were back on the trail, we remounted. While we waited, Athauhnu said, "I will lead the attack. I will take the *fintai* down the trail. When we have cleared the woods, we will turn left and sweep into the enemy. That will put me on the right flank of the attack. You follow the column as it passes. When we turn, you will be on the left. If you want one of these *counai* as a prisoner, *you* will have to catch him yourself. We're killing every one of those *moch* we find."

Ci was up with us in very little time. Athauhnu shouted down the column, "The German *counai* are up ahead, killing our people! We are going to kill them!"

The *Soucanai* growled their concurrence.

"Follow me down this trail," he continued. "When you clear the woods, you will see what they are doing to our people. Follow me! Watch my banner! The trumpet will signal the attack. Once we go in, sweep through and kill every German pig you see! The trumpet will signal assembly!"

The warriors cheered. I realized any attempt at concealing our presence and any hope of tactical deception were now irrelevant to the *Soucanai*. We were going straight in, and Athauhnu actually wanted the *Grunni* to know who was killing them.

Athauhnu unsheathed his sword and yelled, "*Diluhn fi*! Follow me!" He turned his horse and galloped down the trail. The *Soucanai* shouted and followed him. I pulled in behind the last rider.

We pounded down the trail, and no sooner had I cleared the woodline than Athauhnu ordered a halt. He then turned his horse toward the enemy; the *Soucanai* did the same. I watched as his *signifer* unfurled his pennant. It was the same color red as a legionary *vexillum*, but swallow-tailed and long. When a slight breeze off the river caught the flag, I saw there a *draco*, a golden serpent embroidered onto the field of red. Athauhnu raised his sword toward the enemy and yelled something. The troop drew their swords and screamed a battle cry. The trumpet sounded. We charged into the enemy!

It was a massacre.

The German raiders didn't seem to notice our presence until we were on top of them. We chopped them to bits. I was advancing along the edge of the settlement when a German suddenly appeared before me out of some long grass. He raised two empty hands in my direction. I was on him too quickly. Without a thought, I chopped down on him and split his head down to his shoulders.

I swept through the contact zone and was actually past the burning roundhouse. I could see some of the *Soucanai* riders aligned to my right, looking for more raiders to kill. I was beginning to despair of finding the prisoner I had argued for when I suddenly sensed movement to my left.

I looked and saw a German rise from some brush. He was almost comical; he was trying to pull his trousers up from around his knees but refused to let go of a nasty-looking short sword he had in his right hand. He was shouting some gibberish at me; repeatedly, he yelled something that sounded like "*fouc*."

I called out to him in Gah'el to surrender. Again, he screamed back. Again I recognized "*fouc*" and then "*Gallieh*." I realized he was young. It's difficult to tell exactly how old Germans are; their blond hair and light complexions make them look younger than they are. This one looked to be my age, maybe younger.

I tried in Latin, "*Te dede! Ti' parcere volo!* Give up! I won't kill you!"

The boy spit at me. Again, "*fouc!*" He then got a strange, malicious look in his eyes. With his right hand still holding his sword and his trousers, he reached behind himself and dragged something up from the brush. To my horror, I realized it was a young girl, no more than twelve or thirteen. Her dress was torn down the middle, exposing small, pubescent breasts. The left side of her face was red and bruised. She was weeping, trying to tear herself away from her attacker.

The German screamed at me again, "*fouc!*" Then, he turned and drew his sword across the girl's throat as his trousers fell back down around his ankles. Immediately, a red line appeared along her throat where the sword had cut. The girl fell to her knees; blood spurted out of her wound. As the raider tried to pull up his trousers, the girl fell forward into the grass.

I was off my horse. I slammed the flat edge of my sword into the side of the boy's head before he had a chance to react. He fell back, but lifted his short sword up in defiance. To my surprise, his exposed penis was still erect from what he had done to the poor girl. I cut down, severing his sword hand from his wrist. He didn't need a right hand to be useful to me.

Then, to my left, I heard the girl's death gasp as her *anima* escaped from her poor, ravaged body. I looked over at her. She lay on her stomach; her light-brown hair was tangled in the grass, sodden with her blood. Her eyes stared sightlessly at me.

I turned toward my prisoner. He was cradling the ruin of his right arm. Blood covered his chin and his leather *lorica*. He still screamed his defiance at me. I heard that word "*fouc*" one last time, then I slammed the point of my *spatha* up under his chin into his skull. His blue eyes grew wide with shock, then went blank.

I pulled back my sword. The boy twitched once and was still.

The girl still stared sightlessly at me from the blood-drenched grass.

Suddenly, a hand fell on my shoulder. I jumped away and turned in a fighting stance. It was Athauhnu. He quickly backed a few steps away and raised his empty hands toward me. It took me a few heartbeats before I fully recognized him. Then, I relaxed.

He briefly surveyed the carnage and shook his head. "There will be a place for her this day in the Land of Youth. Many from this *dun* will be there to greet her."

Then, he walked over to the dead German boy. Then, he drew his sword and took the raider's head. He wiped his sword on the German's clothes, reached down, and lifted the head, holding it up by the blond hair. "We will leave these *counai* a message of what happens to those who attack the *Soucanai*."

We walked back to the *lawnt* in front of the burning roundhouse. Some of our men were pounding stakes into the ground, on which they were impaling the heads of the dead raiders. Others were gathering the bodies of the *Soucanai* who were killed in the raid for burial. I noticed, a few *passus* down toward the river, our men were trying to comfort the few survivors.

Athauhnu jambed the boy's head down onto one of the stakes.

Then, Ci reported to him, "We suffered no casualties, *a Pen*. These scum were no more than *wuhliad* . . . brigands . . . not a true warrior among them . . . We're collecting their weapons, but it's a sorry collection . . . not worth the effort . . . We should just toss their garbage into the river as an offering to the goddess."

"If it's rubbish, the goddess will not look with favor on the offering," Athauhnu told him. "Throw their weapons into the fires. Leave their bodies to feed the Morgana. The Great Queen relishes such a meal."

"*Shuh!*" Ci agreed and went off to supervise his men.

Then, I heard Athauhnu speaking to me, "Are you alright, Arth Uthr? Were you wounded?"

I realized then I was shaking. I couldn't get the vision of the girl's dead eyes out of my mind.

"No," I told him. "I'm not hurt."

Erratum.

My body was untouched, but my *anima* would never recover. After thousands of fights in hundreds of nameless places, I still see those dead eyes staring at me in my dreams.

When the main body of the Roman delegation reached the site of our fight, I could tell that Publicola was disappointed that we had taken no prisoners, but even he understood the rage of the *Soucanai* at those who were murdering their people. After I reported to him, he simply said, "*Bene gestum, Decurio*, well done. Please, convey my compliments to your Gauls."

After he walked away, Troucillus placed his hands on my shoulders and said, "What you did here is a thing that must be done if we have any hope of preserving our people."

Metius and his thug, Bulla, were nowhere to be seen.

That night, Publicola rewarded us with a feast. We ate; we drank; then, we fell into a stupor while his Roman troopers guarded our campsite.

During the fourth hour of the next day—my head pounding and my stomach doing flips—we reached Vesantio. My first act on reaching the walls of the *dun* was to lose my breakfast into the defensive ditch.

XII.

Vesantio

VESANTIO

*V*esantio was a fortress under siege.

Like most Gallic towns, it wasn't a town at all, at least not by Roman standards. It began its existence as a *dun*, the stronghold of a local chief. Its original purpose was to provide security for the chief's family, his *fintai*, and other hangers-on. It was also the center of the farmlands that supported this population. So, besides the main hall—a roundhouse where the chief, his family, and his servants lived—there were pens for farm animals, a corral for the horses of his *comitatus*, a smithy, workshops for the leather goods and for the farm equipment, and storage bins for the crops. All this was surrounded by a defensive ditch backed up by brambles and, later, by timber and earthen ramparts.

Initially, the chief's *fintai* had slept in the feasting hall of the roundhouse. However, as the troop grew, this arrangement became somewhat inconvenient. The soldiers took wives and soon their children were pelting around the chief's house, upsetting things and getting in the way. Even worse, the younger warriors began to take interest in the women of the chief's household, even the daughters of the house. Soon, the married men and their families were given huts of their own within the compound. The randier troopers were exiled to huts outside the compound, where their comings and goings could be watched.

A community, somewhat similar to the *vicus* of a legionary *castrum*, eventually grew up around this central compound. Soon, the budding market attracted merchants, who established shops, warehouses, and residences in the outer compound. Since Vesantio was situated on a river and near the Gate that joined the Rhenus Valley with that of the Dubis, inns were established for travelers, docks for the river traffic, sheds to store and repair river barges, stables for the land traffic, smithies and repair shops for the horses and carts passing along the roads, and, of course, *cauponae*, taverns, where visitors could find a meal and all the inhabitants could indulge in beer, mead, and, eventually, wines imported from the Roman lands to the south.

When the ruler of the town recognized the value of the community that had grown up around his *dun*, he had it surrounded with walls for its protection, and he stationed his soldiers at the gates to collect duties for admittance and for the privilege of conducting business within the new town. Soon, tolls were being collected from barges moving up and down the river, docking fees were levied for stopping, and duties were tacked on to whatever was unloaded at the docks.

When we arrived at Vesantio late in the month of *Sextilis*, during the consulship of Lucius Calpurnius Piso Caesoninus and Aulus Gabinius, it was a town of close to four hundred inhabitants protected by the *fintai* of Bran mab Cahal, the *Cadeuhrn* of Vesantio. It was also a town that realized it lived under the looming threat of Ariovistus. When Ariovistus moved west with his hordes of bloodthirsty *Grunni*, Vesantio was directly in his path.

When we came within sight of the walls of Vesantio, I held the Sequani back to allow Publicola and the Romans to catch up. Athauhnu sent Rhodri and Drust ahead into the town to announce our presence and coordinate our entry. Protocol demanded that, although we were now the allies of the *cadeuhrn*, we needed to await his invitation to enter his town. Once the invitation was issued, we were then *gouestai*, his guests, and under his protection according to the laws and traditions of the Gah'el.

By the time Publicola was up to our position, Rhoderi and Drust were returning from Vesantio with a detachment from the garrison. I recognized their officer from our brief encounter in Caesar's camp, Dai mab Gluhn, a leader of ten.

Dai approached Publicola, who was decked out in his full regalia, highly polished armor and a broad purple-striped tunic, and announced the formula of invitation, which Troucillus translated. Through Troucillus, Publicola accepted the invitation of the *cadeuhrn* to enter Vesantio as his *gouesta*.

Troucillus was attired as a Roman *eques*, displaying on his white tunic the narrow purple stripe of the Order of Knights. But, he was also prominently displaying his golden torcs and armbands, identifying him as a *pendefig* of the Elvai. Athauhnu and I were stationed behind Publicola, slightly to his rear. Despite our Roman armor, we both wore the five-strand golden torcs of chiefs.

Publicola had decided to enter the town accompanied by Troucillus and the Sequani riders. The Roman troopers were instructed to locate a camp site outside the walls of Vesantio and wait there for further instructions. Cerialis would enter the town with Publicola, and, once the *cadeuhrn* agreed, he would conduct a survey of the town's defenses.

Metius, as was his wont, was nowhere to be seen.

We entered the town through its western gate. Unlike a Roman town, Vesantio was a city of wood. I imagined that this was how Mediolanum had appeared when it was still the Medhán of the ancient Insubres, my ancestors. My moment of nostalgia ended abruptly as I realized how easy it would be for a besieging army to set the whole pile on fire.

Some of the inhabitants stopped what they were doing to stare at us as we rode toward the *dun* of the *cadeuhrn,* which was situated on a bluff overlooking the river. I imagined their initial reaction was relief that the Romans had finally arrived, then disappointment, even despair, when they realized how few Romans there were.

We followed the road from the gate up through the town to a fork. The way straight before us went downhill, while the fork to the right led upwards. As we took the upper road, I heard Dai explain to Troucillus that the lower road led to the river and the docks. After the climb to the top, we arrived at the gate of the *dun*, the *arx* and citadel of the town. As we passed around the entryway, I saw the hall of the *cadeuhrn*. I was sure the building began its existence as the roundhouse of a minor Sequani lord, but it had been expanded extensively over the years so that it seemed to sprawl all about the *dun,* reaching into every corner of the fortress.

The *cadeuhrn,* with his *comitatus,* was standing on the *lawnt* before the entrance to his hall. To his left stood a dark-haired, somewhat portly woman. She was richly dressed and smiling, but her eyes seemed to retain a sharp edge. I assumed that she was his wife.

To his right, stood a tall, well-equipped warrior, who looked like a younger replica of the *cadeuhrn.* I took this to be his *pendefig,* heir and son. Next to the *pendefig* stood another tall man wearing long, brown robes and holding the staff of a *barnuchel,* high judge of the law. Standing slightly behind the *barnuchel* was a short, swarthy man in black robes holding an oaken staff, a *derwuhd,* a speaker of the gods.

Finally, to the left of the *cadeuhrn's* wife stood a man I recognized, Aneirin mab Berwuhn, a leader of a hundred, and, I assumed, senior officer of the *cadeuhrn's fintai.*

Publicola rode to within two *passus* of the *cadeuhrn.* I saw Troucillus lean over and whisper something to him. Publicola nodded and dismounted, handing his reins to Troucillus. He removed his helmet, tucked it under his left arm, and approached to within two *gradus* of the *cadeuhrn.*

"*Ave, Dux!*" he saluted stiffly. "*Tertius Gellius Publicola, Tribunus Militium, te salutat in nomine Gaii Iuli Caesaris, Proconsulis Galliarum et Imperatoris!*"

The *cadeuhrn* seemed to have a slightly inscrutable smile on his face as Troucillus translated Publicola's greeting into Gah'el: "Greetings, Duke! Tertius Gellius Publicola, Military Tribune, greets you on behalf of Gaius Iulius Caesar, Proconul of the Gauls and Victorous General."

When Troucillus finished, the *cadeuhrn* bowed his head slightly and said, "*Tribune! Ave et salve! Beneventus ad Vesantionem. Vobis meae arae et foci!* Greetings and wellbeing! Welcome to Vesantio. My hearth and home are yours!"

The *cadeuhrn* extended his arm toward Publicola, who had to first overcome the shock of being greeted in Latin by someone he had taken for an ignorant barbarian living on the edge of the known world. He took the *cadeuhrn's* proffered hand. The *cadeuhrn* laughed and slammed his left hand down on Publicola's right shoulder, obviously enjoying the look of surprise on the Roman's face.

I could certainly understand Publicola's astonishment. If someone were to ask a Roman who had never traveled north of the *Campus Martis* to paint a portrait of a Gallic barbarian, that portrait would be Bran mab Cahal, the *Cadeuhrn* of Vesantio.

He was tall, at least two *palmi* taller than Publicola, who was tall for a Roman. Although Bran was a man I considered "old" in those days, well into his late thirties, his luxuriant mustachios and tightly braided hair were a deep reddish-brown, with no betrayal of gray. Broad at the shoulders and narrow at the waist, he carried his chainmail *lorica* as well as a man, well, as well as a man of my age then. He wore a long, woolen *sagum* and *bracae* in the blue over green colors of the Sequani, patterned with a bright red design, which I took as the sign of his clan. His *bracae* were bloused into boots, strapped well above his calves, and of a highly polished reddish-brown leather. He carried heavy, golden armbands on his biceps and a five-strand golden torc around his neck, with a locking catch in the shape of a wolf's head with two red gems as eyes.

His glory, though, was the *spatha* that hung at his left hip. It was over a *gradus* in length, encased in a red leather *vagina*, which was wrapped with twisted golden wire woven in diamond shapes. The hilt was all business, dogfish skin secured tightly with leather straps; the balancing pommel was gold, formed in the shape of an eagle's head, again with red gems for its eyes.

Behind him, his *vexillarius* displayed his pennant hanging from a cross-piece guidarm; on a blood-red field was a black raven's head, the symbol of Bran mab Chlir, the wounded god, who led the nations into the isles at the setting sun.

I could almost sympathize with Publicola; he was as far from a candle-lit reception on the Palatine as a Roman patrician could get.

The *cadeuhrn* gestured that we should enter his hall. As we began to enter, Athauhnu and I were intercepted by Dai, who said he would show us where our *fintai* was to be quartered in the *dun*. Before we could move off, however, Troucillus returned and said that Publicola wanted us to attend the *cadeuhrn's* briefing on the situation along the Rhenus. We delegated the quartering of the troop to Guitheru and entered the hall.

We were led into a large room to the left of the main dining hall, obviously one of the later additions to the original roundhouse. The wattle and daub walls were reinforced with heavy timbers and covered with tapestries showing primitive arcadian scenes of nymphs, satyrs, and shepherds. The fire pit, cold now that it was summer, was surrounded by platform tables and chairs, where we were invited to sit. The tables were curved, creating a circle around the hearth, so we didn't understand the protocol of seating.

Bran recognized our confusion and said, "Just sit anywhere, *m'amici*! This isn't an audience."

While Bran's son acted as his shield bearer and helped him out of his *lorica*, we found seats. I was a bit surprised that Bran's wife remained in the room. The women of the Gah'ela were considered, in many ways, warriors and social equals to men, but I had lived long among Romans, who certainly didn't share this belief.

When we were all seated, servants brought us pitchers of wine, freshly baked bread, and bowls of radishes, sliced apples, and red carrots. There were even a few bowls of *garum*. Bran poured himself a cup of the wine, as did his wife. Then, they hesitated before drinking. Hospitality demanded that the guest drink first. Troucillus bowed his head toward Publicola, who nodded and lifted his cup.

"*Gratia deorum totis circum focum*! The blessings of the gods on all in this place," he said in Latin, roughly translating the proper Gallic sentiment.

Bran lifted his cup and said, "*Beneventos totos*! Welcome all!"

We drank and got down to business.

Publicola started, "Please tell me . . . uh . . . *Rex* . . . What is the situation with Ariovistus and the east?"

Bran wiped some wine away from his mouth and answered, "Please, call me Bran . . . We are allies now, no? May I address you as Publicola?"

Publicola nodded and again asked, "What is going on with the Germans?"

"Not good," Bran shook his head. "Ariovistus has recruited thousands from across the Rhenus . . . He has settled his *Suebii* in the valley of the Rhenus, but all the western tribes . . . the Harudes, Marcomanni, Triboci, Vangiones, Nemetes, Sedusii, and even some Saxoni from near *Oceanus* have crossed over to him, hungry for land, plunder, slaves, and blood . . . Here, I have no more than a hundred in my *fintai* . . . If I levy the people, I can put no more than five hundred in the field against him. But, if I were to raise the red flags, I doubt a hundred would respond . . . They are hiding in the hills, trying to protect themselves from the German raids . . . Our position here might be able to withstand a direct assault, but if the raiders disrupt the harvest, we could not hold out longer than a few weeks, at the most."

Publicola responded, "We saw evidence of the German raids as we came up the Dubis from the Arar. We did not see any evidence of your troops."

Bran shook his head sadly, "As a soldier, Publicola, you know a defender cannot be strong at every point. I have three primary responsibilities: preserving Vesantio, defending the Gate, and protecting the valley of the Dubis. With the resources I have, I can defend Vesantio for a time; I can screen the Gate to anticipate any German movement in this direction; I have no troops left to protect the farmers."

Publicola nodded, then asked, "What do you know of Ariovistus' intentions?"

Bran shrugged, "They're Germans. I doubt they have a strategy other than to sieze, kill, and burn. Executing any coordinated maneuver with that many—"

"Just tell him, husband!" his wife interrupted.

Bran looked at his wife and just nodded to her, "Please, tell our guests, Rabria."

Rabria! Why does the wife of a Gallic chief ruling a town within spitting distance of the Rhenus have a Roman name? I wondered.

Rabria began, "We were approached by Ariovistus' 'agents.' They told us that he plans to sweep down the Dubis, down the Arar, and into the Rhonus valley before the wheat turns yellow. He offered us our lives and the lives of our people. We could keep the rule of this city. He and his people have no interest in cities or trade. They just want the land. Our people would be enslaved to work the land for their German overlords. His condition was that we do not resist him or ally ourselves with the Romans."

Publicola was shocked equally by the news and by the fact that it was delivered by a woman in the council of men. But, he recovered enough to ask, "Is that all?"

"No!" Rabria shook her head. "I got his messenger boys drunk, and one of them shared with me that Ariovistus' true objective is not the Gauls, but Caesar. Ariovistus' primary goal is to destroy Caesar and his entire army."

There was silence around the table as Bran nodded in agreement.

Rabria continued, "It's a fool's bargain that Ariovistus is offering. Once he has destroyed Caesar, he will destroy us. What need will he have for Vesantio as a trading center when all trade has been destroyed?"

Troucillus asked, "Have you given Ariovistus your answer? Have these agents returned to Ariovistus?"

"Ariovistus' agents come and go," Rabria answered. "They call themselves 'merchants.' Some actually are. They're mostly Greeks and Romanized Gauls from the Roman *provincia* along the Rhonus. I'm sure a few of them are in the lower town, even as we speak. As far as our answer, we have been prevaricating as best we can. We have sent Ariovistus gifts and messages of friendship, which I'm sure he is not buying. But, we are running out of time. Our choice is to die now or die later. Our only true hope would be that neither comes to pass."

This woman, whom I mistook for a dowdy matron, is an equal partner in the ruling of Vesantio! If Bran is its virtus, its strong right arm, she could certainly be its mens, its intelligence. The Macedonian was by far the most intelligent and ruthless woman I have ever met in my life. She ruled Egypt as Pharaoh in her own right and was able to offset the ambitions of Rome and Parthia for decades. Her strategy against Octavius came to within weeks of success. Rabria of Vesantio could certainly give her a run for her money.

Rubria's voice brought me back from my reverie. "So, the elephant in this room, Tertius Gellius Publicola, is what is Caesar's intention? Does he plan to defend Vesantio with his army? Are you offering us the choice between being either German slaves or Roman slaves?"

The directness of Rabria's question was beyond what was acceptable under the customs of Gallic hospitality, which was probably another reason why Bran was allowing her to take the lead in this discussion. Publicola was certainly a bit flabbergasted. Not only was he being given a strategic military assessment by a woman, but now she was demanding a response from him!

"I . . . uh," he started, "Caesar demands that Ariovistus send his German allies back across the Rhenus . . . He must promise to restrict himself to the lands granted him by the Sequani . . . cease raiding friendly territory . . . return the hostages he has take—"

"And that will happen when?" Rabria interrupted, "When pigs fly? What are Caesar's true intentions for us?"

Troucillus bailed Publicola out. "*Matrona*! Lady! Caesar's army is already on the march. We expect that he is no more than a week behind us. He intends to enforce his ultimatum to Ariovistus, which he has tasked me to deliver."

Rabria's eyes widened. "You are going to ride into Ariovistus' camp and deliver *that* message? You must truly be a brave man, Gai Valeri Troucille, or a complete fool! Ariovistus will cut the meat from your bones and feed it to the camp dogs while you watch!"

Troucillus shrugged, "I certainly hope not, Lady."

Rabria just shook her head.

Bran asked, "You say Caesar will be here in a week with his army? That is indeed good news! May I tell my people? We have been living under the threat of Ariovistus for weeks!"

Troucillus shrugged his shoulders. "Our arrival, I'm sure, has let the weasel out of the bag, but if Ariovistus' agents are still in the town, such a proclamation may be, let's say, too unambiguous. Let's see if we can keep them guessing about the Roman commitment to Vesantio for a few more days, shall we?"

Bran nodded, "That makes sense . . . but we will feast you and your party this afternoon! With the Helvetii rampaging to the south and the Germans threatening us from the north, our people have had little to celebrate this summer."

When our *consilium* ended, Aneirin led Cerialis off on a tour of the town's defenses. They were followed by one of Cerialis' slaves doing his best to balance a number of *tabulae* to notate Cerialis' assessments.

Later in my career, I read Gellius' account of the death of the Greek mathematician, Archimedes, during the Second Punic War. When the city of Syracuse fell to the legions of Marcus Claudius Marcellus after a two-year siege, Roman soldiers broke into Archimedes' house. Without looking up from his work, Archimedes said, "*Noli turbare circulos meos* . . . Don't disturb my circles," just before some *muli* plunged his *gladius* into the back of his neck.

I would have considered that account ridiculous had I not met men like Cerialis, who could become totally preoccupied with his work. I could easily imagine Cerialis still taking careful and precise measurements of the thickness of Vesantio's walls while Ariovistus' Germans burned the place to the ground.

Publicola was saying to Troucillus, "I want Metius to identify Ariovistus' agents among the merchants staying in the lower town . . . We don't want to tip our hands too soon and have the Germans through the Gate before Caesar arrives."

Metius searching for traitors, I thought. *That's a bit like sending a rat out to track down the other rats.*

Troucillus shrugged, "I'm sure Ariovistus is already aware of our presence in this valley. Having Metius arrive independently of us may have at least given him the cover he needs; the other merchants may still confide in him. What do you intend to do if we do identify Ariovistus' agents? I must caution you; this is not Rome, and Roman ways of dealing with certain situations are not acceptable. We are subject to the Gallic laws of hospitality here. Any acts of violence would reflect badly upon the *cadeuhrn.* He would be responsible for ten times the head price of anyone murdered while under his protection."

"I will instruct Metius to be . . . discreet, let's say," agreed Publicola. "We will need Bran's goodwill and cooperation. Vesantio will be critical to us as a supply base and fortress if we plan to operate in the Rhenus valley."

Publicola walked off to coordinate his operation. I approached Troucillus. "Do you think Metius can be trusted?" I asked in Gah'el.

"Trusted?" Troucillus responded. "Trusted to serve his own purposes like any of the *Rhufeiniaid.* I wish I had a clearer idea of what Metius is up to. Whatever Caesar knows about him . . . he's holding his dice in a closed hand. As long as Metius holds that brute, Bulla, in check until we get out of Vesantio, I will be satisfied."

And, that almost happened.

We were called to the *cadeuhrn's* feast at the ninth hour. We assembled in the main hall. As is the custom, we surrendered our swords before entering the hall. My Sequani were used to the practice and trusted the law of hospitality to protect them as the *cadeuhrn's* guests. The Roman boys were not as confident. I had a time convincing Manius Talus that he and his men would be safe in what they saw as a sea of drunken, blood-thirsty *pilosi*. He finally submitted when he saw Publicola and Troucillus surrender their swords.

Since it was late summer, no fires were lit in the center of the round hall. The food was prepared in the cooking shacks behind the main building. Bran mab Cahal, his wife, and his *comitatus* were seated on a raised platform farthest from the main entry doors. To Bran's immediate right was Publicola and, next to him, Troucillus. Rabria was seated to Bran's left. Manius Talus and his Romans sat at the tables closest to the main doors. I imagined they wanted to be in position for a quick exit if things got ugly. No one told them that the food was normally served from the front to the rear, so they would be the last served.

Athauhnu and the Sequani were seated at tables directly below the *cadeuhrn's* platform, a place of honor. I decided that I would sit with my *turma*. I took a spot on the bench between Athauhnu and Guithiru, took out my *pugio* to cut my meat, and took a look around.

Most of the benches near the platform were filled with warriors from the town garrison. Toward the rear, I noticed civilians from the town, noticeable by their dress. I imagined that these were the merchants upon whom the *cadeuhrn* depended for his revenues. Among these, I caught sight of Metius. I looked around but could not spot his thug, Bulla. I wasn't sure what was better, seeing Bulla in a crowded place where a *sica* could be slipped into someone's back without much notice or not knowing where he was at all.

As is the custom of the Gah'ela, women freely mixed with the men for the feast. *Another barbaric custom Publicola has to get used to*, I thought.

The *cadeuhrn* clapped his hands and a dozen servers entered the hall carrying large, ceramic pitchers of beer, mead, and wine. They stopped at the ends of their assigned benches and waited. Then, Rabria stood and walked around to the front of the main table. She took a pitcher from one of the servants, went to where Publicola was seated, and filled his cup. For a few heartbeats, Publicola did nothing, until Troucillus leaned over to him and said something in his ear. Publicola nodded, picked up his cup, offered it first in the direction of Bran, his host, and then to Rabria, his hostess. Then, he drank. It was Gallic beer. Publicola's face turned as red as a legionary's tunic as his Roman tastes coped with the bitter Gallic brew, but he managed to get it down and not commit any gross violations of local custom.

After Publicola had choked down his drink, Rabria filled Bran's cup. Then, she turned to the hall, lifted the pitcher and announced, "*Gadeooch i'r ouleda uhn dechrau*. . . Let the feasting begin!"

The hall answered her with a cheer. I doubt my Roman friends understood Rabria's words, but they did understand her meaning. I saw Manius Talus take the pitcher from the server standing near his table and begin filling the cups of his men.

After a few trips back and forth with pitchers of drink, each table had a few filled pitchers to work on. Then, the servers started bringing out the food. We were treated to roasted pork and chicken; stews of river fish and pork with cabbage, kale, leeks, turnips, beets, and broccoli; bowls of raw radishes, carrots, and cucumbers; baskets of apples, pears, berries, and sliced melons. I looked back to see how our Romans were faring, and I noticed that Rabria had even managed to find some *garum* for them.

Bran allowed us to eat and drink uninterrupted until finally there seemed to be a lull in the babbling, the scraping of knives across plates, and the clunking of ceramic pitchers against earthenware cups. Not a few of the diners were sitting back, away from the table, with sated and content looks on their faces and their hands folded across their bellies. I saw Rabria call over a servant, whom I took to be her master of ceremonies, and say something to him. The man nodded and walked back to where the servers were entering the hall from the kitchens.

Soon, a man, dressed in a long, forest-green robe and holding a triangular, Gallic harp, stepped up onto the front of the platform. The man bowed to Bran and Rabria, then again to Publicola. He turned toward the crowded hall, played a loud chord, which everyone ignored. Then, he shouted, "'*Rando*! '*Rando*! '*Rando*! . . . Listen! Listen! Listen!"

In a few heartbeats, the hall quieted down. The man played another chord and began to sing. This, I realized, was Bran's *pruhduhd*, his bard. He sang the lineage of Bran and the history of his people, starting with Bran and tracing the history of the people back to when they descended from the high places and conquered the valley in which we now all sat.

Somewhere between the account of when one of Bran's heroic ancestors conquered the cannibalistic giants, who originally occupied these hills, and the building of the magnificent palace in which we all now sat, somewhere in the journey through blood sacrifices and multiple enchantments, I realized that Manius Talus and the Roman boys in the back were probably not understanding a word of it. I slid off my bench and quietly made my way back to where the Romans were sitting.

I slid in next to Manius, filled my cup up with beer from a pitcher the Romans were doing their best to ignore, and asked in Latin, "You guys getting any of this?"

Most of them just shrugged. One trooper said, "My woman's been trying to teach me, but my Gallic's not that good . . . I got lost somewhere after a shining sword got broken and the crops wouldn't grow."

By this time, the *pruhduhd* had finished the history lesson. The warriors in front were banging their fists on the tables in support of Bran's lineage and the glories of their tribe; they demanded another story. Bran nodded to his bard. The *pruhduhd* played another chord to quiet the place down. Then, he announced that, in honor of our host, he would sing the tale of Brangouen and the *Pen uh Bran*, the head of Bran.

I told the Romans what the bard had said, then translated the story for them:

Matolooch, king of the western isle, sails to the middle lands to speak with Bran mab Chlir, the Brenn'uchel. He asks for the hand of his sister, Brangouen, in marriage, to forge an alliance between him and Bran.

Bran grants Matolooch's request, but the celebrations are interrupted when Efnisien, a son of Bran's mother, Penardun, angry that Bran did not discuss Brangouen's marriage with him, steals Matolooch's horses, which were the swiftest and most valiant in the western isle. Matolooch is enraged and about to start a war with Bran.

In compensation for his loss, Bran offers Matolooch one of the seven sacred treasures of his kingdom, the Coire Na Beata, a cauldron that can restore the dead to life. Matolooch accepts the gift, and he and Brangouen sail back to the western isle.

Brangouen gives birth to a son, Guern, but Matolooch is still angry over Efnisien's insult. He mistreats Brangouen. She is given the most menial tasks to perform and is beaten every day.

Brangouen tames a raven and sends it across the sea with a message to her brother, Bran. The brenn'uchel, with his brothers, Manawuhdan, Nisien, and Efnisien, and seven times seven thousand warriors sail to the western isle to rescue Brangouen.

Matolooch, upon seeing Bran's host landing on his shores, offers to make peace. He builds a hall big enough to house Bran and all his warriors. In it, he places seven times seven thousand coffers, supposedly containing gold and treasures, but actually concealing armed warriors who are to kill Bran and his warriors when they sleep. Efnisien, suspecting a trick, enters the hall before Bran and kills the warriors.

The war between Bran and Matolooch is renewed. They fight for seven years; that is when Efnisien discovers that Matolooch is using the Coire Na Beata to revive his dead warriors. After a battle, he hides himself among the dead and destroys the cauldron, but the cauldron sucks out his life force and he dies.

To decide the issue, Bran challenges Matolooch to a single combat. Although Bran kills Matolooch with his sword, Duhrn Wuhn, "White Hilt," Matolooch wounds Bran in the thigh with his spear, Gae o Boen, "Spear of Pain," whose wounds fester and never heal.

All the warriors of the western isle are killed. Only seven of Bran's fintai survive the war, among them his brothers Manawuhdan and Nisien; Bran's son, Caradoc; and Taliesin Awenuht, Arth mab Uthr, Peredir mab Evraoug, and Pruhderi mab Pouhll. Even Brangouen dies of a broken heart, blaming herself for the war and the slaughter of her people.

Bran tells his surviving warriors that he will never recover from his wound. In order that his gruhm buhwuhd, his life force, not perish with his body, they are to cut off his head, where his life force resides, and return it to his kingdom.

For seven years, the seven survivors stay in the hall that Matolooch built for Bran, which they call Ard Lech because it sits on a high cliff. There, they are entertained by Pen uh Bran, the Head of Bran, which continues to speak to them. While they remain in the hall, the Pen uh Bran magically provides them with lavish feasts, beers, and mead, all of the best quality.

After seven years, they sail away from the western isle at Bran's command, leaving Bran's nephew, Guern, to rule the western isle. They land on a fog-enshrouded island, where they live for seventy years without perceiving the passing of time. Eventually, the fog lifts, and they see the coast of Bran's kingdom across the sea and feel a deep sadness and longing to return to their homeland.

They return and take the Pen uh Bran to Gwuhn Fruhn, the "White Hill," where they bury it facing east to guard them from their enemies beyond the river.

Peredir mab Evraoug is given guardianship of the Pen uh Bran, which is to be passed down to his descendants for all times. Surrounding the burial place of the head, Peredir builds a great hall and an impregnable dun, which is visible only to the brave and worthy. Thus it remains to this day.

After the saga was ended, Mani Talus said, "That was quite a tale . . . Do the Gauls really think this head thing'll protect 'em from the *Grunni?*"

I shook my head, "When I first heard the tale from my Gran'pa, the western isle was Sicily, and the head faced east against the Romans . . . Can't say it worked too well."

Manius laughed, then said, "Maybe we should offer one of our songs to our host in compensation for this grand feast!"

I wasn't sure I liked where this was going, so I asked, "What do you plan to do, Mani?"

Manius ignored my question and called down the table, "Hey! Croci! You sober enough to sing a song?"

Now, I was really concerned. A singer named Crocius: "Croaker"?

A rider about my age got up and stumbled over to where we were sitting, "Sure am, *Capu'*! My singin's better after a few belts. Whadda ya wanna hear?"

"What was that thing you was singin' the other night?" Manius asked. "The one about that Cartheginian broad who offed herself?"

"Ah! *Lamentatio Didonis* . . . 'The Weepings of Dido,'" Crocius nodded, "Comin' right up, *Capu'*!"

Crocius started to climb up on the table, but Manius pulled him down. "Not here, *stulte*!" he told him. "Up in front!"

Mani grabbed Croaker by his elbow and herded him up the aisle toward the dias. "You better come with me," he told me over his shoulder. "I may need you to explain this to them Gauls."

As the three of us made our way toward the platform as best we could, trying to stear Croaker and laboring under the burden of a pitcher or two of the *cadeuhrn's* finest booze, the place quieted down. I saw a slight look of panic on Publicola's face; Troucillus just looked curious.

"*Domine mi!*" Manius announced to Bran with a bow. "My Lord! We humble troopers of the cavalry *turma* of the grand and glorious Ninth Legion would like to offer you a wee bit of good Roman entertainment."

Publicola was about to stand, but Troucillus shook his head and put his hand on Publicola's arm.

Bran was a good host and a good sport. He stood and answered Manius in Latin, "*Decurio*! Please, come up on the platform."

We managed to help Croaker up onto the dias without killing ourselves or anyone else. When we stood before the main table, Rabria asked, "And, what are you going to perform?"

Crocius bowed and almost followed his head right down into the floor. As Manius and I steadied him, he said, "*Matrona bella* . . . I'll sing the tragic and pitiful weepings and wailings of Dido, Queen of Carthage, as she laments her abandonment by her lover, the perfidious and pious Aeneas of Troy!"

I winced at Crocius' "perfidious and pious," but realized that there was no turning back now.

Rabria seemed not to notice. She inclined her head toward Crocius and said, "Please! Proceed!"

Crocius turned and faced his audience. I was sure money was changing hands over whether he'd finish or pass out first. My money would have been on his taking a header off the platform before he got too much further. Crocius raised his hands out toward the hall, which fell silent.

He began the performance:

Elissa! Sweet Elissa.
What brings you to this place?
Why is your face so pale, my sister?
Why do tears cloud your eyes?
Elissa! Sweet Elissa!
Tell your sister, do!

Amazingly, Crocius seemed to sober up the instant he began singing. His voice was mid-ranged and pleasant. I realized his *cognomen e virtute* was another example of the ironic humor of Roman *muli*. This Croaker could sing.

Thy hand, Anna! Give me thy hand.
Darkness o'ershadows my soul.
Coldness grips my heart.
He is gone, Anna, gone!
Without so much as a farewell.
Without so much as a parting kiss.

Crocius sang the tale of the abandonment of Dido by her lover, Aeneas. I knew the story, but had never heard this *lai* of despair and tragic death. Today, it is never heard. *Princeps noster*, our first citizen, frowns at anything that might cast the legendary founder of our race, Aeneas, in a disfavorable light.

When I am laid in my tomb, my sister,
When the black earth swallows my body,
Offer libations to my restless spirit,
Chained to this earth by its forlorn passion.
Offer libations to my restless spirit;
Let my fate be a warning of hopeless love.

Our Augustus wants Romans to see the tale of Dido as an exemplum of Roman *pietas*. Aeneas is the hero, the founder of our civilization, one who must break the chains of earthly pleasure, abandon the luxury and lavishness of Carthage, and the lure of Dido's bed, to remain faithful to the will of the gods, all in order to protect the posterity of his son, Ascanius, and fulfill the destiny of the Roman nation.

> *This cold sword is all he left me;*
> *I will take it to my breast in his place.*
> *Remember me, oh remember me, Anna,*
> *As a woman who placed her love and hope,*
> *In the care of a faithless man,*
> *A cold and faithless man,*
> *Who will beget a cold and faithless race.*

For Gauls, Dido is the tragic victim of an uncaring and heartless lover. Contrary to the Romans, Gauls see no "eastern perversions" in a woman ruling a kingdom in her own right or making her own choice with whom to share her bed.

The Macedonian was in many ways a second Dido. Dido loved Aeneas, as Cleopatra loved his putative descendant, Caesar. Dido trusted Aeneas and gave herself and all that was hers to him, and he betrayed her. Cleopatra's tragedy was that Caesar died too soon and bequeathed his domain to a successor who admired Aeneas' betrayal of a trusting and loving woman.

> *With drooping wings, the Cupids come,*
> *To lay their offerings on her tomb.*
> *With drooping wings, the Cupids come,*
> *To weep their bitter tears.*
> *And on the portal of her marble house,*
> *These two words alone, "Remember me."*

When Croaker finished his song, there was silence throughout the hall. Rabria rose, came around the table, put her hands on Crocius' shoulders, and kissed his cheek. I saw her wipe a tear from her eye. I had to reach over and steady Crocius; his song over, he was back to being drunk, and Rabria was the only thing holding him up.

Then, Rabria turned toward the hall and raised Crocius' arm toward the audience. The Gallic warriors stood, pounding the tables and shouting their appreciation. How they understood the Latin, I had no idea. Troucillus came around the table, shook Crocius' hand, and handed him a purse. Bran himself stood, removed one of the armbands from his right arm, and presented it to the singer. Publicola clapped his hands and seemed to nod.

The feast lasted well into the eleventh hour. Bran and his *comitatus* left the hall soon after Croaker finished his *lai*. They swept Publicola and Troucillus along with them. But Bran, being a good host, ensured that the booze continued to flow.

As soon as Crocius had gotten back to his table, he lay his head down on his arms and was almost immediately snoring. Manius Talus looked over at him and snorted, "Lightweight!" I stayed with the Roman boys for a while, until Manius reached into his *marsupium* and pulled out his dice, looking for a sucker to clean out.

When I got back to where the Sequani were gathered, I saw Guithiru was in much the same condition as Crocius, except Guithiru was laid out on his back on top of our table, rumbling like Mount Etna. Periodically, one of our boys would toss a radish at him, trying to get it into his open mouth. I think there was money changing hands over it. Athauhnu seemed alright. He was sitting up straight as a rod, with a stern, far-away look in his eyes. When he tried to speak, however, all he seemed to be able to say was, "Good party."

I didn't know whether we were planning to move east in the morning. If we were, most of us would be sobering up in the saddle. So, I decided to call it a night. I filled my cup from a pitcher of beer and walked as best I could out of the hall.

The sun had just sunk below the western hills, for which I was thankful. In my condition, sunlight would have been painful. I could still see a good twenty *passus*, but the shadows were lengthening and deepening.

There was a sentry standing near the entryway to the *cadeuhrn's* hall; what the poor sod had done to get stuck with guard duty on the night of a feast was anyone's guess. I had been drinking beer most of the afternoon, so I asked him where the latrine was. He pointed me toward the riverside of the *dun*, which was just below the top of the hill and behind Bran's hall, so the area was now obscured in darkness. I thanked him with a lop-sided, drunken grin, handed him my cup of beer, and walked across the courtyard like a sailor in a storm.

Once I entered the shadows, I was able to follow my nose to the jakes. It was basic Gallic sanitation: do your business off the side of the bluff; try to hit the river; don't fall in. I seemed to have the place to myself. I pulled up the hem of my tunic and was fumbling with my skivvies when, for reasons I still to this day do not understand, I seemed to sense movement behind me in the shadows. I turned back to my right—my right hand still searching my drawers—and I caught the knife that was intended for my kidney under my armpit in my bicep.

I froze, unsure of what had just happened. I saw the shape of a man in the darkness. He pulled his knife back with his left hand and was about to strike again. Instinctively, I again turned to my right. The knife crossed in front of my abdomen. Something tore as the knife went in; I felt nothing.

The knife withdrew again. I needed space, but I was standing almost at the edge of the river bluff. I tried to maneuver, but the figure shadowed my moves, keeping me back against the cliff.

I reached for my *pugio*. It was not there! I had left it back on the table in the feasting hall. My right hand ripped open the buckle of my leather belt, and grasping the buckle, I flicked the end at my attacker's face. When he flinched, I moved in.

I dropped the belt and drove my left shoulder into his chest. I grasped the wrist of his knife hand with my right. I was going to take the knife with my left when I realized something was terribly wrong. When I drove into the man, he had not moved. I realized that even his arm was immobile, despite both my hands now grasping his forearm. It was as if I had driven myself into a marble statue.

The man remained totally still for a heartbeat. I could smell sweat, *garum,* and garlic. Then he hissed, "*La Matrona* has offered five *librae* of gold for your balls!"

It was Bulla!

He flung me back toward the cliff, as if I weighed no more than a pillow. I had to grasp and scramble to keep from going over the edge.

Bulla moved in on me slowly, as if he was relishing my fear. I imagined I could see the blade of the *sica* cradled in his left hand. I looked around for a weapon. There was none. Even my belt was now out of reach somewhere in the darkness.

Bulla was almost on top of me. I heard a crash. Some drops of liquid hit me in the face. I smelled beer. Bulla stumbled. I heard a voice in the shadows, "You! You there! 'Alt! 'Alt, in the name of the *Cadeuhrn* of Vesantio!"

Bulla recovered. He cursed and quickly moved past me. *To where?* I wondered. *There's only a straight drop down into the river.*

A hand reached out of the darkness and touched my shoulder. "You alright, *a Pen*?" I heard a voice ask. I saw a drawn *spatha*. It was the sentry I had passed.

"I saw someone follow you down to the latrine," he was saying. "At first, I'm thinkin' it's just another drunk goin' to take a leak . . . No offense, sir . . . But somethin' just didn't seem right about 'im . . . so's I followed 'im on back . . . I saw you two goin' at it . . . and 'im with that nasty little knife o' his . . . 'e was about to do for ya, so'd I flung me beer cup at 'im . . . the one you gave me . . . I think 'e went over the cliff."

The sentry helped me to my feet. I stumbled. I felt a burning pain in my right arm. I looked down. I could see what looked like streams of black liquid running down my arm.

The sentry was looking down over the bluff. "'E went right over 'ere . . . Can't see a thing down there . . . too dark."

I joined him. I made sure I was a bit behind him, and I placed my hand on his back to steady myself. I didn't know whether it was the beer or the shock, but I was dizzy and didn't feel like joining Bulla in the river.

Straight below us, it was pitch black. To our right, burning torches marked the river docks. The Dubis ran black and smooth in the torchlight. There was no sign of Bulla.

We watched for a few heartbeats as if we expected Bulla to appear dripping wet out of the black river. Then, I said, "Please . . . walk with me back to the hall . . . I must report this incident."

We found my disgarded belt, and the sentry brought me back to the hall. As he handed me over to one of the internal guards, I thanked him and asked his name so I could commend him to the *cadeuhrn*. The inside guard took me back to the same room where we had our first audience with the *cadeuhrn* that afternoon. As I entered, I must have been a sight: my military belt over my shoulder, my tunic ripped and shredded, and blood flowing down my arm.

Publicola rose. "*Mammas Veneris, Decurio*! What happened to you? Were you in a fight?"

"Bulla!" I said. "It was Bulla."

Rabria told the guard in Gah'el, "Quickly! Get my surgeon! Bring him here!"

She came around the circle of tables and helped me onto the bench. She pulled up what was left of the sleeve of my tunic and examined my wound. Without so much as a word, she reached over, took a cup of wine, and poured it over my wound.

The pain struck in a flash of light, first yellow, then red, finally white as it exploded in my head. I had to screw my eyes closed, suck in my breath, and clench my teeth shut to keep from making a sound. Even so, a strange combination of grunt and whimper escaped my lips. I felt a single tear roll down my right cheek.

As the flashes of pain began to recede, I remembered the cut I had taken to the abdomen. I looked down, fumbling with the shreds of my tunic, terrified that my belly had been sliced open. Most of the damage was to my garment; there was only a shallow scratch across my stomach.

Then, I heard Publicola's voice, "What do you mean, 'Bulla,' *Decurio*? Has he been hurt? Is he involved? *Nuntia, Decurio*! Render a proper military report!"

"I was attacked *by* Bulla, Tribune," I began. "Down by the river bluff where the latrines are." I told the story, making sure I named for Bran the sentry who had saved my life.

"I've had enough of this *merda* about that thug, Bulla," Publicola said. "Where is Metius?"

"The last I saw, he was in the back of the hall with the merchants," Troucillus said.

"I'm going to get to the bottom of this if it takes all night," Publicola announced. He looked around the room for someone to dispatch on the errand to fetch Metius, then realized there was no one to send. Finally, he got up and went to the door himself. He practically collided with Rabria's surgeon.

Rabria nodded toward me, "The Roman officer . . . knife wound . . . right, upper arm."

The surgeon lifted my shredded sleeve and examined my wound. "A sharp, thin blade," he muttered to himself. "Not too deep . . . No major blood tubes cut."

Then, "Did you pour wine on it, my lady?"

"Of course," Rabria nodded. "This is not my first dance."

The surgeon nodded. "No stitches, I think . . . just a tight binding."

As the surgeon fumbled around in his *capsa*, Bran said, "*Gratias dis!*" Then, he asked Rabria, "Should I summon the *barnuchel*?"

I then realized that a grievious breech in hospitality had been committed. A guest had been attacked and injured while under a host's protection—not just a guest, but a Roman officer.

"No need, *a Pen*," I said in Gah'el. "I make no claim against you. This was a . . . a Roman issue . . . We ourselves brought this trouble under your roof, and we alone are to blame . . . In fact, it was your guard who prevented my death."

Bran nodded. In front of witnesses, I had released him from any liability. The gods and the law were satisfied.

Publicola burst back through the door. "No sign of Metius . . . I sent the least drunk of Manius' troopers down into the lower town to look for him."

The words "look for him" awoke Bran. "Guard!" he shouted.

A warrior stuck his head into the room. "Yes, *a Pen*!"

"Dai mab Gluhn is the officer of the guard this evening," Bran stated. "Have him report here to me immediately."

The sentry nodded and left.

Publicola was talking, "I don't understand why Bulla would attack you, Insubrece. Do you have any ideas?"

I gritted my teeth as Rabria's surgeon tightened a wrapping around my arm. "*Nescio, Tribune*," I shrugged. "I don't know. Unless it has something to do with what happened outside your tent the other night."

Publicola shook his head. "That seems to be a pretty flimsy reason to murder someone . . . especially a Roman officer."

"He did mention something about '*La Matrona*,'" I offered. "And a bounty of gold."

"'Her Ladyship,'" Publicola shook his head. "Certainly this thug was not referring to the lady of this hall, Rabria."

Dai then entered the room and reported to Bran. "Take a detail of your men with torches," Bran told him. "I want you to search for this Roman . . . He may be in the water, so commandeer some boats from the fishermen . . . Go about a mile downstream . . . If he's still alive, bring him here to me."

I gave Dai a description of Bulla, and he left on his mission. I knew he would not find Bulla, not alive anyway.

Troucillus was speaking, "Back to your earlier comment, Publicola. The Latin word '*matrona*' could also refer to a 'patroness,' could it not?"

"A woman patron, Troucillus?" Publicola dismissed the suggestion. "That would be ridiculous. What Roman man would submit to the authority of a woman?"

Troucillus shrugged, "Be that as it may, Bulla is my lead suspect in the murder of the Aeduan trooper before we crossed the Arar. I suspect his motive is to disrupt this embassy. So, according to the *lex parsimoniae*, the simplest and, therefore, the most likely, explanation for this act is that Bulla attempted to murder young Insubrecus here to drive a wedge between us and the *cadeuhrn* and weaken our position in our inevitable confrontation with Ariovistus."

"Why would a *Roman* do anything to advance the cause of a barbarian?" Publicola challenged.

"Publicola, you speak of *Romans* as if they were one in mind and goal," Troucillus dismissed the objection. "We know that is not the case. Cato and the rest of the so-called *Optimates* in the senate, the 'Best-Ones,' are not Caesar's friends. They understand that military success in Gaul would greatly increase Caesar's *dignitas* in Rome and his political advantage. The defeat of a *German* threat would establish Caesar as a new Marius! Caesar's fellow *triumvir*, Pompeius Magnus, certainly does not want to share his repute as Rome's foremost general. He certainly would not lose any sleep if Caesar were embarrassed, or even killed, by Ariovistus and his rout. So, the simplest explanation is that Bulla is an agent of Caesar's enemies in Rome."

It seemed that Publicola and Troucillus had put the shadowy *La Matrona* figure totally out of their calculations. I could not. The memory of Gabi ordering her henchman to cut my throat in front of her, so she could see it was "done right," was fixed in my mind. She had also alluded to the gangster, Milo, and seemed to hint that she had taken over part of his organization.

Suddenly, I realized that both Troucillus and Publicola were looking at me expectantly.

"*Quid est?*" I stammered. "What is it?"

Publicola gave me a somewhat patronizing smile, "Do you have any questions? Perhaps the shock of your being attacked is affecting you."

That comment made me feel obligated to ask something, anything, just to show that patrician gobshite I wasn't losing it because I had a scratch on my arm. "I . . . er . . . Trocille . . . you lost me when you referred to a *lex parsimoniae*. The law of frugality? What is that?"

Troucillus smiled and nodded. "It's a concept used by lawyers based on a reading of Aristotle's *Analytika Hystera*: 'All other things being equal, we may assume the supremacy of the determination derived from the fewest assumptions or guesses.'"

"In other words, the simplest explanation is the best," I suggested.

Troucillus nodded, "Close enough!"

At that point, Metius entered the room. He nodded toward Bran, ignored Rabria, and asked Publicola, "You summoned me, Tribune?"

Up to this point, I had not closely observed Metius. He was of average height, about five Roman *pedes* and five or so *unciae*. His hair was dark brown, shot through with gray. He had heavy, dark eyebrows. He was a bit jowly from a few too many evenings in a *caupona* and had a face that looked like it had never learned to smile. He wore a dark green, Roman-style tunic with half-sleeves over a pair of light woolen Gallic *bracae* of a brownish color. His boots were Roman *caligae* but lighter than the military issue. He wore a wide, brown belt with a silver buckle. From his left hip hung a *pugio* in a plain leather sheath; from his right, a small leather *marsupium*.

In other words, our lead spy was in the costume of a Roman merchant in eastern Gaul.

"Where's Bulla?" Publicola demanded.

"Bulla?" Metius actually looked surprised by the question. "Why would you want to know where Bulla is?"

"Why I want to know is none of your affair, Meti," Publicola pushed him. "Just tell me where he is!"

Metius shrugged, "I don't know."

I was beginning to suspect that Metius was ignoring the intent of Publicola's question.

"When's the last time you saw him?" Publicola pressed him.

"The ninth hour, just before I escorted my contacts here to the feast."

Contacts! There was that word again. Now I was sure Metius was hedging.

"And, where was that?" Publicola pressed.

"In one of the *cauponae* in the lower town . . . the sign of the three horses, I think," Metius stated.

"Have you seen him up here since?" Publicola asked.

"Up here?" Metius challenged. "I've already answered that question, Publicola . . . What is this all about?"

"Your man, Bulla, attacked a Roman officer," Publicola spat. "And you will address me as 'Tribune,' *Insitor!*"

Insitor? That was a term usually reserved for dishonest traders, grifters, con men. Publicola was playing his nobility card a bit heavily here.

"Bulla did what?" Metius started. "Bulla would not act on his own unless—" Whatever Metius was about to say, he thought better of it.

But, he wasn't going to ignore Publicola's barb, "You forget yourself, Publicola! Your mission here is to mesmerize the *Grunni* with your broad purple stripe and your flashy armor, like a peacock charms a peahen with its feathery ass . . . My portfolio comes directly from Caesar himself."

"Are you sure of that, Meti?" Troucillus interrupted. "Caesar, and not someone else down in Rome? Pompeius, perhaps?"

Metius' face turned corpse-white. His hand actually dropped down to the hilt of his *pugio*. Then, he seemed to recover himself. "I have no idea where Bulla is," he stated. "I have not seen him since the ninth hour."

With that, he turned and left.

We did not move east the next day. Publicola announced that he wanted to rest the horses one more day. I suspected the real reason was he didn't want to risk running into a horde of Germans with a hungover troop.

Bulla was not found along the riverfront. Bran ordered a search of the lower town, but I was sure that Metius' hitman had escaped. To where, I had no idea.

XIII.

De Itinere ad Castrum Bellum
OUR MARCH TO BELFORT

We started east toward the Gate at the first hour of the next day. It was *dies Veneris*, the day of Venus, the day of the capricious goddess, always an inauspicious day to begin a new enterprise.

I had spent most of the morning the day before at our horse lines in the camp of the Roman cavalry *turma* outside the walls of Vesantio. I was determined to train the black stallion that I had taken from the Boii *thegn* at Bibracte.

This was also the horse that had almost killed me by kicking me in the head. And, *he* apparently had not forgotten.

At times, the horse would obey me. I would ride him in circles and figure eights around the grassy fields with my hands in the air, and he would react to the promptings of my heels, knees, and thighs as if he had been in the Roman army since he was a colt.

Then, he'd pull something.

Six or seven times, he stopped suddenly, throwing me forward into the horns of my saddle. Once, he fell forward onto his front knees. I went tumbling past his right ear and into the turf. Luckily, my fall was cushioned by the long grass and a pile of freshly dropped horse *merda*. When I recovered my feet, the horse was standing, his head down in my direction. He shook his head violently and snorted at me as if he were snickering. I wondered for a heartbeat whether the horse had actually aimed me at that pile of shit.

176

And, so the game continued.

There was a boy from the town watching our antics. He was about eight years old, tow-headed, and wearing the brown, rough-spun tunic and trousers of a *dar fu'thir*, a slave. He seemed to be enjoying the show.

I was doing circles at a canter when the horse suddenly stopped and threw his hindquarters to the left. As I tumbled forward, the left front saddle horn caught me below the ribs, knocking the wind out of me. As I fell, I managed to plant my left heel in the ground as my body spun around, and I landed initially on my arse. As I tumbled down onto my back, my body folded and my knees almost slammed into my chest. As usual, the horse watched my gymnastics then snorted at me. I then realized that this was the way the perverse beast laughed.

Naturally, the boy was laughing. "He good Kraut! He try kill you, Roman!" he said in a guttural Gah'el.

I was bumped, bruised, embarrassed, and still struggling with the aftereffects of last night's drinking, so I wasn't in the mood to be mocked by a slave.

"You could do better I suppose, boy?" I snapped back, brushing clods of turf and grass off my military tunic.

"Where you have horse?" he asked.

"Have horse?" I repeated. Then I felt the need to boast: "Oh . . . I took him in battle . . . from a German chief."

"Ah! Him Kraut horse," the boy nodded.

The boy, all four *pedes* of him, marched directly over to the black stallion, who actually backed up three or four steps at his approach. I was about to intervene, thinking the huge black beast would stomp the kid into mush, when he said in a load voice, "*Hors!*"

The stallion stopped and seemed to come to attention. His ears came straight up, and he dropped his head to look directly at the boy. "*Aet stande!*" commanded my little rescuer.

The horse raised his head and froze. The boy jumped up into the saddle. Talking to the stallion in what I now recognized as a dialect of German, the boy put the horse through the same paces I had been attempting with little success.

Finally, the boy walked the horse over to me and jumped down from the saddle. "Him Kraut horse! Talk him Germanly; him listen you good!"

The boy handed me the reins and walked back in the direction of the town. As he walked away, he called over his shoulder, "Him name '*Beorn*'... 'Hero'... Him listen you now ... maybe."

I decided that I had had enough for the day without having to contend with a German-speaking horse named Beorn who was part of a Gallic cavalry unit serving the Roman army.

I had just finished brushing Beorn down when Manius Talus found me. "There you are, Insubrece! I've been lookin' all over for yas. They want ya down at headquarters, *stat*'!"

"*Stat*'?" I asked. "Something up?"

"You could say that," Manius nodded. "Some merchants come up river with a tale that Caesar's army's mutinied. They're sittin' outside o' Ventum *Cavillonum* refusin' to march another step. They say the Krauts have them soilin' their loincloths!"

Manius and I practically double-timed back to the town and up the hill to the *cadeuhrn's dun*. We found Publicola and Troucillus in the meeting room with Bran, his wife, and Aneirin. They were questioning a civilian, a merchant by his dress. It took me a few heartbeats to recognize him. It was Grennadios, the Greek from Massalia, whom I had detained north of Bibracte.

"I tell you," he was saying to Publicola, "it's true ... Caesar's army is in revolt ... They refuse to go a step farther ... Even the military tribunes are keeping to their tents ... The centurions are refusing to assemble their troops ... They're demanding that Caesar return to the *provincia* and leave off chasing the Germans back over the Rhenus."

Bran's face was as gray as a corpse. If Caesar did not arrive, he and his people were finished.

"What do you think, Publicola?" Troucillus asked.

Publicola hesitated, then shrugged. "I am a Roman soldier with orders that I will obey unless they are rescinded. I will send a section of Manius' cavalry back to Caesar for instructions, but until I receive new orders, I will continue my mission."

"That is madness—" Grennadios started.

"I thank you for your information, Merchant!" Publicola stopped him. "You may go now!"

Grennadios shrugged, got up, and walked toward the doors. Then, he saw me. As if expecting to meet me, he placed a hand on my shoulder and quietly said, "Evra said you would be here . . . How she knows what she knows, I have no idea . . . She wants to speak to you . . . She says it's important . . . Come to us tonight . . . We are stopping at a *caupona* in the town at the sign of the green stag . . . Ask anyone . . . They'll know the place."

I nodded and repeated, "The green stag."

Publicola was speaking, "It's about time you got here, *Decurio* . . . You've heard?"

I nodded, "Mutiny . . . Do we have any proof of this?"

Publicola shook his head, "Just the tales carried by these merchants . . . I plan to depart first hour tomorrow . . . Both of you . . . brief your men . . . I want no panic . . . Tell them these are just wild tales, not to be believed . . . Caesar and the army are on the march behind us."

Both Manius and I nodded, "*A'mperi'tu!*"

"*Bene!*" Publicola nodded. "Mani *Decurio*! I want you to detail five men . . . your fastest horses . . . Get them back to the army and find out what's really going on back there . . . Their rally point with us will be in the Gate . . . at *Castrum Bellum* . . . Do that *stat'*!"

"*A'mperi'tu!*" Manius snapped and bolted out of the room.

When he had gone, Publicola asked me, "Insubrece *Decurio*! Do you anticipate any problems with the Sequani?"

I shrugged, "Over rumors? No! The Sequani are committed to Caesar by his gifts . . . They will go forward." Then, I hestitated.

"*Quid vis dicere, tu?*" Publicola prompted me. "What else?"

"If the *Grunni* break through to the Arar and Caesar does not stop them, the Sequani will look to their own people first," I stated.

I saw Troucillus nod and say, "That's only to be expected."

Publicola was not happy with the answer, but he shrugged and said, "I will not make a military decision based on rumor . . . We depart for *Castrum Bellum* and the Gate tomorrow . . . first light."

At the tenth hour, I was in the lower town, looking for the green stag. It was easy to find, right off the main road leading up to the *cadeuhrn's dun* from the city gate. I entered the main room. After my eyes adjusted to the lamplight and the fumes from the rancid lamp oil, I spotted the *caupo*, the landlord, across the room. He was behind a plank bar, watching over the beer kegs and the cash.

I was halfway across to him to ask after Grennadios when I felt a touch on my elbow. I turned. It was Evra, the woman from the island of the dead. In the dim, smoky light of the *caupona*, I could see her eyes were a blue so deep that they seemed to fade into black.

"You come . . . good," she said in a heavily accented Latin. "Follow."

She turned and walked back into the *caupona*. She stopped at what appeared to be a curtained alcove, drew back the drape, and stared back at me. It was then I realized that I had remained standing in the middle of the tap room. As I walked over toward her, she disappeared behind the curtain. I followed her in.

She sat in the shadows at the back of the darkened alcove, a cave really. A single lamp sputtered on a wooden table.

"Sit," she told me.

I did as I was told. She stared directly into my eyes for a few heartbeats, then placed a white stone on the table. It seemed to glow with its own light, more translucent than white. It seemed to promise blue and purple depths.

"Hold stone in hand," she told me.

I did. It felt warm, either from Evra's touch or a heat of its own, I couldn't tell.

"*Nunc da mi!*" she demanded, thrusting her open right hand at me. "Now give to me!"

I handed the stone over to her.

She closed her fingers tightly around it and brought her hand to her breast. She closed her eyes and appeared to drift away to another place. All the noise of the *caupona* seemed to fade away with her. Our darkened alcove became an endless black cave, a universe of darkness. I felt as if I were looking at our ineffective lamp across a great, gloomy chasm. We remained like this almost beyond time. Then, with a moan, she drew in a great breath. Her eyes were open, staring straight into mine. Somehow our faces were only inches apart.

"Anu has spoken!" she began, but her voice did not seem to enter through my ears; it was present in my mind. "Anu has spoken . . . Anu, god mother . . . sister-self, Eriu . . . red-haired queen . . . She holds you close to her breast . . . The great queen must lose a son . . . Morgana, sister-self must have blood . . . The black-haired queen weeps in darkness . . . Go to the east . . . dark forests await . . . dark hills . . . cold places . . . Dark ones will not come near you . . . The land of sun is danger . . . In the east . . . the queen of the sun tears at her hair . . . Beware the fair one, son of Caesar . . . Protect the dark one, son of Caesar . . . The red-haired queen will find you . . . a death to be avenged . . . a death to be appeased . . . Bring to the light, son of Caesar . . . Death becomes life."

She shuddered and opened her hand. The white stone was gone, as if it had merged into her breast.

Then, she was gone.

I didn't see her slip out of the alcove. It was as if I had blinked her away.

I rose and pulled back the curtain. I was back in the taproom of the green stag. I could hear the click of ceramic jugs on drinking cups, the muffled voices of drinkers, the rattle of dice on wooden tabletops. Evra was gone. No one seemed to notice me. I wondered whether Evra's spell had rendered me invisible.

Then, Grennadios called my name and brought me out of my reverie. I looked across the room and spotted him at a table along one of the walls. He was holding up a cup, inviting me to drink.

As I sat down, he asked, "Has Evra seen you?"

"Evra!" I said. "Was she not just here? Did you not see her?"

"No," Grennadios answered, pouring wine into the cup for me. "I did not see you come in either."

"We were there! In the alcove," I said gesturing across the room. "She just left me. You must have seen her."

Grennadios just shook his head. "The woman comes and goes like smoke. What did she say to you?"

I tried to recall what she had said. "I'm . . . well . . . I'm not sure . . . Anu . . . a red-haired queen." The whole incident was fading from my memory like a dark night's dream in the light of the day.

"Ah . . . Anu," Grennadios was saying, "that is one of her people's goddesses. I cannot make sense out of them. Her gods are all contradictions . . . The good that is evil . . . Death that is life . . . irrational . . . dark . . . Give me Apollo . . . or Aphrodite . . . gods a man can understand . . . not these dark, shadowy *daimonai* from that mist-shrouded island of hers beyond *Oceanus*."

What had happened in the alcove continued to fade; now it was more a feeling than a memory. I could almost believe I dreamed it. Some of the old ones, the dark goddesses of my ancestors, were shape shifters, never constant, like dark smoke in a breeze. They revealed themselves in contradictory trinities . . . Even the Romans had their three-faced Hecate. These were mysteries not open to mortals, not accessible by reason, entities best ignored, never evoked, best left in dark places.

I realized that I was rubbing the *Domina Fortuna* medallion hanging under my tunic.

Grennadios was talking: "If Caesar does not come, what will happen to Vesantio?"

"Vesantio?" I returned to the tap room. "Vesantio will be gobbled up by Ariovistus . . . Why do you think will Caesar not come?"

"I think nothing," Grennadios shrugged, pouring himself another cup of wine. "Four days ago, I passed Caesar's camps west of the Arar . . . The fourth hour of the day and the army had not moved . . . What Roman army stays in camp that late? The Aedui told me the soldiers refuse to move . . . refuse to march east and face *hoi Germanoi* . . . I saw this . . . That is why I ask."

"The Aedui told you this?" I asked. "We're moving east toward the Rhenus in the morning, carrying Caesar's message to Ariovistus."

"You're *trelos* . . . *blameno* . . . mad," Grennadios shook his head. "There is no hope! Ariovistus has eyes everywhere. He'll already know about the Roman mutiny. You will have no . . . no *pleonektima* . . . no leverage to bargain with him."

"Bargain?" I snorted. "We are not here to bargain with Ariovistus! We're here to provoke him."

I realized I was revealing too much to Grennadios, so I changed the subject. "What do you know of a Roman merchant named Marcus Metius?"

"Metius?" Grennadios snorted. "Metius is no merchant . . . He is *iktis* . . . *mustela* . . . a rat-eater . . . He would trade his mother's honor for a clipped drachma . . . He *trades* in information . . . He works for whomever will pay . . . He serves only himself."

"Do you know anything about a Roman, who travels with him?" I asked. "A thug called Bulla."

I thought I saw Grennadios's eyes widen, then he shuddered. "That one? That one has no . . . no *psyche* . . . no life force in him . . . He is the bringer of death . . . That one you stay away from, *phile mou*."

Stay away from him? If only I could.

"Have you seen him?" I asked Grennadios.

"Seen him? Here in Vesantio?" Grennadios made a sign with his fingers to ward off evil. "No! *Eucharisto tous theous*! No!"

Thank all the gods, indeed! I wondered what is worse: the evil you can see or the evil you cannot? The gods act in ways enigmatic to mortals.

"What will *you* do, my friend?" I asked him.

"Me?" Grennadios shrugged. "War is coming to Vesantio. Whether Caesar arrives or not, war is coming. Evra and I will return to Massalia. We'll lose some business, but better to lose a few drachmai than your head." Grennadios drew his thumb across his throat for emphasis.

I said farewell to Grennadios. With Bulla possibly lurking about, I wanted to get back to my billet in Bran's *dun* before sunset.

The next morning during the first hour, we were on the road east. Troucillus asked me to ride with him, so Athauhnu was commanding our point element, Guithiru's *ala*, and a contingent of riders from Vesantio under the command of Dai mab Gluhn. Ci's troop rode as our rear guard. Most of Manius' boys rode in the main column behind us. Manius and about ten of his troopers rode behind Publicola to our front. As usual, Metius seemed to be missing.

Troucillus was saying, "I am now convinced that it was Bulla who murdered that Aeduan trooper west of the Arar, and despite Metius' blustering, Bulla attacked you in Vesantio. I examined the bluff overlooking the river where he jumped, and I'm convinced he could have survived it. It's not really a cliff, but a sandy bluff descending steeply down to the river. So, we must assume that Bulla's still out there somewhere. Who this *La Matrona* is, I have no idea."

"It's Gabi," I told him. "It has to be. Gabinia Pulchra *Matrona* . . . the daughter of the consul, Aulus Gabinius."

Troucillus stared at me for a few heartbeats. "The consul's daughter? You have accumulated some interesting enemies for one so young. Why would this Gabi of yours want you dead?"

I told Troucillus the story of what had happened in Massalia. He shook his head and laughed, "So, you have your own personal Tisiphone stalking you . . . It makes sense . . . My sources tell me Bulla has, or had, connections with the gangster Milo down in Rome . . . That would make him Pompeius' man, the same camp your Gabi seems to be in . . . So, what does that tell us about our friend Metius?"

"That he can't be trusted," I inserted.

"No man can be *trusted*, as you say, until you discover where his interests lie," Troucillus said. "We have to discover what his agenda is. We may not have to worry about it very long if Caesar doesn't get the legions up here."

I nodded. *Seditio*, mutiny, is an ugly word, almost as ugly as *decimatio*, decimation. I remember Strabo, my training officer in basic, telling my squad that mutiny and cowardice in the face of the enemy were crimes for which a legion could be decimated, *decimum quemque occicere*, every tenth man beaten to death by his mates.

I knew the army was restive about Caesar's determination to move east this late in the campaigning season. To these men, Caesar was still an unknown entity, and his release of the Helvetii, allowing them to go back to their homelands instead of selling them off to the slavers for profit, won him no friends among the *muli*. Even worse, the *veterani* understood that Caesar had led them into a trap at Bibracte; only *Bona Fortuna* and Labienus' capacity to maneuver the *acies tertia*, the third line, the army's "forelorn hope," prevented a complete disaster.

Now, Caesar wanted to drive them east toward the Rhenus, to face the Germans, the giant, blood-thirsty monsters from a Roman's worst nightmare.

"I tried to convince Publicola to wait until his messengers return from Caesar's camps," Troucillus was saying, "but he would have none of it . . . He had his orders, and if Caesar wanted to countermand them, Caesar would have to send word to him . . . as if Caesar didn't have enough on his plate with his army refusing to march . . . Sometimes these *patricii*, these tight-assed Roman aristocrats, don't understand that they are not the center of everyone's universe."

This was the closest I had seen Troucillus come to breaking with the decorum of authority. I think he caught himself, though, because he suddenly changed the subject. "It reminds me of an old joke . . . What's the difference between a Roman patrician and the god Iove?"

"*Nescio*," I shrugged. "Not a clue."

"Iove doesn't think he's a patrician," Troucillus chuckled.

We arrived at the Gate by the fifth hour of the next day. We had followed the Dubis to a point where it turned back on itself toward the mountains to the south. Then, we continued north and west, following a tributary the Sequani called *Afon Merchsoucana*, the "Daughter of Soucana," which meandered down from a valley. Finally, we arrived at what appeared to be a wide ridge between highground to the north and a line of mountains to the south. The *cadeuhrn's fintai* had established a base and an observation point here, overlooking a valley to the east.

Troucillus and I rode forward to where Publicola was positioned. "Welcome to *Castrum Bellum*, gentlemen" he announced. "The valley you see before you is the valley of the Rhenus. If Ariovistus wishes to invade Gaul, he must pass through here."

The name *Caer Harth*, or *Castrum Bellum*, must have been some ironic joke.

The views *were* beautiful. The valley of the Rhenus stretched out before us, fading into distant blue mists in the northeast. The Gate itself seemed to rest on the southern shoulders of the mountains of the hunting god, Vosegus, whom the Romans call Mercurius. Across its southern flank marched the *Montes Iuria*, the mountains of the forest god, *Ioros*.

Tactically, *Caer Harth* was beautiful, according to our military engineer, Cerialius. His boys were already staking out the fortifications Caesar's *muli* would dig when—or if—they arrived.

But, there was no *caer*, no fortress. The Sequani from Vesantio had set up some lean-tos for shelter while they overwatched the Rhenus. Other than a few shepherds' huts, there was nothing here to prevent an army from just strolling through on their way down the Dubis into the valley of the Arar and eventually the Rhonus.

This was, indeed, the gateway to Gaul, and the gates were wide open.

At the eighth hour, Metius made his appearance, *from the east.* He was accompanied by a dozen riders. Their horses were first rate, but their equipment was mixed. Most didn't have helmets or *loricae.* What body armor they had was of boiled leather and padded jackets; only two had chainmail, but the steel rings were rusted and broken. Four of five carried swords of various vintages; the rest carried lances, of which only six or seven had iron points.

Most of Metius' escort wore unkept beards, which were braided to keep them out of the riders' faces. Their hair, also braided, hung down their backs. They were mostly blond, with some shades of red and light brown. In other words, Krauts!

They dropped back a few *passus* from our encampment, unsure of their welcome and hesitant to find out. It was probably good judgment on their part, for as soon as they appeared, Dai's men were on their feet, hands to their sword hilts. My Sequani quickly reinforced their compatriots from Vesantio. If Caesar wanted a war with Ariovistus, we could have easily started it right there.

Metius, however, understood the Gallic protocol and began waving a wooden wand of negotiation. The Sequani relaxed a bit, but did not move their hands far from their weapons.

Publicola walked over to Metius, who dismounted at the edge of our encampment. They talked briefly. Metius nodded, then called over to his escort in a guttural language I assumed was German. One of them, a rider wearing a helmet and a chainmail *lorica* and carrying a *spatha*, answered Metius. Then, the rider, who I now assumed was their leader, gave a few guttural commands to his troop, who dismounted but did not come any closer. The Sequani spread out across their avenue of approach to our camp, but also held their ground.

Publicola and Metius walked into our camp, Publicola calling for Troucillus. As Troucillus replied, he beckoned to me to go with him. As we approached together, I hung back to the left of Troucillus. I had no desire to get any closer to Metius, or Publicola for that matter. I saw Manius Tallus walking over to us uninvited. Publicola gave him a patrician "who-invited-you" look down his long Roman nose, but decided not to further challenge his presence.

"Ariovistus has agreed to meet with Caesar's emissaries," Metius announced. "The day after tomorrow at the sixth hour at a place called *Collis Pecorum*, the Hill of the Flocks."

"How far?" Publicola asked.

"Two hours northeast," Metius responded. "Ariovistus' *Suebii* will guide us."

Manius snorted when he heard that. Publicola gave him a dirty look, but was even more displeased when he heard me call out in Gah'el for Dai.

Dai walked over to us from his impromptu picket line facing the *Suebii*. "You wish to speak to me, *a Pen*?" He addressed me in Gah'el, giving Troucillus a nod, and then, after a heartbeat, acknowledging Publicola's presence.

"Are you familiar with a place called *uh bruhn uh gouarteg*?" I asked him, translating "Hill of Flocks."

Dai shrugged, "There are many. It's any place where the herders shelter their sheep and cattle from the heat . . . That is, before the troubles started."

"This one's about a two-hour ride into *duhvruhn uh Rhain*," I added.

"The valley of the Rhenus," Dai nodded, then thought. "Yes . . . I know the place . . . We use it as an observation point when we're scouting against the *Almaenwuhr*."

"Is it defensible?" I asked.

Dai shook his head. "There is line of sight only to the east and south. North and west, there are wooded hills and ridges, which could hide an army."

"So," I surmised, "if we were to approach this place directly from here, we could be seen, but we could not see what was on the hill or behind it."

Dai affirmed, "We never come in from the south . . . We would be visible for miles and would not know what we were riding into . . . From here, *uh bruhn uh gouarteg* should only be approached from the west, and even then very carefully . . . The *Almaenwuhr* could come down from the north and not be seen."

Troucillus was translating for Publicola and Manius. "It's a bloody death-trap," Manius snorted. "We'd be ridin' into a shaggin' ambush by a superior force, and we'd have nowhere to withdraw."

Publicola was just about to speak when Troucillus interrupted, asking Metius, "What did you share with Ariovistus concerning our mission or Caesar's situation?"

Metius responded, "I only told him that you are delivering a message from the Roman proconsul." Metius's face was unreadable.

"So," Troucillus continued, "you said nothing about the nature of the message or the rumors of a Roman mutiny?"

"I've already answered that question, Trocille!" Metius dismissed it.

Troucillus decided not to challenge the answer, but continued, "I don't like it. Publicola, I recommend we hold here until we hear from Caesar. Even if we assume that Ariovistus knows nothing of Caesar's situation or his message, when we deliver it, he may decide to answer it with our heads in a sack."

Publicola shook his head. "We have already had that discussion, Trocille. A Roman officer obeys his orders, and *I* will obey mine."

Troucillus' shoulders sagged. Then, he said, "Let me at least suggest this. First, send those *Suebii* back to Ariovistus. Even if they are not part of a conspiracy against us, I can't promise that the Sequani will not try to cut their throats if they have to look at them for two days. Dai's troopers can lead us to the meeting."

Metius seemed to be about to say something, but Publicola said, "*Tecum consto* . . . agreed."

Troucillus continued, "Also, we won't wait almost two days for Ariovistus to arrange a reception committee for us . . . First hour tomorrow, we'll send out a contingent of our Sequani *auxilia* troopers under Insubrecus here . . . They can work their way around from the west and keep the meeting place under observation until we arrive."

Again, Publicola nodded. Metius' face was stone.

I was translating Troucillus' Latin for Dai. When I translated the phrase "under Insubrecus here," my literal third-person translation stuck in my throat. *I* was advancing into the territory controlled by Ariovistus, not some faceless Roman officer named "Insubrecus."

"*Constamus!*" Publicola announced. "We are in agreement. Metti! Dismiss these . . . these *pilosi barbarici* . . . Send them back to their master."

Then, he walked away.

Metius grumbled and walked toward the dismounted *Suebii*. After some discussion with their chief, which sounded to me like pigs grunting, the *Suebii* remounted and withdrew toward the northeast. They were obviously displeased with this change in *their* plans. I wondered briefly if Metius felt the same way.

Troucillus, Dai, Manius, and I watched the *Suebii* disappear down the ridgeline. Then, Troucillus said, "Dai! *A Pen*! Give them an hour; then take a patrol straight down their path. I don't think they'll go too far. Sweep them away. I don't want them to see Arth's advance tomorrow, and I definitely don't want them dogging our tracks when we go to meet Ariovistus."

Then, Troucillus turned to Manius. "*Decurio*! Detail a couple of your men, ones whom you trust, to keep an eye on Metius and his entourage. They are not to leave our encampment before we depart to meet with Ariovistus. If any of them try to leave, or if they should suddenly *disappear* from our camp, tell me immediately."

"Even Marcus Metius, sir?" Manius asked.

"*Especially* Marcus Metius!" Troucillus confirmed.

XIV.

De Calamitate in Colle Pecorum
THE DEBACLE AT THE HILL OF FLOCKS

His mandavit Caio Valerio Trocillo et Marco Mettio quae diceret Ariovistus
cognoscerent et ad se referent quos cum apud se in castris Ariovistus
conspexisset exercitu suo praesente conclamavit quid ad se venirent an
speculandi causa conantes dicere prohibuit et in catenas coniecit

"Caesar instructed these men, Gaius Valerius Troucillus and Marcus
Metius, to find out what Ariovistus had to say and to report back
to him. When Ariovistus saw them in his camp, among his army,
he cried, 'Why have they come here, if not to spy on us?' Ariovistus
gave them no chance to reply, but threw them into chains."

(from Gaius Marius Insubrecus' notebook of Caesar's journal)

The next day, as soon as it was light enough to travel, I was off on
my detail to the Hill of Flocks. I rode with Guithiru's *ala* and two
guides from Dai's *fintai*. I also took our *exploratores*, Rhori and
Drust, our scouts. I anticipated a need for their skills as hunters and trackers.

Athauhnu stayed behind with Ci's *ala*. He would screen the rear of Publicola's
party as they approached the meeting place with Ariovistus.

Publicola had decided to put on a real Roman dog-and-pony show for what he anticipated to be an encounter with a ragtag collection of barbarians who would be overawed by Roman military grandeur. Manius' boys spent the entire day before their departure polishing and cleaning their kits for what they hoped would merely be a long parade through the woods.

Dai's *fintai* would hold our position in the Gate, while Ceriales continued to survey locations for our eventual fortifications.

Troucillus had been right about Metius' *Suebii* escort. They had only ridden a couple of thousand *passus* back down the trail and seemed to be hunkering down to wait for Publicola's advance. When Dai's boys came up on them, the *Grunni* were at first not inclined to attack or retreat. Finally, when their leader realized that any advantage they might have had was lost, they reluctantly withdrew to the northeast. Dai dogged their trail until he was confident that they were gone.

Still, as we rode out that morning, I kept my scouts and Dai's guides well ahead of my main column, just in case any of the *Suebii* were still lurking about. None were, and by the third hour, we were following a narrow trail north through a wooded valley. My advance party was waiting for me along the trail.

"*A Pen*," one of Dai's scouts, a warrior called Duglos, addressed me. "*Uh bruhn uh gouarteg*, the place you seek, is east and north of here on the other side of this ridge."

"How are we going to get the horses up over this bloody mountain?" I asked him.

"About two hundred *passus* to the north, there's a gap," he answered. "We can walk the horses up a trail between the hills. Near the top of the pass, there's an open area that is well screened from the Hill of Flocks. We can leave the horses there, climb the hill directly to the east, and from the top we can watch the valley below."

"You've seen this place?" I asked him.

He nodded, "Many times, *a Pen*. We use it to watch for the *Almaenwuhr* who are foolish enough to approach *Caer Harth* directly."

"Lead us there, Duglos!" I agreed.

Duglos went ahead with Rhodri and Drust. He left his mate, Ewuhn, to guide us. We soon came to the trailhead leading up into the gap. It was narrow and winding, so we dismounted and led our horses in a single file.

Clamriu was not at all happy with this new development; she kept shaking her head, snorting at me, and trying to pull me back down the trail. It was her way of asking me whether I had totally lost my mind. I can't say I blamed her much. There were less than twenty of us deep in the woods bordering the valley of the Rhenus, which was reportedly filled with hordes of Ariovistus' blood-thirsty *Grunni*. And, they had a pretty good idea we were coming.

We soon reached a level area surrounded by high wooded hills to the east and west. The trail that we had been following continued, descending downward between the hills to the south and east. Dugos and my scouts were waiting for us.

"The trail continues into the valley of the Rhenus," Duglos said. "We leave the horses here and climb the hill on the east. From the top, we will be able to see the valley below."

I nodded and called to Guithiru. "*A Pen*, secure the area and establish our horse lines here. I'm going up on top with the scouts to see what we've got."

Guithiru nodded, and we began our climb to the top of the ridge. Duglos was right. From the top, we had a clear view into the valley of the Rhenus. Below us, less than a thousand *passus* away, was the Hill of Flocks. Its approaches from the south and east could be clearly seen, but to the north and west, directly below our position, the terrain was heavily wooded. Hannibal and all his elephants could be hiding there, and we would never see them.

I sent Drust back down the hill to get Guithiru while I studied the terrain below me. Finally, Guithiru joined us.

"Our primary job," I began, "is to ensure that the *Rhufeiniaid* are not walking into a trap. If you were going to set up an ambush with the Hill of Flocks as the primary kill zone, how would you do it?"

After a few heartbeats, Guithiru offered, "I would conceal my men in the forests . . . foot soldiers . . . Horses would not abide those woods . . . I would lure the *Rhufeiniaid* to the top. Then, I would spring it."

Everyone nodded in agreement. Then Duglos added, "I might position some cavalry on top of the hill or just to the east of it in order to prevent the *Rhufeiniaid* from escaping to the south."

"Then, our primary job is to detect any movement by the *Almaenwuhr* into the north and east flanks of the hill," I concluded.

There was no disagreement.

"We cannot do that from here," I announced. "We need to advance scouts into the terrain we cannot see. Duglos and Ewuh, you work your way around the north side of the hill. We'll send another two-man team, Rhodri and Drust, straight down to cover the west flank. That will seal off any approach to those two danger areas. Does that make sense?"

Again, no disagreement.

"This is very important," I continued. "Avoid contact with the *Almaenwuhr*. If you detect movement into the area, you get back here and report."

Still, agreement.

"This will be our main command and observation post, I continued. "Guithiru and I will be here. Unless you're prevented, you withdraw to this point. Any questions about that?"

There were none.

I kept going, "Guithiru! Send a couple of the men down the trail, south into the valley below. I want to be sure that the trail is open in case we need it as an escape route. Tell them to scout it all the way down, but they are not to break cover. I do not want our presence here to be detected by the enemy. We'll also send two men back to the trailhead to make sure that the enemy doesn't infiltrate in behind us."

Guithiru nodded.

"We'll leave a couple of men down the ridge to secure the horse lines. The rest will be up here."

Then, I turned to Rhodri, "Do you have your hunting horn?"

"*Shuh, a Pen,*" he said. "It's tied to my saddle."

"*Mai huhnnu uhn da,*" I answered. "That's good. Bring it here. A series of three quick blasts on the horn is our signal for immediate assembly. You hear that, you get back here as fast as you can. Meet us here or at the horse lines below.

Four blasts will mean we're totally screwed. Four blasts and forget about us. Just get back to friendly territory any way you can."

Cogitant homines; rident di. Men plan; gods laugh!

I was feeling cocky, confident that I had it all figured out. But, *Domina Fortuna's* wheel had already spun and stopped. Nothing I could have done would have changed what was to happen the next morning.

Looking back on these events, I realize that *Fortuna* had nothing to do with it. It was my own lack of experience as a soldier, especially in facing the *Grunni.*

Romans are masters of the open field. If they can entice an enemy into opposing them in a set-piece battle, especially when they pick the time and the place, they are invincible. But, they dread the forests, the constrained, dark places where their battlelines cannot be established and the enemy can creep up on them without being seen.

The *Grunni* are masters of the forests. They can move under the gloomy canopy of its trees swiftly and silently. They can strike quickly, then fade back into the shadows. In those obscure, constricted places, Roman tactics–even the size of their armies–can put them at a disadvantage.

On one policy *Augustus* and I agree: Roman legions must never cross the Rhenus, except on punitive raids, and then they must quickly withdraw. If the *Grunni* want a fight to the death, let them come to us.

That next day on the Hill of Flocks, Ariovistus gave me my first lesson in fighting Germans; a few days after that, Caesar gave Ariovistus his final lesson in fighting Romans.

Our recon parties had equipped themselves as if they were setting out on a hunt. They stripped off their armor and went down into the forests, armed only with *pugiones* and *gaia* javelins. They reasoned that the weight of their armor would just slow them down. If the *Suebii* detected them in the woods, all the steel in the world wouldn't save them, but stealth and swiftness might.

The rest of that first day up on the ridge overlooking the Hill of Flocks was peaceful, almost pastoral. Except for the almost languorous wind drifting across the long grasses, nothing moved in the valley, which stretched away into the distance toward the golden mists of the Rhenus.

Guithiru and I took turns keeping watch from the ridge. It was a warm, dozy late summer's day, and the songs of the cicadas and the warm breezes whispering through the trees lulled me to sleep.

The next day started as if it were going merely to replay the day before, until sometime during the second hour, when we detected movement in the valley below. A troop of riders–some thirty or so–approached the hill from the northeast. From their equipment, they seemed to be from the same bunch who had escorted Metius to our camp at *Caer Harth. Grunni*!

They swept around the Hill of Flocks and rode up to its summit from the south, which was clear enough to accomodate a troop of mounted men.

"Smart!" I heard Guithiru's voice behind me. "*Uh Gweleduth*, the Seer, does not want any surprises waiting for him on the hill when he arrives."

After a while, the *Suebii* sent a small detachment of six riders south, to screen for the advancing Romans, we assumed. After they disappeared up the valley, we again settled down to wait: we on the ridge, the *Suebii* on the Hill of Flocks.

I was just crossing over into Morpheus' dark realm when Guithiru grabbed my shoulder. "Arth . . . to the north . . . riders!"

I quickly recovered my wits and looked out into the valley. At first I saw nothing. Then, I sensed movement out beyond the Hill of Flocks. Eventually my perception of movement resolved itself into distinct figures, then the figures into distinct individuals. I saw riders, this time heavy cavalry, well-armored men on big horses.

"They are not *Almaenwuhr*!" I heard Guithiru say. Then, I heard his breath whistle through his teeth, "They are Gah'el! Gah'el who fight for *uh Gweleduth*!"

As the troop drew closer, we could see their tartan colors . . . They were *Aineduai* . . . *Aineduai* fighting with the *Almaenwuhr* . . . We had at last discovered the *fintai* of Deluuhnu mab Clethguuhno, the renegade prince of the *Aineduai*!

This was a major development. I was sure the Romans were not expecting to encounter heavy cavalry. The *Grunni* fought on foot; there was no use for cavalry in their forests. Their horsemen on this side of the *Rhenus* could barely stay atop their horses. Their equipment and weapons were primitive; they were used mostly for reconnaissance and raids. When they fought, they dismounted, to fight on foot. But, these were trained, well-equipped Gallic horsemen, and Publicola was riding straight into them.

"I need to send back a messenger," I hissed to Guithiru. "Do we have anyone who can speak Latin?"

"*Possum . . . solum me . . . parvus paulum*," Guithiru answered in his faltering Latin. "I can . . . just me . . . a little bit."

"Then you it is!" I told him. "Ride back to Publicola . . . Report what we've seen here . . . Take one of our boys with you . . . Avoid the *Almaenwuhr* scouting up the valley . . . Get to Publicola."

Guithiru nodded, then moved back over the ridge down to where we had established our horse lines. I continued to watch the valley below.

The *Aineduai fintai* established a loose cordon to screen the southern approach to the Hill of Flocks. Military order quickly broke down among them. They dismounted and let their horses graze freely. The men formed informal groups; I saw the pantomime of conversations; some broke out rations and began to eat; others just stretched out on the grass and slept while their horses cropped the grass around them.

We were well into the fourth hour when we spotted another group of riders approaching from the northeast.

Ariovistus had arrived!

He was obvious among the approaching troop. He rode a large, white stallion, and a long, flowing, gray, hooded cloak hung from his shoulders. On his left rode his standard bearer. On his banner I could see the shape of a red serpent cut into pieces on a jet-black field. Below the flag, attached to the staff, were nine small, wooden crosspieces, one for each of his allied tribes.

On Ariovistus' right rode Deluuhnu mab Clethguuhno. Behind him, his standard bearer carried the colors of the *Wuhr Blath*, the Wolf clan *Aineduai*, a snarling wolf's head with blood-red eyes on a field of the tribal plaid. I was a bit surprised; displaying that banner was the privilege of the clan leader, Deluuhnu's brother, Duuhruhda, the *Uucharix* of the *Aineduai* and the supposed ally of Caesar. Behind Deluuhnu rode six well-equipped and well-mounted riders of his *custodes*, his personal bodyguard.

Ariovistus also surprised me. I had expected to see a Germanic giant, with piercing blue eyes, a bristling red beard twisted into braids, gilded plate armor, and a high-crowned helmet sprouting eagle's wings. His muscular arms should have been covered in thick, golden armbands, daring enemy warriors to try and take them from him in battle.

Instead, I saw a smallish man—even by Roman standards—dark-haired and barefaced. He wore no helmet. I could see no armor and no sword. He wore a gray robe and carried no visible weapons, only a long, wooden staff. Then, to add to my surprise, I saw a small, gray-haired woman riding behind him.

Ariovistus's physical stature did not seem to undermine his authority. As he approached the Hill of Flocks, the *Suebii* horsemen came down to greet him. I was not at all familiar with the protocol of the Germanic tribes, but by the standards of the Gah'el—even by Roman standards—Ariovistus' followers seemed subservient, even submissive. They dismounted before him and bowed low as he approached, not daring to meet his eyes, as if he were one of their gods come down into the middle lands.

Even as the *Aineduai* who had arrived earlier rose to their feet, they focused on Ariovistus and not on their own *penefig*, Deluuhnu.

I watched as Ariovistus gave instructions to his men. They nodded repeatedly, bowed again, remounted, and ascended the Hill of Flocks. Ariovistus, his standard bearer, and the old woman followed them.

Deluuhnu remained behind, giving instructions to his *fintai*. Then, he, his *signifer,* and his *custodes* followed Ariovistus up the hill. The *Aineduai* who were left behind took control of their mounts and straightened their picket line in front of the hill. Most did not remount, but remained, waiting in place.

Soon, I saw the *Suebii* scouts who had gone in search of Publicola's party galloping toward the Hill of Flocks. As they passed through the Aeduan picket line, the Gallic riders began to remount. The scouts mounted the hill. I could see them address Ariovistus and his party, who stood on the south-facing slope.

One of my men grabbed my right forearm and pointed south up the valley. It took me a few heartbeats, but finally I noticed the flash of sunlight shining off polished steel.

Publicola was approaching the Hill of Flocks.

As the Roman party resolved into recognizable shapes, I could see a lead unit of ten Roman troopers arranged in a *cuneus*, the wedge formation called the "pig's snout." On the Roman left flank, facing the forested high ground, Manius had arrayed another ten men in a column to protect that flank against ambush. On the right flank, he had formed yet another ten-man *cuneus*, ready to manuever around an enemy's flank should the lead or flanking units make contact.

Publicola was riding immediately behind the forward wedge. His highly polished armor and helmet sparkled as if he had just descended from Olympus itself. To his right rode the signifer of the cavalry *turma*, his blood-red dragon pennant snapping jauntily in the breeze. To Publicola's left rode Mani *Talus*, and behind Manius, the *cornicen*, the trumpeter of the *turma*.

Troucillus rode a few *passus* behind the command party. He wore no armor, just the white toga with the narrow purple stripe of a Roman knight. Metius, wearing only a dark green tunic, rode slightly behind Troucillus. Behind Metius rode Guithiru, who remained aloof from the Roman groupings.

Gratias dis! I thought when I spotted Guithiru. *The Romans had been warned of the Gallic cavalry.*

The *Aineduai* who were screening in front of the Hill of Flocks straightened their picket line as the Roman party came into sight.

This movement was seen by the Romans. Manius moved forward to the leading *cuneus* and put his men into a canter in order to open some distance between them and the main party. As soon as he had a good tactical separation in which to manuever his troop, he brought them back to a trot. Manius was too good an officer to wind his mounts while approaching possible enemy contact.

I was beginning to relax, knowing that Guithiru had gotten through and warned Publicola of the presence of a heavy cavalry on the objective. Then, I heard a horn blast. Although it came from the Hill of Flocks, I thought for a heartbeat that one of my men had sounded it. Then, I heard the signal again from Ariovistus' position.

I wondered whether this was some sort of welcoming signal that the *Suebii* use in situations like this . . . if not a welcome, a sign of a truce. Then, I heard movement climbing toward me from the ridgeline below. A voice called in Gah'el, "*A Pen*! It's me! Duglos!"

The man entered the clearing, his face bright red from the exertion of climbing the ridge almost at a run. He doubled over, panting.

"*A Pen*," he gasped. "*Almaenwuhr* . . . many . . . on foot . . . north . . . north of the hill—"

"What?" I countered, not wanting to believe what I had heard. "*Almaenwuhr*! Where?"

Duglos straightened up and pointed beyond the Hill of Flocks. "Coming through those hills . . . coming fast . . . We barely escaped them."

I looked where Duglos had indicated and saw only the tops of the trees, but I could visualize what was about to happen below. Ariovistus would draw the Roman party onto the hill where they would be overwhelmed by his infantry pouring out of the trees.

"Where's Ewuhn?" I asked Duglos.

"He goes . . . he goes to collect Rhodri and Drust . . . before they're trapped!"

I looked down into the valley below. The Roman point element was less than a hundred *passus* in front of the Aeduan picket line. I had to keep them from getting closer! They must not climb the Hill of Flocks! It was Ariovistus' death trap!

I realized then that Manius and I had coordinated no danger signal . . . no signal to tell the Romans to clear off . . . retreat immediately . . . danger close!

Still, I ordered one of my troopers to sound assembly. Perhaps Manius would understand that he needed to withdraw . . . immediately!

As the hunting horn sent out its three blasts, the heads of the troopers below us in the valley – Romans and *Aineduai* alike – turned toward my position.

My assembly signal continued to sound.

Still, the Romans advanced toward the Hill of Flocks.

Ariovistus gestured with his staff. The solid cordan of Aeduan troopers split in the middle, moved back, and reassembled on the forward flanks of the slope. The Roman wedge entered the gap, which the *Aineduai* had made. Publicola, Troucillus, and Metius advanced behind them toward the hill.

They were entering into the maw of Ariovistus' trap.

I turned to Duglos. "I am taking the *fintai* into the valley below to make contact with the Romans. When Rhodri, Drust, and Ewuhn get here, follow behind."

"*Uhr wuhf uhn dealch*," he nodded. "I understand."

I grabbed him by the shoulder, "Come quickly!"

I ran and slid down the ridge to where we had left our horses. Slowly, much too slowly, my men assembled. I did a quick count. I had only twelve.

"Is this everyone?" I asked.

I got nods and affirmative grunts as my answer.

"The *Almaenwuhr* and their *Aineduai* lap-dogs plan to kill the Romans in the next valley!" I shouted. "We are riding down this trail to kill them! Follow me! Stay close!"

With that, I vaulted onto Clamriu's back. She was a war horse. She knew she was going into battle. The narrow, dark, forested path that would have normally panicked her now had no effect. She galloped down the trail toward the battle.

In what seemed like no time at all, we broke out of the forest into the open river valley. I had to lead my men a few *passus* out onto the plain to get a visual contact with the Hill of Flocks.

Two things were immediately obvious.

First, Ariovistus had sprung his trap. I could see the Roman advanced party in a confused melee with the *Suebii* on the front slope of the hill. Below that, the *Aineduai* had closed the gap and were engaged with the Roman cavalry still in the valley.

Second, our mounts were winded from our dash down from the ridgeline. We needed to pause and give them time to get their wind, or they'd be clapped out by the time we made contact with the enemy.

My initial impulse was to try to force my way through the center of the *Aineduai* line and come to the aid of Troucillus and the Romans on the hill. I arranged my small detail into a *cuneus* wedge behind me and was about to start walking the horses toward the fight when I saw a rider galloping toward me from the rear of the Roman line.

It was Guithiru.

He galloped up to me. "*A Pen*! The Roman chief wants you to reinforce his left. The *Aineduai* are threatening to turn that flank."

"But, we're needed on the hill," I began.

Then, I noticed that Manius' assessment was correct. The *Aineduai* in the valley had the Romans fixed, engaged across the entire front of their battle line. I could see the *Aineduai* taking advantage of their superior numbers by shifting a force of riders around the Roman left, a point of contact where the swords of the defenders were masked by their shields and bodies. If the *Aineduai* pushed the Roman flank back and got in behind them, it would be a massacre.

This battle was not being fought as a typical cavalry engagement. The cavalry, as opposed to the infantry, normally does not stand up against an enemy attack. The strength of the cavalry is in its speed and maneuverability. Most cavalry fights are short, vicious brawls, after which both sides disengage.

The situation before me was different. The outnumbered Romans would ordinarily have disengaged, retreated up the valley toward my position, and found favorable terrain to continue the fight should the enemy pursue. But, these were Romans, and they refused to abandon their commander and their comrades trapped on the hill above them. So, they stayed engaged with the superior force and fought on unfavorable terrain, even if it meant they too would be annihilated.

For a Roman soldier, death is better than having to live knowing you abandoned your mates on the battlefield.

I realized that Troucillus and the rest of the *turma* on the hill would have to hold their own for a while. My point of attack needed to be directed where Manius wanted it, toward the Roman left, in order to turn back the enemy flanking movement.

But, there was yet another hope for us.

"Guithiru," I said. "Ride back up the valley . . . Find Athauhnu . . . He should be no more than a thousand *passus* back . . . Bring him here quickly!"

"But, *a Pen*—" he began. No Gah'el with his blood up wants to abandon a fight.

"Go quickly, *a Pen*," I told him. "Or none of us will survive this fight!"

If I could stabilize the Roman line on the left, then Athauhnu could break through the center to the hill above us when he arrived.

Reluctantly, Guithiru nodded, then turned his horse up the valley to find Athauhnu.

My troop was still in a *cuneus* wedge. We shrugged our shields off our backs and drew our *spathae*, our cavalry sabers. Then, we began to trot our horses toward the Roman left flank. I could see the end of the Roman line and the movement of the *Aineduai* toward it. Judging the distance and the potential speed of our attack, I targeted a point of contact with the enemy.

I ordered my *fintai* to the canter. Once the horses were moving comfortably, I ordered my *cornicen* to signal our approach with his hunting horn. After a couple of blasts, I could see the heads of the Roman troopers on the left turn toward us. They were veterans and immediately understood my intent. They began to fold back their line to give me a clean shot at the flank of the advancing *Aineduai*.

As the Roman flank folded back, I ordered my troop to the gallop. My men started whooping and screaming the battle cries of their clans.

Despite the clamor, the *Aineduai* were so intent on turning the Roman flank that they didn't see us until it was too late for them. We tore through them as easily as a sword plunges into water. As we swept through, I got a flashing impression of a shocked face under a helmet on my right, too far away to reach with my *spatha*. An *Aineduai* on my shield side made an ineffectual swipe at me with his sword before he was ridden down by one of my troopers.

Then we were through. We were in their rear!

I immediately realized that I had a clear path to the top of the hill a few hundred *passus* to my front!

I have since learned that battles are not won by the leader with the best plan; battles are won by the leader who takes advantage of the opportunities that present themselves on the battlefield. Once combat is joined, decisions made solely according to predetermined strategies are useless the moment the boot of the first soldier steps out toward the enemy. The battle plan is rendered useless by the unexpected and unpredictable dynamics of the battlefield; decisions made during the battle must be based on the immediate prospects at hand. A seasoned combat leader makes these opportunistic decisions immediately and instinctually, based on experience, audacity, and confidence.

And, that is where I proved fatally inadequate in that fight.

Given our position between the *Aineduai* cavalry and the Hill of Flocks, we could either continue our advance up the hill to reinforce our trapped mates, or we could turn and attack the rear of the *Aineduai* who were still engaged with Manius.

My gut urged me to attack the hill, despite the need to attack uphill across open ground against a superior force with the enemy both in front and to the rear.

An experienced combat leader would have immediately seized on the second option: attack downhill and cut through the backs of the unsuspecting enemy.

Instead, I did the worst thing any leader could do in combat. I froze!

Almost immediately, I saw two riders gallop toward me from the hill. They were Romans. I recognized the second rider as a senior officer. It had to be Publicola. He was bent over his saddle horns and could barely keep his mount. The lead rider was a Roman trooper. He was leading Publicola's horse.

The trooper was Crocius.

"*Decurio*," he panted, "get the tribune to safety . . . He's badly wounded . . . Refused to leave his men . . . Can't do a thing for them . . . a trap."

He tried to hand me the reins. I could see Publicola sagging forward over his saddle horns; under his helmet, his face was pasty, greenish white. I was immediately reminded of Madog at Bibracte.

"Stay with him, Croci!" I ordered. "Get him back to safety!"

"No, *Decurio*!" Crocius shook his head. "My *contubernales* on the hill . . . my mates . . . they need me."

I was about to order him to stay when the *Suebii* on the hill stole the option from me. About twenty of their light cavalry charged down the hill. Instead of engaging my troop, they pulled up about halfway down the slope. Then, I saw that each rider was dragging a foot soldier who was hanging on to a saddle horn. As soon as the infantry detached itself from the cavalry, the riders tossed down wicked-looking long spears to the foot soldiers. The infantry formed a line facing us. They locked their shields and raised their pikes to form a *contra equitatum*, a counter-cavalry picket line, between us and the Hill of Flocks.

I realized then that I couldn't go forward. I had broken the momentum of the attack and now had a solid wall of *Suebii* infantry to my front. In fact, with the *Aidenuai* to my rear and flank, I was effectively trapped.

No sooner had I realized my predicament than a Sequani hunting horn sounded from the south. It was immediately answered by a Roman *cornu*.

Athauhnu had arrived!

The *Aineduai* immediately disengaged from the Romans and began to melt back toward the Hill of Flocks. In no time Manius was up to my position.

"Insubrece *Decurio*," he began, "we are pullin' back to the Sequani line to reorganize."

Then, he spotted Publicola slouched forward over his saddle horns. "*Verpa Martis*! Excuse me . . . I mean . . . Tribune! What are your orders?"

"I don't think Publicola's in any condition to give orders, Mani *Decurio*," I answered him. "Let's get him back to the troop."

I looked up over the heads of the *Suebii* pickets toward the Hill of Flocks. The fight up there was now over. I could see no sign of further struggle. But, Ariovistus, on his white stallion, was surveying the battlefield below with that gobshite of an *Aineduai* traitor, Deluuhnu mab Clethguuhno, mounted next to him.

There was nothing I could do for the Roman troopers who had gone up that hill, nothing I could do for Troucillus.

Although the *Aineduai* had withdrawn, the *Suebii* infantry on the front slope of the hill were becoming aggressive. I could see more foot soldiers descending the hill to reinforce their mates along the shield wall. As soon as their battle line was strong enough, I was sure they would sweep down on us.

So, we withdrew up the valley, toward the position where Athauhnu had established his picket line. As we moved back, we used the opportunity to recover our dead and wounded.

The Romans believe that without the proper burial rites, the *limures* of the dead are doomed to wander the middle worlds forever. To leave the bodies of mates unburied, to allow them to be stripped and abused by the enemy, would be a dreadful failing, a violation of *contubernium*, comradery, as culpable as cowardice. So, our dead were recovered, and our wounded helped to retreat as we withdrew.

I could only imagine how the Roman troopers felt about the bodies of the mates they had to leave behind on the Hill of Flocks. The thought that Troucillus was among them only exacerbated my feelings of failure; I had failed to carry out my *officium obligatum*, my pledged duty.

We reached the relative safety of Athauhnu's line. The *Suebii* did not yet seem inclined to pursue, but had moved their shield wall down to the base of the hill and halted. We took stock of our situation. Manius had lost eight and four were wounded. Nine of his troopers were missing on the hill, along with Troucillus and Metius. I counted two dead and three wounded from my Sequani. Some of our wounded needed to be helped on their journey across the river with a single downward thrust of a *pugio* in the hallow between throat and collarbone. The rest were mounted as best they could for the march back to the Gate.

Publicola would have been a candidate for a merciful dispatch, except no one in the troop would strike a patrician. He had taken a spear thrust just below the right armpit, where his plate armor didn't protect him when he raised his sword. He was having difficulty breathing, and the wound in his side bubbled with every breath he took. He was fading in and out of the *somnis vulneris*, the "wound sleep," a stupor that the gods sometimes send as a mercy to badly injured soldiers. The Sequani *medduhg*, our only medic, packed Publicola's wound with his *sudarium*, his military scarf, and tied his right arm down to his side to seal it. We secured Publicola to his horse the best we could.

The *Suebii* advanced about fifty *passus* toward our line. They tried to be threatening, but kept a healthy distance. They began to taunt us. The expected stuff: screaming insults in languages we didn't understand, baring their bottocks. It had little effect on the men. But, when they began flaunting the body parts of our dead mates at us—heads, limbs, and even penises—Manius decided it was time to get out of there before our boys did something stupid.

The retreat back to the Gate was a short journey, but a nightmare nonetheless.

We moved across the open ground of the valley in an *orbis*, a hollow square formation. One of Manius' *alae* was the point element and the other, the right flank; that was all he had the manpower for. Ci was on the left and Guithiru the rear. We put the wounded in the center. Manius remained with the point element, while Athauhnu and I kept the flank and rear elements closed up and tight. It was a difficult formation to coordinate, and it moved slowly, but it provided us with security on all sides.

The *Suebii* took advantage of our slowness to dog our line of march. They didn't attempt to attack our *orbis* directly. They mounted archers with their light cavalry and moved around our flanks, waiting in ambush along our route of withdrawal. They would find a covered position and strike uphill from us so that we could not get any momentum to counter attack. Since we were marching up the valley, they had many opportunities to attack us. Typically, the first indication we had of their presence was an arrow thudding into a man or a horse.

Luckily, our chainmail *loricae* defeated most of the blows from the *Grunni's* arrows, which were poorly constructed and shot out of short hunting bows. But, sometimes they got lucky. Manius' boys suffered wounds to their legs and arms; one lost an eye. I lost one of my Sequani troopers to an arrow in the throat; it severed one of his major blood tubes; he bled out before we could do anything to help him.

The real impact of these attacks was not from the casualties they inflicted, but from the torment of the constant harassment. When we were fortunate enough to catch one of those *cunni*, he didn't die quickly.

As we climbed the valley toward the Gate, the forests closed in around us, and we could no longer maintain the *orbis*. Soon, we were marching in a column and the *Suebii* were concentrating on our flanks.

I imagined that I could hear the approach of the two arrows that were shot at me. One smashed into my upper-right chest, and the second hit Clamriu in her right shoulder. The arrow that hit me became wedged in the iron rings of my *lorica*. The arrow head buckled, and I was merely stung. But, Clamriu was lamed. The Sequani *medduhg* examined her wound while I covered his back with my shield. He assured me that he could remove the arrowhead from her once we got back to camp, but there was nothing he could do for her there. He clipped the arrow shaft, leaving only about an *uncia* protruding from her flank. He told me I should walk her, to relieve the pressure on her leg. Then, he moved down the column to examine his next patient. For the rest of the march, I remained near the front of our formation, just ahead of the wounded. Clamriu soldiered through her pain like a trooper.

My personal nightmare on that retreat was not the constant harassment, or even the wounding of my horse, but it was the trauma of having lost Troucillus and the certainty that I had failed him and my mates.

My mission had been to prevent what had just happened. So, in my judgment, my mission had failed. If I had only arranged some sort of signal with Manius to warn the Romans away from the Hill of Flocks, I could have prevented the ambush in which Troucillus and the Roman troopers had died. Not only had I failed to warn them off, but I had also failed to detect the enemy advance until it was too late. Then, at a critical moment in the battle, I froze. I chastised myself for even considering an attack up onto the Hill of Flocks. If only I had reacted more quickly and turned around, I may have been able to change the outcome. I might have reached my mates in time.

As I write this memoir, I have been living with the memory of that fight for over twenty years. I know now that by the time I had arrived on that battlefield, it was already too late to do anything to influence events on the Hill of Flocks. Had I attacked up the hill, I would have only made matters worse by getting myself and all my troopers killed. My only reasonable option might have been to attack the *Aineduai* rear. But, even that would only have accelerated their disengagement from Manius' troop, which, in the end, was caused not by anything I did–or could have done—but by the timely arrival of Athauhnu's *fintai* on the battlefield.

But, as we limped back toward *Caer Harth*, I was seventeen and still a very green junior officer. I was guilty of that hubris that allows youths to believe that they, and they alone, are the sole cause of some significant event. So, I firmly resolved to resign my commission and request reassignment back to the legionary line of battle as a *mulus*.

We were, by my estimation, less than five hundred *passus* away from the Gate when instead of the hiss and thud of another Kraut arrow, I heard a voice ahead of us call out in Latin, *"Cons'tit' vos! Qu'estis?* Halt! Who are you?"

Manius slipped down from his mount and responded, *"Amici!* Friends!"

The voice challenged him for the password. "*Ursus*! Bear!"

"I do not have the password," Manius asnswered. "I am Manius Rabirius, *Decurio* of the Ninth Legion, now in command of the *vexillatio* of Tertius Gellius Publicola, under the direct orders of the *Imperator*."

There was a brief silence, then the voice challenged, "What is your shield symbol?"

Manius responded, "*Taurus*, the Bull!"

Then, the voice, "*Maneas illic tu, Decurio*! Please stay where you are, sir!"

I thought addressing Manius as "sir" and requesting him to stay put, instead of ordering it, were good signs that whoever was out there accepted our *bona fides*.

Then, I heard, "*Tesserari*! *Stationem quinque*! Officer of the guard! Post five!"

I walked up to where Manius was standing, and as I joined him, a Roman soldier appeared on the trail ahead. He was soon backed up by five additional *muli*. All were equipped as *velites*, skirmishers, stripped down to their *subarmales*, the padded jackets legionaries wear under their armor, and armed only with *gladii* and *pila*.

"*Ave, Decurio*!" the first said. "Greetings, *Decurio*. I'm called Rufius, *Tesserarius* of the Fifth Century, Third Cohort of Caesar's Tenth Legion. We had been told to look out for you!"

I saw Manius' shoulders sag a bit as he realized that he had finally gotten his people back to safety.

"*Ave, Rufi*," he responded. "This is Gaius Marius Insubrecus, Commander of the Sequani cavalry and *Decurio Praetorius* of the *Imperator*. Please . . . lead us to camp . . . quickly . . . We have wounded."

XV.

De Nece Reducitur Amicus

A FRIEND BROUGHT
BACK FROM THE DEAD

---

*Postea quam in vulgus militum elatum est qua arrogantia in conloquio
Ariovistus usus omni Gallia Romanis interdixisset impetumque in nostros
eius equites fecissent eaque res conloquium ut diremisset multo maior
alacritas studiumque pugnandi maius exercitui iniectum est.*

"Later, when our rank and file found out about Ariovistus' arrogance
during the conference and how he forbade Romans any access to Gaul and
how he attacked our delegation in order to break up the negotiations, our
army was more than ready and raring to fight the Germans."

(from Gaius Marius Insubrecus' notebook of Caesar's journal)

---

e limped back, arriving at the Gate during the tenth hour; it was
immediately obvious that the Roman army had arrived.

Standing before us was a ten-foot *vallum*, a wall of earth topped
by a wooden parapet and fronted by a *fossum*, a defensive ditch dug to the
regulation six *pedes* in depth. A screen of fully armed *muli* stood along the ditch,
while their mates, stripped down to their red military tunics, placed *lilia*, "lilies,"

foot-traps of sharpened *sudes* stakes, down in the ditch. As we approached the conventional folded gateway, I saw the red *vexillium* of the Tenth Legion waving from the battlements.

A sentry on top of the gate called down our approach into the *castrum*. Almost immediately, a group of soldiers came out to meet us. I was surprised to see the legate, Labienus himself, leading the group. Behind him marched Tertius Piscius Malleus, the Hammer, *Centurio Primus Pilus* of the Tenth Legion, his *vitis* staff clamped firmly under his left arm.

"*Gratias dis*," Labienus was saying. "Thank the gods you made it back . . . Caesar sent messengers to recall you, but they didn't get up here in time!"

Then, Labienus searched among our banged-about, ragtag assembly, "But . . . where's Publicola? Troucillus?"

Manius, as our *de facto* commander, responded, "Legate! Manius Rabirius, *Decurio*, reports—"

"Forget the military formalities, *Decurio*," Labienus stopped him. "Please, just answer the question."

"Legate! The tribune, Tertius Gellius Publicola, is badly wounded . . . He's back with the column . . . The envoy, Gaius Valerius Troucillus, is missing and presumed dead."

"And Marcus Metius?" Labienus continued.

"Missing . . . presumed dead, Legate!" Manius repeated.

"How many wounded with the column?" Labienus asked.

"Ten . . . six Romans, four Sequani," Manius answered.

Labienus turned to one of the soldiers with him, a *muli* dressed in only a red tunic with a *tabula* tucked under his arm, one of his *scribae*, headquarters clerks. "Quickly, Quinte! Run back and get Spina . . . Tell him we need him and as many of his *capsularii* as he can spare . . . Stretchers and wound kits . . . up here QC! *Quam Celerrime*! ASAP!"

The man handed his *tabula* to one of his mates and ran back through the gate.

"How many dead, *Decurio*?" Labienus continued.

"Seven Romans confirmed dead, nine Romans missing and presumed dead, not counting Troucillus and Metius, and five Sequani," Manius reported.

Labienus sucked air through his teeth, "Twenty-three out of only two *turmae*! Did you recover the bodies?"

"We have all the Sequani, but we could not reach nine of our *contubernales*... Their *lemures* await our return to the place of their final battle," Manius said.

"They will not have to wait long, *Decurio*," Labienus said, reaching out and gripping Manius's shoulder. "Please, lay our comrades outside the ditch, as is with custom. We will collect what we need for the pyre and honor them at sundown."

Then, Labienus noticed Athauhnu, "Adonus *Dux*! I assume you will honor your dead according to your customs."

Surprisingly, Athauhnu shook his head. "They died as Romans. Let them accompany their comrades in smoke to the blessed place."

Labienus nodded.

Then, Spina burst through the gate. "Tribune! What's goin' on heah? I hoid ahr patrol got back . . . Dare's wounded . . . My boys are on dare way."

"Uh. . . *bene* . . . *Medice*," Labienus started, translating Spina's Aventine-Hill gibberish into coherent Latin. "Please . . . see to the tribune."

Spina looked around, "What tribune? I dohn see no tribune."

One of Manius' boys finally led Publicola's horse up to the front of the column. Spina and the trooper untied Publicola and eased him down to the ground. I thought for a heartbeat that Publicola had already crossed the river. His face was pasty white and his body was as limp as a child's stuffed doll. There was a trail of blood from the side of his mouth down to his chin. Then, I saw he was still breathing.

Spina looked at the binding under Publicola's right arm and the bright-red blood down his chin. "A lung wound . . . Dair's nuttin' I can do fer 'im here . . . I gotta take 'im back to da shop."

Spina's medics had finally appeared. He grabbed two and a stretcher. They eased Publicola onto the stretcher and tied him down.

"Get 'im back to da shop, *stat*'," Spina instructed his boys.

"*Cornices pascet*," Athauhnu muttered aloud as they lifted the stretcher. "He'll be feeding the crows."

One of the *capsularii* shot Athauhnu a dirty look, either because of the comment itself or because it came from a Gaul. I was continually impressed with

Athauhnu's growing mastery of Latin idioms and military slang; I would have to talk to him about his timing, however.

Labienus was speaking to Manius: "Get your men settled in, *Decurio*. I will take your formal report during the first watch tonight."

Then to me, "Insubrece *Decurio*, come with me to the *principia* . . . We have things to discuss . . . Adone *Dux* . . . you will come too, please."

Labienus turned and walked back toward the gate.

I spotted the Sequani *medduhg* and handed Clamriu over to him. "Please take care of her, *vuh frind*," I said to him in Gah'el.

The man nodded. "I'll have this old girl prancin' like a pony in no time, *a Pen*," he reassured me. To further reassure me, Clamriu nuzzled the man's neck despite her pain.

As the *medduhg* led Clamriu away, I felt a heavy hand on my shoulder. I turned to see the Hammer scrutinizing me with a humorless grin, "Looks like you earned your *sestertii* today, *Decurio!*"

Then, he turned and marched back into the *castrum*.

Coming from a *centurio primus pilus* that was high praise. High praise, indeed.

I only wished I had earned it.

Labienus had erected a small tent in the center of the *castrum* to serve as his *principia*. As we walked through the camp, it was obvious that it was not manned by a full legion, although the dimensions of the camp being built would eventually accommodate one.

Labienus was explaining as we walked, "We're a *vexillatio* of the Tenth . . . We experienced some delays on the march, so Caesar put two cohorts from the *acies prima*, the first battle line, on horses, the First and the Second, and sent them ahead to secure the Gate . . . Put me in command with Malleus as my number one . . . You should have seen those *muli* clinging to their saddle horns while trying to hold on to their infantry shields and *pila* . . . Would have been hilarious if we weren't so worried about Ariovistus getting to Vesantio before us . . . Those boys were so glad to get off those horses that they didn't bitch about having to dig an entire legionary *castrum* with only two cohorts . . . Even the First Cohort boys, who are immune from digging, were happy to be firmly planted back on mother earth and playing in the dirt . . . The boys took it in good humor, though . . . After the role the Tenth Legion played in resolving some problems we had on the march, they boasted that, not only did Caesar appoint them his *singulares*, his chosen ones, but he also assigned them to the cavalry."

"Problems on the march," I repeated. "Are you referring to the mutiny, Legate?"

"Mutiny?" Labienus echoed. "So, you heard about that, eh? There was no mutiny . . . Just another one of Caesar's schemes . . . I thought it had worked out pretty well, but by the looks of you, it may have backfired a bit."

When we arrived at his headquarters tent, Labienus invited Athauhnu and me to drop our *loricae* and relax. We helped each other out of our armor and found some camp chairs to drop onto. One of the clerks brought in a pitcher of *posca* and some clay cups. I took a long swig and almost choked on it as it burned its way down my throat. It was indisputably the vinegar of the Roman army.

I briefed Labienus on our mission: the murder of the Aeduan trooper by Bulla, the hearing before Troucillus's *barnuchel*, our conversations with the *cadeuhrn* in Vesantio, Bulla's attempt on my life, Publicola's insistence on obeying his orders to the letter and confronting Ariovistus, and the fight at the Hill of Flocks.

"So, you have no idea where this Bulla has gotten to?" Labienus asked when I was done.

I shook my head. "He wasn't with us when we passed through the Gate. He may be lying low in Vesantio . . . or he may have drowned in the Dubis. . . But I don't think so."

"A Roman *sicarius* this far north," Labienus said absently. "Strange . . . very strange. Why do you think he attacked you, Gai?"

"I don't know," I shrugged. "Maybe he thought I showed him up when he attacked one of Manius' troopers . . . He did say someone called *La Matrona* wanted me dead."

"*La Matrona,*" Labienus repeated. "*Quam insolite* . . . quite bizarre . . . a woman, obviously . . . Did you jilt one of your many girlfriends, Gai?" Labienus asked jokingly.

I had no energy left to remind Labienus about Gabi, her crazed brother, and the network of vengeance and deceit that seemed to reach all the way to the consul and Pompeius himself. So, I just grinned at Labienus' ribbing and shook my head.

"Well, we have bigger issues to deal with than a missing Roman thug and a mysterious *femme fatale*," Labienus stated. "Let me catch you up on Caesar and the army."

"As we marched east, Caesar realized the men weren't completely behind his plan to move against Ariovistus, so he decided to kill two birds with one arrow . . . get the men with the program and purge the army of cowards and politically untrustworthy elements. We were in camp, two-day's march east of Bibracte, when Caesar sent his own agents, mostly junior legionary-grade officers, to spread rumors among the *muli* about the *Suebii* . . . how huge they were . . . how they ate their captives . . . how just looking at a one of them would freeze a man like the Medusa . . . Caesar's idea was to flush out any agents who were working for his rivals back in Rome or who were just not up to the job.

"It worked like a charm . . . The very next day, the men refused to march . . . Some of the narrow-stripers wouldn't even leave their tents out of fear . . . By midday, Caesar had a comprehensive list of the unreliables, either because they were in the pay of his political enemies and were magnifying the rumors that Caesar's agents started or because the very thought of a Kraut made them soil their loincloths.

"Then, Caesar produced a bit of theater . . . During the ninth hour, he summoned his legates, his tribunes, and his first-line centurions to a meeting between the camps . . . This, of course, drew in a huge crowd of *muli* . . . Caesar read them the riot act . . . He told them they had no business calling themselves Roman soldiers because Romans never give in to fear and refuse to obey their orders . . . He told them that Ariovistus was nothing more than a pumped up swamp-rat leading a rabble of disorganized savages . . . All the legions had to do was show up, and the *Grunni* would be climbing over each other to swim back across the Rhenus . . . He declared that the Roman cause was just . . . Ariovistus had attacked Rome through her allies . . . He had stolen land, cattle, and slaves that were under the protection of Rome . . . If the legions didn't act, they shamed themselves . . . They shamed Rome!

"Then Caesar pulled off his master stroke . . . As arranged, Malleus and all his senior centurions from the Tenth Legion fell to their kness, seeming to weep . . . Can you imagine Malleus weeping? If I hadn't seen it with my own eyes, I would have said it couldn't happen! They implored Caesar to forgive them . . . They swore that they would wipe away their shame like the tears they were shedding . . . They would march east that very moment, even if they had to face the *Grunni* alone . . . it was better to die in glory than to live in shame . . . They begged only that Caesar would lead them.

"Caesar descended from his platform . . . Right on cue, one of his praetorians brought him his white stallion and red general's cloak . . . He mounted and rode over to where Malleus and his boys were kneeling . . . He took the Tenth Legion's standard and raised it up . . . He told Malleus and his officers to rise, to stand like Romans, and follow him . . . Caesar declared that the Tenth Legion was now his own legion . . . his strong right arm . . . He would be proud to lead them on an assault against Hades itself!

"Caesar turned his horse east, but before he could ride, the rest of the assembled officers surrounded him . . . They took hold of his reins . . . They begged him not to leave them behind in shame . . . begged that he take them with him to the Rhenus.

"Caesar pretended to soften . . . He welcomed them back into the fold . . . He told them they would march east at dawn . . . an unstoppable Roman juggernaut to push the Krauts back over the Rhenus.

"Meanwhile, Caecina and a detail of praetorians were working through Caesar's list of unreliables . . . Some snot-nosed military tribunes were sent packing back to Rome . . . The legionary-grade officers were given a choice . . . either swear personal allegiance to Caesar himself or be cashiered right then and there in the middle of *Gallia Comata*, without pension or burial funds . . . Most saw the writing on the wall and swore the oath.

"Now that Caesar had purged his army of its disloyal elements, the legions were eager to march with him against the *Suebii* . . . It was a master stroke . . . They believed that destroying the Krauts would wipe out their shame . . . but it did cost us a couple-of-day's march . . . We thought we could make the time up, but once we got across the Arar, the terrain was abysmal . . . lousy roads, narrow valleys, marshes . . . But you already know that . . . So, Caesar sent me and Malleus ahead to cancel your mission and to block the Gate against Ariovistus . . . I expect the rest of the army up here late tomorrow . . . the day after, at the latest."

I nodded my head. So, our army was coming. But, it was too late for Troucillus and the Roman troopers who died on the Hill of Flocks because of *my* incompetence.

I stood up before Labienus and assumed the position of attention.

"Legate!" I stated. "Gaius Marius Insubrecus, *Decurio*, has a request!"

Labienus sat up straight, blinked twice at me, and then responded, "*Quid voles tu, Gai? What do you want?"

"Legate!" I continued. "The *decurio requests* that he be relieved of his commission and returned to the ranks!"

Labienus was taken aback by my request. Even Athauhnu sat there with his mouth hanging open. "Why would you ask me to do such a thing?" Labienus asked.

I told Labienus of my failings: how I failed to detect the infiltration of the German infantry; how I failed to warn Publicola in time; how I failed to attack the Hill of Flocks when I had the chance. By the time I was done, I was no longer rendering a battle report like a Roman officer. I was near to joining Malleus in tears and begging for forgiveness.

When I ended my tirade, Labienus stared at me for a few heartbeats. Then, he looked down at the ground. When he lifted his head again, he was grinning. "At times, I forget how young you still are, Gai . . . What . . . seventeen now?" he asked.

"Sir!" I began to protest.

Labienus held up his hand to stop me. "Let me finish what I have to say to you, Gai."

Labienus paused again for a few heartbeats to get his thoughts together. "First, your commission comes directly from Caesar himself. It is not within my authority to relieve you. If Caesar wishes to do so, he will. But, until he does, you will continue to serve this command in the role Caesar has assigned you."

Labienus continued, "If anyone has to shoulder blame for the Hill of Flocks, it's Publicola. He was the commander in the field. It was his decision to procede against Ariovistus without support . . . Certainly, he was . . . uh . . . is a *brave* officer, but rigid . . . inflexible . . . and that can be a deadly combination in a commander. He models himself after the noble Roman heroes of myth . . . Mucius Scaevola plunging his hand into the fire . . . Publius Horatius Cocles defending the *Pons Sublicius* against overwhelming odds . . . the sort of nonsense children read in their history books . . . school-boy *Romanitas* . . . When he heard the rumors of mutiny, he should have waited until he received further instructions from Caesar, instead of confronting Ariovistus without an army to back up his bravado . . . But I believe that Publicola has paid the price for his mistakes . . . Unfortunately, he took too many brave Romans with him."

"Did you make mistakes?" Labienus mused. "I imagine you did. But, you're only seventeen! You're on your first campaign! The only man who does not make mistakes is the man who does nothing! The gods have granted us awareness of our errors for good reason . . . to teach us! Learn from yours! The only thing I ask of you or any officer is not to repeat his mistakes. Learn from them! Become a better leader!"

"Finally," Labienus continued, "that you have regrets about the men who died on the Hill of Flocks and your possible role in it is a good thing . . . a good thing *after* the battle is over. If you stay with the army, you will have to make decisions that will send men to their deaths . . . You should never make those decisions lightly . . . A good leader is one who always balances the lives of his men with the needs of the mission . . . After the battle, you should feel elation for your own survival . . . If you win, celebrate your victory . . . but you should also mourn its cost."

"My advice to you, young Insubrecus," Labienus concluded, "is just leave it alone. Get some food in your belly and get some rest. If Caesar needs to follow up with you on this, he will. If I were you, I wouldn't confront him with this issue . . . He has enough on his plate at the moment. Perhaps, in a couple of days, the gods will offer you the chance to revenge your loss. It won't bring your friend back, but it's the only satisfaction the gods allow."

I just nodded.

Labienus was right, of course.

When I look back at this episode through the lens of almost two decades of war, I am amazed at how naïve I was—and strangely, how much I now wish for just a whiff of that innocence.

I was, of course, wallowing in self pity.

I thought I had lost a friend. Since that day, I have lost so many mates, men as close to me as brothers, that if I allowed myself to dwell on it, I'd go as mad as a Greek priestess. I lock these memories up in a place deep within the darkest recesses of my *anima*. Occasionally, one escapes; a face unexpectedly appears before me. It confronts me. If I'm alone, I may even weep a bit. But, I immediately wipe my tears and slam the door on the memory. I must get on with the life *Domina Fortuna* has granted me.

Like a child, I poured out my sins, *me' culpae*, to Labienus, my *confessio*. I was disappointed in myself because I wasn't perfect. I needed absolution, forgiveness. Labienus gave it to me.

Early in my career, the gods granted me the blessings of good mentors: Caesar, certainly, Troucillus, Macro, but especially Labienus. Their advice and their example helped me when I had to deal with great challenges and lesser men, men who only thought of *themselves* as remarkable: Pompeius Magnus, Marcus Cicero, Sextus Pompeius, Brutus, Cassius, Antonius, and even our current "first citizen," Octavius *Augustus*.

To this day, I miss Labienus and regret the circumstances of his death.

When Caesar finally broke with Pompeius and the *Optimates* who dominated the senate against him, Labienus broke with Caesar. It wasn't personal. Despite his advice to me that day, there was a bit of Scaevola and Horatius left in Labienus' sense of *Romanitas*. When Caesar defied the senate and defied ancient tradition, marching his army south of the *Rubico* into *Italia* itself, Labienus rallied to the cause of *his* Rome.

Labienus fought for Pompeius in the First Civil War, and after Pompeius was murdered in Aegyptus, for Pompeius's sons. Despite that, I believe Caesar would have gladly pardoned him, as he did Lucius Vipsanius Agrippa and many others. But, that was not what the gods decreed.

Labienus fell at Munda, the last battle of the First Civil War. Munda was a blood bath. It was said that you could walk across the entire battlefield on the bodies of the slain. I believe that.

On that day, I was Caesar's *centurio ad manum,* commanding his praetorian bodyguard on the right flank of the army. Caesar's Tenth Legion, his strong right arm, was pressed hard and was beginning to bend back under the enemy pressure. To rally his men, Caesar picked up a shield and joined the battle line. I went in with him, as his *geminus*, his battle-partner, and guarded his open side. We fought the enemy, shield-to-shield as *muli,* until the enemy finally collapsed. We pursued them beyond their camps all the way to the walls of Munda itself.

Later, in Caesar's tent, we were given the day's butcher's bill. We had lost about seven thousand, the equivalent of almost two legions. The Pompeians had lost over thirty thousand, and we had captured all thirteen of their eagles. Both Sextus and Gnaeus Pompeius were on the run. The wars were over, finally over.

Despite his great victory, Caesar was despondent. He never relished killing Romans; he had just killed thousands and disgraced thirteen Roman legions. Then, someone broke the news to him: Labienus' body had been discovered near the enemy camps. He had tried to rally his cavalry against Caesar's decisive flank attack and was overrun.

Caesar's face went deathly pale. Despite all the carnage, this one death robbed him of any sense of relief that his long struggle against the Pompeians was finally over. This one death seemed to tip the scales against Caesar.

That day, Caesar's soul was wounded. Even the Macedonian, who had trailed after him to Rome with the boy she claimed was his son, asked me about it. She could sense Caesar's pain, as only a woman and a lover could. Something in him had died. I can almost imagine that a year later when Brutus plunged his *pugio* into Caesar's breast in the theater of Pompeius, Caesar felt relieved that his dark labors were finally over.

Caesar was never much of a drinker, but that night after Munda he drank heavily. I finally had Spina, who was then Caesar's personal physician, slip a few drops of *liquor papaveris*, the juice distilled from eastern poppies, used to ease the wounded or to send them mericifully to the boatman, into Caesar's cup to prevent him from having one of his spells.

Before he slipped off to sleep that night, Caesar said something to me: "If there were never a Caesar, there still would have been a Labienus. If there were never a Labienus, never would there have been a Caesar."

After leaving Labienus, Athauhnu and I found where our boys had set up for the night. They had scored some food from the *muli*: *buccellata*, jerky, and *posca*. The *buccellata* was so hard that even legionary *posca* couldn't soften it. I ate it anyway; I was starved.

I then searched out the *mudduhg* to ask after Clamriu. He said that the Kraut arrow hadn't gone deep; the head came right out. The wound looked clean, and she should be fit in a couple of weeks.

I then went to check on our wounded. I found Spina's "shop" right where the medics always set up in camp, just down toward the *porta decumena* from the *principia*. There were still lamps burning as I approached.

My mind was on Publicola.

I found Spina sitting at a table, his head in his hands over a half-filled wine cup. He lifted his head and saw me looking at his pitcher. "Wine's a medical necessity," he announced. "It goes everywhere wid me . . . You come to check on ya tribune?"

I nodded.

"Well, da good news is he's still wid us," he shrugged. "De'udder news is I don't know fer how long . . . Come on back."

Spina got up and led me back to a *cubiculum* in the rear of the tent. There I saw Publicola lying on a cot. He was asleep, and if anything, his color looked better. He also seemed to be breathing more easily.

"Dat speah or stick dose *Grunni* stuck 'im wid opened up his lung cavity," Spina was saying. "Da lungs woik like a bellows . . . Open up da cavity and de'air and da blood collapse 'em . . . Ya can't breathe . . . Gotta clear out da cavity and seal up da hole . . . I used a nice, thick piece a parchment to seal him up wid an' tied it down tight . . . Looks like it's woikin' . . . So far dat is."

I was about to ask Spina how he "cleared out dah cavity," when on the ground next to Publicola's cot I noticed a piece of brass tubing and a bowl that looked like it was filled with blood and pus.

Spina saw me look. Then, he said, "*Cac't*! Can't get good help dese days . . . Mawkay! Get yer sorry ass in 'ere and clean dis mess up!"

Wiping his eyes, Marcus, one of Spina's *capsularii*, stumbled in and collected the bowl. "Sorry, Boss . . . must a dozed off."

"I'll doze ya off, *ingnave*! Ya lazy bum!" Spina chided him. "I'll have ya cleanin' out latrines till ya start likin' da smell a shit!"

"Seen a lot a dis when I woiked in the *ludus*, dah gladiatorial school, back dair in Rome," Spina continued, nodding toward Publicola. "Dem gladiators'd take one in da chest . . . My master'd try to patch 'em up best he could . . . Ya gotta close da hole up before too many *daimones* get in and poison da blood. . . Your Sequani horse doctah did a pretty good job on dat . . . but if too many blood tubes're cut, dere's nothin' to be done . . . Da lungs'll just fill up again . . . We'll see about dis one . . . If he's still around in da morning, he's got a chance."

I nodded. I took Spina's wine cup out of his hand, drained it, and handed it back to him. "Thanks, Doc. That'll help me sleep."

The next morning, I got two surprises. The first was that Publicola was "still around." The other was that Caesar had arrived during the fourth watch of the night at the head of a flying column.

As the eastern skies were beginning to pale, I was summoned to the *principia* and found Caesar, Labienus, and Caecina already there. Caesar looked up as I entered the tent, "Ah! Insubrece! You have a bit of catching up to do on my daily journals. Much has been happening, and it has been happening quickly."

I was trying to process that piece of unexpected and seemingly irrelevant information as Caesar continued, "Labienus has briefed me on your mission . . . You and Manius Rabirius are to be commended . . . Not many officers have been cut off by a superior force in enemy territory and lived to tell about it . . . *bene gestum!*"

Bene gestum, I thought. *A thing well done. That's it in Caesar's mind. Bene gestum to the past; now let's get on with what we have to do next.*

Caesar was speaking: "Ariovistus has committed a strategic error by not getting to Vesantio ahead of us . . . Agrippa is back there now, establishing our logistics . . . We can bring our supplies right up the Dubis by boat . . . The Sequani in Lugdunum and the Aedui along the river were more than happy to swap their river barges for Roman silver . . . Once our supplies arrive at the docks in Vesantio, Agrippa's *frumentarii* can haul them on wagons up through the Gate and into the Rhenus valley . . . So, we have Ariovistus right where we want him . . . his back's to the Rhenus, and we're sitting in the Gate . . . Let's finish this thing before the leaves fall and it gets too cold up here to be wandering around without trousers . . . eh?"

Labienus was nodding. Caesar continued, "First things first . . . I expect the army to arrive early this afternoon . . . We're not stopping here . . . We'll pick up the two first-line cohorts of the Tenth and drop off a third-line cohort of the Twelfth to finish up the work here and secure the Gate . . . Labienus . . . pick a reliable tribune to command here . . . an *angusticlavus* will do just fine . . . I want you up with me and the army."

Labienus was scribbling on a *tabula* as Caesar went on: "We have to fix the location of Ariovistus's mob . . . That's where you come in, Insubrece . . . I need you and the Sequani back in the saddle . . . Take an *ala* of riders under that *Dux Bellorum* fellow, the war-chief of Vesantio's man . . . What's his name . . . Daius?"

Close enough, I thought. *Dai.*

"Yes, *Patrone*," I said.

"*Bene*," Caesar said. "That should give you a full *turma*, about thirty men . . . enough for this job . . . Find out where Ariovistus is . . . Shouldn't be hard . . . They'll be straight up the valley, sitting right out in the open with their wagons . . . You should be able to see the smoke of their fires from five thousand *passus* away . . . Rejoin the army before dark at this Hill of Flocks . . . That's the goal of today's march . . . We'll stop there . . . honor our dead . . . It will be good to stir the men up, seeing what those *cunni* did to their *contubernales* . . . Then they'll go after those *Grunni* with blood in their eyes . . . Which reminds me . . . Gai, Cerialis is in camp . . . Take him out with you . . . He's to locate potential battle sites . . .Five legions in *acies triplex* . . . just about two-thirds strength . . . No more than four cohorts of each legion on the front line . . . good flank security . . . Our backs to the east for a morning fight; our backs to the west in the afternoon . . . A good supply of fresh water . . . He knows the drill."

"*A'mperi'tu, Patrone,*" I agreed.

"*Bene . . . bene,*" Caesar nodded. "Get it done, Gai! *Miss'est!* You're dismissed . . . and don't forget . . . As soon as things settle down a bit, there's a pile of my journals on your desk to get through!"

By the sixth hour, we were tucked deep in the *Silvae Vosegi*, the forests of Vosegus, overlooking the valley of the Rhenus, well north of the Gate at *Caer Harth*.

We had an *ala* of Dai's horsemen with us, about twelve riders. Since they knew the terrain better and were riding lighter, I gave Dai the lead. He knew where to look for the *Suebii* and had ridden north to confirm that they were still there.

I had established our rally point on a ridgeline about twelve thousand *passus* beyond the Hill of Flocks. Cerialis was out and about with Athauhnu, using Guithiru's *ala* to survey the terrain for potential battlefields. Ci and I were keeping watch from a ridgeline near the edge of the forest.

Earlier, when we passed west of the Hill of Flocks, I was hard-pressed not to ride over into the valley and look for Troucillus' body. I knew at this point I could do nothing for him, but seeing his body would at least give me some closure. Perhaps I could quickly put him in a shallow grave to protect him from the crows and other carrion eaters. As we passed the trail that led up over the ridge into the valley of the Rhenus, I stopped and stared at it for a while. Athauhnu saw me and guessed what I was thinking.

"We go this way, *Arth*," he said, gesturing to the northeast with a nod. "Tonight, when we rejoin the Caisar, you can bid farewell to your friend."

I lingered there for a few more heartbeats, sighed, and nodded. Then, I followed our *fintai* up the trail leading north.

With Clamriu recouperating from her wound, I was riding the black German stallion, Beorn. So far, he was behaving, but I didn't trust him. In combat, he might still prove the traitor and deliver me to the enemy by somehow flinging me out of the saddle. All that morning, I imagined I could see a shifty look in his eyes. He was just waiting for an opportunity to do me in.

Below us, there was a small, wooded hill in the middle of the valley between our ridgeline and a small river flowing north. The hill created a bit of a blind spot. I didn't think it at all critical, but I was feeling restless waiting for Athauhnu and Dai to return. In truth, I didn't want to be idle, thinking about what had happened on the Hill of Flocks.

"Ci," I said, "I'm taking four men to check out that hill down there."

Ci looked down at the little hill and shrugged, "*Am ba resoum, a Pen? Why, Boss?*"

I just shrugged in answer, "It's there."

I gathered my four riders. I noticed that one of them was Arion mab Cadarn, the man who had been absolved of Rhuhderc's murder by Troucillus' *barnuchel*, Aderuhn mab Enit. Somehow this vague connection to Troucillus comforted me.

Even moving tactically, our ride to the hill took us less than an hour. We secured our horses under the shade of the trees on the western slope. I left a man to guard them, and we climbed to the top. From there, I had a better view of the small river and the valley beyond the hill, but as Ci intimated, it gained us nothing. The terrain was empty.

Regardless, the day was warm, the shade comforting, and I felt that I was doing something. So, I decided to settle in there for a bit. I must have dozed off because suddenly I felt Arion's hand shaking my shoulder. As I became fully awake, he pointed toward the river below us.

It took me a while to perceive what Arion was indicating, but soon I could see movement down along the river bank. Riders! *Suebii!* About a dozen. They were moving south, making good use of the terrain to cover themselves from the hills to the west.

They stopped almost directly below our position, about two hundred *passus* away. There was some conversation. Then, eight of them rode off towards the south. The remaining four stayed in position. I saw more conversation. Then, one pointed toward our hill. They turned and rode directly toward us.

Suddenly, I noticed something strange. One of the riders wore no armor. He was dressed only in a green Roman tunic. He had short hair and no beard. It was Metius!

They were probably riding over to get into the shade and wait for their companions. They would then be sitting right below us with no idea we were there. We had equal numbers and the advantage of surprise. All the better! I had a score to settle with that *Irrumptor*, Metius.

"Let them settle in," I hissed to my men. "Then, we'll jump them. I want the Roman alive."

Metius and the *Suebii* soon reached the bottom of the hill. Then, they did something I hadn't anticipated. Instead of just settling in to wait, they sent one rider up the hill, either to be sure it was clear or to keep a look out. I could hear him climbing the hill directly toward us. I made eye contact with a trooper. I put two fingers across my lips: *Silence!* I pointed down toward the German approaching us: *Him!* I then drew my thumb from ear to ear: *Kill!*

My man nodded and unsheathed his *glev*.

The Kraut broke into the open almost immediately to my right. He saw me, and his eyes widened; he froze. A hand snaked around his mouth from behind, pulled his chin up, and a flash of steel slid quickly across his throat. A gout of hot blood splashed onto my face and down my *lorica*. The hand kept the Kraut silent and upright until his body spasmed, accepting its death. Then, the hand lowered the body to the ground.

There was never a sound to warn his companions below us.

I wiped my face and chest with my *sudarium*. Again, I placed two fingers across my lips. I signaled my men to follow me in file down the hill. I followed the path the German had made climbing the hill.

Soon I could hear the sound of men talking below. They heard us descending, and a voice called out a word that sounded like "Fulfgar."

I drew my short sword. I ran down into the Germans. The one who had called out was facing me, his hands empty. Before he could react, I ran at him and plunged my *gladius* up under his ribs, twisted the grip, stepped back, and pulled out the blade with a sucking sound. The man's heart blood followed my sword blade, drenching my hand, forearm, and chest.

As the man went down, I jumped to the side and assumed a fighting position. But, there was no fight to be had. The other Kraut was down, and Metius was still standing, his face contorted in terror at the bloody, murderous apparitions that had suddenly leaped out of the forest.

"*No sliath me! Ich eam thas searwes man!*" he cried out, showing us his empty hands. Then, he seemed to recognize our armor. "Do not kill me! I'm a friend of Caesar!" he repeated in Latin.

"They don't understand Latin, you stinking *verpa*!" I answered him, lowering my sword point to his abdomen.

Metius blinked twice and finally recognized me through the blood. "Insubrece! *Gratias dis*! I have a message for Caesar! Take me to him!"

"Tell me your message, and I'll kill you quickly, *perfide*! Traitor!" I hissed. "Or, I'll take my time with you."

"Don't be a fool, Insubrece," Metius challenged. "I am Caesar's man!"

"As far as Caesar knows, you're already dead . . . killed on the Hill of Flocks with Troucillus and the Roman soldiers you betrayed to your Kraut master!" I accused.

Metius stared at me for a heartbeat. "Troucillus? Troucillus isn't dead! Ariovistus has him. That's what I need to talk to Caesar about!"

I didn't kill Metius. I couldn't. Not with Troucillus' life in the balance.

But, I didn't treat Metius with any gentleness. I had my boys truss him up like a side of beef from the cattle market. Then, when he wouldn't shut his bloody gob, I had them gag him for good measure.

We left the *Grunni* where they fell for their mates to find. Hopefully, they'd think Metius had something to do with it. One man's traitor is every man's traitor. I've heard Germans, despite being treacherous bastards themselves, like to take revenge for blood spilt through treachery.

We withdrew back to Ci's position on the ridge, taking the Germans' horses and whatever decent weapons we could salvage. We did all we could to cover our trail away from the hill.

We got back up on the ridge by about the eighth hour. Dai was still out, but Athauhnu had returned with Cerialis. When I kicked Metius off his horse, Athauhnu looked at him with surprise.

"Are we at war with the *Rhufeiniaid* now, *a Pen*?" he asked facetiously.

"We are with this one," I answered.

Ceriales would have no part of it. "He's a Roman citizen," Ceriales protested. "Only Caesar can legally restrain him." So, I released Metius. Not because I gave a dried turd for Ceriales' protestations; I just got tired listening to him bitch at me.

Dai returned during the ninth hour. In case only a few of us made it back to Caesar, we all shared his intelligence.

Dai's *fintai* had discovered Ariovistus' encampment about fifteen thousand *passus* to the north, just beyond two large mountains in the *Silvae Vosegi*, called *Tethi'Abnoba*, the "Teats of Abnoba," the consort of the forest god, Vosegos. The *Suebii* and their allies were camped at the confluence of the river that ran north toward the Rhenus—the *Afonolilis*, Dai called it, the "River of Lilies"—and some nameless stream that ran down from the western mountains.

The Germans weren't moving, but their camp seemed to be stirred up in preparation for their move toward the Gate. Dai couldn't guess their numbers, but they were there in the thousands.

"They have hundreds of wagons with their women and children, so they will not be able to move quickly," Dai explained.

I translated this for Cerialis, who asked, "On which bank of this . . . this *flumen liliorum*, this "river of lilies," will they march?" Cerialis asked.

When I asked Dai, he just shrugged and said, "Both . . . on the march they will need access to water for their people and animals."

"How far can they march in a day?" Cerialis asked.

"No faster than an ox can travel," Dai said. "No more than ten thousand *passus* a day, at most."

I turned to Metius, who was obviously eavesdropping on the conversation. "Do you have anything to add, *mentula*?" I asked.

"My message is for Caesar's ears only," he snorted.

I was about to slap him when I caught Cerialis' look.

We were back at the Hill of Flocks during the twelfth hour. Caesar's legions—all six of them—had built their camps around the hill. As was his preference, Caesar had established his headquarters with his Tenth Legion.

As Athauhnu, Dai, Ceriales, and I approached Caesar's *principia*, I saw Labienus briefing a gaggle of narrow-stripers. I had a fistful of Metius' tunic and was pushing him along. When Labienus was finished, I shoved Metius forward. "A gift for the *Imperator*," I announced. "The traitor, Metius!"

With a shocked look, Labienus caught Metius and steadied him. I assumed Labienus' shock was Metius' unexpected survival.

Erratum! I was wrong.

Labienus said, "Meti! *Laus dis!* Praise the gods! Caesar thought you were killed! Go straight through . . . Caesar will be delighted to see you!"

Metius turned toward me, shot me a look of arrogant triumph and entered Caesar's tent. I was about to say something, but Labienus silenced me with a look and a shake of the head.

I waited a few heartbeats, but could no longer restrain myself. "That *mentula* is a traitor!" I protested. "He led us into a trap."

Labienus held up his hand. He took me aside so the others wouldn't hear. "That may be, Gai, but he's *our* traitor!"

"*Quid? Quid dicis tu?*" I stammered. "What are you saying?"

"You're correct, Gai. Metius is on Pompeius's payroll to spy on Caesar," Labienus explained. "But, Metius went to Caesar and offered his services to him also. Now Metius tells Pompeius only what Caesar wants him and his enemies down in Rome to know. And, Pompeius trusts Metius. Why? Because the more you pay for something, the higher you estime its value, and Pompeius pays Metius well . . . very well indeed."

I wasn't willng to let go. "But, that *cunnus* is selling us out to the Krauts."

Again, Labienus held up his hand. "I'm sure Metius is working a few deals of his own with Ariovistus . . . Duuhruhda of the Aedui thinks Metius is in his *marsupium*, too . . . For all I know, Metius was selling information to the Helvetii . . . Metius has almost as many connections up here as that Greek friend of yours, Grennadios . . . In fact, Pompeius' agents among the *Suebii* use Metius to convey their information south, which, of course, Metius delivers to Caesar . . . Caesar doesn't begrudge Metius a few business deals on the side, as long as it doesn't interfere with Caesar's business . . . That's how these things are done . . . When Metius is no longer of any use to Caesar," Labienus shrugged, "let's just say, I'll be telling a different tale."

I was stunned. But, I had learned another useful lesson in *Romanitas*. A well-placed double-agent was worth more to a Roman commander than the lives of a score of his troopers.

Just at that point, Ebrius stuck his head out of the tent flap. "The boss'll see you now," he announced.

When we entered Caesar's *cubiculum*, he was looking at his campaign map. Metius was sitting off to the side with a look of smug satisfaction equal only to an Egyptian's pet cat after a good brushing.

Caesar turned as we entered, "*Bene*! Where is Ariovistus? Is he moving?"

I quickly explained to Dai how to read a Roman map. He walked up to it, examined it for a moment, and then pointed to a spot north of our current position. "*Uhno! Mae'r Almaenwuhr uhno*," he said. "There! The Germans are there."

As Ebrius marked the German position on the map, Cerialis spoke up, "*Imperator*! May I point out some critical inaccuracies on your map?"

Caesar nodded, "Of course, Cerialis! That's why I sent you north."

Cerialis took a piece of blue chalk from a box on the floor and drew a line running from north to south between the Rhenus and the forests of Vosegus. "This is a river the natives call . . . uh . . . the *Ilia*."

I didn't correct Cerialis' error. Getting the name of some minor river in the boondocks of Gaul wasn't critical.

Cerialis continued, "This river essentially cuts our area of operation in half . . . It's fordable in a number of places, but in others too deep to cross without bridging . . . I've located a number of battle positions for us, mostly on the west bank of this river because the ridgelines and hills that extend from the mountains offer opportunities to anchor our flanks. . . The native scouts believe that the Germans will move along both sides of this river . . . That poses a problem for us in securing our flanks . . . If we establish a battleline anywhere on the west bank, the Germans on the east bank can easily move past us and get between us and the Gate."

Caesar nodded, then asked, "Cerialis, in your opinion, where would be the best place to offer battle to the Germans?"

Cerialis thought for a few heartbeats, then pointed to a spot on the map. "Right here, *Imperator*. There's a spur of forested highground on the west to secure our left, and the right can be secured on the river. There's a small stream flowing down from the west on which we can align our front . . . That would force the Germans to cross the stream and climb its bank to attack us . . . and the stream will supply us with fresh water . . . But the problem with our right flank remains . . . If I were commanding the Germans, I'd just move past our battle position, across the river along the east bank . . . Then, we would have to retreat to prevent them from getting across our supply lines."

"Or, even worse," Labienus added, "they could hold our battleline in place with a frontal assault on the west bank and envelop us from the right by moving down this east bank and crossing the river behind us."

Caesar stared at the map with his arms folded across his chest. Then, he nodded, "Well . . . let's hope Ariovistus is not as clever as you gentlemen are . . . I think his problem will be controlling his force once the battle begins . . . They may be numerous, but they are barbarians . . . They'll all rush to attack our front . . . If they do attempt a flanking movement, we'll be able to detect it in such open country . . . Occupying that battle position before Ariovistus reaches it is now our immediate objective . . . How long will it take the army to reach this position, Labiene?"

Labienus shrugged, "With a forced march, we could be up there by sundown tomorrow . . . With regular marches, by the sixth or seventh hour the next day."

"I prefer not to force march into a battle," Caesar said to Labienus. "I want the men fresh when we make contact . . . Have Caecina issue orders . . . The army leaves this position tomorrow during the first hour . . . Order of march: Tenth, Ninth, Twelfth, Seventh, Eleventh, the *impedimenta*, then the Eighth . . . Legates march with their legions . . . Place the auxiliaries—the archers, slingers, and light infantry—between the Twelfth and the Seventh . . . I will be with the Tenth . . . How are our auxiliaries acclimatizing since they came up from Massalia, Labiene?"

Labienus looked up from his *tabula* and shrugged, "As well as can be expected, Caesar. The slingers from the Balearics and the infantry from *Hispania* are doing fine . . . All these hills and forests are making the archers from Syria a bit nervous, but they'll get over it."

Caesar nodded, "They'd better . . . We're moving light and fast . . . Strip the *impedimenta* of anything unnecessary . . . Just carry rations and water for the troops . . . fodder . . . I want a full complement of artillery: *ballistae, scorpiones,* and bolts . . . nothing more . . . We'll stockpile our stores at *Castrum Bellum* in the Gate . . . If the Germans get around us, our first fallback position will be here, so we'll leave these fortifications intact . . . Our final fallback position before Vesantio will be *Castrum Bellum* in the Gate . . . Who does Agrippa have forward to work supply?"

"Uh. . . a second-line *centurio prior,* formerly with the Seventh," Labienus answered, "name of . . . uh . . . Opilio."

"Good man?" Caesar asked.

"Agrippa seems to have confidence in him," Labienus shrugged.

"That's good enough for me then," Caesar agreed. "We march the normal twenty thousand *passus* tommorrow. . . The *exploratores* report the terrain is fairly open and flat . . . should bring us about here by the seventh hour," he pointed to a position on the map. "Have the scouts and engineers up ahead to locate the camps . . . Any questions?"

"*N'abeo, Imperator!*" Labienus replied. "No, sir."

"*Bene!*" Caesar concluded. "Gentlemen, you are dismissed . . . Thank you for your efforts . . . Cerialis, you may return to your legion . . . Thank you for a job well done . . . Labiene and Insubrece, please remain."

XVI.

De Caesare et Ariovisto

CAESAR AND ARIOVISTUS

Qui nisi decedat atque exercitum deducat ex his regionibus sese illum
non pro amico sed pro hoste habiturum quod si eum interfecerit multis
sese nobilibus principibusque populi Romani gratum esse facturum
id se ab ipsis per eorum nuntios compertum habere quorum omnium
gratiam atque amicitiam eius morte redimere posset.

"Unless Caesar departed and removed his army from Ariovistus' lands,
[Ariovistus] would consider Caesar an enemy, not a friend. Besides, if
Ariovistus killed Caesar, many of the nobles and leading men of the Roman
nation would thank Ariovistus. Ariovistus knew this from their messengers,
who said Ariovistus could win their gratitude and friendship by Caesar's death."
(from Gaius Marius Insubrecus' notebook of Caesar's journal)

After the others left the tent, Metius made a point of giving me a
dismissive snort as he walked by. When we were alone, Caesar
said, "Gai . . . Metius is furious with you . . . Said you treated him
pretty rough out there . . . bound him up . . . Wants me to discipline you."

Before I could respond, Caesar clapped me on the shoulder and laughed, "I told him it was because he played his part so well . . . He should be flattered . . . He fooled you completely . . . I'll throw some silver his way to help him get over his affronted dignity . . . Ironic that a double-dealing spy like him has any dignity at all . . . but there you are . . . I have to keep him content for the time being."

Romanitas, I thought.

Caesar continued, "The good news is that Troucillus is still alive . . . We collected the remains of our people earlier . . . parts and pieces mostly . . . I thought Troucillus was among them . . . Nobody could tell . . . I had already begun composing a letter of condolence to his father . . . Gaius Valerius Caburus is a significant client of mine . . . His people, the Helvii, hold the bank of the Rhonus for Rome . . . They stand between the port of Massalia and the Aedui to the north and the Allobroges to the east . . . I'd hate to have to explain to him that I got his younger son killed . . . which brings me to Ariovistus' message."

Caesar stopped talking and located a pitcher among the *tabulae* on his work table. He poured a cup, then called out, "Ebrius! How's the wine?"

"First rate, Boss," Ebrius' voice sounded from beyond the *cubiculum*.

Caesar sniffed the contents of the cup anyway, then handed it to Labienus. He poured another, handed it to me, and then poured a cup for himself.

"*Sedeamus*," he invited. "Let's sit."

Caesar leaned back into the camp chair, his legs extended straight out. He took a sip of his wine and seemed to sigh.

"It's been a long day . . . Where were we . . . oh, yes . . . Ariovistus . . . He's trying to use Troucillus to leverage me . . . He wants to meet with me to discuss what he calls 'our options' . . . He picked a spot, a hill about twenty-five thousand *passus* up the valley between our armies . . . Said we both should bring no more than a hundred men . . . cavalry, no infantry . . . Meanwhile, both our armies will remain in camp."

"He's just trying to delay us," Labienus dismissed the offer.

Remembering the Hill of Flocks, I added, "Or it's a trap."

Caesar sighed and fell silent for a few heartbeats. "Yes . . . maybe . . . but it won't work. My orders for our move north are being issued . . . As far as an ambush, I have no intention of putting myself at the mercy of this demented

Grunnus who thinks the gods speak directly to him. I'm mounting a cohort of legionaries from my Tenth as my 'cavalry' escort . . . They got enough practice on the way up here that they should be able to pass for cavalry . . . *Roman* cavalry, anyway."

Caesar took another sip of his wine, sighed, and rubbed his forehead between his thumb and middle finger.

"Should I send for Spina?" Labienus offered.

"Spina?" Caesar responded. "Uhh . . . no . . . no, thank you, Tite . . . I'm just a bit tired, that's all . . . Gai . . . explain to me again how Ariovistus pulled off his ambush at the Hill of Flocks."

Again, I told Caesar how Ariovistus infiltrated infantry through the forests north of the hill and how his cavalry supported the movement of his infantry.

When I was done, Caesar nodded and said, "I don't doubt he'll try the same trick again . . . Also, I don't doubt that his masters down in Rome would not be offended were he to kill me . . . According to Metius, that's exactly what they're hoping for . . . Unfortunately, for him and for them, I have no intention of cooperating."

Then, Caesar chuckled, "I doubt Ariovistus realizes that were he to do what the *Optimates* in the senate are paying him for, Pompeius would be placed in command of this army . . . Ariovistus would be hoisted up on a cross before he had the chance to spend a brass *ass* of his blood money."

The next day by the first hour we were riding north. Caesar had mounted up the Second Century, First Cohort of the Tenth. Despite what he had said, as I looked at them riding behind me, they didn't even look like *Roman* cavalry; they looked like sixty-seven Roman *muli* who strongly preferred not to be strapped to the backs of horses.

They were commanded by a first line *centurio prior*, Volesus Salvius Durianus, known among the *muli* as *Durus*, the "Hard Case." Durus was considered Malleus' "number one," to take command of the First Cohort and of the legion when the Hammer either stepped down or was put down in battle.

At the beginning of the fourth watch, the Hammer had left camp in command of a *vexillatio* of Spanish light infantry and the *fintai* of Dai mab Gluhn's cavalry. Their mission was to get in behind the hill where we were to meet Ariovistus and prevent him from pulling off any nasty surprises, while Caesar explained the facts of life to him.

Caesar led our expedition, white stallion and red cloak to ensure that Ariovistus and every *Grunnus* within a thousand *passus* knew it was he. He took his *legatus equitum*, his cavalry commander, Publius Licinius Crassus with him, to "give the boy some seasoning," as he put it.

I was riding with Athauhnu's *fintai*. We had Guithiru on the point and Ci's *ala* on the flanks and rear. Athauhnu rode ahead with Guithiru, but Caesar insisted I remain with him in the main body. So, for that ride to our meeting with Ariovistus, my only entertainment was watching the legionary *muli* try to stay on the right side of their horses.

We arrived at our destination during the fifth hour. Caesar halted a good two-hundred *passus* south of the hill. Durus dismounted his boys and established a doubled battleline, each *contubernium* manning two positions along the front rank, giving it a twenty-man front. Athauhnu placed Guithiru on the right flank, Ci on the left, while Durus' *optio* and *tesserarius* straightened out the ranks of the *muli*. Finally, after a bit of pushing, shoving, and not a few slaps to the backs of helmets–very much to the amusement of my Sequani— Durus got the nod from his *optio*, after which he and the *tesserarius* took their positions to the rear of the formation.

Durus and his *signifer* marched to the center-front of the battleline. Durus bellowed out, "*Centuria . . . Stat'*!" The *muli* stiffened, shields front and grounded, *pila* tucked into the right shoulder.

Then, Durus faced Caesar, "*Imperator*! *Centuria dua, Cohortis Unae, Legionis Decem parat'est*! General! Second Century, First Cohort, Tenth Legion is ready!"

Caesar nodded, "*Laxat*! At ease!"

The *muli* unstiffened slightly. Then, Caesar directed, "Dure! Have your men stand-down in place . . . They can drop their helmets and ground their equipment . . . Water and rations."

"*A'mperi'tu, Imperator*," Durus responded, "Yes, sir!"

Then, Caesar called over to Athauhnu, "*Adone Dux*!"

"*Ti'adsum, Imperator*!" Athauhnu responded as if he been under the eagles his entire life, "Yes, sir!"

"Place one *ala* forward to screen for our visitors, the other to screen the flanks and rear of this position," Caesar directed. "Then, please join me here!"

"*A'mperi'tu, Imperator!*"

As Athauhnu coordinated his *alae*, Caesar jumped down from his horse and pulled off his helmet. Crassus and I did likewise. Caesar ran his hand through his sweat-matted hair, which exposed his rapidly receding hairline.

"*Landica Veneris!* That breeze feels good," Caesar muttered. Then, "*Dure! Ad me venias!* Durus! Please, come over here!"

Durus double timed over to us. "*Ti'adsum, Imperator!*" he bellowed, standing as stiff as a spear.

"*Laxa!*" Caesar cautioned. "Relax, Dure! Save your strength. You may need it. Ah . . . here's Adonus *Dux*."

Athauhnu returned from stationing his riders and dismounted with us. Caesar began, "*Bene* . . . we're all here . . . This next part may be tricky . . . Obviously, Ariovistus has nothing to say to me . . . so why the meeting? My guess is he wants to take a shot at me . . . He may try the same trick he used to snatch up Troucillus . . . If he does, we're going to surprise him . . . Malleus is in postion with the Spani to the north . . . If he engages, he will signal . . . If that happens, we go after Ariovistus . . . Take him down; he's of no value to us as a prisoner . . . If we kill Ariovistus, we probably kill Troucillus . . . I'd like to avoid that, but without Ariovistus, this whole German confederacy falls apart . . . So it's an acceptable trade."

"*Acceptable trade?*" I was stunned. "*Ariovistus for Troucillus?!*" Another lesson in *Romanitas*.

"The code word is *alea*, dice," Caesar continued. "If I yell that, I want every *pilum* we have thrown at Ariovistus . . . Then, go in with the sword . . . If I'm down, Crasse, you give the order . . . If Crassus is down, Durus . . . If we're all down . . . well, if that happens, just do what you have to do, Insubrecus . . . The primary target is Ariovistus. Adone *Dux*! You're mounted and have the best chance of escape . . . If this thing goes to Hades, get back to Labienus . . . Tell him to get here as fast as he can with all that he can . . . Any questions?"

Shaking of heads and negative grunts.

"*Bene!*" Caesar said. "Now we wait."

We didn't have long to wait. At mid-day, one of Guithiru's troopers galloped back to our position. "Riders! *Almaenwuhr*! About two miles out!" he told me.

"*Grunni*! Two thousand *passus* off," I translated for Caesar.

He nodded. "Have the cavalry withdraw slowly to this location. Slowly. Don't lose contact."

I relayed the order and the trooper galloped back to Guithiru.

Soon after the Sequani withdrew to us, we spotted the German scouts. They halted about two hundred *passus* to the east of the hill and waited. Soon, we saw the main body join them. Even at this distance, I could make out Ariovistus' white stallion and the heavily armed cavalry of the Aeduan renegade, Deluuhnu mab Clethguuhno.

"The gods smile on us today," I heard Athauhnu hiss in Gah'el. "They deliver *Aineduai* for us to kill."

The Krauts seemed to gather in some sort of conference. Then, a lone rider galloped in our direction.

"Who the kaisar?" he asked in a guttural Latin.

"That me," Caesar answered mockingly.

The man didn't get the joke. "King Ariovistus say meet the kaisar top hill ten man, no more; come now."

"The kaisar come now," Caesar agreed.

The man said something that sounded like "goot" and galloped back to his master.

As Caesar retied his helmet, he instructed, "Crasse! Insubrece! You're with me. Adone! Here with your riders! Be ready to make a dash up that hill if we're attacked. Dure! Detail one *contubernium* to accompany me. Put them back on the horses. They're supposed to be cavalry. You stay here with the rest of your *centuria*."

"*Imperator*!" Durus protested as Caesar remounted. "My duty is with you!"

"Your *duty*, *Centurio*, is to obey my orders!" Caesar admonished. "Detail your *optio* to command my *contubernium* if you wish, but you remain here with your men."

We waited while the *muli* remounted. It was difficult to tell which were the more reluctant, the men or the horses, but soon they were aboard, and we rode toward the hill. As we pulled away from our party, I could see ten German riders do the same. Ariovistus was in the lead.

We met at the top. Neither party dismounted.

Up close, Ariovistus looked more like a weasel than he did a mystic German warlord. He was still wearing his gray cloak and carrying a long wooden staff. I was surprised to see that one member of his party was the ancient hag I had also seen at the Hill of Flocks. Her hair was an unwashed Gordian knot of grays and black. Her eyebrows were thick and black; her complexion, an ashen, sallow yellow. She wore a shapeless sack of dirty gray linen. Her face was strangely unlined and beaded by piercing blue eyes, which, for some reason, were fixed directly on me.

Ariovistus was speaking in Latin. "Gaius Iulius Caesar! Descendant of the goddess Venus and Roman Proconsul of the Gauls and Illyricum! Welcome to my lands! And, this must be the legate, Publius Licinius Crassus, son of your partner and fellow *triumvir*. And, who might this be?" he asked, fixing his glare on me.

The old woman said something to Ariovistus in German. He nodded to her, and she urged her horse forward toward me.

"Don't be alarmed," Ariovistus cautioned me. "*Da elde moder* wants to make your acquaintance."

Da elde moder, I thought: *moder, mater,* mother?

The woman was next to me. My black stallion tried to shy away, but I steadied him. The woman sniffed me, then the horse. Then, she laughed and returned to Ariovistus.

"*De kild bit uuelle. Ac de hors bit estmere,*" she snickered.

Ariovistus nodded. "A Gallic boy . . . on a German horse . . . Then this must be Gaius Marius Insubrecus . . . Caesar's little scribbler and go-for . . . I believe we have met before . . . the Hill of Flocks?"

It was beginning to sound like Ariovistus' intelligence network was every bit as good as Caesar's. Then I remembered his network was also Caesar's. Metius!

"And the rest must be Roman legionaries pretending to be Roman cavalry," Ariovistus laughed. "Well-played, Caesar. . . well-played, indeed . . . I too have a bit of a surprise for you . . . These men who are accompanying me are not mere cavalry either . . . They are the *reges gentium*, kings of my allied tribes . . . Harudes, Marcomanni, Triboci, Vangiones, Nemetes, Sedusii, and, of course, my Suebi . . . All the major nations of western *Germania* here, under my command . . . They were curious . . . They had heard how tiny Romans are . . . They couldn't believe it . . . so I invited them here to see for themselves."

"*Laden uuara suua uuac lic suua ik cuuath?*" I heard Ariovistus snicker.

The warriors with him laughed and nodded, "*Ya . . . ya.*"

Suddenly, Ariovistus' face turned serious, "So, Caesar, now I must ask you . . . why are you here in my lands with an army? These lands are mine, Caesar . . . I have taken them from the Gauls by the strength of my armies, as you Romans have taken land elsewhere . . . I am here at the invitation of your own senate, which calls me 'friend and ally' . . . So again, Caesar, why are you here?"

Caesar was equally blunt, "Your usefulness to the Roman nation has passed, Arioviste! Despite that, I am willing to allow you to remain, but only after you have released Troucillus, as well as the Sequani and the Aedui you're holding hostage. But, the rest of these barbarian *spuma*, this scum that follows in your wake, must return to the German swamps they crawled out of."

One of Ariovistus' troopers was translating Caesar's words into the guttural gibberish his "kings" understood. They were obviously not liking Caesar's message. As the translator spoke, they actually began growling like hounds. Hands began dropping toward swords. Suddenly, our *muli* dropped from their horses, got their shields up, and planted their feet in a position I recognized. They were readying to launch their *pila*.

Caesar saw the movement also and hissed to the *optio* in command, "*Laxat*."

Ariovistus steadied his own men. "Don't be rash, Caesar . . . You don't want to die on this hill . . . You are facing German warriors . . . men who have never slept under a roof . . . men who live for battle . . . I have conquered these lands . . . I have conquered these people . . . I will do with them as I wish. Do I tell the Roman nation how to treat its conquered peoples? Then, how dare you presume to tell me how to treat mine? Don't be a fool. You are welcomed to do what you want in your part of Gaul . . . Do not dare tell me what I must do in mine."

I realized suddenly that with one well-placed volley of *pila*, Caesar could end this thing. *Ariovistus and all his chiefs are well within range!* I thought to myself. *Is Caesar thinking the same thing? Give the word, say 'alea,'* I thought.

Just then, I heard a Roman *cornu* sound from the north. Ariovistus heard it too. His face went deathly pale.

"Hear that, oh great conqueror?" Caesar mocked him. "That sound means that your ambush will not be sprung . . . Your invincible German warriors are dying under the swords of Roman soldiers."

Ariovistus knew the game was up! And, he was under the spears of a trained Roman *contubernium*. Suddenly, he turned his horse, bending low over its neck.

His men tried to follow, but Caesar yelled, "*Alea!*"

Seven Roman *pila* were immediately hurled at Ariovistus. I saw one split the chest of his translator and another bring Ariovistus' horse down. One of the Krauts pulled Ariovistus up on his horse. Our *muli* surged forward, shields up and *gladii* bared, but the *Grunni* quickly outdistanced them on their horses.

To the east, Ariovistus' *comitatus* saw the fight erupt on the hill. Deluuhnu's troop surged forward, hoping to trap us on the hill. Immediately, Athauhnu and Guithiru charged to intercept them. They were badly outnumbered, but their goal was only to break the momentum of the charge until we could safely withdraw.

I heard our *optio* give the order to reassemble and remount. The *muli* were picking up their *pila* as they jogged back toward their horses. One of the *muli* put his boot on the translator's chest and pulled out his *pilum*. The legionary quickly checked the shaft and nodded; the *Grunnus* twitched once and was still.

We were moving back toward our *centuria* when from below the hill I heard a crash as my Sequani struck the Aedui in the field behind us. In front of us, Durus was forming the men in an *orbis*, expecting a cavalry attack to his flanks and rear. In the distance, I could see Ci's *ala* rushing forward to our aid.

The *muli* opened their ranks so we could pass through to the center of their box formation. Our legionaries dismounted and Durus placed them into the line. Screaming their battle cries, Ci's *ala* thundered past to reinforce Athauhnu and Guithiru, who were engaged with the Aedui.

But, today wasn't a day for dying.

The Aedui covering Ariovistus' retreat withdrew. Athauhnu moved slowly back toward our position, meeting Ci about halfway. It appeared that all of Guithiru's riders were still in the saddle, though a couple seemed to be nursing wounds.

Caesar remained mounted on his horse, scanning the field of battle from the center of the *centuria*.

"*Optime gestum!*" I heard him say. "We missed that *cunnus*, Ariovistus, but that was damn well done!"

As we rode back to our army, I raised my concerns about Troucillus, after what had happened on the hill.

Caesar shook his head. "As long as Ariovistus thinks he can defeat my army, Troucillus is of value to him."

"*In quo modo, Patrone?*" I asked. "How?"

"Troucillus is a prince of the Helvii," Caesar explained. "His father holds the Rhodanus between *tres Galliae*, the three Gauls, and our *provincia*. Ariovistus believes he can trade Troucillus for a safe passage over the Rhodanus. Then, after he has conquered the lands of the Helvii, he has a tame prince to keep the Helvii in line."

"So, as long as Ariovistus thinks he can beat us, Troucillus is safe," I clarified.

Caesar nodded, "That's what Metius reports. But, as soon as we defeat that *mustela*, that little rat-catcher, Ariovistus, we need to act fast if we're going to get Troucillus out alive."

XVII.

De Proelio ad Silvas Vosagonis
THE BATTLE NEAR
THE FOREST OF VOSAGO

Ipse a dextro cornu quod eam partem minime firmam hostium esse
animadverterat proelium commisit ita nostri acriter in hostes signo dato
impetum fecerunt itaque hostes repente celeriterque procurrerunt ut spatium
pila in hostes coiciendi non daretur relictis pilis comminus gladiis pugnatum est

"After [Caesar] himself took command of the right flank because he
considered the enemy weakest on this point, he initiated the battle.
When the signal was given, our troops attacked fiercely. But at once, the
enemy counterattacked unexpectedly, so that the interval needed for our
men to launch their spears was closed. Our soldiers threw down their
spears and engaged the enemy hand-to-hand with their swords."

(from Gaius Marius Insubrecus' notebook of Caesar's journal)

Caesar never had any doubts that he would defeat Ariovistus in an
open battle.

I remembered Labienus explaining to me after Bibracte that barbarian
armies, regardless of how terrifying they seemed, could rarely defeat Romans

242

on open ground. Barbarians were successful only if they had overwhelming numbers or if they could lure the legions into a surprise ambush, in which they could not deploy into battle lines, or if the Roman commanders were complete incompetents.

None of these conditions applied to Caesar and his campaign against Ariovistus. But, Caesar seemed ever eager to tempt the fates.

The army reached the designated battle site during the seventh hour of the *Dies Martis*, the Day of Mars. Caesar immediately deployed his six legions in the *acies triplex*, the triple battle line. But, our *exploratores* reported that Ariovistus' horde, still a good two days away, was spread out over miles and moving slowly down both banks of the river the Romans now called the Ilia.

Caesar took advantage of the time Ariovistus was allowing him. He posted a strong cavalry screen to the north, up both banks of the Ilia, while he set his legions to building a string of *castra* about five hundred *passus* behind the putative battle site. When these were complete, he tasked the third line of the Twelfth Legion with bridging the Ilia about seven hundred *passus* upstream. The *muli* from the Twelfth also built a series of strong fortifications to protect the eastern approaches of the bridging point. If Ariovistus did attempt to flank the Roman battle line, Caesar now had a way of either preventing German crossing or quickly deploying troops to the east bank.

On the third day after Caesar's arrival, the *Grunni* began to arrive on the west bank of the Ilia. They created a strong stockade with their wagons about four hundred *passus* downstream from the Roman lines and did nothing. Labienus estimated they were waiting while their people straggled in and their troop strength built.

The Kraut mob moving up the east bank arrived a few hours later. Despite our fears, they also halted, established a separate wagon stockade, and did nothing.

Some of Caesar's officers urged him to attack immediately, before the German army assembled. Remembering the debacle when he attacked the Helvetian wagons at Bibracte, Caesar refused. He reasoned that if he waited and forced the Germans to attack him, even at full strength, the Romans would suffer fewer casualties.

So, for the next five days, both armies fell into a routine. The Romans would march out of their camps during the fourth watch of the night and form their battle lines facing the Germans along a little stream flowing east into the Ilia.

For the most part, the Krauts remained behind their wagons. The mob on the east bank, using boats, rafts, and anything that would float, began ferrying warriors over to reinforce the laager, which faced the Roman battle line. While this was transpiring, men, women, and even children would climb to the tops of the wagons and scream what we assumed were insults and challenges at the Romans formed opposite them.

Each day, during the early hours of the first watch of the night, when the enemy was deeply into the tuns of beer and mead that they had dragged along with them, the Romans would return to their camps, leaving a strong screen of cavalry and auxiliary troops between themselves and the *Grunni*, now drunk behind their wall of wagons.

Again, Caesar's legates urged him to attack the German laager at night, when they were all drunk. But, the lesson of the fight at Bibracte was still too fresh in Caesar's mind, so he refused. Drunk or sober, his plan was to make the Krauts come to him.

While we waited for the *Grunni* to make up their minds, the *muli* reinforced their front line.

They went to work on the southern bank of the stream with their *dolabrae*, their pick-axes. They cut the bank straight like a *vallum*, the earthen wall of a legionary *castrum*, and then piled the soil on top to heighten it and create a parapet; the stream itself served as the *fosse*, the defensive ditch. When these fortifications were established to the satisfaction of even the first-line centurians, the men started planting *liliae*, "lilies," sharpened *sudis* stakes in foot traps, along both banks of the stream.

This front-line wall was broken every hundred-fifty *passus* or so with an earthen ramp and a wooden bridge across the stream to allow the passage of cavalry and troops. But, in case the Krauts got any ideas about using these openings for their attacks, the Romans placed batteries of *scorpiones*, powerful crew-served crossbows, overlooking the ramps. What might appear to be an opportunity to the attacking *Grunni* would be quickly turned into a death trap by scores of tension-launched bolts. The *muli* marked these *portae*, gates, as they called them, with red pennants, as much to indicate to retreating Roman skirmishers where they were as to dare the Krauts to follow.

Caesar anchored both his flanks with batteries of *ballistae*, artillery pieces which could cover the army's entire front with interlocking fire of steel bolts and small stones. The *ballistae* were setup on small, earthen platforms that jutted out ahead of the Roman lines, so each weapon could fire across the entire front.

Each day, Caesar would ride up and down his battle line, with white stallion, red general's cloak, and full-dress armor. He'd swap jokes with the *muli*; he'd say things to them like, when they beat the Krauts, they could have the women; he just needed some hair. The men would chant back at him, "*Calve! Calve! Calve!* Baldy! Baldy! Baldy!" He told the men of the Ninth Legion that the Seventh bet a bag of silver that they'd beat them over the Kraut wagons. He told the Seventh that the Eleventh had made the same bet. And, so on. The boys loved it. Whatever had soured them with Caesar after Bibracte seemed to be forgiven and forgotten.

About one thing Caesar was serious, however. This was a battle of extermination. Unlike the Helvetii, the Roman nation had no use for *Grunni* on this side of the Rhenus. The *muli* were to kill everyone who didn't manage to swim back over the river. Any they didn't kill were going *sub corona*; they'd be sold to the slavers in Vesantio. Caesar claimed that the sale of German slaves would make the *muli* so rich that when they died, Charon would have to give them a first-class stateroom for their boat ride over the Styx.

Agrippa's *frumentarii* finally caught up with the army after it had been on the line four days. Now, instead of hardtack and jerky, the men had fresh bread, green vegetables, and pork stew, compliments of the Sequani living in the Dubis valley. Agrippa himself was still back in the rear; I was told he was supervising a barge-building project in Lugdunum, so he could float supply north over the river network. The *frumentarii* in the field were commanded by a *centurio posterior* named Opilio, who was invalided by wounds at Bibracte.

During most of this time, I was with the Sequani cavalry *turma*, screening the bridging points on the east bank of the Ilia. It was easy duty. We'd advance to a point on high ground where we could see down into the Kraut wagon laager on that bank. Most of their activity was focused on ferrying warriors over to the west bank. We could also see a steady stream of people, cattle, and wagons still straggling down from the north on both banks of the river.

For the most part, the Krauts ignored us. Occasionally, small groups of young men would mount up and ride out in our direction, but they never approached any closer than a few hundred *passus*. They sometimes swung their swords over their heads, pumped spears up and down, dismounted and showed us their arses, and grunted insults at us in languages we didn't understand. We just watched and did nothing until they tired of the game and returned to the wagons.

On the afternoon of the seventh day, everything changed; the German horde on the west bank came out from behind the wagons. From my position on high ground on the eastern bank, I could see them advancing toward the Romans. There was no discipline or order to their advance. Warriors simply flooded out from between the wagons onto the field.

The Roman *velites*, mostly the light Spanish auxiliary infantry, withdrew before them. The Roman battle line stirred; I heard their bugles sound attention.

The *Grunni* advanced no more than a hundred *passus* toward the Romans and halted. I could see warriors milling about, then gravitating to a number of tribal standards and swirling about the standards in large, disorganized herds.

Athauhnu pointed to the mass closest to the bank of the Ilia, opposite Caesar's Tenth Legion. "That's the *Suebi*," he said. "Ariovistus wishes to challenge Caesar directly."

A cacophonous blast of trumpets sounded from somewhere in the *Grunni* mob. They went still. Then, they began chanting. I recognized it from my fight with the Boii at Bibracte. They were evoking their god, Woden, "Wo . . . Wo . . . Wo . . . Wo."

To the rear of the *Grunni* horde, women climbed to the top of the wagons. Most just screamed out toward the Roman lines; others held up what looked like small bundles. When one of the bundles began kicking, I realized they were children.

The chanting, shrieking, and screaming built for about an hour. The warriors were drumming with an irregular rhythm, striking their shields with the pummels of swords, pounding the earth with their boots and spear butts.

Then, it stopped.

I thought for sure the Krauts would attack.

They didn't. They just turned around and returned to the wagon laager.

Within half an hour, except for crushed grass, the field in front of the Roman line was empty, as if nothing had happened.

The *Grunni* repeated this show for two consecutive days. Out they came, clustering around their standards, chanting, pounding, shrieking. Then they'd go back behind their wagons.

I asked Athauhnu what it was all about. He had no idea. The *Almaenuhr* were barbarians, he said, barely human. No one knows how they think, if they think at all. The only reason that Athauhnu could guess at was that the moon would be full in another couple of days. Maybe their gods fight well only under a full moon.

By the third day, Caesar had had enough.

The *Grunni* moved out from behind their wagons as usual, and while they were milling about trying to cluster around their tribal standards, a Roman trumpet sounded. The *ballista* batteries on the flanks and the *scorpiones* along the line opened up a murderous barrage of steel darts that ripped into the massed formations of Krauts.

Again, the Roman trumpets sounded: "All legions! Advance!"

The first battle line moved down over their carefully constructed parapet and across the stream. As they moved forward and tried to dress their ranks, the second battle line followed them. The third line halted at the top of the earthen wall and extended its ranks to cover the entire battle front. The *scorpiones*, now masked by friendly troops, ceased fire. The *ballistae* on the army's flanks adjusted their line of fire deeper into the mob of Krauts.

As I watched the Roman first line struggling to adjust its alignment after crossing the steam, I imagined that Caesar was counting on the *Grunni* to freeze long enough for the legions to reorganize for an assault.

He was almost right.

The German center and right did freeze. The five legions on the Roman left were able to reform their ranks, advance, launch volleys of *pila* into the massed *Grunni*, and attack with sword and shield.

But, the *Suebii* on the German left flank, opposite Caesar's command group and the Tenth Legion, immediately counterattacked. They moved so quickly that the *muli* in the front line had no chance to launch their *pila*. They barely had time to get their shields up before the *Grunni* smashed into them, pushing them back into their second line, which was still struggling to reestablish its alignment.

The German wave washed over Caesar's command group. I saw the white stallion go down, the red cloak lost in a sea of barbarians. The praetorian detail surged forward to protect their *Imperator*.

My first reaction was to gallop back over the river and attempt to reinforce the Roman flank. Athauhnu must have sensed what I was thinking. He reached over and grasped my right forearm before I could raise it. "It's too late for that, Arth Uthr!" he said in a low voice. "Caesar must fight his own battle. We can do nothing."

The Roman first line was overrun, almost six men deep in places. It began forming the defensive *murus scutorum*, the shield wall, from the rear.

After a few heartbeats, the Roman line seemed to stabilize. Then, the shield wall morphed into a modified *testudo*, the "turtle" formation.

The *muli* engaged directly with the enemy kept their shields forward and locked. The ranks of men immediately behind the forward line of the shield wall raised their shields up over their heads and locked them down at an angle onto the shields of the front line troops. This covered the heads and upper bodies of their mates in the front line from the *Grunni* assault. Then, the *muli* in the third rank raised their shields up over their heads, locked them onto the shields of the second rank and bent forward, creating an inclined roof of shields. The next rank back raised their shields, locked them forward, and took a knee; rearmost rank did the same but fell to their knees and bent forward.

This manuever formed a closed, armored, inclined platform with shields, as if the Romans were preparing to assault over a walled fortification.

Then, the second battle line, which had reformed its ranks behind the *testudo*, began launching their *pila* deep into the German formation in order not to hit their own mates, who were still fighting individual battles in a wild, swirling melee in front of the shield ramp.

The volleys of *pila* had their desired effect. Scores of German fighters went down, while those behind them pulled back to avoid being struck. The momentum of the German attack was disrupted, and the Krauts already engaged with the Roman line were now isolated.

Then, a Roman soldier ran up and over the shield ramp. By the transverse red crest on his helmet, he was a centurion. He leaped from the platform, over the Roman shield wall, and was swallowed up in the swirling melee of *muli* and *Grunni* hacking at each other.

The Roman second line gave up a thundering roar, then followed him, attacking en masse over the shields of their mates in the front line. Athauhnu pointed, and I saw one attacking soldier wearing a bright red *sagum*, the mantle of the commanding general. Caesar himself had joined in the attack.

The *Suebii*, caught between the Roman shield wall and the beaten zone hammered out by the Roman *pila*, recoiled as the men of the fifth, sixth, and seventh cohorts flooded into them over the ramp of shields. The *muli* threw themselves at the Germans, pressing them backward. The Krauts tried to establish a shield wall of their own, but the Romans were on them too quickly. I saw *muli* pull the German shields down with their bare hands as their mates stabbed over their heads into the German rout. Soon, the entire mass of *Suebii* were being pushed back toward their wagon laager by a steadily coalescing line of Roman red.

I was taken out of my role as spectator when one of my Sequani troopers galloped up to my location. He reported to Athauhnu, "*A Pen*! Boss! Guithiru asks you to come. Something is happening in the valley below!"

I thought for a heartbeat that this might be the start of the expected Kraut flanking move to envelop the legions in contact on the west bank.

We rode quickly to Guithiru's position overlooking the German wagon laager on the east bank. From his position, the west-bank laager was also visible.

There was no evidence of a Kraut flanking movement. Just the opposite, in fact. The stream of *Grunni* that had been trickling down from the north for the last few days had not only stopped, but seemed to have changed direction. We could see knots of people, mostly women and children, moving off toward the Rhenus. Germans from the western laager were now trying to cross the Ilia to the east. Some of these seemed to be men of fighting age. The laagers themselves seemed to be breaking up. Farmers were driving their beasts and wagons out of the encirclements and away to the north and east.

"Easy pickings down there," Guithiru suggested. "Should we attack?"

"No," I cautioned. "Let them think the way is clear and they will flee. If they think they're trapped, they'll fight."

Guithiru answered with a grunt.

Athauhnu nodded, then asked, "Where is Ci?"

"His *fintai* is in the trees on that hill there," Guithiru pointed.

Ci was less than two hundred *passus* distant with a clear line of sight.

"Now . . . *that* is interesting," Athauhnu said.

I looked and noticed three enclosed wagons pulled by teams of horses leaving the western laager. These weren't farm wagons. They were guarded by a *turma* of well-equipped riders.

"I believe Ariovistus wants to make sure his loot is safe, just in case things do not turn out well in his battle with the Caisar," Guithiru suggested.

"I agree," I shrugged. "But, our duty is here, screening the army's flank."

"Look there!" Athauhnu said, pointing. "Is that not a Roman?"

I looked and could see a man dressed in a white, Roman tunic. He was closely shepherded by three warriors. By the way he was holding his hands, they were bound in front. Even from that distance, I could see the narrow purple stripe bordering his tunic. It was Troucillus.

"How many men do you have with you, Guithiru?" I demanded.

"Ten, *a Pen*," he responded.

"Are Duglos or Ewuhn riding with us?" I asked.

Guithiru nodded, "Duglos rides with us . . . Shall I summon him?"

I nodded and Guithiru whistled to get his men's attention. "Send up the scout from Vesantio," he instructed.

When Duglos joined us, I asked, "How far is it to the nearest ford that could accommodate heavy wagons?"

Duglos thought for a few heartbeats, then answered, "This time of year, no more than three . . . four thousand passus."

"You know the place?"

"I can find it."

"Athauhnu," I said, "I'm leaving you in command here with Ci's *ala* . . . I am riding to this ford with Guithiru."

I could see that Athauhnu was not happy with my decision. But, Caesar's flank must be protected, and Troucillus was my friend.

"*A'mperi'tu, Decurio*," he responded in Latin.

No loot, no wild ride, no desperate battle, I'm sure he was thinking. To distance himself from his Gallic nature, it was becoming Athauhnu's habit to respond in Latin to decisions that made sense only to Romans.

I nodded and said to Guithiru, "We go!"

"What about the *Almaenwuhr* below?" he asked.

"*Maent uhn fermwuhra!*" I spat. "They're farmers! They'll run from us!"

Athauuhnu didn't miss out on a thing. There was no wild dangerous ride and no desperate battle against overwhelming odds.

As I predicted, when the Germans saw us, they continued to flee, just a bit faster. We reached the ford in just under two hours. We didn't press our horses. We wanted them ready to fight or to flee, whichever option made the most sense for us.

There was a convenient, wooded hillock overlooking the ford on our side of the Ilia. I concealed the main body of my troop there and sent scouts—Duglos, Rhodri, and Drust—across to watch for the wagons. I told them I was only interested in the one with the Roman prisoner; they should ignore the others.

It was almost two hours before the first wagon arrived. It was heavily loaded and guarded by well-mounted and equipped warriors. I imagined they were members of some *thegn's* personal bodyguard, a *gedricht* the Krauts call it. What was most curious was the well-dressed young woman seated on the board next to the driver.

We let them pass, the wheels of the heavily laden wagon digging deep furrows in the mucky soil of the trail leading up from the ford.

The wagon I wanted arrived soon after.

My scouts returned over the ford to tell me it was on its way. They swore they had not been seen by the escort. They were good at their jobs. I took them at their word.

I mounted the *fintai*. I told them we would wait until the wagon was in the middle of the ford before we revealed ourselves. I instructed that, as long as the *Almaenwuhr* offered no resistance, we would let them live. Keeping the *Rhufeinig* alive was our first priority. If one of the *Almaenwuhr* drew a sword, or I gave the word, we would attack immediately. No prisoners. Kill them all, but keep the *Rhufeinig* safe.

The wagon arrived as we expected. I could see Troucillus, his hands bound, riding behind it. He was shadowed now by only one rider.

When the wagon was fully immersed in the water of the ford, we broke cover. The escort froze, not at all sure who we were. We rode slowly toward them. The Krauts realized that we had them at a significant disadvantage. I stopped my horse at the point where the trail began to dip down toward the river and raised my empty hands toward the *Grunni*. I was thankful the black beast I was riding was finally getting with the program. I could just imagine a thought was flickering through his tiny equine brain that this would be the perfect time to turn traitor and dump me in the river.

"Do any of you speak Gah'el?" I asked.

The lead riders looked at each other. Finally, the one to my right shrugged and answered, "Me speaking *Welic*."

I had no idea what *Welic* meant, but I continued. "All I want is the *Rhufeinig*. Give him to me, and the rest of you and your wagon can go."

"Why we give you?" the speaker challenged.

"You give me the *Rhufeinig*, and we don't kill you," I stated bluntly.

There was some discussion. I understood none of it, but I saw no move to draw weapons. I did hear the words "*thas welas*" and "*se Romeh Mann*" repeatedly. I assumed "*se Romeh Mann*" meant "*Romanus*," the Roman, in their Kraut gibberish.

"Good death, good thing," my interpreter finally countered.

"Dying for a *Rhufeinig*," I countered, "is that a good death?"

Again, a grunting discussion. This time, the one I assumed was their leader laughed and said something about *se Romeh mann* and *se gerefa*.

The interpreter nodded, then said to me, "We give you *Romeh Mann*, we go?"

I nodded and added, "You give me the *Romeh Mann alive*."

The leader made the sound, "*Hwat?*"

The interpreter said something about *se Romeh mann*; the leader laughed again and nodded, "*Goot! Goot!*"

The leader called out, "*Dohmealde*," and gave what I assumed were instructions. One of his band brought Troucillus forward. Suddenly, the Kraut drew his knife. My hand dropped immediately to my own sword. But, the German chief raised his open hands in my direction. Then, I saw that "Drohmealde" was cutting Troucillus' bindings. Then, the leader gestured to Troucillus that he should join us above the ford.

When Troucillus had joined us, the chief said to me, "*Al iss goot?*"

Before I could respond, Troucillus, rubbing his wrists, said, "*Al iss goot! Abead halle, Erlvulf.*"

The journey back to where I had left Athauhnu and the rest of the Sequani was more challenging than the journey to the ford. The valley was now awash with *Grunni* fleeing the scene of the battle. Not only were there the obvious farm families with carts, children, and livestock, but also groups of men of fighting age, warriors, some showing wounds. I quickly discovered that, if we veered away from the Germans to the west, they mostly ignored us.

Troucillus was relieved that he was finally free of Ariovistus. He told me many of the Krauts wanted to offer him as a blood sacrifice to their dark gods, but the old woman, whom the Germans called *da ealde moder*, stopped them. She said that the "*Rune Stafas*" told her the gods would not accept human blood in exchange for victory. She claimed that the power of the goddess, Sinthgunt, was waxing with the moon. When the moon was full, they should attack; Sinthgunt and her sister Sunna would ride from Asgard on steeds of fire and ice to lead the peoples of the forests to victory. Then, once *das Romenen* were vanguished, Troucillus and any prisoners who fell into their hands, should be burned as a thanksgiving offering to Moon and Sun.

But, he had heard something else in their camp that disturbed him greatly. He insisted that he had to get to Caesar, QM, *quam celerrime*! I didn't understand his urgency. Battle had already been joined and, from what I could see, won. What information could there be about Ariovistus's intentions that was of importance now?

Troucillus said the Krauts spoke openly in front of him about their plans. "The *Suebii* didn't know that I understood one of their dialects," Troucillus explained. "I know the language of the short-sword people . . . the *Chaucingas* . . . or *Saxones* as we call them . . . They talked right in front of me."

"What of it?" I contested. "Caesar has committed the legions . . . The battle will be decided by the time we return."

"It has nothing to do with the battle," Troucillus insisted. "Ariovistus has a weighted die in his cup . . . Win or lose the battle, his goal is to kill Caesar . . . He has been paid well by Roman interests either to defeat Caesar on the battle field or to kill him . . . They don't seem to care much which he does."

"Kill Caesar?" I challenged. "How is any Kraut going to get close enough to Caesar to stick a *sica* into his ribs?"

"Ariovistus' weapon is not a 'Kraut,' as you call it; it's a Roman!" Troucillus revealed.

"A Roman!" I said. "Metius . . . It must be Metius!"

"I did not hear a name," Troucillus responded. "But Metius's involvement in this wouldn't surprise me a bit."

"Metius is back in camp!" I urged. "We have to get back there . . . We've got to stop him!"

"Metius may not be our problem," Troucillus cautioned.

"What do you mean?" I questioned.

"I know Metius is a rat, but he may not be *this* rat," Troucillus explained. "Ariovistus kept referring to someone he called *se Grekisc* . . . the 'Greek.' Whoever is giving this *sicarius* his orders is called the Greek!"

We continued to ride south, avoiding the Kraut refugees by circling them to the west, until we discovered that we had positioned ourselves almost due north of the eastern wagon laager.

From our position near the bank of the Ilia, we could see that the battle on the west bank was over. Roman cavalry had reached the western laager, and many of the wagons were burning.

The Romans hadn't yet crossed the river, but the eastern laager looked mostly abandoned, with large gaps in its perimeter where wagons had been taken away by their fleeing owners. We decided to ride straight through, but I warned my men no looting. They were to defend themselves only if attacked, but no looting. Our mission was to get Troucillus back to Caesar as quickly as possible.

When we entered the perimeter, we were assailed by the stench of unwashed bodies and human waste. The German cooking fires were still smoldering, and feral-looking dogs were routing about. There were still some *Grunni* skulking among the wagons, looting their own people. But, like the dogs, they scattered out of our way as we passed, some with departing snarls.

When we cleared the laager to the south, I could see a group of riders approaching us. They rode under a red dragon pennant and wore Sequani colors. It was Athauhnu.

"A great victory, *a Pen!*" he announced as he approached. "The *Almaenwuhr* are destroyed!"

I nodded. "We have been watching them flee toward the Rhenus! I must return this man to Caesar quickly! Detail five men to escort me. You hold your station here. The Roman pursuit should begin soon. You may join it if you wish. There will be good hunting!"

"Good hunting, indeed!" Athauhnu grinned. Then he turned and called down his column, "Emlun!"

Athauhnu's nephew rode up the column, "Yes, *a eoua* . . . I mean, *a Pen.*"

"Take four men, and go with Arth Uthr to the camp of the Caisar," Athauhnu instructed.

Emlun's face clearly revealed his disappointment. But, he was maturing as a warrior. "I go, *a Pen,*" he said simply.

We rode to the Roman camps guarding the western approaches of Caesar's bridge. The sentries challenged us with the sign, "*Virtus.*" I gave the countersign, "*Valor,*" and we were waved through.

When we got to the eastern approach to the bridge, we were stopped. A legionary *turma* was galloping toward us across the bridge. They were *venatores,* "hunters." The pursuit of the fleeing Germans had begun.

As soon as they cleared the bridge, I could see another group of riders approaching from the west. The sentry on my side was keeping us in place when Troucillus decided to pull rank.

"Make way for the *vexillatio praetiorianus* of the *Imperator*!" he commanded.

The *mulus* took one look at his narrow purple strip and my purple sash and stepped aside.

As we pounded across the bridge, I yelled, "Make way in the name of the *Imperator*! Make way in the name of Caesar!"

The approaching *turma* pulled up just short of the bridge. As I crossed, I saw it was led by Mani Knuckle Bones.

Manius grinned when he saw me. "The way you were yelling, I thought you were delivering Ariovistus' *coleones* in a golden coffer to Caesar!"

I pulled up. "Good hunting over there, Mani! You have a lot to get even for."

Manius shook his head. "You can never get even, Gai! *Numquam*! Never!"

I nodded. We shook hands, and Manius led his men east to kill Germans.

Caesar would either still be on the field or in the camp of the Tenth Legion. Since we had to pass by the legionary *castra*, I decided to look there first. The sentry at the gate didn't challenge us. He took in our equipment and Troucillus' equestrian stripe, assumed we were Romans, and waved us through with a fist pump and the cry, "*Io! Victoria!*"

I heard one of my boys echo him in Gah'el, "*But'ugoliai!*"

I could just imagine the expression on that *muli*'s face when he realized he had just admitted a bunch of armed Gauls into a Roman *castrum* unchallenged.

I quickly found Caesar's *praetorium*. There was a sentry from his praetorian bodyguard at the entrance to the tent. He recognized me and nodded to Troucillus. He allowed us to pass right through. I told Emlun and my escort to dismount and water the horses lightly, no feed. We might have to ride again soon.

Ebrius was not at his desk; he was probably still on the battlefield with his cohort. When we entered Caesar's *cubiculum*, he was there, seated in a field chair while Spina attended to him. Caesar's face was white and drawn. It was easy to understand why. Spina was stitching a slash that extended almost the entire length of Caesar's right forearm.

"Just a couple mowa n we'uh done heeah, Boss," the *medicus* was saying.

Caesar was taking some anesthetic from Spina's pitcher of disinfectant wine. He looked up as we entered. When he saw Troucillus, his eyes widened, a notably expressive response coming from Caesar.

"Troucillus! *Laus omnibus diis*! Praise all the gods! I was afraid those *cunni* had done for you!" he said, almost pulling his arm away from Spina.

"Hold still theyuh, will ya, Boss?" Spina grouched. "Now dat's goona leave a scaw!"

"Women and voters love scars, doctor," Caesar dimissed Spina's complaint. "Troucillus, it's good to see you back. Gai! I suppose I have you to thank for this?"

As I nodded, Troucillus said, "Caesar! I have urgent information for you."

"What could be so urgent at this point?" Caesar began. Suddenly there was a crash in the outer tent. The flap to Caesar's *cubiculum* burst aside, and a man dressed in a red military tunic and a *subarmalis* jacket entered. His upper right arm was wrapped in a legionary *sudarium*; in his left hand was a *gladius*, red with with fresh blood.

It was Bulla.

Spina tried to dismiss him, "This isn't da medical tent, soljah."

My right hand darted for my sword, but Bulla smashed the pummel of his into my face, and I went down.

"I'll do for you when I'm done with the nob," he snarled. "Now that I got this to thank you for, it aint gonna be quick, *podex*!"

When I shook the tears out of my eyes, I noticed that Bulla had an angry, red, semi-healed slash along his left cheekbone.

"The Greek's *striga*, that Irish witch gave me this," he said touching the wound. "The *cunna* said I was to leave you be . . . Her gods said you wasn't for me . . . I told her to *basìmi culum*, kiss me arse, so she gave me this . . . She can go to Hades . . . Dead, you're worth a sack full of silver to me . . . But first, I'm gonna take care of what I was sent up here to do."

Caesar had risen to his feet. The thread with Spina's needle still attached dangled down his right arm. I saw that Caesar's sword was propped up against his *lorica* over by his campaign maps. His belt with his *pugio* was nowhere to be seen.

"How did you get in here?" Caesar demanded.

"Your security's shit, yer honor!" Bulla told him, stripping the bandage from his right arm. "I walked right through the main gate . . . The sentry thought I was just another wounded soldier comin' back from the fight . . . even wished me good luck . . . The rest o' your boys are either out looking for loot or getting' drunk . . . As far as that *stultus*, the idiot you left outside . . . I walked right up on him, asking directons to the aid station . . . He was being greeted by *Dis* before he realized his mistake."

"I followed ya in from the battle," Bulla boasted. "I thought sure them Krauts did ya when they overran your lines . . . Would'a cost me a bundle if they did . . . but I got lucky . . . I saw your boys bring you back here with that wounded wing o' yours . . . Gave me the idea of wrappin' me own arm . . . Walked right in, like I said."

I tried to reach my knife while Bulla was talking, but all I got for my efforts was the toe of his *caliga* smashed into my ribs. "Wait your turn, *verpa!*" he hissed. "That Hibernian bitch ain't tellin' me what to do . . . Think I'll pay her a little visit when I get back down to Massalia . . . her and that *Graeculus*, that Greekling, who let her cut me. Ya know, I was sitting right there in the *caupona* when you showed up . . . The Greek didn't expect ya so soon . . . Had the *striga* take you into the back room to distract ya while he got me out . . . Hope she did ya up good . . . It's the last you're gonna get."

Bulla looked at Troucillus and Spina, "I got no contract for you two . . . but yer witnesses, and live witnesses are bad for business."

"Are you at least going to tell me who your working for?" Caesar asked.

Bulla laughed, "I work for the silver, yer honor . . . The silver for your little Gaul here comes from *La Matrona* down in Massalia . . . The silver for you—"

Emlun burst through the tent flap, his *spatha* out in front of him. He must have seen the dead sentry. Bulla turned. Emlun saw the *gladius* in Bulla's hand and thrust forward. The blow took Bulla just under his breastbone. He grunted once and was dead before he hit the ground.

Emlun stepped back, his sword still out. He saw Caesar and realized what he had just done. "*Cacu!*" he exclaimed in Gah'el. "Shit! A Rhufeinig! I killed a Roman warrior right in front of the Caisar!"

"*Cac't* indeed, young man!" Caesar answered as Bulla's blood spread around his body. "And this Caisar is forever in your debt!"

XVIII.

De Fine Belli Primi Mei

THE END OF MY FIRST CAMPAIGN

Ita proelium restitutum est atque omnes hostes terga verterunt nec
prius fugere destiterunt quam ad flumen Rhenum milia passuum ex
eo loco circiter L pervenerunt ibi perpauci aut viribus confisi tranare
contenderunt aut lintribus inventis sibi salutem reppererunt

"And so the battle was won, and the entire enemy force turned their backs,
and they didn't stop running until they reached the Rhenus, some fifty
miles away from the battlefield. There, the very few who escaped either
relied on their strength to swim across or found small boats to escape."

(from Gaius Marius Insubrecus' notebook of Caesar's journal)

---

espite Caesar's reassurances, it took me some time to
calm Emlun down. Troucillus embraced him, and Spina
offered him his wine pitcher. Still, Emlun couldn't get
beyond the fact that he had just killed a man he believed to be a Roman soldier
right in the middle of a legionary camp and in front of the commander himself.
Finally, Caesar gave Emlun a Roman handshake, thanked him, and presented
him with a leather purse bulging with *denarii*; I showed him out of the tent.

Spina examined Bulla's body and found a *collegium* mark tattooed in blue ink on his right shoulder.

"Dat's da mawk uh da *Vicus Silani Salientis* boys from up on dee Aventine," he said pointing to a crudely drawn *sica* washed in a spray of water. "Dere's a *caupona* right across from da fountain nee-uh where da crossroad shrine is . . . some *lar vialis,* a roadway god nobody remembers no more. . . Dat's whey'uh you'd find 'em usually . . . Day just stick mostly to strong-arm jobs, cutting purses, selling protection to da locals . . . a beatin' awe two . . . a hit ev'ry now n den . . . Nuthin' much to speak a."

Caesar was sitting back down in his camp chair, cradling the pitcher of wine. Spina's thread and needle were still hanging from his right arm. "I don't need their history back to Romulus, Spina. What's a member of this . . . this "spuming fountain" gang doing here, dead in my tent?"

Spina shrugged, "Da dead pawt's easy, Boss . . . Da kid stabbed 'im . . . Dee utter pawt . . . can't tell ya dat, Boss . . . An dis one ain't doin' much tawkin' . . . Word is, dair hooked up wit' Milo's bunch."

"Milo!" Caesar repeated. "If that's so, this . . . this . . . What did you call it, Spina?"

"A *percussus*," Spina suggested, "A hit."

"Yes," Caesar nodded, "this 'hit' might be traced back to elements in the senate . . . or even to Pompeius."

"Good luck tracin dat, Boss," Spina shook his head. "Unlike certain people in dis tent, the *Vicus Silani Salientis* don't write da memoirs of dare exploits . . . An dair not known for bein' very tawkative."

Ignoring the barb, Caesar just nodded his head as I interrupted, "There's still the matter of the Greek . . . and this *Matrona, Patrone.*"

"Go on," Caesar urged.

"I think the Greek is a merchant I saw down in Vesantio . . . He calls himself Grennadios," I explained. "He was also in the vicinity of Bibracte when we were chasing the Helvetii . . . He has a woman from *Hibernia* who travels with him . . . calls herself Evra . . . She looks and acts like Hecate herself."

"Is this Grennadios still in Vesantio?" Troucillus asked.

"I don't think so," I answered. "He said he was heading back down to Massalia . . . Things were getting too hot for him up here."

"You think dis Greek guy's da bag man for the gangs down in Rome?" Spina asked.

"Bag man?" I questioned.

"Yeah!" Spina explained, "Da bag man . . . da guy wit' dah bag fulla silvah . . . da banker . . . da payroll."

"That makes sense," Troucillus agreed. "A merchant's got access to cash, and no one's going to get suspicious if a merchant's carrying a lot of silver around."

Caesar held his hand up. "I'll send down to Massalia for word on this Grennadios."

Then, he pointed to the needle and thread hanging down from his arm and said, "Spina! You think you could finish this up before it heals on its own?"

"Shoowa ding, Boss," Spina began.

That still left the mysterious "*Il Matrona*" Bulla had mentioned twice. Then, I remembered something Gabi had said to me while she was still bothering to seduce me down in Massalia. She had inherited her dead husband's clients. That would make her their *patronus*, but in Rome, a woman couldn't be a *patronus*, a "little father." She'd be what, a *matrona*? The word meant "missus," a married woman—unless it was a pun: *matrona*, a "little mother," a patroness. For whom? Gangsters?

"*Patrone!*" I said. "I have a thought."

Caesar looked up at me and winced as Spina stuck the needle into his arm. "Go on, Gai."

"This '*Il Matrona*,'" I began, "I think I know who she is."

"'She'?" Caesar challenged. "Despite the name, do you imagine a *woman* capable of . . . uh . . . putting out a hit on a man . . . Did I say that right, Spina?"

"Dead on, Boss," Spina answered, not looking up from his handiwork.

Roman men have a blind spot about Roman women. Although we Gauls wouldn't doubt for a heartbeat that, given the right incentive, a woman would slice off a man's *coleones* and serve them up to him in his stew, a Roman refuses to believe a woman capable of homicide—even as he's eating the hemlock-laced mushrooms she prepared for his dinner.

Romanitas!

I explained to Caesar what had happened in Gabi's villa. How it was she who sent the killer disguised as a slave to kill me down in Aquileia. How she had another *percussor* waiting for me in Massalia. How she told him to kill me in front of her because she wanted "to see it done right this time."

Caesar shook his head. "I can't believe this . . . The woman's the daughter of a sitting consul . . . the widow of a senator . . . My daughter Iulia goes to dinner parties in her home . . . and you tell me she's this *Il Matrona*? The mistress of Milo? A 'patroness' of gangsters in the pay of Pompeius? Do you have a witness for this, Gai?"

"Yes," I answered. "Adonus *Dux*."

Caesar dismissed that. "Adonus *Dux* is a . . . a . . . *peregrinus* . . . a foreigner . . . No one will accept his word against a well-connected Roman woman of the senatorial class."

Then, Caesar realized what he had just said to me and tried to recover, "It's not that I don't believe you, Gai . . . but . . . uh . . . there's a great difference between the hysterics of a jilted lover and the machinations of a criminal mastermind . . . It's just not . . . well . . . It's fantastic . . . incredible."

"*Inromanitate?*" I suggested.

"Yes! Exactly," Caesar agreed. "Not Roman at all."

Labienus returned from the battlefield during the tenth hour to report to Caesar. He unlaced and removed his helmet to reveal his curly, dark brown hair matted flat against his skull. Caesar's body slave helped Labienus remove his *lorica* plates. His military tunic was so wet that Labienus could have been swimming the Rhenus itself in pursuit of the Krauts. He spotted Spina's wine pitcher on Caesar's field desk. He picked it up, swirled the liquid around and sniffed. He grimaced and asked Caesar's slave to fetch him some water. He was about to put the pitcher down when he shrugged and took a swig anyway. Then, Labienus sunk into a field chair with a sigh.

Labienus reported that the *Grunni* were totally defeated, and those who had survived the battle were either still fleeing toward the Rhenus or were penned up waiting for the slavers. There was no sign of Ariovistus and no trace of his reputed hoards of silver and loot, but the men were still searching.

Caecina then reported that Roman casualties were considered light to moderate. "We went into the fight with a battle-line strength of 18,787 across the six legions. At current count, we lost 2,177 dead and 1,075 wounded, of which about 350 will probably not make it. The hardest hit was the Tenth Legion, which took the brunt of the Suebian attack on the right. Do you need the breakdown, *Imperator*?"

"No . . . that can wait," Caesar said. "Are any of the legions not mission capable?"

"No," Labienus offered. "But, the men are exhausted . . . They need rest. I recommend a two-day stand down before we pursue the enemy."

Caesar shook his head. "We're not pursuing. Good riddance to any Germans who get back across the Rhenus. Sweep up any survivors on this side. If they surrender, they go *sub corona* . . . If they resist, kill them. Let the allied cavalry take the lead on this . . . I'm sure the Sequani have a few scores to settle with their erstwhile guests . . . Our legionary cavalry can back them up . . . Give the mop-up job to young Crassus . . . I want this side of the Rhenus cleansed of Germans . . . The legions can stand down, unless they're needed."

Labienus took notes on a *tabula* while Caesar continued. "Officers' call tomorrow during the third hour . . . Let the boys sleep in a bit in the morning . . . all legates, broadstripers and *primi pili* . . . Crassus excepted . . . He's to stay in the field with the cavalry . . . We'll conduct funeral rites for our fallen the day after tomorrow at dawn . . . Have the prisoners build the pyres, one for each legion . . . Dump the dead Germans into a pit . . . Unless Crassus runs into trouble, we pull out the day after that."

Labienus looked up from his tabula, "Back to the *Provincia*?"

"No," Caesar shook his head. "The army will winter in Gaul . . . I want two legions stationed along the Dubis between the Arar and the Gate. They'll be quartered outside Vesantio . . . They're to strengthen the fortifications in the Gate . . . I want at least three cohorts manning that position . . . Their other tasks are to improve the road along the Arar and up to the Gate . . . and to bridge the Arar at the fords above *Ventum Cavillonum* . . . The legionary engineers should be adequate to the tasks . . . Have them fortify the heights above the confluence of the Arar and the Dubis on the eastern bank . . . Cerialis has already staked out the site . . . One cohort should be enough to man it . . . They'll probably have to raze that fly-bitten native village there . . . I'll speak to the *Dux Bellorum* of Vesantio about it when we pass through."

Labienus looked up from his notes. He kept a straight face, despite the fact that Caesar had essentially announced that the Roman presence in Sequani lands was permanent, "Which legions should be assigned, *Imperator*?"

"The Seventh and Ninth, I should think," Caesar responded. "They're good, veteran formations . . . They won't soil their loincloths at the prospect of spending the winter isolated up here in *Gallia Comata* . . . Put Vatinius in command . . . I think he's up to it . . . Do you agree?"

It took Labienus a heartbeat to realize that Caesar was asking for his concurrence to Vatinius's assignment, not the stationing of the legions. "Yes," he nodded "Vatinius has developed into a good field officer . . . He should be fine . . . And those legions have experienced, veteran centurions to support him . . . Quiricus, the 'Oak,' will keep things in line."

"*Bene*," Caesar continued. "I'm sending the Twelfth back to the *Provincia* . . . They'll be assigned to Agrippa . . . He has a road to construct and some boats to build . . . That'll keep that bunch busy all winter . . . The Tenth and the Eleventh will winter at Bibracte . . . That leaves the Eighth . . . They're for Lugdunum . . . The Eleventh will improve the road from Bibracte to Ventum Cavillonum . . . the Eighth the road from Lugdunum to Ventum Cavillonum . . . Between those places I'd like at least a *via terrena* that can accommodate a march four *muli* abreast and loaded supply carts . . . Let's assign Crassus to the Eighth . . . I'd like to see how that young man handles an independent command."

Labienus nodded, "And the Tenth?"

"The Tenth will be my reserve," Caesar said. "We'll keep them together at Bibracte, in case I need immediate reinforcements anywhere . . . Meanwhile, they can sit on Diviciacus and the Aedui . . . I don't trust that *verpa* as far as I can see in the dark . . . and that brother of his is still in the wind."

Labienus nodded over his notes.

"Tite," Caesar continued, "I'm leaving you in command of the army up here, while I go down to Massalia to try and straighten out the mess with the civilian administration in my provinces."

Labienus looked up, blinked twice, nodded, and continued scribbling.

"Gai," Caesar addressed me, "I need you to stay up here with Labienus . . . You've made some good contacts with the Sequani . . . You'll be my eyes and ears with them while I'm down in the *Provincia*."

Labienus spoke up, "Is there anything that concerns you Caesar?"

"Nothing specific," Caesar shook his head. "The priority for our intelligence are the Aedui . . . They are the keystone to my Gallic policy . . . Keep an eye on our friend, Diviciacus . . . I want to know everything he does, down to what he has for breakfast every morning . . . Troucillus has agreed to serve as my personal representative to Diviciacus . . . He will be granted the rights and privileges as my *legatus ad manum*, my personal ambassador to the Aedui . . . And if Dumnorix, the king's brother, shows his ugly kisser anywhere near Bibracte, put him in chains and send him to me . . . in pieces, if you have to."

Labienus nodded and noted.

"One last thing," Caesar continued. "Metius has shared some disturbing information with me concerning the Belgae."

For a heartbeat, I wasn't sure what shocked me more, the fact that Caesar now had his eyes on the Belgae or that Metius wasn't rotting in some dungeon.

"He says one of their tribes . . . a bunch called the Nervii . . . are stirring up trouble against us . . . Metius is on his way to a place he calls Durocortum, the main town of a bunch called the Remi, one of the smaller Belgian tribes . . . The Remi are *culti*, he tells me . . . "civilized" . . . at least by Belgian standards . . . Been trading with us for years . . . They claim to have descended from Remus, the brother of Romulus, if you can believe that . . . So they're "brothers" to the Romans . . . Be sure to pass any information from Metius on to me *QM* . . . I believe we may have to deal with these Nervii sooner rather than later."

POST SCRIPTUM

So, at the end of the campaign season in the consular year of Lucius Calpurnius Piso Caesoninus and Aulus Gabinius, with the Helvetii defeated and forced back to their native lands and Ariovistus utterly destroyed, Caesar was already looking north for his next adventure, a campaign against the Nervii.

Until the end of his life, Caesar swore that it was never his intention to bring Gallia, Aquitania, and Belgica under the *imperium Romanum*. He claimed it "just happened that way."

Caesar used to explain himself by comparing his campaigns in Gaul to a game of multi-stone *latrunculi*. A player may have a plan at the opening of the game, but despite his assumptions about how his opponent will play him, he has to be able to counter threats and take advantge of opportunities as the game progresses. Where he actually is at the end game may not at all reflect where he thought he'd be at the beginning. The critical goal is winning.

Caesar once shared with me that, in Gaul, he would have been content with merely establishing a peaceful and stable confederation of tribes friendly to Rome. Eventually, two things drove him to reducing Gaul to a *provincia*: the need to contain the Krauts east of the Rhenus and Vercingetorix.

To that, I would add one additional reason: Caesar's obsession with the isle of the *Pretani*.

I'm not sure what was driving Caesar in this matter. Servilia, who knew better than anyone Caesar's insecurities, doubts, and fears, once confided in me that Caesar believed beyond *Britannia* lay the isle of the dead, a portal to the other world. His encounter with Evra had somehow planted that seed in his mind. Somewhere, in the dark recesses of Caesar's *anima*, he was driven by the idea that he, by virtue of his descent from the goddess Venus, would someday land on the shores of Dis's kingdom on a far western island under the setting sun.

But, more about that later.

So, at the end of our first campaigning season in Gaul, Caesar was convinced that our presence there and our victories over the Helvetii and the *Suebii* put us on an unavoidable collision course with the Nervii. And, Caesar was not a man to flinch.

For me personally, my encounter outside of Massalia ended my fantasies of a life with Gabi.

The Gabi I knew was dead. She had been replaced by Gabinia Calpurnia Pulchra Matrona, a vicious, frenzied, murderous harpy from the depths of Hades.

After a few years, she seemed to lose interest in having me gutted and mounted, *laus diis totis*! Her many and varied "interests" in Rome took up most of her time. She managed to ingratiate herself with Caesar after Pompeius fled east. She even had a brief flirtation with one of the *Liberatores* after Caesar's murder. When Octavius and Antonius destroyed Caesar's murderers, she managed to nestle under Antonius' wing for a while. Now, she's *in fidem Liviae*, under the protection of Livia, Octavius' wife.

Our *Augustus* is much too proper and decorous to be associated with the likes of Gabinia Pulchra. His wife, Livia, is a different matter altogether.

Publicola did survive his wound, but he was invalided out of the army and returned to Rome. He was never the same man. Just walking across a room too quickly left him short of breath. Through the influence of his father and Pompeius Magnus, he was appointed to the senate, but he was never well enough to attend its sessions or to accept any of the magistries in the *cursus honorum*. Every winter, when the coughing sickness inflicts itself on the young and the weak, Publicola would be laid up for weeks, wheezing, feverish, hardly able to breath.

In *Februarius*, during the year of the consuls Sergius Sulpicius Rufus and Marcus Claudius Marcellus, Publicola ended his struggles by lighting a brazier full of charcoal in a closed room and going to sleep. When I heard of his death, I was with Caesar near Alesia of the Mandubi, trying to patch the army back together after the Vercingetorix campaign. Although I could never get myself to like Publicola, I could still remember Troucillus' counseling me about

Publicola's conflict between his ingrained sense of *Romanitas* and his deep-seated desire for *humanitas*.

That evening I offered both bread and wine as *viaticum*, travel rations, for his *lar* on its journey across the river and prayed to the *di inferni* to allow his shade to abide in the fields of Elysium.

For now, my financial concerns about establishing the *vigiles* force in Mediolanum seemed to have evaporated. Rufia had secured all the funding needed, and then some.

I don't know whether it was her sense of civic duty or her desire to get her husband, my friend Macro, out of the house, but she invited all the major players in Mediolanum to a soirée at her old place of business, the blue-door *lupinarium*—my dear cousin Naso included. I don't know what was said or done there–an ignorance with which I'm quite content–but as a result, not only had all needed funds been pledged, but Rufia had matched them!

So, now the queen of the Mediolanum underworld was funding its law enforcement.

Romanitas, I guess.

A free eBook edition is available with the purchase of this book.

To claim your free eBook edition:

1. Download the Shelfie app.
2. Write your name in upper case in the box.
3. Use the Shelfie app to submit a photo.
4. Download your eBook to any device.

Shelfie

A free eBook edition is available
with the purchase of this print book.

CLEARLY PRINT YOUR NAME ABOVE IN UPPER CASE

Instructions to claim your free eBook edition:
1. Download the Shelfie app for Android or iOS
2. Write your name in **UPPER CASE** above
3. Use the Shelfie app to submit a photo
4. Download your eBook to any device

Print & Digital Together Forever.

 Snap a photo

 Free eBook

 Read anywhere

Morgan James makes all of our titles available
through the Library for All Charity Organizations.

www.LibraryForAll.org

Printed in the USA
CPSIA information can be obtained
at www.ICGtesting.com
JSHW021956150824
68134JS00055B/1024